M000280117

ELIZ~~~~~ ~~~~
LANDSCAPE IN SUNLIGHT

ELIZABETH MARY FAIR was born in 1908 and brought up in Haigh, a small village in Lancashire, England. There her father was the land agent for Haigh Hall, then occupied by the Earl of Crawford and Balcorres, and there she and her sister were educated by a governess. After her father's death, in 1934, Miss Fair and her mother and sister removed to a small house with a large garden in the New Forest in Hampshire. From 1939 to 1944, she was an ambulance driver in the Civil Defence Corps, serving at Southampton, England; in 1944 she joined the British Red Cross and went overseas as a Welfare Officer, during which time she served in Belgium, India, and Ceylon.

Miss Fair's first novel, *Bramton Wick*, was published in 1952 and received with enthusiastic acclaim as 'perfect light reading with a dash of lemon in it ...' by *Time and Tide*. Between the years 1953 and 1960, five further novels followed: *Landscape in Sunlight*, *The Native Heath*, *Seaview House*, *A Winter Away*, and *The Mingham Air*. All are characterized by their English countryside settings and their shrewd and witty study of human nature.

Elizabeth Fair died in 1997.

By Elizabeth Fair

Bramton Wick (1952)

Landscape in Sunlight
(1953, published in the U.S. as *All One Summer*)

The Native Heath
(1954, published in the U.S. as *Julia Comes Home*)

Seaview House
(1955, published in the U.S. as *A View of the Sea*)

A Winter Away (1957)

The Mingham Air (1960)

ELIZABETH FAIR

LANDSCAPE IN SUNLIGHT

With an introduction
by Elizabeth Crawford

DEAN STREET PRESS

A Furrowed Middlebrow Book
FM15

Published by Dean Street Press 2017

First published in 1953 by Hutchinson

Cover by DSP
Cover illustration shows detail from
Tea at Furlongs (1939) by Eric Ravilious

ISBN 978 1 911579 35 9

www.deanstreetpress.co.uk

INTRODUCTION

'DELICIOUS' WAS John Betjeman's verdict in the *Daily Telegraph* on *Bramton Wick* (1952), the first of Elizabeth Fair's six novels of 'polite provincial society', all of which are now republished as Furrowed Middlebrow books. In her witty *Daily Express* book column (17 April 1952), Nancy Spain characterised *Bramton Wick* as 'by Trollope out of Thirkell' and in *John O'London's Weekly* Stevie Smith was another who invoked the creator of the Chronicles of Barsetshire, praising the author's 'truly Trollopian air of benign maturity', while Compton Mackenzie pleased Elizabeth Fair greatly by describing it as 'humorous in the best tradition of English Humour, and by that I mean Jane Austen's humour'. The author herself was more prosaic, writing in her diary that *Bramton Wick* 'was pretty certain of a sale to lending libraries and devotees of light novels'. She was right; but who was this novelist who, over a brief publishing life, 1952-1960, enjoyed comparison with such eminent predecessors?

Elizabeth Mary Fair (1908-1997) was born at Haigh, a village on the outskirts of Wigan, Lancashire. Although the village as she described it was 'totally unpicturesque', Elizabeth was brought up in distinctly more pleasing surroundings. For the substantial stone-built house in which she was born and in which she lived for her first twenty-six years was 'Haighlands', set within the estate of Haigh Hall, one of the several seats of Scotland's premier earl, the Earl of Crawford and Balcarres. Haigh Hall dates from the 1830s/40s and it is likely that 'Haighlands' was built during that time specifically to house the Earl's estate manager, who, from the first years of the twentieth century until his rather premature death in 1934, was Elizabeth's father, Arthur Fair. The Fair family was generally prosperous; Arthur Fair's father had been a successful stockbroker and his mother was the daughter of Edward Rigby, a silk merchant who for a time in the 1850s had lived with his family in Swinton Park, an ancient house much augmented in the 19th century with towers and battlements, set in extensive parkland in the

Yorkshire Dales. Portraits of Edward Rigby, his wife, and sister-in law were inherited by Elizabeth Fair, and, having graced her Hampshire bungalow in the 1990s, were singled out for specific mention in her will, evidence of their importance to her. While hanging on the walls of 'Haighlands' they surely stimulated an interest in the stories of past generations that helped shape the future novelist's mental landscape.

On her mother's side, Elizabeth Fair was the grand-daughter of Thomas Ratcliffe Ellis, one of Wigan's leading citizens, a solicitor, and secretary from 1892 until 1921 to the Coalowners' Association. Wigan was a coal town, the Earl of Crawford owning numerous collieries in the area, and Ratcliffe Ellis, knighted in the 1911 Coronation Honours, played an important part nationally in dealing with the disputes between coal owners and miners that were such a feature of the early 20th century. Although the Ellises were politically Conservative, they were sufficiently liberal-minded as to encourage one daughter, Beth, in her desire to study at Lady Margaret Hall, Oxford. There she took first-class honours in English Literature and went on to write *First Impressions of Burmah* (1899), dedicated to her father and described by a modern authority as 'as one of the funniest travel books ever written'. She followed this with seven rollicking tales of 17th/18th-century derring-do. One, *Madam, Will You Walk?*, was staged by Gerald du Maurier at Wyndham's Theatre in 1911 and in 1923 a silent film was based on another. Although she died in childbirth when her niece and namesake was only five years old, her presence must surely have lingered not only on the 'Haighlands' bookshelves but in family stories told by her sister, Madge Fair. Another much-discussed Ellis connection was Madge's cousin, (Elizabeth) Lily Brayton, who was one of the early- 20th century's star actresses, playing the lead role in over 2000 performances of *Chu Chin Chow*, the musical comedy written by her husband that was such a hit of the London stage during the First World War. Young Elizabeth could hardly help but be interested in the achievements of such intriguing female relations.

Beth Ellis had, in the late-nineteenth century, been a boarding pupil at a school at New Southgate on the outskirts of London, but both Elizabeth Fair and her sister Helen (1910-1989) were educated by a governess at a time when, after the end of the First World War, it was far less usual than it had been previously to educate daughters at home. Although, in a later short biographical piece, Elizabeth mentioned that she 'had abandoned her ambition to become an architect', this may only have been a daydream as there is no evidence that she embarked on any post-schoolroom training. In her novels, however, she certainly demonstrates her interest in architecture, lovingly portraying the cottages, houses, villas, rectories, manors, and mansions that not only shelter her characters from the elements but do so much to delineate their status *vis à vis* each other. This was an interest of which Nancy Spain had perceptively remarked in her review of *Bramton Wick*, writing 'Miss Fair is refreshingly more interested in English landscape and architecture and its subsequent richening effect on English character than she is in social difference of rank, politics, and intellect'. In *The Mingham Air* (1960) we feel the author shudder with Mrs Hutton at the sight of Mingham Priory, enlarged and restored, 'All purple and yellow brick, and Victorian plate-glass windows, and a conservatory stuck at one side. A truly vulgar conservatory with a pinnacle.' Hester, her heroine, had recently been engaged to an architect and, before the engagement was broken, 'had lovingly submitted to his frequent corrections of her own remarks when they looked at buildings together'. One suspects that Elizabeth Fair was perhaps as a young woman not unfamiliar with being similarly patronised.

While in *The Mingham Air* Hester's ex-fiancé plays an off-stage role, in *Seaview House* (1955) another architect, Edward Wray, is very much to the fore. It is while he is planning 'a "select" little seaside place for the well-to-do' at Caweston on the bracing East Anglian coast that he encounters the inhabitants of 'Seaview House'. We soon feel quite at home in this draughty 'private hotel', its ambience so redolent of the 1950s, where the owners, two middle-aged sisters, Miss Edith Newby and widowed Mrs Rose Barlow, might be found on an off-season evening darning guest towels underneath the gaze of the late Canon Newby, whose portrait 'looked down at his daughters with a slight sneer'. By way of contrast, life in nearby 'Crow's Orchard', the home of Edward's godfather, Walter Heritage, whose butler and cook attend to his every needs and where even the hall was 'thickly curtained, softly lighted and deliciously warm', could not have been more comfortable.

Mr Heritage is one of Elizabeth Fair's specialities, the cosseted bachelor or widower, enjoying a life not dissimilar to that of her two unmarried Ellis uncles who, after the death of their parents, continued to live, tended by numerous servants, at 'The Hollies', the imposing Wigan family home. However, not all bachelors are as confirmed as Walter Heritage, for in *The Native Heath* (1954) another, Francis Heswald, proves himself, despite an inauspicious start, to be of definitely marriageable material. He has let Heswald Hall to the County Education Authority (in 1947 Haigh Hall had been bought by Wigan Corporation) and has moved from the ancestral home into what had been his bailiff's house. This was territory very familiar to the author and the geography of this novel, the only one set in the north of England, is clearly modelled on that in which the author grew up, with Goatstock, 'the native heath' to which the heroine has returned, being a village close to a manufacturing town that is 'a by- word for ugliness, dirt and progress'. In fact *Seaview House* and *The Native Heath* are the only Elizabeth Fair novels not set in southern England, the region in which she spent the greater part of her life. For after the death of Arthur Fair his widow and daughters moved to Hampshire, closer to Madge's sister, Dolly, living first in the village of Boldre and then in Brockenhurst. *Bramton Wick, Landscape in Sunlight* (1953), *A Winter Away* (1957), and *The Mingham Air* (1960) are all set in villages in indeterminate southern counties, the topographies of which hint variously at amalgams of Hampshire, Dorset, and Devon.

Elizabeth Fair's major break from village life came in 1939 when she joined what was to become the Civil Defence Service, drove ambulances in Southampton through the Blitz, and then in March 1945 went overseas with the Red Cross, working in Belgium, Ceylon, and India. An intermittently-kept diary reveals that by now she was a keen observer of character, describing in detail the background, as she perceived it, of a fellow Red Cross worker who had lived in 'such a narrow circle, the village, the fringes of the county, nice people but all of a pattern, all thinking on the same lines, reacting in the same way to given stimuli (the evacuees, the petty discomforts of war). So there she was, inexperienced but obstinate, self-confident but stupid, unadaptable, and yet nice. A nice girl, as perhaps I was six years ago, ignorant, arrogant and capable of condescension to inferiors. Such a lot to learn, and I hope she will learn it.' Clearly Elizabeth Fair felt that her war work had opened her own mind and broadened her horizons and it is hardly surprising that when this came to an end and she returned to village life in Hampshire she felt the need of greater stimulation. It was now that she embarked on novel writing and was successful in being added to the list of Innes Rose, one of London's leading literary agents, who placed *Bramton Wick* with Hutchinson & Co. However, as Elizabeth wrote in her diary around the time of publication, 'it still rankles a little that [the Hutchinson editor] bought *Bramton Wick* outright though I think it was worth it – to me – since I needed so badly to get started.'

However, although Hutchinson may have been careful with the money they paid the author, Elizabeth Fair's diary reveals that they were generous in the amount that was spent on *Bramton Wick*'s publicity, advertising liberally and commissioning the author's portrait from Angus McBean, one of the period's most successful photographers. Witty, elegant, and slightly quizzical, the resulting photograph appeared above a short biographical piece on the dust wrappers of her Hutchinson novels. The designs for these are all charming, that of *The Native Heath* being the work of a young Shirley Hughes, now the doyenne of children's book illustrators, with Hutchinson even going to the extra expense of decorating the front cloth boards of that novel and of *Landscape in Sunlight* with an evocative vignette. Elizabeth Fair did receive royalties on her second and third Hutchinson novels and then on the three she published with Macmillan, and was thrilled when an American publisher acquired the rights to *Landscape in Sunlight* after she had 'sent Innes Rose the masterful letter urging to try [the book] in America'. She considered the result 'the sort of fact one apprehends in a dream' and relished the new opportunities that now arose for visits to London, confiding in her diary that 'All these social interludes [are] extremely entertaining, since their talk mirrors a completely new life, new characters, new outlook. How terribly in a rut one gets.' There is something of an irony in the fact that by writing her novels of 'country life, lightly done, but delicately observed' (*The Times Literary Supplement*, 1 November 1957) Elizabeth Fair was for a time able to enjoy a glimpse of London literary life. But in 1960, after the publication of *The Mingham Air*, this interlude as an author came to an end. In her diary, which included sketches for scenes never used in the novel-in-hand, Elizabeth Fair had also, most intriguingly, noted ideas for future tales but, if it was ever written, no trace survives of a seventh novel. As it was, she continued to live a quiet Hampshire life for close on another forty years, doubtless still observing and being amused by the foibles of her neighbours.

Elizabeth Crawford

CHAPTER I

ON FINE DAYS, at an hour towards evening—which varied, of course, according to the season of the year—the sun reached the little window of the vicar's study. This window, set rather high in the wall and serving no useful purpose (since the room was adequately lighted by a larger window facing north), had been filled with stained glass by a former vicar of Little Mallin, who fancied himself as an amateur glazier. A local tradition maintained that he had found the glass stored in the crypt of St. Luke's at Mallinford and had removed it under the very nose of the rector, who was only interested in mediaeval manuscripts; but other people said the vicar had made the glass himself. Red, blue and yellow predominated in the window, which might be regarded as an early example of *pointillisme*.

To Mr. Custance, the present incumbent, the red, blue and yellow rays which streamed into the room when the sun reached the little window served as a reminder that he had not yet done the dusting. Like theatrical spotlights they illuminated the principal ornaments of his mantelpiece and revealed his own neglect. On this particular evening, the first fine day after a succession of cloudy ones, the dust was very noticeable. In fact the study had not been dusted for some time, for without the sun's illuminating rays he did not perceive that dusting was necessary.

But though the reminder came late in the day, it was not yet too late. He kept his own duster tucked away in a drawer in his desk, and owing to this precaution no one of his family—or so he believed—knew that he usually dusted his study after tea.

He began with the mantelpiece. The principal ornaments were a glazed earthenware tobacco-jar, a model of the Parthenon carved out of olive-wood, and a small bronze bell hanging in a bamboo frame, and alleged to be a Burmese gong. Behind and among them lay a miscellaneous collection of letters, bills, bits of string and stubby pencils, which he left undisturbed.

The small table by his easy chair and the ink-stained, flat-topped desk received summary treatment, but he lingered over the round table in the middle of the room, for he knew that his wife would look at it if she came in. Its appearance had often caused her to have the whole room 'turned out', and his books and papers ruthlessly displaced and rearranged, so that it had taken him a long time to find the ones he needed.

It was partly this dislike of having things disturbed which had made him volunteer to do the dusting himself in this room. But he was also a kindly man, and he regretted the burden of domestic work which fell on his wife and daughter; for the vicarage was large and his stipend small. Had circumstances permitted he would have undertaken other tasks, but as it was he had to confine himself to chopping the kindling and occasional assistance with the washing-up. The work of his parish and his literary labours left him no time to do more.

The round table had now acquired a satisfactory gleam, and Mr. Custance judged that the rest of the room would do very well as it was. He put the duster away and looked at his watch. There was still half an hour to spare before the Literary Institute meeting.

One side of the room was lined from floor to ceiling with bookshelves, and towards these laden shelves he now advanced, searching his pockets as he went for the envelope on which was written a quotation he wished to verify. The quotation had come into his mind quite suddenly, in the middle of a conversation with Eustace Templer about belts and braces, and Eustace had supplied a pencil, as well as the envelope itself, so that he could write it down.

Eustace Templer might be eccentric, thought Mr. Custance, but he had a practical side to him too—always had a paper and pencil handy and never minded lending them. It was lucky he had been with Eustace when he thought of the quotation, because if he had not written it down at the time it would have been lost for ever. The human mind, he thought, is a curious thing; for he could clearly remember borrowing the pencil and pressing the envelope against the top bar of the gate while he wrote, but the quotation itself had vanished from his mind as if it had never been there.

It took him a few minutes longer to realize that the envelope had vanished too. Another search of his pockets, a hopeful inspection of all the places he had dusted, a look at the duster itself and the drawer where he kept it (for envelopes and other small objects could play the most curious tricks on Mr. Custance), and he was reduced to standing still and trying to recall his conversation with Eustace Templer. He knew it was no good trying to remember the quotation itself, but if he could reproduce the sentence that had prompted it some hidden association might bring it back to him.

"They're more comfortable," Mr. Custance said aloud, speaking his own part in the conversation.

Stooping and slightly bending his knees—for Eustace Templer was a head shorter—and assuming a high-pitched staccato voice, he retorted: "Comfort! If it's comfort you're after, why not a siren suit like Churchill? No braces *or* belts—just a zip!"

"My dear Templer, consider my cloth. What would the Bishop think?" he remonstrated; and then he faltered, for even in his rôle of Eustace Templer it seemed a sort of *lèse-majesté* to repeat the next part of the conversation. Eustace Templer was no respecter of bishops. But he was approaching the important moment, the keyword was on the tip of his tongue, and after a pause he continued, carefully emphasizing the Templer characteristics to make it clear that this was not his own opinion.

"What the Bishop thought—if he is capable of thinking—would be so obscurely expressed that you wouldn't know if he approved or not. Until you found that he'd adopted the idea and was passing it off as his own. And I must say, Custance," he added shrilly, "the sight of the Bishop in a siren suit would be a phenomenon not without its own bizarre attraction."

"Edward!"

His wife's voice, breaking in on this dramatic duologue, was not the only thing which brought Mr. Custance to a stop. The keyword had done its work, and he looked round for a pencil and paper.

"Edward?" Mrs. Custance repeated, her voice hovering between anxiety and reproach.

"Phenomenon," said Mr. Custance. He got it down on paper—the key-word and the first three words of the Greek quotation it had inspired. He placed the bit of paper carefully in the tobacco-jar and turned to face his wife.

Mrs Custance was fond of saying that she was just an ordinary woman, and in saying it she contrived to suggest that this was much the best thing to be. She was constantly on the watch lest her nearest and dearest should do anything markedly unusual; for an ordinary woman, to be consistent, must have an ordinary family circle surrounding her.

It was therefore extremely disconcerting to find her husband decrying his bishop, speaking aloud in a high unnatural voice, and addressing himself as Custance.

Her first thought, that he might be ill, was quickly suppressed; for twenty-seven years of married life had taught her that if Edward were ill he would tell her at once and not waste time writing things down on bits of paper. When he popped the paper into the tobacco-jar she knew instantly that it was something to do with his book, and this increased her annoyance.

She came into the room and closed the door carefully behind her—a familiar action which warned Mr. Custance that he was about to be rebuked. Except for themselves the vicarage was empty, but Mrs. Custance, in moments of stress, behaved as if there were a large staff of inquisitive servants clustered in the hall.

"What you *imagine* you're doing—" she began.

"I was being Eustace Templer," Mr. Custance murmured unhappily. It was no good trying to explain things to Amy, and even in his own ears the explanation sounded a bit thin. Clutching at a straw, he added that Eustace Templer seemed very pleased with Cassandra and had said she was doing wonders with Leonard.

"That doesn't sound like him," Mrs. Custance said coldly. "And it isn't what you were making him say when I came in."

Nevertheless, the atmosphere grew lighter. Few ordinary mothers can resist hearing their daughters praised. Edward Custance, guiltily aware that he was using Cassandra—and not for the first time—as a red herring, hoped it would be forgiven him. The thing to do now was to go on talking about Cassandra and Leonard, and so distract his wife's attention from Eustace Templer and the Bishop.

"She seems to like the boy," he said.

"Cassie is very fond of children," said Mrs. Custance. "I hope she'll have some of her own one day."

Though he was careful to conceal it, Mr. Custance gave a little sigh. His manoeuvre had been all too successful, for Amy had forgotten her annoyance and was now embarking on her favourite subject: her hopes for Cassandra's future.

"She's young. We don t want her to marry in a hurry," he said soothingly.

"She's twenty-five. I was younger than that. And of course I could have married much earlier. I had plenty of opportunities," said Mrs. Custance, tossing her head coquettishly, "but poor Cassie has so few. Sometimes I think we're wrong to keep her at home."

Mr. Custance was fond of his wife, but there were moments when she irritated him excessively. He knew perfectly well that she had been twenty-eight when she married him, that she had been leading a humdrum existence in her father's country rectory and had been glad to leave it, and that it was to please her that Cassandra remained at home.

But his peace-loving nature—for so he chose to think of it—prevented him from challenging this collection of mis-statements. He remained silent.

The silence itself might have produced a disagreement, but fortunately an interruption occurred. The sound of Cassandra's footsteps on the path outside, as she wheeled her bicycle along to the stables, attracted Mrs. Custance's attention.

"There she is!" she exclaimed. "And it's time for your meeting, Edward." She looked at her husband, who was looking at himself in the mirror above the mantelpiece and gently smoothing his hair. It was a pity Edward was going bald, but it could not be helped. It was a pity Cassie had to be a governess, but at least she lived at home and could be nursed when she had a cold.

Just for a moment Mrs. Custance's life seemed perfectly satisfactory, her worries and grievances receded, and she fell into a happy trance, in which her mind was occupied by thoughts of a new summer hat, a day by the sea, and a roast chicken for Edward's birthday.

It was in this benign mood, a few minutes later, that she went out to greet her daughter. Cassandra had come in through the back door and was washing her hands at the kitchen sink. "The chain came off my bicycle twice," she said. "I might just as well have walked."

"It wants tightening up. You must take it to Bryce—or perhaps I could do something myself."

Mrs. Custance spoke with assurance, for she had a remarkable talent for repairing mechanical defects. The vicarage clocks, the wireless, the family bicycles and even the aged car responded obediently to her ministrations. Since neither Edward nor Cassandra was mechanically minded they regarded her as a sort of minor magician.

"Oh, do try," Cassandra said. "Bryce always takes such ages. Has Father remembered his meeting?"

"He's just gone. Rather late, I'm afraid."

"They'll all be late, except Mrs. Midge. No one in Little Mallin has any sense of time."

Mrs. Custance, who was punctuality itself, might have queried this, but she had something else to think about.

"Mrs. Midge?" she repeated. "Surely she isn't on the committee?"

"Elected last time. Didn't Father tell you? I suppose he forgot."

"That wretched boy," Mrs. Custance said obscurely. "And anyway, why *should* she be on? She hasn't been here very long."

Cassandra knew that her mother was a kind woman, always ready to help people in practical ways as well as giving good advice. Though she demanded conventional behaviour from her family she did not insist on it in her friends; Eustace Templer's eccentricity, his sister's extreme vagueness, the somewhat predatory outlook of Miss Fenn and Miss Daisy Fenn, were broadmindedly accepted. But this did not mean that her mother was completely tolerant, it simply meant that her tolerance was unpredictable. If one tried to define it, it would be like the graph of a fever temperature, rising to remarkable heights and sinking to alarming depths.

For no valid reason Mrs. Custance simply refused to like certain people; and prominent among these social outcasts was Mrs. Midge.

It was no good trying to argue Mrs. Custance out of her prejudices, but Cassandra, in spite of her twenty-five years, had not yet given up trying.

"Oh, Mummy, she came in the war," she said. "And Lukin isn't so bad really."

Lukin was the wretched boy.

"She's on the make. One of those social climbers. One reads about them, you know."

Mrs. Custance was rather given to thinking in slogans, and such phrases as 'a typical English family', 'people like ourselves', and 'the backbone of the country' served her well. Like formal abbreviations they stood for ideals which she did not trouble to put into words.

"I don't see much future for a social climber in Little Mallin," Cassandra said. "We're all much of a muchness, and anyway the Literary Institute is quite plebeian. Look at Bryce."

"Ah, but she won't stop at that. I wish Eustace Templer had never let her have that house."

"I believe he wants it back."

The remark slipped out, and Cassandra at once regretted it. As daily governess to Eustace Templer's younger nephew she spent a good deal of time under his roof, and heard, from Lily and Felix if not from Mr. Templer himself, a good deal about his intentions. But she was usually careful not to spread stories, partly because she thought it bad manners and partly because she knew that her mother, if her interest was once roused, was all too likely to take action.

"Of course that's only an idea of mine," she added quickly. "No one has said anything."

Mrs. Custance nodded comprehendingly. She was familiar with village life; she knew it wasn't necessary to say anything, the news circulated as if it were carried by the wind. "I expect he wants Prospect Cottage for his brother-in-law," she remarked.

Prospect Cottage was where Mrs. Midge resided. It belonged to Eustace Templer, who lived at Prospect House farther up the hill. For years and years Prospect Cottage had been let to two old sisters. But in the middle of the war the sisters, unable to cope with housework, had retired to a private hotel, and though there were several people available locally who would have made good tenants, Mr. Templer had let the place to a total stranger. Nothing was known of Mrs. Midge except that she came from London, that she had a young son who was supposed to be delicate, and that she worked in a Government department which had been evacuated to Mallinford.

At the end of the war the Government department returned to its own home, but Mrs. Midge stayed on. While the war lasted Mrs. Custance had accepted her as part of the war-effort and had hardly troubled about her; it was only in the past year or two that Mrs. Midge had been transferred to the category which Mrs. Custance described as 'people we could manage without'.

Cassandra, still hoping to lessen the effect of her remark, said that Prospect Cottage might not suit Colonel Ashford.

"It's quite small, and awfully inconvenient," she pointed out.

"It could be modernized," said Mrs. Custance. "I don't suppose he wants a large house; Army pensions don't go far. And of course it would be nice for Isabel Templer to have her sister so near."

Her expression suggested that it would be nicer still to get rid of Mrs. Midge.

"Well, don't *say* anything, Mummy, to Miss Templer or anyone, in case they think I've been gossiping."

"Of course not, darling," said Mrs. Custance, who believed herself to be the soul of discretion. "Did you have a nice day?"

In the excitement of hearing about Mrs. Midge being on the Literary Institute committee and possibly going to be evicted from Prospect Cottage, she had forgotten to ask her daughter this customary, and rather irritating, question.

"Quite nice," Cassandra answered. This was the customary reply, equally irritating to her mother who would have liked a detailed account of everything Cassie had said and done and eaten. But this evening Cassandra relented and added the information that they had had a boiled fowl for lunch and that Felix was not going back to school that term.

Mrs. Custance said she knew that; Mrs. Truefitt had told her in the post-office, both about the hen and about Felix. The doctor said he had been working much too hard and must have a complete rest, which was silly because boys of Felix's age simply did not overwork.

"I think it was the measles too," said Cassandra.

"I hope you won't have to teach him as well as Leonard."

"Oh no, he's not to do any work. Anyway, I couldn't take them both. Leonard is only just ten and Felix is nearly fifteen."

Cassie had had a good education and Mrs. Custance believed her to be very clever and fully capable of instructing boys of fifteen. Nevertheless, she hated to think of her daughter being a governess. Of course, if Eustace and Isabel had not wanted a governess for Leonard, Cassie might have had to take a post in some school instead of living at the vicarage; and perhaps she might still have to do that, next year when Leonard grew too old to be taught at home.

Mrs. Custance, who had had the sketchy sort of education that was thought suitable, in her generation, for the girls of a large and impoverished family, and had managed very well on it, sometimes wished that Cassie had not been quite so lavishly educated; for without all those examinations and certificates no one would have wanted her as a governess. She had not foreseen, when she wrote for prospectuses and sewed name-tapes on three sets of everything and economized to pay the school fees, where it would all lead; she had simply wished for an intelligent and lively daughter who would shine in any society.

Things had turned out differently, but she had not yet given up hope. If only there were more young men in the neighbourhood, if only Cassie showed more interest in them, if only she did not have to be a governess! Thinking of Cassie's occupation, her mind went back to Prospect House and its occupants. Eustace Templer was a bachelor, but he was sixty-six and thoroughly unreliable. Colonel Ashford had a wife already, and Felix, an orphan and presumably Eustace Templer's heir, was only fifteen.

"I wish Felix was a little older," she said.

"I think he's rather a nice age," said Cassandra. "He'll probably be very silly when he grows up."

Mrs. Custance sighed. The trouble was, Cassandra so often seemed to find the male sex silly when it grew up.

CHAPTER II

FOR THE PAST WEEK the weather had been, as Mrs. Midge expressed it, unkind. A succession of damp, drizzling days and chilly nights had made a fire essential, though she usually stopped fires on the first of May. But today had been lovely, a real summer's day at last. Even now, though the dying gleams of the sunset were fading from the sky, the air was still warm, and it hardly seemed necessary to close the windows. But she was a methodical creature; this was the hour for shutting up, and she went from room to room as usual, not neglecting her own bedroom or Lukin's.

Mrs. Midge paid lip-service to the virtues of fresh air, but in her heart she believed that too much of it was not beneficial to the human body. Fresh air in the daytime was well enough but fresh air when you dressed and undressed was dangerous and might lead to chills. So the bedroom windows were shut and latched, to be re-opened last thing at night when she got into bed, and that only in settled weather.

When she had finished it was quite dark in Prospect Cottage, because the curtains dated back to the war years and were all lined with blackout material. She had made them when she came here, and she had made them to last.

Ten years at Prospect Cottage, which had no electricity, had accustomed her to moving about in the dark. It was a nuisance to have to carry a lamp or candle every time one left the sitting-room, so she and Lukin had developed a cat-like aptitude for managing without lights. This was not difficult, since everything in the cottage was always in its right place and the position of the furniture was never altered. Mrs. Midge's liking for order and tidiness was so pronounced that her surroundings had an oddly immovable appearance, the very ornaments seeming glued in place and the books permanently confined in glass-fronted cupboards.

But tonight, just as she was turning to leave Lukin's room, she stumbled against something heavy and solid which was lying on what ought to have been an unencumbered strip of carpet. It had been so nearly dark when she entered the room that she had not noticed the obstruction.

"Ouch!" she said aloud. She was more startled than hurt. She groped her way across the room and lit the candle that stood on the bed-table. The obstruction revealed itself as a square wooden box, the box in which Lukin kept his collection of stones and seashells, and which ought to have been pushed back against the wall by the fireplace.

Mrs. Midge sighed. Dear as Lukin was to her—her only child, her ewe lamb—she did not hesitate to rebuke him when she felt rebuke was needed. And this careless misplacement of the box could have had serious consequences. She might have fallen, she might have broken her leg and been laid up for months, and what would have happened to him then?

Filled with the righteous indignation of one who knows herself to be indispensable, she contemplated the future as it might have been: she saw herself crippled, unable to work, unable to pay the rent and therefore at the mercy of her landlord who was already seeking to evict her from Prospect Cottage. She saw Lukin, her darling child, thrown out in the road, with nowhere to go, no understanding parent to guard and feed him. (She herself was not in the road with him but immured in some dingy hospital, facing pain and disaster with her usual fortitude.) It was a dismal picture.

But she did not dwell on it, for she prided herself on being practical, and she was more concerned with what she was to say to Lukin—how she was to bring it home to him that his offence had been serious, and yet do it in such a way that no ill-humour should result.

"The bond between us is very close," she used to say to her friends. The bond was compounded of mutual appreciation and dependence, and of a fixed determination to avoid hurt feelings, on both sides. They were two sensitive creatures, each had found the world unkind, and it was tacitly agreed between them that angry voices and shrill recriminations should not be used.

Having restored the box to its proper place Mrs. Midge went downstairs and lit the oil-lamp in the kitchen. She closed the kitchen window but left the blind undrawn, and the lamp-light shone out into the summer night as a signal that supper was ready.

Prospect Cottage stood on the hillside, sheltered from the north by the long gentle slope behind it, and open to the south and west. The lane which led to it continued up the hill to Prospect House and a farm beyond, but these were out of sight, hidden behind a line of trees. The garden lay to one side of the cottage, a long, narrow garden with a small paddock beyond it which was included in the tenancy. At the far end of the garden was a wooden shed which Lukin used as a workroom. Mrs. Midge sometimes spoke of it as his 'atelier', and she had furnished it with wicker chairs, and had encouraged him to decorate the interior walls with a series of geometric designs, executed in bright colours and symbolizing the procession of the seasons throughout the agricultural year.

A light was burning in the workroom, a beacon answering her own. She had meant the place to be a daytime retreat for Lukin, and the lamp was an innovation of which she did not wholly approve. During the week she was away all day, and it was nice for him to have his workroom where he could do as he pleased without sullying the neatness of Prospect Cottage or having to listen to the garrulous old woman who came in to clean and scrub. But it was not so nice that he should want to be there in the evenings when his mother was at home. She wondered whether to amplify her lamp's mute summons by ringing the cow-bell. But even as she watched, the light in the workroom was extinguished, and she turned away from the window.

Supper was already set out—hard-boiled eggs, cheese and salad—and she lit the oil cooker and put the milk on to heat for the cocoa. She and Lukin were both very particular about what they ate. They had weak stomachs and could only digest certain things, but luckily their tastes, or their stomachs, were alike. Hard-boiled eggs and rubbery cheese, washed down with very thick sweet cocoa, agreed with them admirably.

Presently the door opened and Lukin appeared.

"*There* you are!" Mrs. Midge greeted him. "Just time for supper."

"Lovely supper!" Lukin responded, eyeing the table.

These phrases meant nothing and were simply a manifestation of goodwill. Friendship, as Lukin and his mother understood it, was not conducted in silence; silence was disturbing and usually implied that something was wrong. Therefore they kept up a constant patter of talk, like the chirrups and twitters of little birds in a hedgerow, to tell each other that they were together and that no danger threatened.

"They're Doris's eggs, and one of Dorcas's."

The Midges had six hens, each of whom was, so to speak, a personal friend with a name, a character, and a recognizable style in eggs. They lived in the paddock at the end of the garden, and all were now elderly and hardly worth their keep. But neither Mrs. Midge nor Lukin could contemplate killing and eating them, and though they did not provide many eggs they were useful as a subject for conversation.

"Wonderful Doris," Lukin said devoutly. "She must have laid every day this week."

"Yes, her long rest has done her good."

The amiable talk went on while Mrs. Midge made the cocoa and Lukin washed his hands in the scullery.

"Ought I to comb my hair?" he asked, standing in the doorway between the two rooms.

Lukin's sensitive nature was so highly developed that he responded like a good barometer to the slightest atmospheric change. Not only was he easily hurt but he could foresee the probability of his being hurt, long before the wounding words were spoken. And now, although everything was outwardly genial, he had a premonition of trouble to come.

There were several ways of dealing with such a situation. The easiest, the one he adopted instinctively and almost without calculation, was to put the hands of the clock back and become little Lukin again.

It was little Lukin who asked whether he should comb his hair.

Mrs. Midge smiled at him, seeing—as she was meant to see—the little boy with scratched knees and grubby finger-nails. Her little boy. "Darling!" she said; seeing also, in the sort of double vision common to mothers, a young man with crinkly hair, blue eyes, and a small unobtrusive chin. She had once hoped he might grow taller, but it was not to be. However, though short, he was trim and well proportioned, and his face bore a strong resemblance to her own.

In her youth Mrs. Midge had not lacked for admiration, and by a curious process of transference she admired in Lukin the very things for which she had once been praised—the ingenuous blue eyes, the pouting mouth, and above all the appearance of innocent and engaging youth.

It was sometimes quite difficult for her to remember that Lukin was no longer a little boy but twenty-five on his last birthday.

"Dear Mama," he said, investing it with a sort of wistful wonder which was quite in character. They exchanged loving smiles, and Lukin's delicate barometric needle registered a lightening of the atmosphere.

"Never mind about your hair," his mother said. "The cocoa's getting cold."

After supper they went into the sitting-room. It was warm enough to do without a fire and they settled themselves in the bay window, with a table between them for Lukin's knitting and Mrs. Midge's embroidery. Lukin only knitted occasionally but Mrs. Midge embroidered nearly all the time. She made tea cosies, tray-cloths, even bedspreads, and sometimes, as a 'special order', a quilted satin cushion cover or a set of monogrammed table mats, destined for a Mallinford wedding present.

Mallinford was the small town where she worked, in an arts-and-crafts shop. Her acquaintance with Mrs. Imber, the shop's owner, had begun during the war, soon after her arrival at Prospect Cottage, when she was a clerk in a minor Government department which had installed itself in Mallinford Grange. Mrs. Imber had seen a tray-cloth which Mrs. Midge had contributed to a local hospital bazaar, had sought her out and offered to buy some of her work for the shop, and had ended by offering her a job.

By that time the war was nearly over, the Government department was full of rumours of redundancy, and Mrs. Midge was glad to exchange her hard chair and trestle table for the comforts of Mrs. Imber's establishment in Church Lane. In her war-work she had been anonymous, a stranger whom no one bothered about, but since becoming Mrs. Imber's assistant she had begun to feel herself at home. She was no longer an evacuee but a resident, people remembered her name, and she had already made one or two friendships which she described to herself as 'useful'.

She was not, in point of fact, a resident in Mallinford. The parish of Little Mallin was separated from Mallinford by the river and a toll-bridge. Although it was only a few miles from the town, the toll-bridge had prevented much building development on the north bank of the river and Little Mallin had remained a small and very rural community. A scanty and inconvenient bus-service linked it to the town, and Mrs. Midge, faced with the uphill walk from the village to her cottage, had sometimes wished she could find a house in Mallinford itself.

She wished it more often in winter. In summer she quite enjoyed being where she was; moreover she felt that there was a certain distinction in living outside the town. She liked being able to talk about her country cottage, and she had taken to wearing robust country tweeds and strong low-heeled shoes, though she still cherished her complexion and had not been able to break herself of carrying an umbrella in wet weather.

This mild contentment with Prospect Cottage had lately been fanned into a blaze of possessive love by the suggestion that she might have to leave it.

The suggestion had been made by her landlord, Eustace Templer, at their last meeting. Not in so many words—for he was never explicit—but clearly enough to arouse in Mrs. Midge a feeling of insecurity. Eustace Templer had a brother-in-law who had recently retired from a career abroad; he was staying with the Templers at Prospect House, looking for a house of his own, and 'rather fancied this part of the country'. The words by themselves were not significant, but there had been a sinister gleam in Mr. Templer's eye—or so Mrs. Midge had imagined—and his cherubic smile had boded nothing but ill.

Since that day Mrs. Midge and Lukin had had plenty to talk about. Seldom an evening passed without their indulging in a lively disparagement of the Templer family, and wild surmises about the future. This particular evening was no exception. As soon as they had settled in their chairs, and while Mrs. Midge was still sorting out her embroidery silks, Lukin cocked his head and said:

"Listen, Mama! Do you hear anything odd?"

Mrs. Midge listened, and could hear nothing. But unfortunately she was a little deaf; not deaf to ordinary conversation but deaf to those faint and mysterious sounds which Lukin often heard.

"What do you mean?" she asked.

"There!" said Lukin. He cupped his hand to his ear, giving a dramatic rendering of a man who is hearing something odd. "*There*," he repeated. "Outside in the garden. I think there's someone prowling round."

"You don't mean—"

"I do."

They gazed at each other, indignation sharpening their features and increasing the resemblance between them.

"Not *again*!" said Mrs. Midge. "Well, really, that's—that's the limit."

She could not hear the unlawful sounds but she took Lukin's word for them. Someone was walking about their garden, and they were both convinced that it was their landlord. Or an emissary of their landlord's, which came to the same thing. It had happened before, quite soon after Eustace Templer had dropped the hint about wanting Prospect Cottage for his brother-in-law.

"What *can* he be up to?" Mrs. Midge asked, addressing this question less to Lukin than to the protecting walls around her.

On the other occasion it had not appeared that he was up to anything; a scrupulous examination of the garden, the next morning, had revealed no signs of damage. But perhaps that had merely been a reconnaissance. Mrs. Midge laid down her work, the better to concentrate on what was happening outside. But in the tense silence she could only hear the dripping of the scullery tap and the mooing of a distant cow.

"Of course he's mad," she said.

"Do you think I ought to go out?"

"Certainly not, darling. He might hurt you."

With a mad landlord it was better not to take risks. They waited for some time, but nothing more was heard, and at last it seemed safe to assume that the enemy had retired.

"Well," said Lukin, "I suppose that's the sort of thing we shall have to put up with."

Mrs. Midge pursed her mouth and sighed.

"We shall have to bear it," she said nobly.

Everyone knew that Eustace Templer was eccentric. He had been eccentric for years and they had borne it without much difficulty. Until recently Mrs. Midge had been on good terms with her landlord, and the worst she could find to say about him, when she chatted with Mrs. Imber in the little room behind the shop, was that he was rather peculiar. She used to tap her head as she said it, till she realized that this sort of gesture did not go with the country tweeds and that Mrs. Imber was a friend of Eustace Templer's sister.

But now, looking back, it seemed to Mrs. Midge that she had had a great deal of trouble, far more trouble than other people whose landlords were stable and ordinary. The memory of past grievances made the present situation more alarming; in her eyes Eustace Templer was no longer eccentric, but mad, and his nocturnal sorties in her garden were an absolute proof of it.

"I suppose he can't turn us out," Lukin said doubtfully.

"Certainly not. Not as long as we pay the rent."

Her knowledge of the law was not extensive, but she had a fixed idea that no landlord, however mad and ruthless, could turn you out as long as you paid the rent, and that once you got into arrears you might be summarily evicted.

This belief made the preservation of her own good health an essential duty; she remembered how easily she might have injured herself, falling over Lukin's wooden box, and determined to speak to him about it before the day was over. But the subject must be approached with tact, and the right moment chosen with care; for the present she went on talking about Mr. Templer and their position as his tenants, with a slight emphasis on the need to be scrupulously prompt about paying the rent and not putting themselves in the wrong.

Half-past ten was their bedtime. They were both light sleepers, and late hours did not suit them. Mrs. Midge extinguished the lamp and Lukin lit a taper, with which he led the way out of the room and up the narrow stair. The lighting of the taper was a traditional rite, dating from the time when they had first come to Prospect Cottage and had not accustomed themselves to moving about in the dark.

They washed in the bathroom, Lukin first, then his mother, who undressed slowly to give him plenty of time. Their toothbrushes and mugs, sponges and face-flannels, were arranged on two shelves, with two rails underneath for their towels. Mrs. Midge noticed that Lukin's shelf had been left in extreme disorder and that his towel was flung over a chair instead of being folded in three and replaced on its rail. Allowing herself to feel slightly annoyed she paused to restore everything to its right place, while she rehearsed what she was to say.

When she was ready she went along the passage and tapped lightly on the door of his room. The tap, like the taper, was traditional; she did not wait for an answer but walked into the room as quietly as if he were still a sleeping child. She went to the window and drew back the curtains, then she crossed to the bedside and bent to kiss him.

"Goo' night," he murmured.

This was normally the end of the ceremony, but tonight Mrs. Midge lingered. She had already extinguished the candle, but there was a full moon and she could just see Lukin, who was lying curled up in a posture suggestive of overwhelming sleepiness.

"Lukin," she said gently.

He made a faint and inarticulate response.

Just as Lukin, to forestall or deflect criticism, adopted the character of a small boy, so did Mrs. Midge, in moments of crisis, adopt the third-person and the lofty personification of herself as 'Mother'. At such moments it was not her everyday self who spoke, but a Superior Being inspired solely by an anxious devotion to duty, and therefore entitled to respect.

She assumed this guise only on rare occasions, for it would not have done to make Mother a too familiar figure in their daily life. But Lukin's carelessness might have had serious consequences; it was necessary that he should be brought to see and acknowledge his fault.

She sat down on the edge of the bed and laid her hand on his shoulder.

"Lukin, Mother has something to say to you. . ."

CHAPTER III

WHEN EUSTACE TEMPLER, in a fit of petulance, had decided to retire from his profession, he had acted without delay. His comfortable home in Hampstead was put up for sale, his tradesmen were paid and his furniture sent to store, within a week of the decision. He was a bachelor, which made it easier, and the sister who kept house for him was happily relaxing in Switzerland. He wrote to her on the eve of his departure from London, explaining what he had done but omitting to say where he was going.

Some sisters might have taken it badly, but Isabel Templer had learned to be philosophic.

"Oh well," she said, "if it's done, it's done." Her companion on the holiday, a woman friend of her own age, urged her to return, to seek out Eustace and expostulate. But Miss Templer preferred to stay in Switzerland and make the most of what time remained, for, as she said, she would never dare to go abroad again.

"As for Eustace, it's his own money. He'll find a house somewhere, and I shall be back in time to help with the moving in. I wonder where we shall live."

"But it's absurd," said her friend. "A great artist can't renounce his art and retire, like—like a stockbroker or a civil servant!"

"A great artist certainly couldn't," Miss Templer said calmly. "Eustace is a fashionable portrait painter."

All by himself, on a sunny autumn morning in 1930, Eustace found Prospect House. It had stood empty for some time; the garden was neglected, the bathroom archaic, and there was a gimcrack studio of wood and glass, built out from the back drawing-room. But he liked the house, and he liked the district. It was rural, but not in the least picturesque; it was not the sort of place to attract painters, nor were there any other studios visible in the locality. He found that the property included a field and a second dwelling, known as Prospect Cottage, which was let on a long lease to two old ladies. It stood farther down the hill and could not be seen from Prospect House.

Eustace Templer did not look particularly shrewd but he haggled briskly over the price and eventually got the property for rather less than he had been prepared to pay. He at once arranged to have the studio pulled down and every trace of its existence removed.

By the time Isabel arrived on the scene nothing was left of the studio but the brick footings and a stone-paved floor, and after some argument Eustace agreed that these might remain to form the groundwork for a small walled garden.

"I shall have those little clipped trees in tubs," she said, "and perhaps a sundial in the middle."

At this date Miss Templer intended to take up gardening seriously. Nearly ten years younger than her brother, she was still under forty and her new existence stretched rather bleakly before her; there would be plenty of time, she thought, to learn all about gardening. But somehow she never managed it, the time passed more quickly than she had expected, and she gradually came to look on the tangled vegetation that surrounded Prospect House as a normal, and indeed as a pleasant, background.

For the young Templers, the niece and nephews of Eustace and Isabel, the story of the move to Prospect House was family history, something that happened in the remote past before they were born. What gave it its interest was that Prospect House was now their home and Uncle Eustace and Aunt Bella their guardians.

Only Lily, the eldest, could remember their parents clearly and so compare her present life with what it might have been. It was an agreeable fantasy to pretend that if her father had not been killed in a motor accident and her mother had not died at Leonard's birth, she herself would have been much happier and better prepared for the trials of modern life.

Without wishing to disparage Aunt Bella's efforts, Lily felt that she was not really fitted to bring up three sensitive children. Or perhaps two sensitive children and an imperturbable third; for from the earliest age Leonard had shown a sturdy indifference to his surroundings. But in her less exalted moments she found her present existence quite pleasant and Aunt Bella both kind and tolerant.

With Uncle Eustace, of late, her relations had been less satisfactory.

"Life with Uncle Eustace would hardly be bearable," she said, "if it weren't for the element of mystery."

She said it to her brother Felix, who like herself, and unlike Leonard, took a deep interest in human nature.

"You mean the mystery of his past?"

"Past and present. Is he really eccentric, or does he simply enjoy foxing us?"

"To enjoy pretending to be eccentric is, in itself, a sort of eccentricity," Felix suggested.

"But what he really enjoys, perhaps, is our reactions to the pretence."

"Then he must awfully enjoy having Uncle Henry here. *His* reactions leave ours quite in the shade."

Lily shook her head. "But he doesn't, and one really couldn't expect it. Uncle Henry, as an audience, is too disapproving and prejudiced."

The young Templers were sitting at the breakfast table, alone except for a tortoiseshell cat which was drinking milk from Lily's saucer. Their uncle Henry Ashford had already breakfasted. Eustace, Isabel and Leonard were still to come. Breakfast at Prospect House was a casual meal, with coffee keeping warm by the fire and porridge waiting over a spirit-lamp on the sideboard. Porridge, with toast and marmalade to follow, was all that Miss Templer provided. She and Eustace had always found it enough, and the children had never complained. It was only Colonel Ashford who sometimes looked hungrily about him, deceived by the smell of fried bacon in the hall. The smell came from the kitchen, where Mrs. Truefitt was cooking her own breakfast.

The morning was warm and sunny. A fire was hardly necessary; but in this room, later on, Leonard would do his lessons with his daily governess, who was said to feel the cold. For the sake of Leonard's education breakfast had to be cleared away by half-past nine, and it was now after nine o'clock. From overhead came sounds which showed that the late sleepers were stirring.

"We'd better begin," Lily said. "They will soon be upon us."

She poured out the coffee, Felix helped them both to porridge, and they divided the morning paper between them.

Isabel Templer was the next to appear. Plump and short, with thick grey hair swept into a coil, which began the day by being dignified but soon became wispy, she no longer strove to look youthful, but she still wore the sort of clothes she had liked in her youth, clothes whose bright colours and flowing lines had once proclaimed her modernity, but which now appeared as quaint and old-fashioned as the velvet jackets and peg-top trousers of an earlier Bohemianism.

With a vague but affectionate gesture Miss Templer kissed her niece Lily. Remembering that boys of that age are supposed to dislike such demonstrations, she refrained from kissing her nephew Felix.

"Here are the letters," she said. "The postman came to the front door this morning. I wonder why?"

Felix said the postman had quarrelled with Mrs. Truefitt and daren't go near the back door, though it was shorter for him.

"A letter from Bonny. Now what can she be writing about?"

Miss Templer played a sort of guessing game with her letters, finding out as much as she could from their outward appearance before reading them. While she turned Aunt Bonny's letter over to make out the date of the postmark the door opened and Eustace Templer walked briskly in.

"Good morning, Uncle Eustace," said Lily.

He did not reply at once but stood still, looking meditatively about him at the sunny domestic scene. The fire flickered cosily, the cat was washing its face, the faces of Lily and Felix were adequately welcoming, and through the open windows came the first warmth of summer and the noisy drone of a motor mower. It was the windows that held his attention; and after a long careful look he went across the room and slammed them shut. Then he helped himself to porridge and took his place at the breakfast table.

Miss Templer looked up from her letter and said mildly, "It's too early for your thin shirts, Eustace."

"Not at all. It's no good making rules about what one ought to wear. In England one must dress to match the weather."

To match this particular day he was wearing a faded green shirt and over it an old knitted cardigan, unbuttoned because most of the buttons were missing, and a blue spotted scarf instead of a tie. But as if to contradict this informality he had put on the trousers of his best suit.

"Ne'er cast a clout till May be out," Felix said sagely.

"Exactly," Miss Templer agreed. "Just listen to this." She held up the letter. It was, as she had already announced, from her sister Bonny, who was the wife of Colonel Ashford.

"Uncle Henry," said Felix.

"What, dear?"

"Perhaps we should fetch him. A more fitting audience than ourselves."

"He heard from her yesterday. That's why I was surprised." But the mention of Henry Ashford suggested something else to Miss Templer, whose mental processes were largely based on the association of ideas, and she continued triumphantly:

"Oh, was it the mower, Eustace? I thought at first you were cold."

"I'm never cold. If you dressed to match the weather you wouldn't be either."

"Personally I rather like the sound of it. But perhaps not at breakfast."

"What has breakfast got to do with it? Though as to liking . . ." Eustace stopped eating and listened intently. The noise of the mower, now that the windows were shut, had diminished to a faint buzzing.

"Perfectly insignificant," he declared. "Neither likeable nor dislikeable. A neutral sound."

"Surely silence would be—" his sister began.

"Henry means well. Or if he doesn't, we must give him the benefit of the doubt. But only a man who had spent his life in the tropics would try to mow the lawn at this hour. Don't they have dew in the tropics?"

Lily and Felix remained mutely ignorant.

"Dew," he repeated. "One can't mow long grass in heavy dew."

"Till Uncle Henry bought the mower we couldn't mow the grass at all," said Felix, coolly impartial. Lily, who on the whole preferred her Uncle Eustace to her Uncle Henry, said:

"I don't think there can be dew in the tropics, or he would have told us about it."

"The things Henry tells us," said Isabel, "are never the things one wants to know."

"At our age, my dear, we don't want to know any more than we know already. Our minds are closed—sealed—however much we pretend they're not. We've stopped growing."

"I want to know one thing. If you're not cold, and not disturbed by the mower, why did you shut the windows?"

In his normal good-humoured voice Eustace replied:

"Scorpions."

He helped himself to more coffee, stirred it, tasted it, and added another lump of sugar.

"Scorpions," he repeated. "This weather, you see . . ."

Eustace Templer had one peculiarity which stood out rather above the rest. He disliked, he had a positive horror of, scorpions.

Luckily they were, even in his imagination, few and far between. And in actual fact, as Miss Templer had often pointed out to the children, non-existent. Had he lived in the tropics, or in southern Europe, it might have been different, but here in England there were none. It was just one of his foibles.

Miss Templer said, "I'll get some more D.D.T."

She never argued about the scorpions. It was as though, long ago in the past, they had come to an agreement; her hand-done Christmas cards, blotters and lampshades, the whole messy paraphernalia of her artistic hobbies, in exchange for the scorpions and a few other figments of his imagination.

The promise of more D.D.T. seemed to satisfy him. "I'll get it myself," he said agreeably. "I'm going into Mallinford to see Armitage. A tin, I suppose."

Taking a pencil and a crumpled bit of paper from his trouser pocket he wrote, 'Tin—large', while Lily and Felix exchanged glances of guarded suspicion. The arrival of Leonard came as a not unwelcome interruption to a silence that threatened to be prolonged, and the youngest Templer was received with cordial greetings from everyone.

Leonard was ten years old and did not lack perception. Aware that by being late he had somehow contrived to be useful, he took advantage of his temporary popularity to ask Miss Templer for a holiday, for himself and Miss Custance, one day next week.

"But, Leonard," she said, "you had a holiday *last* week."

"That was not a gifted one. Miss Custance had a cold. It was wasted, because I didn't know it was to be one."

"Eat your breakfast. Miss Custance will be here before you've finished." As she glanced at the clock Isabel's mind took another leap. "Are you going to Mallinford?" she asked Eustace. "You'd better hurry if you're going on the bus; that clock is always six minutes slow on Fridays."

He shook his head. "Doesn't matter if it is. What's Time?— leave Now for dogs and apes. I shall walk; it's too fine a day to hurry after a bus."

"Surely a vain pursuit," said Felix.

"I shall walk slowly down the lane. I want to have a look round."

Isabel sighed. The scorpions were harmless enough, their stings as imaginary as the rest of them, but a visit to Mallinford might mean trouble. Mr. Armitage was Eustace's solicitor—his current solicitor—and she thought immediately of Prospect Cottage. It was on the way to Mallinford, and it might well be the thing he wanted to look round at.

"Are you going to alter your will?" Lily asked boldly. Uncle Eustace permitted and even encouraged a little teasing; he was in some ways a conscientious guardian and he had established an uncle-and-little-niece convention which still coloured Lily's behaviour.

"Yes, Miss. I'm going to cut you off with a shilling." His bright eyes twinkled at her, and there was a gleam of malice in them. It could have been true.

"Aunt Bella, may I have my holiday?"

"Perhaps. I must think about it."

"But *I* have to think about it. I have to make a plan. It's no good saying perhaps,"

"I must ask Miss Custance."

"But she knows. We want to go on an expedition."

"Very well," said Miss Templer, hoping that an expedition sponsored by Cassandra would have cultural value. Torn between her wish to please Leonard, for whom she had a weakness, and her anxiety to be impartial, she looked appealingly at Felix, who had assumed the face of an elder brother.

"I never had holidays," he said.

"You are having one now," said Leonard.

"Convalescence from an illness brought on by overwork is not the same thing as a holiday coaxed from an indulgent aunt," said Felix.

"It lasts much longer."

"An obvious distinction, but not the only one. As Uncle Henry would say—"

"Oh, I wonder if Henry wants anything in Mallinford," Isabel interrupted. "You might go and ask him, Lily."

She stood up and began to gather the cups and plates together. Lily fetched the tray from the sideboard.

"Henry must do his own shopping," Eustace said blithely. "If he wants to live in rural England he must learn to behave like the natives. No turbaned minions here to fetch and carry for him. I'm nobody's minion, am I, Lily?"

"You would look very fine in a turban."

"Too hot," he objected. "Stuffy."

He never wore a hat. His hair was white, but soft and silky like a baby's hair, and it grew with youthful exuberance. He was rather proud of it.

Lily carried the tray to the kitchen. The back door stood open, Mrs. Truefitt was peeling potatoes, the dog Barker, who was supposed to be a watchdog, was lying in his basket. The kitchen bore the stamp of Mrs. Truefitt's personality and was quite different from the rest of the house.

"On the table, please," said Mrs. Truefitt. She was a tall, gaunt woman, encased in late-middle-age since Lily could first remember her. Towards her employers she maintained an attitude of strict neutrality, and among the children she favoured Felix.

Feeling that she was not wanted Lily did not linger, but walked out through the back-yard into the sunlit garden. There were tasks awaiting her indoors, but they were tasks that could be done later.

The discipline of the boarding-school she had so recently left had had little effect on Lily; the virtues of punctuality, method and thoroughness had somehow failed to take root. She had not been unhappy at school, but she was glad to have finished with it. She was thinking about it as she walked through the garden, and the memory of past summer terms, of mornings as fresh and inspiring as this when she had been bound to a dull routine of lessons and school-walks, made idleness a pleasure in itself.

Until Colonel Ashford's arrival no one at Prospect House had attempted to look after the garden. Behind the house, sloping uphill to a belt of coppice, was a neatly cultivated enclosure dedicated to vegetables; this part belonged to old Todd the gardener, just as the kitchen belonged to Mrs. Truefitt. But Todd cared only for vegetables, and the rest of the garden was a wilderness of overgrown bushes and matted grass where long-neglected flower-beds bulged above the surface like small grave-mounds. Although Todd had periodic fits of conscience about the front of the house, during which he weeded the rutted drive and pruned the straggling roses, he had not the time—as he explained to Colonel Ashford—to get things back as they ought to be.

"As they ought to be" was a misleading expression; for Eustace and Isabel liked the garden as it was. The uninteresting and rather dingy walls of Prospect House were hidden by Virginia creeper and rambler roses, the soft, tussocky grass was enclosed by rhododendrons and some fine old trees, and such flowers as had managed to survive grew luxuriantly—clumps of iris on the sloping bank above the lane, sheets of daffodils and bluebells on the higher ground, and foxgloves and willow-herb among the tangled thickets of the shrubbery.

That most of these flowers were not flowers at all, but weeds, in the eyes of a true gardener like Colonel Ashford, was no reason for despising them. They were no trouble. Each, at its proper season, recurrent and dependable, made its gay contrast with the green wilderness of grass and trees, and year after year they appeared in greater profusion.

The whirr of the mower had stopped. Lily came round the corner of the house and saw her uncle Henry Ashford squatting beside his precious machine, with a spanner in his hand and an expression of vexed resignation on his face.

CHAPTER IV

YEARS OF foreign service had given Colonel Ashford the shrivelled appearance of an elderly walnut, but had not impaired his natural energy. He had always taken plenty of exercise. He believed in it. He also believed in method, discipline and punctuality. His present struggles with the garden at Prospect House gave him the exercise he needed and bore witness to his zeal. Each strip of mown grass, each newly-weeded bed, was a symbol of civilization. That Eustace and Isabel preferred the garden as it was did not occur to Colonel Ashford, who had the single-mindedness of a pioneering missionary and no doubts as to what was best for everyone.

For the past few years he had held an administrative post in a native dependency, where his words, though not technically law, had inspired great respect and a large measure of obedience; and to find his life now linked with Eustace Templer's was strange and disturbing. At Prospect House people listened to him if they felt like it, but it made no difference to their actions. But at Prospect House, as he constantly had to remind himself, he was a guest; and for guests, as for everyone else, there was a rigid code of behaviour. He said as little as possible and tried not to show what he thought. The effect of this self-repression on a character which for many years had developed on autocratic lines was mildly disastrous.

Looking up from his struggles with the mower he saw Lily walking towards him. She was wearing white linen trousers and a bright green shirt. Her hair was short and waved, and with the enthusiasm of seventeen she had covered her mouth with scarlet lipstick and her nails with dark crimson nail-varnish. This dazzling colour scheme was a reaction from the dullness of school uniform and healthy schoolgirl complexions, but Colonel Ashford did not know it. He thought she looked quite deplorable.

"'Morning, Lily," he said, straightening himself from his labours. "Had your breakfast?"

"Oh yes," Lily replied, happily impervious to sarcasm. Seeing him standing idle she asked helpfully, "Won't the mower work?"

The owner of a mower which will not work does not care to have its delinquency pointed out to him. Colonel Ashford replied coldly that the grass was too wet.

"Of course you're used to the tropics."

He had long ago given up telling them that his native kingdom had not lain in the tropics, so he let this remark go unanswered.

"Do you want anything in Mallinford?" Lily continued. "Uncle Eustace is going in this morning."

"Is he? I'm going in myself. I'll take him in the car."

In addition to owning a motor mower, Colonel Ashford owned a shiny and almost-new car, which he had bought on his return to England. When he spoke about his car his voice betrayed an unexpected warmth and enthusiasm, and he was always eager to use it and to give lifts to anyone who could be persuaded to accompany him.

When Lily explained that Eustace wanted to walk Colonel Ashford became morose again. It seemed to him a clear example of Eustace's perversity that he should never do a hand's turn in the garden and yet should choose to walk into Mallinford when he might have had a ride in a car.

"Aunt Bella had a letter from Aunt Bonny," said Lily.

Colonel Ashford sighed. His wife Barbara—whom her family insisted on calling by her childhood's name of Bonny—was still in a nursing-home recovering from an operation. It was on her account that he had had to retire a year before his time was up, and that they had come back to England with no plans for the immediate future.

Lily thought the sigh must mean that he was grieving over Aunt Bonny's illness. This was true, but not quite in the way she supposed. Colonel Ashford was one of those healthy, unimaginative men who find it hard to sympathize with ill-health. He did not grudge Barbara her nursing-home, but he could not help wishing that, if she had to be ill, she could have postponed it for another year. If she had not fallen ill he would not now be marooned at Prospect House.

Thinking of this, he sighed again.

"Perhaps Aunt Bonny's much better," Lily said. "Perhaps she'll soon be coming out. I'm sure she must be longing to get away from the nursing-home."

She said it to cheer him up, but it did not have a very good effect. He remembered that in her last letter his wife had mentioned she would have to live quietly for a few weeks and had suggested that they should stay on at Prospect House during her convalescence. The idea of it appalled him.

"Well . . ." said Lily, whose kind impulse to cheer her uncle up had already diminished. All conversations between Colonel Ashford and his relatives had a way of ending in inconclusive silences and an atmosphere of things carefully unsaid. She smiled politely, to show that she was still listening if he wanted to go on talking; but Colonel Ashford was looking at his watch.

The morning was too fine to be wasted on an uncle, and without saying any more Lily drifted away. She walked round to the other side of the house, where she found Felix lying on a rug and reading a detective story.

"And what are your plans for the future?" Felix asked, in a not-very-successful imitation of his Uncle Henry.

"If you mean for today, none at all."

"Don't you find it very dull, doing nothing?"

"I find it heaven, after school."

"Well, I don't," said Felix. "I thought I should, but the pleasure has worn off. I shall ask to do lessons with Leonard."

"Don't be silly," his sister said kindly. She was fond of both her brothers, and especially of Felix, but she had lately come to feel that they were much younger than herself.

"But one must do something. You ought to get a job, or you'll turn into an Uncle Eustace."

"Of course I shan't."

"Or Aunt Bella—worse still. Unless of course you find someone to marry."

"I shan't get married for a long time," Lily said firmly. A year ago she would have discussed anything with Felix, but now there were subjects she did not care to discuss. She sometimes wished that instead of brothers she had a sister of about her own age, or a dear sympathetic female friend, with whom she could have long, cosy talks about the future.

Although at present she was content to do nothing, Lily had no intention of settling down at Prospect House. Little Mallin was too quiet, and all the people who lived there had known her since she was a child and still treated her as a child; and then they were mostly middle-aged or elderly people. When she announced that she did not mean to marry for a long time, she spoke the truth. But in her imaginary talks with the imaginary female friend she admitted that she would like to be admired, and perhaps sought in marriage. It did not seem probable that this would happen to her if she remained in Little Mallin.

She lay back on the grass and closed her eyes, slipping happily into the daydream of becoming a charming, amusing creature and going to a lot of parties where she excelled in brilliant conversation. The kind of parties she envisaged were held in large sumptuous rooms, and though music and dancing took place, as it were, in the background, brilliant conversation was their *raison d'être*. Women in elegant gowns, men in evening dress, strolled through the rooms (there were always several rooms, connected by double doors or velvet-hung archways), or formed groups about some witty and intelligent speaker whose sallies held them enthralled. And the centre of one such group, of course, was Lily herself.

She knew quite well that it was a fantasy, a dream picture of what she would like the future to be. Brilliant conversation, unfortunately, was not a thing at which she excelled, but she believed this was due to her present youth and inexperience.

At home there was no one to talk to, for Uncle Eustace preferred to do the talking himself, Uncle Henry was morose, her brothers too young, and Aunt Bella too absent-minded. But now, lying on the grass and enjoying the stimulating heat of the sun, it occurred to Lily that she might gain experience and poise by talking to other people. Even if the inhabitants of Little Mallin were stupid and dull, they would do to practise on, and even if they thought of her as a child, in common politeness they would have to listen to her. It was a good idea; and she wondered where she should begin.

There were the Custances. She could try Cassandra; but Cassandra, by being Leonard's governess, was perhaps too nearly one of the family. There were Miss Fenn and Miss Daisy Fenn, rather excitable and both great talkers themselves. There were the Brighams at Mallin Hall, Sir James and his son George, promising material but unfortunately rather inaccessible, since Mallin Hall stood a mile the other side of the village and she had no good reason for going there. Regretting the distance that separated her from the Brighams—for she felt that a male audience would perhaps be easier—she suddenly remembered Lukin Midge.

Lukin had several defects but one obvious advantage: he was close at hand. She would not have to invent reasons for a stroll down the lane, and Mrs. Midge was always away on week-days. Lily had an impulsive nature, and no sooner had she thought of this interesting scheme than she yearned to put it into practice. She sat up and brushed the grass from her bare arms.

"Would you like my other book?" Felix asked.

"No, thank you. I'm just going for a walk."

"A sign of boredom. One goes for walks in the country to fill in time."

Lily did not bother to answer this. Her walk had a more important purpose than filling in time, but she was not going to say so to Felix. Halfway across the lawn she thought it might be better if she changed her old canvas plimsolls and touched up her face before setting forth, and she turned back towards the house.

Felix was deep in his detective story, but this digression did not escape him.

"Don't put on any more lipstick," he called. "The cows don't really notice it."

Colonel Ashford pushed his motor-mower round to the shed in the back-yard. He came into the house through the kitchen, where Mrs. Truefitt was making pastry.

"There's a cup of coffee for you, sir, if you want it," she said. "Shall I bring it through?"

Colonel Ashford said he would have it in the kitchen, and sat down at the other end of the well-scrubbed table. He liked Mrs. Truefitt. She listened to him with the respectful attention to which he had long been accustomed. She called him 'sir', she studied his ways, she made no demands; and she had the additional merit, which his native subordinates had lacked, of not being temperamental.

When he had first come to Prospect House he had thought it odd that people like Eustace and Bella should have such a respectable henchwoman as Mrs. Truefitt. She was not only a good cook but she knew how to behave. The more he saw of her, the more he realized how ill-suited she was to her present position; without putting it clearly into words he had come to believe that she was much too good for Eustace and Bella. She was just the kind of cook he would like in his own house.

In company with Mrs. Truefitt, though he would not have admitted it, Colonel Ashford passed his happiest hours at Prospect House. The conventions, of course, were strictly observed; there was no mention of the Templers, never a hint of disapproval or regret. Even when he spoke of his struggles with the garden he implied that it had fallen into ruin through the mere accident of time, and Mrs. Truefitt gave him moral support by taking the line that without a motor-mower gardening would be quite impossible.

If Colonel Ashford had a weakness it was a passion for motors and mechanically-propelled vehicles. This passion, and his irritation at the sight of the neglected garden, had led him into buying the motor-mower; of course he would take it with him when he got a house of his own, and in the meantime, he assured himself, it would help to fill in the hours of enforced idleness.

He was thinking about the mower now, as he sat sipping his coffee. It was not behaving itself. It had already broken down twice, and showed a horrid tendency to tear up the grass by the roots or else to bound along over the matted surface without cutting anything. It was perhaps the fault of the grass; but he had a touching faith in the power of man, and of man-made machines, to conquer all obstacles. He decided to call at the shop where he had bought the mower and have a talk with the enthusiast who had sold it to him.

"I'm going into Mallinford," he told Mrs. Truefitt. "Anything I can do for you?"

Mrs. Truefitt said she would be glad if he would visit the ironmonger's and find out if the mincer had been mended yet. In saying this she showed tact. Colonel Ashford liked being given a task to perform, since it made him feel that his visit to Mallinford was necessary as well as enjoyable, but he also like the task to be something simple and straightforward, not taking up too much of his time. As he was going to the ironmonger's anyway, the present task was perfectly chosen, and they parted with smiles.

He closed the kitchen door behind him and immediately found himself back in the Templer *ménage* where there was always something to irritate him. The big, square hall faced south and was now full of sunlight. The sunlight showed him, as it had shown Mr. Custance, that the place had not been dusted that morning. Or perhaps for several mornings.

Colonel Ashford paused, trying to work out who should have dusted the hall, and when. The trouble at Prospect House was bad organization; there was no plan, or if there was, they did not stick to it. He took a small note-book from his pocket and wrote down a list of the rooms, and opposite them a list of names.

Mrs. Truefitt did the cooking and cleaned the dining-room and the back premises and her own bedroom and the bathroom. Probably she did other work he did not know about; he ticked her name off as being fully occupied. Eustace and the boys did nothing, but it was impossible to include them in any plan and expect it to work. There was a garrulous old woman who came on certain days to clean brasses, scrub the stone passages, and turn out rooms. Except when she turned out a room she did not do any dusting, so he put her name at the bottom of the list with a question-mark. That left Bella, Lily and himself.

It was Bella and Lily who disorganized the plan. They were for ever exchanging duties, saying "I'll do that", or simply leaving some task undone. Dusting the drawing-room was nominally Lily's work, and Eustace's library, Bella's. Since his arrival Colonel Ashford had made himself responsible for the upper passages and the stairs, and had polished all the brass door-knobs which were not on the official brass-list. The hall was debatable territory, a sort of no man's land where Bella and Lily made occasional sorties when they thought about it.

Colonel Ashford studied his list. If the hall could have been exactly divided by a chalk line down the middle, half for Lily and half for Bella, or if Eustace could have been persuaded to accept it as his task, things would have been pretty equal. But as it was, the only solution seemed to be to dust it himself.

He looked at the clock and decided that it was too late to begin now. It was, in fact, rather later than he had thought. He went into the cloakroom and washed away the traces of his struggles with the mower. When he came out, his sister-in-law was standing in the hall.

She was wearing a raffia hat, decorated with a bunch of woolwork flowers, and over her summer frock a picturesque blue cape lined with yellow silk taffeta. A raffia bag to match the hat was looped over one arm, and she was further encumbered by a cluster of lampshades and an untidy paper parcel. Colonel Ashford looked at her, and his heart sank. She was obviously coming with him to Mallinford.

"Mrs. T. told me you were going in the car," she was saying. "So I thought it would be a grand chance to take some stuff to Mrs. Imber. So difficult on the bus."

He nodded glumly. Then, pulling himself together, he offered to carry the lampshades. After all, she was Barbara's sister, and his hostess.

"Thank you, but I think not," Miss Templer replied. "They crush so, you see."

Colonel Ashford said nothing. They walked in silence to the converted stable where the car lived. He settled the lampshades on the back seat and his sister-in-law on the front one. He wiped over the windscreen, which was already spotless, and got in himself. He pressed the self-starter and the car started at once.

The car's obedience was soothing. In his late career he had been able to impose neatness and discipline on his surroundings, and even on his subordinates, while here everything seemed to defy him. The long wet grass that would not let itself be cut, Lily's regrettable appearance, the dust in the hall—these were but minor instances of what he had to bear. But now, steering carefully down the steep drive, making the car stop at the gate, making it proclaim its coming with loud blasts on the horn, he felt happier. The car at least was his own, and would do as it was told.

His heart softened towards Bella. He really enjoyed giving people lifts; it made him feel powerful and benevolent, like a well-disposed djinn with a particularly luxurious magic carpet.

Bella did not deserve a lift, for the last time she had been in the car she had spilt a bottle of ink on the floor, and the time before she had lured him into taking a short cut which had ended, as he might have foreseen, in a farmyard. It was for these reasons that he had disliked her coming this time, but now that she was here he was prepared to make the best of it.

They passed the belt of trees and saw below them the trim red roof of Prospect Cottage. As they approached it Miss Templer asked suddenly:

"Would you really like to live there, Henry?"

Colonel Ashford felt that the question needed a careful answer. He was not sure whether Bella wanted him at Prospect Cottage. He was not even sure whether he wanted it himself.

"Nice-looking place," he said judicially. "Just the right size, too. Must see what Barbara thinks about it."

Miss Templer rightly took this to mean that he had not yet made his mind up about Prospect Cottage.

"Lovely roses," she remarked. "And they're always so prompt with the rent. It seems rather a shame."

Colonel Ashford said nothing. He could not see what the roses had to do with it.

CHAPTER V

THE TOLL-BRIDGE dated from the early years of the nineteenth century. It had been built, at great expense, to replace an ancient ferry and to provide a direct road between Little Mallin and Mallinford. But it served, paradoxically, to keep them apart.

Mallinford was a thriving country town. It had a small carpet factory, a brewery, two corn mills, and a flourishing weekly market; and in addition it had some attractions for summer visitors, who came for the fishing and sailing in the estuary below the town. But to get there from Little Mallin it was necessary to pay the toll: a halfpenny for pedestrians, fourpence for a cart, and sixpence for a car. The high cost of communications kept Little Mallin isolated and rural, and was a great grievance to the more ambitious members of the community.

If the toll-bridge were free, they argued, their village would become a prosperous extension of Mallinford. But as it was, the council houses, the new shops, and the projected new county school were all to be built at the other side of the town; and Little Mallin still had no main drainage.

The progressive element in Little Mallin was not very large. But although the majority of the residents did not yearn for a new housing estate and were quite content with the existing sanitation, almost everyone grumbled a bit when it came to paying the toll. Perhaps the only exceptions were the Misses Fenn, who lived in a house close to the toll-bridge itself and found it both convenient and enjoyable to have an unhurried view of everything that crossed the river.

If they wanted a word with any of their friends they had only to keep an eye on the road; for everybody, sooner or later, had some shopping to do in Mallinford. At the end of the bridge was a white gate and a small hut for the toll-keeper; this official did his business in a very leisurely way and there was usually time for Dossie or Daisy to run out of her own gate and intercept the person she wanted to speak to. It was, as they often exclaimed, "so handy being right on the spot".

Their house stood on the river bank and was called The Moorings. It was one of a pair of small brick villas which had been built about fifty years ago, rather spoiling the approach to Little Mallin. Its twin brother, The Anchorage, nestled alongside; the houses were detached, but only just, and the tarred wooden fence that separated them was a continual source of trouble. The fence belonged to Bryce, the owner of The Anchorage, and needed repairs. It threatened to fall into the Misses Fenns' garden. Again and again they had spoken to Bryce about it, and he had said he would see to it as soon as he had time. But nothing ever got done.

It was not the only thing that Bryce neglected, and the maddening part was that he was perfectly capable of mending the fence. In the village it was generally believed that Bryce could do anything, if he cared to turn his hand to it.

He was not noticeably idle, but he was always busy with something else. This morning he had gone to look at the engine of a motor-boat. The workshop where he was often to be found stood locked, and outside the door some hopeful person had dumped a sewing-machine, with a label tied to its handle saying 'Urgent'. This was convincing evidence of his absence; for had he been there the sewing-machine would have been admitted to join the ranks of bicycles, pots and pans, parts of engines, and other objects awaiting repair. Though deaf to cries of urgency, Bryce never refused a job.

Miss Templer turned away from the workshop door and re-traced her steps to the car. She had remembered, as they drove through the village, that both the sash-cords of her bedroom window were broken, and she had asked Henry to stop while she had a word with Bryce. It was a triumph to have remembered about the broken sash-cords while she was in the vicinity of the workshop, and an additional disappointment that Bryce should now be absent.

"Perhaps he's having a morning at home," she said to Henry Ashford. "We might just look in on the chance."

Colonel Ashford looked instead at his watch, and the significance of this gesture was not lost on Isabel. Poor Henry, always thinking about the time, always worrying about being late—it was a dreadful nervous habit which seemed to be growing on him. Probably, she thought kindly, it was the strain of those years in the tropics and the great burden of responsibility that had lain on his shoulders. She did not feel a strong affection for her brother-in-law, but she was ready to make allowances for him.

"It won't take a minute," she said. "His house is at the other end of the village, close to the bridge. I'll just pop across and see him while you're getting the toll ticket."

"Doesn't take a second to get the ticket. And I can't wait out there on the bridge, holding up the traffic."

"There's never much traffic and anyway there's plenty of room. And old Birley loves a chat."

Colonel Ashford knew this. He had already had several encounters with old Birley, who seemed to think the duties of a toll-keeper included finding out the destination and business of all who crossed the bridge. But he knew also that Bella, though forgetful and feather-brained, could be dreadfully obstinate. He would have to stop at the toll-gate, and nothing but force could prevent her getting out of the car and 'popping across' to see this Bryce. Resigning himself to the inevitable he said curtly:

"Don't be long."

"I shan't be a minute," she replied inaccurately. They were approaching the bridge as she spoke, and almost without a pause she added: "Oh, Henry, stop here! There's Mrs. Custance, I must just speak to her."

"I can't stop here."

"Then I'll just run back. I want to ask her to tea."

Exercising remarkable self-restraint, Colonel Ashford said nothing. He drew up by the toll-keeper's hut, and Miss Templer got out of the car and walked back to meet Mrs. Custance. Old Birley was talking to the driver of a car coming the other way; it really didn't matter, Colonel Ashford thought, if the feller kept him waiting twenty minutes. For Bella would certainly keep him longer than that.

The sun glinted on the water, gulls sailed overhead, and the air smelt faintly of tar and salt. Below the bridge the river broadened into a long, winding estuary, and in the distance he could see a dinghy tacking downstream. He did not care for sailing, but he thought how satisfactory it would be to have a motor-boat, something quite small and handy which he could manage himself, and in which he could escape from Prospect House and all its inhabitants.

Colonel Ashford was a practical man, and it was not often that he indulged in such longings. The car and the lawn-mower were useful things; a motor-boat would be a luxury. Nevertheless, he wondered how much they cost, and whether they used much petrol. The dream had progressed no further when a voice in his ear, coming from the outer world and not from his conscience, said loudly:

"A penny for them!"

Turning his head he found himself facing, at close range, the beaming smile and flashing teeth of the younger Miss Fenn.

"A penny for your thoughts," she repeated, to make it quite clear. She laughed to show that it was a joke. "I saw the car— rushed out to catch you—but I must say you don't seem in a hurry."

"I am waiting for my sister-in-law," he replied.

"Then you'll be here for ages. Dear Miss Templer, she's an angel, but absolutely no sense of time. Where is she?"

"She went to see Bryce."

"Then she'll be unlucky—he's out. But whatever it is, it's no good asking Bryce. Dossie and I have been at him for a year to get the fence mended, but he won't do a thing!"

Though still conscious that he had a grievance, Colonel Ashford began to feel more cheerful. Miss Fenn's brisk voice and her contemptuous dismissal of Bryce suggested that she shared his views on sloth and procrastination. He said that everyone in the village seemed to him only half-awake, and she agreed that it did seem like that sometimes.

"When I came home after the war I just couldn't believe it," she went on. "I mean, being in the Services does teach you to make it snappy."

He nodded, feeling that the woman spoke sense; though her use of the plural was rather puzzling. She could hardly have been in more than one Service. He wondered which one, and was about to ask her when she turned away to speak to old Birley, who had finished his conversation with the driver of the other car and was now ready to start all over again.

"Lovely day," she shouted. She worked on the assumption that old people were always rather deaf.

"Aye. Going to 'ave a fine summer at last."

Birley always had a lot to say about the weather, but this time he was not allowed to say it. Miss Fenn cut him short, thereby establishing herself in Colonel Ashford's eyes as a woman of character.

"Where's Bryce got to?" she demanded.

"Mr. Bryce 'e went down to Shingle Street. Says 'e 'ad to look at a motor-boat that's a-laid up down there."

"There you are!" Miss Fenn said triumphantly, turning back to Colonel Ashford. "Got a whole workshop full of jobs waiting for him, and he has to go pottering off after an old boat that won't be wanted till the holiday people come. Typical, isn't it?"

Colonel Ashford agreed with her. But he was more interested in the motor-boat than in the iniquities of Bryce. "Do they hire it out?" he asked.

"They use it to run people across the river from Mallinford, in the summer. There's a café place at Shingle Street, but of course it's miles from anywhere, except by boat."

"Very pretty it is, down at Shingle Street," old Birley put in. "You oughter 'ave a look at it, sir, when you got time. You goes down there along the footpath—"

"*There's* Miss Templer coming now, with Mrs. Custance. Is Mrs. Custance going with you to Mallinford?"

"I expect so," Colonel Ashford said gloomily. He liked giving people lifts—but he liked to be the one to offer the lift. Too often Bella behaved as if the car were her own, making him stop and offer lifts to people he had never seen before and never wanted to see again, people who banged the doors, dropped cigarette ash on the carpet, and asked to be set down at very inconvenient places.

He wished Mrs. Custance good morning and learnt without surprise that she was coming with them to Mallinford.

"It will save me going in this afternoon," she said. "I've only got to get the fish, so it won't take long."

He was glad to hear it. Moreover, Mrs. Custance knew him to be the owner of the car and asked him where she should sit.

"We'll sit together in the back," Miss Templer interposed. "Just help me to move these lampshades to the front. Or do you want to come too, Daisy?"

Miss Fenn said she was too busy, she had just come across to tell Colonel Ashford there was a house for sale over at Witling, because she'd heard he was looking for a house; of course it wasn't her business but one couldn't help hearing things, and the house at Witling was the old rectory and was being sold by the ecclesiastical commissioners because it was three miles from the church and too big for the present rector.

"Then I expect it would be too big for me," he said.

"You might buzz over and have a look at it. It wouldn't take you long in *this* car," said Miss Fenn, giving the car an admiring glance as she spoke. "Let me know if you're going, and I'll tell you how to find it, it's a bit off the map. Or I could come with you."

Colonel Ashford was not a vain man. Admiring glances directed at himself would have left him unmoved; but to have his car admired was a different matter. He could not resist it, and quite unexpectedly he found himself saying that he might run over to Witling that afternoon, and that it would be a pleasure if Miss Fenn would accompany him.

"Love to," she answered heartily. "Three o'clock suit you? Right. I'll meet you at the other end of the village, by the criss-cross. No point in you coming down here, 'cos we have to go up the other road past the Brighams. Bye-bye for now."

In the back seat of the car Mrs. Custance and Miss Templer exchanged smiling looks, but Colonel Ashford was not aware of it. "Sensible young woman, that," he observed, as they drove across the bridge.

Neither of his passengers disputed it, though neither of them, with Cassandra and Lily for comparison, would have described Daisy Fenn as young—or even as sensible. The Misses Fenn had retained a girlish exuberance which caused them to be known, behind their backs, as 'Fizz and Pop'. But they had lived in the village for most of their life and had come to be tolerated and accepted. Mrs. Custance liked them both, and what she alluded to as 'their little ways' drew from her no more than a shake of the head and a mild wish that they would learn to settle down.

"The rectory at Witling is hopeless," she said to Miss Templer, speaking in a low voice so that Colonel Ashford should not hear. "About twenty rooms, and it's never been modernized. When Mr. Scrope was there—the old rector, you know—he let it get full of birds."

"Birds," Miss Templer said thoughtfully. "Do you mean in aviaries?"

"Oh no, real birds out of the garden. Mr. Scrope was devoted to birds. He used to feed them and talk to them, and gradually they got very tame, and then they started coming into the house. Of course, that was after his wife died, and I suppose he was lonely. There were robins nesting in the bedrooms, and jackdaws in the chimneys, and chaffinches all over the place, and bluetits in the dining-room clock. Of course it made rather a mess."

"But very charming. Why did I never get to know Mr. Scrope?"

"He was a recluse. He never went anywhere—except, of course, to the church, and that, I'm afraid, not as often as he might have done. Very difficult for his successor, and I hear he's rather High which won't make it any easier."

Mrs. Custance had strong views on parsons who were High, but to Miss Templer's volatile mind they sounded like pheasants that had been hung too long. The wheel came full circle, for the pheasants recalled the palatial outside-larder of her grandfather's country house, and this, through some trick of Gothic perspective, reminded her of the ugly protruding porch of Mallin church.

"Edward gave us a very good sermon last Sunday," she said. "Really most interesting, only I did wish I'd had a map because I'm so bad at geography."

"Geography?"

"Where St. Paul went—all those islands and places in the Mediterranean, or was it the Aegean?"

"Oh, *ancient* geography," Mrs. Custance said disparagingly. "My dear, what's the good of learning that?—it's all altered since then. And after all, it's what St. Paul *said* that matters."

After they had delivered the lampshades at Mrs. Imber's shop Miss Templer offered to accompany Mrs. Custance to the fishmonger's. There were three fishmongers in Mallinford, but the one they patronized was the smallest and most obscure, situated in a narrow lane off the High Street and hiding its excellence behind a frosted window on which the words ISH ONGER were faintly visible. The lane in which it stood was a blind alley, and Miss Templer told Colonel Ashford that they would leave him to do his own shopping and meet him near the market cross in twenty minutes' time.

"It's no good asking Henry to bring the car down here," she said, as they picked their way along the cobbled pavement. "He can't turn it, and he's not very clever at backing it. I sometimes wish he hadn't bought such a large car, but it's nice being able to give people lifts."

"Very nice," Mrs. Custance agreed. "Our car always seems to be full of things, and then all the springs are sticking through the back seat, so it's not very comfortable."

They came to the fishmonger's. By this time it was too late to expect a wide choice of fish, but Mrs. Custance bought some smoked haddock and a pair of kippers and professed herself satisfied. "No queue at all," she said. "We haven't been nearly twenty minutes. I might as well go to the post-office and get some stamps."

Miss Templer remembered that she needed some white tape. Both stamps and tape could have been got in Little Mallin. But it would save time to get them now, said Mrs. Custance, walking briskly away from the market cross where Colonel Ashford sat looking at his watch.

The post-office was at the other end of the High Street, and on the way they stopped to buy the tape, and to examine some rolls of material for summer dresses. Neither of them needed a new summer dress that year, but they had Lily and Cassandra to think about.

"Cassie never seems to bother," Mrs. Custance said fretfully. "I don't want her to be vain, but I do wish she cared for clothes."

"She always looks very nice."

Naturally, thought Mrs. Custance, her daughter looked very nice. That was not what she had meant, and it was stupid of Isabel to misunderstand her. Cassie looked nice because she could not help it, and therefore it was no credit to her.

Mrs. Custance sometimes felt that she would not have minded Cassie's indifference to dress, if she had been an ugly girl. It would not have seemed such a waste. But pretty daughters were a tradition in her family. She had been one herself (though with the disadvantage of having three sisters who rather outshone her), and Cassie had the Maitland eyes, the Maitland mouth, and the classic oval face, and in fancy-dress would have borne a striking resemblance to her great-grandmother who had brought these good looks into the Maitland family. The trouble was that she had inherited the Maitland looks without the Maitland character.

Mrs. Custance regarded herself as a happily married woman, and except in moments of exasperation she was devoted to her husband. This did not prevent her from imputing all Cassandra's shortcomings to her Custance blood. Unable to believe that any young woman could really prefer comfort to elegance, or care more for a new book than a new hat, she put it all down to laziness. Edward was lazy. Of course he was clever too, but the laziness was a fatal bar to achievement. Cassie had inherited it, which explained, though it did not excuse, her refusal to take trouble over her clothes.

Thinking sadly of Cassie's laziness, while she fingered the material and wondered if the blue would fade (eight-and-eleven was not much in these days), Mrs. Custance became aware of a familiar voice wishing her good morning. She looked up and saw that it was George Brigham.

"Good morning, George," she said curtly.

A few years ago he would have had a warmer greeting, but a combination of circumstances had caused her to do a thing foreign to her nature. She had changed her mind about George.

Though such a change was, for her, an unnatural action, she had done it thoroughly. From being a first favourite in her affections, the son of her old friend and neighbour Sir James Brigham, a motherless boy who needed mothering, and just the right age for Cassandra, he had become ungrateful and conceited, a disappointment to his father, a man with very odd friends, a man who got engaged to Italian countesses. His fall from grace had been so complete that she hardly ever thought about him, and although he sometimes came to church their acquaintance had dwindled into an exchange of good mornings and conventional comments on the weather.

Apart from these Sunday occasions she seldom saw him nowadays, and to meet him in Baxter's shop was an unpleasant surprise. A man of his age, Mrs. Custance thought, should be at work and not loitering about in close proximity to a display of ladies' underwear.

Miss Templer shared her surprise, though not her displeasure.

"What a funny place to meet you, George," she said. "What are you buying?"

"Darning wool," said George. He showed it to them, and Mrs. Custance could not help thinking it was very inferior darning wool. But Miss Templer was more struck by its colour.

"It's very bright," she said. "Are your socks really that peacock blue?"

"Well, no," he admitted. "It was all they had. But it always gets dirty while I'm doing the darning, so that'll tone it down a bit."

Time was when Mrs. Custance had gone through all George's clothes, darning and mending them, before he went back to school. She wondered if he still made as many holes in his socks, and what the resulting darns looked like.

But she had no wish to continue the conversation, and she was glad to see that he was in a hurry to be gone.

"I eat at that café near the station," he was telling Miss Templer. "The food's not bad but you get very small helpings if you're late."

"Oh, dear!" Miss Templer exclaimed. "Is it lunch-time already?"

George said it was nearly one o'clock. Even Mrs. Custance was surprised that the morning had gone so quickly. "Cassie will be home before me," she said. But it did not really matter, for Edward had to be in Bramchester that day and she and Cassie were only having cold boiled bacon and salad, so there was no cooking.

"I'm afraid we've kept Henry waiting," said Miss Templer. This did not matter either, although Henry would probably think otherwise. But after all, he had no other occupation.

At the door of the shop they parted, George Brigham going one way, the ladies the other. Watching him stride off up the street Miss Templer remarked that he was really very handsome. But of course Sir James was a handsome man too, if only he didn't stoop so badly.

"Handsome is as handsome does," said Mrs. Custance.

"Yes, I think George has been a disappointment to his father. What a pity he doesn't marry and settle down."

"Well, he's been engaged for months. I suppose he's bound to get married soon."

"But he isn't engaged," said Miss Templer. "There was some mistake about that, or else it's off now. I forget the story exactly, but Lily was talking about it the other day."

"These Italians!" Mrs. Custance said sharply.

"Oh no, Amy, this one wasn't an Italian. That was the first one, Contessa Something-or-other, but that didn't last very long. I expect it was just being in Italy and the war being over, you know. I nearly got engaged myself once in Italy, and not to the nobility either, and I was much older than George."

"'Nearly being engaged' isn't the same thing at all, and anyway it's quite different for a woman," said Mrs. Custance. "I don't approve of men who play fast and loose. The war spoilt George Brigham."

Nevertheless, the thought of George darning his own socks, and the news—if it was accurate—that he was no longer engaged to be married, had somewhat oddly combined to make her sorry. Not sorry for George (who did not deserve to be pitied), but sorry that she had had to change her mind.

CHAPTER VI

THE TEMPLERS and the Midges had never become friends, and relations between Prospect House and Prospect Cottage were based on mutual forbearance rather than on esteem. Since Mrs. Midge had gone to work at the Gifte Shoppe she had seen more of Miss Templer than she had done in the past, but she did not like what she saw; Miss Templer's lampshades and Christmas cards were surprisingly attractive, but Miss Templer herself, vague, untidy and inefficient, was the sort of woman she had been brought up to despise.

Her poor opinion of the Templers was shared by Lukin, whose sensitive nature felt itself slighted by their lack of interest. Lily, Felix and Leonard were much younger than himself, but on the occasions when they met he found himself at a disadvantage. They treated him neither as a comrade nor as a responsible elder, but rather as a native of some distant and backward country for whom allowances must be made.

On her side, Lily was accustomed to hearing Lukin Midge laughed at or pitied for being simply the appendage of a possessive and adoring mother. It was possible to like or dislike Mrs. Midge, but it was not possible to feel strongly about Lukin. In all the years they had lived at Prospect Cottage she could hardly remember seeing him apart from his mother; and for the last year she had not seen him at all. At Christmas he had been ill, and in her summer holidays he had been away from home. The intervening periods, of course, she had spent at school.

Now that she had left school for ever she felt that the time had come to make a new approach to Lukin Midge; and indeed to all the people she knew. She wanted conversational experience, but she also wanted to find out what Lukin was really like. She was no longer a child, and to mark her independence it was necessary that she should form her own judgements and not accept, unquestioningly, those of her family and friends.

Resolutely unprejudiced, Lily entered the trim garden of Prospect Cottage and advanced towards the front door. It was opened, before she had had time to knock, by Mrs. Nutting. Mrs. Nutting was the daily help, who, as well as obliging Mrs. Midge, came twice a week to Prospect House and had known Lily since she was ten.

"Well now, what a surprise!" Mrs. Nutting said cheerfully. "You give me quite a start, you did indeed, Miss Lily. Jest coming out to give this old rug a shake—not that it reelly needs it, but she likes 'em shaken out every day, wet *or* fine!" She threw the rug down on the step and folded her arms comfortably across her bosom, ready, as always, for a nice long chat.

Lily was disconcerted. In her hurry to gain poise and experience she had forgotten that Mrs. Nutting would be here. For a moment it seemed that the expedition was doomed to failure, but luckily, in the spate of talk which now filled the air, she was able to snatch at a plausible excuse for her own presence.

"Brought a message from your auntie, I s'ppose," Mrs. Nutting was saying. "If it's a note, you give it me and I'll put it where she sees it when she comes 'ome. Top of the dresser with an egg-cup on it, that's where I always puts it. But it's no good you giving it me by mouth, because I never sees 'er, on'y Saturdays when she doesn't go to the shop. If it's by mouth, Miss Lily, you'd better come in and write it down. There's a pad and pencil in the kitchen, and if it's anything private like, I dessay I could take an envelope from 'er writing-desk. She won't mind that, not for once, though mind you she's *that* fussy—"

"Actually, it's a message for Mr. Lukin," Lily said loudly. "Is he at home?"

"'E's down there in that shed of 'is, bottom of the garden, where 'e always is." Though she obviously longed to know what the message was about, Mrs. Nutting appeared to accept it as genuine. "Shall I call 'im, or will you go down there?" she asked. "I can easy call 'im, there's a sorter bell, ever so funny it is, 'anging in the kitchen—"

"I'll go and find him."

Having shaken Mrs. Nutting off—a process which took time— Lily walked down the garden towards the workroom. Its windows faced the house, and she could see Lukin moving about inside. But he did not notice her approach, and as she came nearer she saw that he was engaged in some form of gymnastic exercises, raising his arms above his head, stretching up towards the ceiling, and then performing a complicated kind of jump.

This was not what she had expected. Though she was determined to make a new start it was not possible to obliterate all she knew and had heard of Lukin, and she had imagined him as an indolent person, a static contrast to his mother's bustling energy. Surprised at what she saw, Lily forgot the intelligent remark with which she had meant to begin the interview. Arriving at the open door of the workroom she exclaimed abruptly: "Hullo! What are you doing?"

She was not the only one to be surprised. Lukin, at the difficult climax of his gymnastics, lost his balance and staggered towards her, overturning a chair in his progress. Confronted by an unknown young woman, and confused by the clatter of the falling chair, he involuntarily spoke the truth.

"I'm trying to get taller."

To Lily, full of schemes for her own improvement, this appeared a laudable venture. But she wondered whether it would succeed. "Can you?" she asked doubtfully. "I mean, shouldn't you have begun earlier?"

At the second glance Lukin had recognized his visitor. Lily Templer was not a person he would have chosen to confide in, had he recognized her sooner. But at least she was not laughing at him. She looked quite serious.

"I've got a book about it," he said cautiously.

"I suppose you are rather small, but does it really matter?"

The words, spoken harshly, might have wounded him, but her voice was reassuringly sympathetic. Besides, she was small herself, so that in her company he was not reminded of his lack of inches.

"Hadn't you noticed it?" he asked. "I always imagine people notice it, but then I'm painfully self-conscious."

"Oh," said Lily, not knowing what else to say. None of her other acquaintances in Little Mallin would have confessed to being self-conscious, nor would they have tried to make themselves taller. His sulky dignity was a little absurd, but she found him interesting. She felt that the conversation had begun well.

"I thought you were delicate," she went on. "But those exercises look awfully strenuous."

At this allusion to his health Lukin thawed perceptibly.

"I *am* delicate," he said, as if he were rather proud of it. "I had a very unsettled childhood, and I'm highly strung. I get bronchitis in the winter, but I had the Schwenk-Stenhouse injections last year and they really did a lot of good."

"Oh," she repeated. As a comment on his complicated ill-health it sounded inadequate. "Then you must be looking forward to the summer," she added.

Lukin smiled sadly. "I can't stand the heat," he said. "It gives me insomnia."

"Well—but those exercises—"

"Oh, they don't harm me. Nothing to do with the nervous system, you see. And if I got taller the psychological effect would be helpful. I believe my bronchitis is really a form of frustration."

Lily had read novels in which the hero or the heroine suffered from frustration, but it had never taken the form of bronchitis. Nevertheless, she was impressed. She wished she could produce some ailment of her own to compare with the many ills which afflicted Lukin, but although she and Felix considered themselves sensitive, discerning creatures, it had not affected their health. True, Felix had had the measles very badly last term, but he had had it at school in company with numerous other boys, and an epidemic of that sort could hardly be said to count.

"I suppose it was the war," she said hesitantly.

The war, in the novels she had read, had frequently had a disastrous effect on the character of the hero or heroine, and it seemed safe to ascribe Lukin's unsettled childhood, his frustration, and even his bronchitis, to this universal upheaval.

"That's the obvious answer," he replied. It was fairly clear that he could supply a better one if he chose to confide in her, but for the moment he restrained himself.

Lily had been standing in the doorway, and now she stepped inside. She did not like being told that her remarks were obvious, but she wanted the conversation to continue. Lukin, who had seemed so dull and stupid in his mother's company, was a different person when one got him alone.

She had met few young men, and she was accustomed to being talked to as a child, a schoolgirl whose interests were limited and juvenile. The elder brothers of the school-friends she sometimes visited had treated her like that; and it had been difficult, under the critical gaze of Mary Thompson or Betty Sinclair, to appear grown-up and sophisticated. But Lukin addressed her as a contemporary, and this was so flattering that she longed to know more of him.

The only difficulty was, that she could not think of anything to say. In her imagined future there were no awkward silences, but in real life it was not so easy. In real life the person to whom she was talking often seemed to lose interest, or to suffer from the same paralysis of thought at the same moment. Perhaps that was what was happening to Lukin.

"I haven't seen you since last Easter holidays," she remarked desperately. "I mean the one a year ago, when I was still at school. You were away in the summer."

She wanted to make it quite clear that she had now left school for ever. But Lukin ignored the information.

"I was at Pentalloch in the summer," he said.

Lily wondered where it was. She dared not assume that it was in Wales, since it might equally well have been in Scotland. She ventured to hope that he had enjoyed himself there.

"An interesting experiment, but useless for anyone like myself. Jealousy and squabbles. A total absence of the communal spirit, and far too much destructive criticism. I haven't got the vitality for that sort of thing."

The heretical thought smote Lily that Lukin showed few signs of having the communal spirit either. But she was obliged to confess that she had never heard of Pentalloch.

"It's a school," he informed her. "Not like the one you've left. A school of painting. Of course you've never heard of it, no one down here knows a palette from a paint-box, and actually it's quite a small place and it hasn't been going very long. It was started by a man called Kropkin, but you won't have heard of him either. He's scarcely known outside Czechoslovakia."

"Have you been to Czechoslovakia?" she asked, grasping eagerly at this conversational plum.

"Of course not. I've just been telling you, he lives at Pentalloch. He left Prague because of some trouble over a portrait he'd done— political trouble, I suppose, but I don't know much about it because he can hardly speak any English."

"Then how can he have a school?"

"That's quite different. He doesn't profess to teach languages," Lukin replied decisively. Lily felt baffled; she still could not see how Kropkin could instruct pupils who did not understand him. But that was just a detail. The important, the fascinating thing was, that Lukin was a painter.

She ought to have guessed it sooner; but she had been so occupied with Lukin himself that she had hardly looked at the workroom. Now, glancing round, she saw that its walls were covered with bright, complicated designs, and she moved forward to examine them.

"Relics of childhood," Lukin said loftily. "Don't pay much attention to them, they're morbidly escapist. An unhappy attempt to blend meaning and abstract thought."

Nevertheless, he pulled a chair away from the wall so that she should have a better view. The few people who had seen his pictures had all shown a curious disposition to underrate them, but Lily's admiring gaze, her obvious interest, persuaded him that she would prove a worthier audience than the jealous fellow-students at Pentalloch.

Lily walked from one wall to the next, wishing she knew which bits of work were meaning and which were abstract thought. To her uninstructed eye the murals looked much alike—a succession of geometric patterns repeated in slightly different colours and proportions. "Why did you want it to mean anything?" she asked at last.

The question appeared to please Lukin, who nodded his head significantly.

"Yes, it was a mistake. I wasn't being true to myself. It wasn't possible at that time. In fact, it isn't always possible now."

He looked so dejected that Lily felt quite sorry for him, and in a flash of sympathetic intuition she asked:

"You mean, you were influenced by someone else?"

"It's not possible to avoid it, not possible even now," he repeated. "One can only externalize it, and at that stage I hadn't begun to."

She felt it would be unwise to say more, for it had somehow become clear to her that the unavoidable influence came from Mrs. Midge. But her opinion of Lukin himself grew ever more favourable, and she commended herself for her enterprise in seeking him out.

"Let me see what you're painting now," she begged.

Lukin looked across the room to the farther window, where a picture stood on an easel, covered over by a piece of cloth. Seeing him in profile, she noticed the little, beaky nose, and the confident —almost arrogant—expression. She noticed also that he was sadly lacking in chin, but in her present mood this did not deter her from admiring him.

"Not at present," he said. "I've covered it up, as you see. I don't want to look at it myself just now. It needs a fresh eye."

A long silence followed, while Lily wondered what to say next. It was obvious that Lukin took his painting seriously, and his reference to destructive criticism suggested that it would be all too easy to say the wrong thing.

Of course, he was painfully self-conscious. Remembering this useful phrase, she decided that what Lukin really needed was to meet more people. Shut up at Prospect Cottage, seeing no one but his mother, it was not surprising that he should be self-conscious, and rather bad-mannered.

Even Felix, she thought, would have offered me a chair. She looked about her. The chair that Lukin had upset was still lying on its back, and the other one was piled with books. The only thing left to sit on was a stool, and he had just taken it for himself. He was gazing into space, rather as if he were indulging in abstract thought. She might not have been there.

"Spring, summer, autumn, winter," he said suddenly. "Trivial actions of sowing and reaping—people doing things. One might as well paint posters for the Underground."

From his scornful gesture Lily grasped that he was referring to the murals. She had not dreamed that they were meant to represent people doing things, and for a moment she had a frightful desire to laugh. Fortunately Lukin had his back to her, so her struggles went unobserved.

"Do you ever paint portraits?" she asked. She feared the question was foolish, but she did not feel capable of discussing the murals at that moment.

"I thought you'd say that. I suppose you want me to paint yours."

It was true that when she had discovered he was a painter Lily had instantly thought of herself as a model. Long ago, when she was very small, Uncle Eustace had made a water-colour sketch of her—the only painting he had ever done, as far as anyone knew, after his official retirement. Aunt Bella had rescued the sketch from the nursery, and had had it framed and hung in her bedroom. It had been a source of pride to Lily, and she had often wished that Uncle Eustace would paint her again. She was, she considered, no less paintable now than she had been then; and naturally she could not help hoping that Lukin would see this too.

But her first glimpse of his work had shown her he was not that sort of painter. She did not want to be blended with abstract thought into a quite unrecognizable pattern; and the complacency in his voice annoyed her.

"No, I don't," she replied, momentarily forgetting his sensitive nature.

"Just as well. Portrait painting—the thing *you* mean—is finished anyway."

Lily began to wonder if Lukin was as agreeable as she had thought at first. She knew she was ignorant, but she had not come here to be treated as a child.

"It's a pity you can't paint portraits," she said. "I'm sure your mother would love you to paint her. Why don't you try?"

The mention of Mrs. Midge had a curious effect on Lukin. It was as if, by speaking of her, Lily had evoked an invisible but authoritative presence. In his mother's company he had always been the kind of son Mrs. Midge wanted him to be, and now he reassumed that familiar rôle. Abandoning his air of superiority, he gave a little pouting smile, pleading for Lily to be kind to him.

"Mama doesn't know much about all this," he said. "I mean, she knows about the painting—of course she sent me to Pentalloch, last year—but—Well, she'd expect a portrait to be a photograph. Do you understand?"

The pouting smile made its effect. Lily did not see him as a little boy, but as a contemporary, someone of her own age who was misunderstood by his nearest and dearest. She also had the pleasure of feeling that she had gained his confidence.

She nodded sympathetically. "But doesn't she want to know what you're doing?"

"I do lots of things," Lukin said vaguely, pointing to a work-bench under the window. "She doesn't realize that painting is the Important Thing."

Lily longed to hear more, but at this moment, from the distant cottage, came the tinkling summons of the cow-bell.

"That's for my lunch," he said. "I must go." Evidently Mrs. Midge had brought him up to be punctual.

"When can I see your picture? I mean the new one?"

"Oh . . . sometime."

It was not a very satisfactory answer, but she felt that on the whole the morning had been a success.

Cassandra was wheeling her bicycle down the steep drive from Prospect House. On Tuesdays and Thursdays she spent only the mornings there, since Leonard was supposed to be old enough to manage some of his homework without supervision.

"Hullo," Lily said. "Felix wants to do lessons with you. Will you teach him?"

"I've got enough to do to teach Leonard. Have you been to Mallinford?"

"No. I've been to see Lukin."

"Prince Finnikin and his Mama," said Cassandra. She did not ask Lily the reason for her visit; she knew from her own experience that it was sometimes tiresome to be forced to give explanations and reasons.

"He's not really like that at all," Lily protested. "He's awfully interesting. He's got great possibilities."

She half regretted telling Cassandra of the visit, yet she wanted to talk about it. Unfortunately, Cassandra was now preparing to mount her bicycle without waiting to hear more about Lukin's possibilities.

"I've always thought him rather dull," she said.

"Oh no! Of course, he's rather difficult to talk to. He's painfully self-conscious, for one thing, and then he doesn't meet enough people. I think Mrs. Midge represses him, not intentionally of course—"

"Look, Lily, I'm frightfully sorry but it's after one and I must fly."

"You're as bad as Lukin. He had to rush off to his lunch the minute Mrs. Nutting rang the bell."

"I thought you said he *wasn't* bad. Or is his punctuality due to his being repressed?"

Lily was forced to laugh. "But Lukin really *is* interesting," she said. "Do you know, he paints extraordinary pictures!"

"Gracious, does he? Tell me all about it tomorrow." Over her shoulder, as she sped away down the hill, she called back, "Don't tell your uncle!"

Lily quite agreed with her. It would not do to tell Uncle Eustace that there was a painter at large on his property. He was a man of strong feelings, and painters, like scorpions, were a species he could not abide.

CHAPTER VII

THE CHURCH at Little Mallin was both large and ugly. It had been built in a spirit of thanksgiving at the end of the Crimean war, but before it was completed the money had run out and it had been necessary to make drastic alterations to the original plan. The most noticeable effect of these economies was that the church had no spire.

Where the spire should have been there was instead a dwarfish protruding stub, which did not even taper to a point but finished abruptly, as if it had been sawn off, a few feet above the ridge of the roof. To make up for this deficiency a later benefactor had added to the west door the large, cavernous porch, which reminded Miss Templer of her grandfather's larder. The church resembled a long barn with a lesser outbuilding attached to it and a peculiar excrescence at one end of its roof. Inside, it was equipped with pitch-pine pews, a big cast-iron stove in one corner and a pseudo-marble font in another, and numerous Gothic embellishments wherever there was room for them.

Sir James Brigham, in whose gift the living lay, was perhaps the only person who really admired Mallin church. His grandfather had fought at Sebastopol, and had subsequently given the land for the building, and a large sum towards its cost. Three windows in the north aisle commemorated this hero and other Brigham worthies, and there was an unappropriated window next to them which he hoped might one day commemorate himself. So he enjoyed a proprietary interest in the church, and this enabled him to view it in a favourable light. Sir James had the happy belief that the things which belonged to him were somehow better than the things which belonged to other people.

He had invited Edward Custance to become vicar of Little Mallin because he was the brother of the John Custance whom he had known at Cambridge, and on occasions when the vicar annoyed him he had been heard to say that families did not always run true to type. Mr. Custance in his turn was annoyed by having his sermons adversely compared to the non-existent masterpieces of his brother John, who, not being a parson, had never preached a sermon in his life.

But on the whole the squire and the vicar were on good terms, and on Sundays, at the end of the morning service, Sir James usually waited to have a word with his parson (for so he thought of him) before returning to Mallin Hall and the degenerate modern substitute tor a Sunday joint.

This particular Sunday was fine and warm, and Sir James did not linger in the porch but walked out into the churchyard and began a desultory inspection of the epitaphs on the tombstones. Presently Mrs. Custance emerged from the porch and joined him.

"Where's Cassandra?" he asked, after the first greetings had been exchanged. Mrs. Custance said Cassandra had gone straight home by the footpath across the fields. Every Sunday either she or Cassandra had to go straight home, to see to the lunch, but it was no good explaining this to Sir James, who had a masculine inability to understand domestic details.

"Who was that young woman in the hat?" he asked next, but Mrs. Custance could not answer this question. She had come to church in good time, her pew was right in the front, and she was too well-mannered to turn round and stare. But she understood that he must be alluding to some particularly striking hat, for Little Mallin was an old-fashioned place and all the female members of the congregation would certainly be wearing hats of some sort.

"Perhaps it was Dossie or Daisy Fenn. They both like bright colours."

"No, Amy, no. I may be getting on," said Sir James, leaning more heavily on his stick, "but I'm not too blind to recognize Dossie and Daisy Fenn. And *all* their hats. Know them by heart."

"You're not blind at all," Mrs. Custance said resolutely; for it did not do to let him embark on the subject of his failing years and increasing decrepitude. "You see a great deal more than most people. Now, what was this wonderful hat like?"

"Big flat yellow thing—straw, y' know—with a bright blue ribbon all round and hanging down a bit at one side. And where the ribbon hung down there was a bunch of cornflowers. Or some sort of blue flowers—can't be sure they were cornflowers. Might have been scabious."

"Then I know who you mean. Miss Templer was telling me about that hat on Friday."

"Good Gad, it wasn't her. Couldn't possibly have been. Not old enough, and then—"

"No, it was *Lily* Templer."

"It wasn't a child either. A young woman—quite got up, y'know—red mouth and all that sort of thing."

"It was Lily," Mrs. Custance repeated firmly. "She's left school now. She's seventeen, and frankly her taste is appalling. Miss Templer is quite worried about it, but as I tell her, Lily will soon learn."

"Seventeen, is she?" said Sir James. "Well, well, we're all growing older. Pretty little thing."

A pang of maternal jealousy seized Mrs. Custance, for Lily was not as pretty as Cassandra. She had a lively agreeable expression, a good skin, and nice hands, but her eyes were a nondescript hazel, and like all the Templers she was short and plump. Of course it was partly her age, thought Mrs. Custance, trying to be fair; it was puppy-fat and she would thin down later on. But it was hard to hear her called a pretty little thing, and she could not bring herself to agree with Sir James.

Luckily at this moment Mr. Custance came out of the vestry door, and the subject was dropped.

"Not a bad sermon this morning, Custance," Sir James said approvingly. "Didn't stick to your text, though. Why bring in Pericles?"

Mrs. Custance could have told him that Edward simply could not help bringing in Pericles, or another of those tiresome Greeks whose exploits meant so much more to him than the exploits of living men. But Mr. Custance dodged the question by hurrying off to have a word with one of his parishioners who was waiting at the gate to catch him. It was not often that this parishioner, a garrulous seeker for sympathy, found it so easy to gain the vicar's attention.

"Doing his duty, eh?" said Sir James, who liked to see a parson earning his stipend. He stared after Mr. Custance with a critical gaze. "Not in very good shape, is he? Looks as if he could do with a change of air."

"He hasn't really got over Easter," Mrs. Custance replied. She was a devout churchwoman, but insensibly she had come to view the major festivals of the Church as being, in some degree, tests of stamina. "He had the 'flu very badly at the beginning of April, and he wasn't really fit by Easter. It was a great strain on him."

"Getting a bit bald, too, poor chap."

Sir James spoke with sympathy, but his hand went up to caress his flowing white moustache. Eight years older than Custance, and he still had plenty of hair—though of course it wasn't a question of moustaches, since parsons had to be clean-shaven. "A good change, that's what he needs," he declared. "You should take him away, Amy. Get him to a place like

Brighton, or—or—What's that place George did his training at, when he was first called up?"

"Salisbury Plain. But I don't think—"

"Damn' cold place, that. I went over to see him there. Never been so cold in my life, not even in France in the other war. But of course that was in December, and I remember I said at the time, 'This place would be very bracing, George, if it wasn't always raining'. A bracing place—that's what Custance needs."

"I don't think we shall be going away this year. Edward will soon pull round, if we get a fine summer."

Mrs. Custance was on much better terms with Sir James than her husband was. Or perhaps on rather different terms; for Sir James could not help thinking of Edward Custance as 'his' parson, and therefore as a man whom he could direct and, if necessary, admonish. But although Mrs. Custance was treated as an old friend and addressed as Amy, while her husband had to be content with Custance, she knew that the friendship must not be strained by allusions to poverty, or to any other circumstances for which their patron felt himself even remotely responsible. Sir James could be very generous, but he disliked what he called 'being hinted at', and he was quick to imagine hints where none had been intended.

Years of practice had taught Mrs. Custance to avoid these misunderstandings by saying as little as possible about financial difficulties, and she would not have dreamed of admitting that she and Edward could not afford a holiday this year.

"It looks like being a fine summer," she went on. "So hot already, and it's only May. I must tell Bryce we shan't need the heating any more, if it's like this next week."

She was alluding to the cast-iron stove in the church. It was fortunate that Bryce was a churchwarden, for no one else really understood the stove's temperament, and even Bryce could not keep it completely under control. This morning, though it was hardly necessary to have heating, the stove had got red-hot and one of the congregation had fainted.

"George says that stove's worn out," said Sir James.

Mrs. Custance might have asked how George knew, seeing that he came to church so seldom, but she contented herself by suggesting, in a mild and friendly voice, that before George condemned the stove he had better think of a way of raising money to buy a new one.

Sir James inclined his head in a very melancholy way. "Money," he said sonorously. "That's all he *does* think of. Money. Going off like that—hr-rmph! Setting up as a corn merchant! D' y' know, the other day I saw a waggon—lorry—or whatever they call it— standing in the High Street in Mallinford, and his name—*my* name—painted on the side! Brigham and—and—"

"Tukes," said Mrs. Custance. It was Tukes and Brigham, but she was too tactful to say so.

"Tunk," said Sir James, who determinedly mis-pronounced the names of people he did not like. "Brigham and Tunk. . . . What d'you think of that feller, eh?"

Mrs. Custance said nothing, but looked sympathetic. It was getting late and she did not want to keep Edward waiting by beginning a lengthy discussion of the character of Mr. Tukes.

"Between you and me, Amy, George is a great disappointment to me."

As he spoke these words Sir James puffed out his cheeks and hunched his shoulders despondently, leaning on his stick in the attitude of a stricken father. Not once, but many, many times had he proclaimed his disappointment in George, and he had brought the business to a fine art.

"Sir James thought you needed a holiday," Mrs. Custance said at lunch-time. "No, not you, Cassie. Your father."

"He does look rather thin," Cassandra agreed.

"And he's getting bald. Sir James noticed it."

"But a holiday wouldn't restore his hair. Could you manage a holiday, Mummy?"

"Not this year, I'm afraid. We shall have to save up to have the car re-bored, it really can't be put off much longer."

"If you went somewhere not far away?"

"Sir James suggested Salisbury Plain."

Cassandra laughed and said it was the last place she would have expected him to choose; she would have thought Brighton or perhaps the south of France.

"He went to Salisbury Plain when George was training there— that must be quite ten years ago. In the war, you know, before George went to Italy."

"North Africa," Cassandra said quickly. "It was long before the Italian landings."

Geography, whether ancient or modern, was not a subject Mrs. Custance took seriously, because, as she had told Miss Templer, it was always changing. To her it hardly signified whether George had gone to North Africa or the North Pole. Wherever he had been to begin with, he had ended up in Italy; and that was all one needed to know. So she did not pay much attention to her daughter's correction, except to wonder, for a fleeting moment, if there was any importance in Cassie's remembering such a minor detail of the distant past. But probably it was simply due to her liking for accuracy and her excellent memory for facts.

While approving, in theory, of accuracy, Mrs. Custance sometimes wished Cassandra would let well alone, for her pedantic insistence on truth inspired a horrid fear that she might, one day, turn into a 'real' governess, an enthusiastic, earnest creature with no interests outside the schoolroom. It was the thought of this transformed Cassandra, a dreadful blend of all the school-marms she had read about in books and the few she had encountered in life, that kept Mrs. Custance awake at night, wondering where she could find an eligible young man and how she could persuade her daughter to take an interest in him.

She was happily confident that it would not be difficult to persuade the young man, when found, to take an interest in Cassandra.

"Anyway, I don't fancy Salisbury Plain," Cassandra was saying. "For you, I mean. You'd both get so very bored."

"But, darling, if any of us needs a holiday, it's *you*," Mrs. Custance protested. "Everyone knows that teaching is exhausting. I thought perhaps in August you might go to Aunt Mary for a week or two. Not a very exciting holiday, I'm afraid, but it would be a change of air."

Mr. Custance, who had been sitting in a waking dream in which he was only half-conscious of the conversation going on around him, suddenly came to life and announced that he for one would prefer to stay at home.

"I shall be perfectly happy here," he said generously. "You two go off and enjoy yourselves. 'Gather ye rosebuds while ye may . . .'"

Cassandra and her mother had been about to begin an argument over the merits of a visit to Aunt Mary, but they now united to assure Mr. Custance that he could not possibly stay at home unattended, and that the whole question of holidays had started because Sir James had said he was looking run down. Cassandra added that she herself did not need a holiday at all, but if she went anywhere she might join Joan Baker-Wright, who had the use of a caravan which belonged to her brother-in-law and which was kept in an old gravel-pit not fifty miles away. She pointed out that it would be a nice cheap holiday, and she wouldn't have to bother about clothes because it was right in the country and Joan never minded what she wore.

If it had not been Sunday, a day she had been brought up to respect, Mrs. Custance would have spoken her mind about this suggestion. The combination of Joan Baker-Wright and a caravan right in the country was the exact opposite of what her daughter needed.

Joan had been Cassie's dearest friend at school and she had often stayed at the vicarage. She had been a lumpish child with a talent for arithmetic, and she was now a lumpish young woman who taught mathematics at a girls' school where they wore scarlet-and-white blazers and pretended to be boys. At least, that was how Mrs. Custance thought of the school; her knowledge of it had been gleaned from Joan herself who, as a newly-appointed junior mistress, had spent her half-term at Mallin and had never stopped talking, from morning till night, about Smithers and Cox and Smallweed; about the prefect system and the common-room; about the Lower Fourth kids and a hefty jape they had played on poor old Brownie. It would be just the place for Cass, she had told Mrs. Custance. The staff were all young and there was always something going on.

No, Mrs. Custance thought, a holiday with Joan Baker-Wright would not be a good thing at all. Apart from being a silly waste of time (for they would meet no one, but would spend the days reading books in the seclusion of the gravel-pit), it would give that dreadful Joan a chance to unsettle Cassie, to persuade her that life in a common-room with Smithers and Cox and Smallweed was better value than life in a vicarage with her father and mother.

She sometimes thought it was a mistake to keep Cassie at home, but she was quite sure it would be a worse one to let her go to a place where romantic tendencies were actively discouraged, and where the ideal woman seemed to be an all-England lacrosse player with dusty hair and an Honours degree.

Cassandra and her father were now discussing a holiday in Greece. A legacy from his godfather had enabled Mr. Custance to visit Greece in 1920; he had spent a month touring the country, on foot and in rickety motor buses, and he still thought of this as the highlight of his youth. Of course Cassandra knew all about it, but she was a good daughter and she listened with a fair show of interest.

Her mind, however, was not concerned with Greece. She was wondering whether she was wasting her life.

Cassandra did not share her mother's views on matrimony as a career, and she had outgrown the dreams that beguiled Lily Templer, of being rich and amusing and a social success. But she had lately begun to tell herself that her life was being wasted and that she ought to leave Little Mallin and get a job where she would be of some use to the community.

Put like that, it became almost a moral obligation. She was qualified to teach, she liked teaching, and there was really nothing to prevent her going. Nothing but the obstinate other-half of herself, that clung to Little Mallin as if it were a life-belt in a stormy sea.

Unlike Lily, she did not yearn for a female friend in whom to confide; she wished instead that she could be a single-minded person with a single set of hopes and ambitions. But she was still young enough to believe that wisdom lay ahead, and that by clear thinking and lucid arguments one part of herself would vanquish the other.

"We looked down at the plain from the top of the pass," Mr. Custance continued. "Up there, we were in shadow from the peak, and it was all bare rock. But the plain was in full sunlight . . . a wonderful golden light, indescribable. And the olive trees, mile on mile of them, rippling and shimmering in the sunlight. I'll never forget it. We came over the pass and there it was. The plain of—the plain of . . ."

He paused, and a look of mild distress replaced the happy expression he kept for memories of Greece.

"What was the name of the plain?" he asked.

"Salisbury Plain," Cassandra said dreamily.

But Mrs. Custance had gone into the kitchen to begin the washing-up, and Mr. Custance, being subject to verbal errors himself, was not the man to attach much importance to a mere slip of the tongue. He did not even notice that his daughter was blushing.

"No, no," he said. "I'm speaking of Greece."

"I meant Thessaly, of course," said Cassandra.

CHAPTER VIII

Sir James Brigham was, as Mrs. Custance had remarked, an observant man, and when he was with other people he was constantly reminded that he was getting on in years. He noticed such things as grey hairs and wrinkles, and these signs of age in his contemporaries served as a yardstick by which he could measure his own decline. In a melancholy way he enjoyed comparing himself with slightly older, or slightly younger men, and seeing who came off best; but he did not like it when other people made the comparison and told him, with the best intentions, that he was looking wonderfully well and far fitter than old So-and-so who was ten years his junior. He preferred a more respectful attitude, a blend of sympathy and admiration for one who had had much to bear.

When he was alone he thought much less about his age, and although he always carried a stick he often forgot that it was needed to assist his faltering steps.

On this fine Sunday morning he had chosen to walk to church. He had come by the road, walking slowly and stopping here and there to rest while younger and brisker church-goers overtook him. But after his talk with Mrs. Custance he returned to Mallin Hall by a path across the fields and along the edge of a wood. The path was uphill most of the way and there were several stiles, but since he was alone he made good progress, and when he paused at the edge of the fir plantation it was less because he needed a rest than because he liked to look at the trees and assure himself that they were doing well.

The fir plantation was called the New Wood, and it had been established nearly forty years ago, shortly after Sir James had succeeded his father at Mallin. It had been his own idea to have a wood at this particular spot. He had thought at first he would plant beeches, but beeches are slow-growing trees and he had wanted a wood he could enjoy in his own lifetime, for even then he was conscious of time's wingéd chariot at his back. So he had planted Norway spruce and Scots pine, with a belt of larches at one end where he could see it from his bathroom window at Mallin Hall.

The New Wood was now an integral part of the landscape, and it gave him great pleasure to look at it and to feel that he was responsible for its existence. The trees were tall and vigorous; unlike human beings, they did not develop wrinkles and grey hairs or complain of rheumatics or asthma, and so he was able to contemplate them with hardly a twinge of melancholy.

This morning, in the heat and the sunshine, the trees were looking their best, and his walk home put Sir James in a good temper. He strode quite smartly across the last field, only using his stick to slash at some thistles in his path. The old cook-housekeeper, watching his approach from the kitchen window, said to the old house-parlourmaid that the master was frisking across the paddock and she had better hurry up and get the table laid.

Mallin Hall had once been maintained by a staff of seven, and Sir James was considered an uncommonly fortunate man for still having two resident servants to look after him, when other houses were reduced to daily help or even to no help at all. Some people said he did not deserve it, and others pointed out that it was always easier where there were only men in the family, and that as soon as George Brigham got married—if he brought his bride to Mallin Hall—the two treasures would quickly depart. Everyone said it must be wonderful to have resident maids, even if they were rather decrepit, and that there was nothing like old family servants when it came to loyalty. .

Sir James and his son agreed, in public, that they were very lucky, but each of them thought privately that old family servants had disadvantages only known to those they served.

Mrs. Dixon and Sarah Ede were both difficult characters, and the passage of time had not mellowed them. They were both very proud of themselves for having stayed so long in one place, and they wore their old-fashioned white caps rather as if they were haloes. They were close friends and enjoyed a happy, comfortable life, and neither of them ever thought seriously of leaving; but by threatening, in an allusive roundabout way, to give notice, they exacted tributes of praise and a gradual enfranchisement from duties they did not care to perform, such as answering bells and cleaning shoes.

To the veiled threat of leaving they had lately added suggestions of mysterious infirmities which prevented them from doing as much cleaning and polishing as they would have otherwise have deemed it their duty to do. A bad back kept Sarah from turning out rooms, and pains in her knees made it essential for Mrs. Dixon to have the gardener in to scrub the kitchen floor. In fact, they did pretty much as they pleased, and regarded themselves as irreplaceable, which they might be, and faultless, which they certainly were not.

Mrs. Dixon did not usually trouble about having meals exactly to time, but on Sunday afternoons she and Sarah went out together and so they liked to get lunch over as early as possible. She did not approve of Sir James going to church by himself, he always got talking after the service and that made them all late. But today was not so bad, it was only ten to one and by the time Sarah got the table laid—which she might have done earlier if they hadn't sat so long over their tea—she would have everything dished up.

She took the baking-tin out of the oven and picked out the crispest of the potatoes for herself and Sarah. The joint could hardly be called a joint at all; she reminded Sarah to be sure and tell the master it was all they had, so that he should leave enough for themselves.

She had thoughtfully made two fruit pies, because she and Sarah preferred their pie hot and Sir James had an unnatural liking for cold ones. But he would have to put up with the custard being warm, as there hadn't been time for it to cool. Cheese and biscuits to follow—well, no, he couldn't have biscuits, the tin was nearly empty and she and Sarah had to have dry biscuits to take to bed with them, something to chew in the night when they felt hungry. She got out the loaf instead; it was rather stale because the baker didn't come Saturdays, but it would do.

"Here you are, Sarah," she called. "That's the lot, now hurry up with that gong."

The gong had been moved into the kitchen passage so that Sarah should not have to walk all the way to the front hall. A baize-covered door shut off the passage from the rest of the house and the gong's summons now sounded subdued and muffled, like the cry of a humbled giant in some deep dungeon. It reflected the sad change that had taken place in the Sunday menus.

The dining-room was impressive rather than beautiful. It faced east and the windows looked out on to a shrubbery; the greenish light that filtered through a bank of rhododendrons and laurels made one feel one was dining in an aquarium. There was a black marble chimney-piece supporting a grey marble clock, the walls were papered in fading crimson flock but were almost entirely covered with obscure oil paintings in massive gold frames, and the length of the room was filled by a handsome table which could have accommodated sixteen people.

Sir James sat at the head of the table and George sat on his right, in what would have been the next chair but one had the table been fully occupied. There was thus no need for them to look at each other and they could eat in silence if they felt like it. But today Sir James was in a talkative mood.

"You ought to have been at church," he declared, as soon as he had finished carving the joint and helped himself to vegetables. George was preparing to defend himself against a charge of spiritual indolence, when his father continued:

"Stove got red-hot. Nearly blew up. One of those Gidding girls fainted—went a horrible colour and they had to carry her out. Quite an excitement."

"It must have been," George said gravely. "Where were you?"

"Middle of the second lesson. Oh—where was I sitting? In the warm corner. But I shall have to move up next week. It's not often I can move up in May."

All the pews in the church were free, and theoretically anyone could sit anywhere, but in practice the regular church-goers kept to their own seats. Sir James was unique in having two seats, one for summer and one for winter. The summer seat was directly under the pulpit, where he unnerved Mr. Custance by taking out his watch at the beginning of the sermon and placing it on the ledge in front of him, allowing the vicar exactly twelve-and-a-half minutes of eloquence before he started coughing.

"It won't last," George said. "Probably be freezing next week."

"It's going to be a good summer. Old Birley says so, and he's not a bad prophet."

"Haven't talked to him for ages, except to say good morning. I've developed a technique for fending him off."

This remark reminded Sir James that George went across the toll-bridge every day on his way to his business in Mallinford, and he gave a deep sigh. Brigham and Tunk. If George really wanted something to do why didn't he choose some respectable profession? —he could have stayed in the Army, or he could have gone to Cambridge at the end of the war and read for the Bar or turned himself into one of those scientists or professors with letters after his name. Even a professor had a certain standing; and there had been a Brigham cousin of his grandfather's who had written learned books and given lectures, which seemed to prove that it ran in the family.

But of course, he thought, George didn't need an occupation. He was not dependent on an allowance; he had his mother's money. It was nothing but obstinacy—sheer pigheadedness—that had driven him into the corn-merchant's business and brought disgrace on the family name.

George's mother had died when he was five, and from that day to this Sir James had never been able to understand why she should have left her money to her son instead of to himself. For of course it would have come to George eventually, or would have been used to maintain and improve the estate which George was to inherit. He had not known, until after her death, that she had made a will, and although she had been an admirable wife he could not acquit her of deception.

A gentle woman, a woman who was, if anything, too shy and retiring, a woman who never argued and even chose her dresses to please him—who would have dreamt of her going off to a lawyer by herself and making a will without consulting her husband? Making a will, in fact, which simply ignored her husband; for he had not even been appointed a trustee for her estate. It was an action so inexplicably out of character that it could only be described as a woman's whim—an impulsive thing done on the spur of the moment and for no reason at all.

By thinking of it as a woman's whim, he managed to elude the criticism of himself which the will implied, and he had long ago forgiven his dead wife for her unintentional treachery. But he had never quite been able to forgive George for being, in defiance of tradition and propriety, a son who could afford to defy his father.

George knew quite well that his father was thinking of the corn-merchant's business and his own damned obstinacy. The deep sigh, the expression of melancholy calm, were unmistakeable symptoms. He wished his father would give up sulking and realize that they had come to a stage of history when even Brighams had to work for their living.

"I hear Witling rectory is up for sale," he said. His father had been ready to talk when they sat down to lunch, and it seemed a pity that they should sink back into this distressful silence.

"Can't think why," Sir James responded gloomily. "Good Georgian house—good stables and garden. What do they want to sell it for?"

"It's a bit big. Old Scrope only used a corner of it, and I suppose the upkeep's pretty heavy."

"Scrope was an old man, a widower. This new man is quite young—only been married a year. How do they know how many children he'll have?"

"Well, no," said George. "I don't suppose even the Bishop knows that."

"May have six—a dozen—children. A parson over at Long Hampton, when I was a boy, had a dozen children. No reason why this chap shouldn't. And where'll he put 'em all, in that red brick doll's house he's living in now? No, no, George, it's a great mistake getting rid of these old places just because they're roomy. Parsons tend to have large families—I've often noticed it."

Having dealt with Witling rectory, Sir James began eating his pie. After the first mouthful he turned round in his chair and peered into the corner of the room where Sarah sometimes lurked behind the screen that masked the service door. But Sarah, who was training them to wait on themselves, had gone back to the kitchen to eat her own lunch.

"This custard's *hot*! D' y' know, George, it's been like this three times out of four, lately? If there's one thing I can't stand it's a hot fruit pie. But I'm not sure it's not worse having the pie cold and the custard hot!"

"Mrs. Dixon likes them both hot."

Sir James gave an indignant snort. "Well, what if she does? I don't have to like what Mrs. Dixon likes, do I? Good Gad, what does she mean, sending in a hot custard?"

"She means you to get used to it. And when you've got used to it, you'll have to start getting used to a hot *pie*," George explained. "Just as I've had to get used to last night's toast for breakfast."

They looked at each other.

"D' y' know," said Sir James, "it's quite time one of us *spoke* to Mrs. Dixon."

George did know it. He also knew that his father had no intention of being the one to do the speaking, and that if he did it himself and Mrs. Dixon and Sarah gave notice it would all be his fault. So he said tactfully that perhaps Mrs. Dixon was still suffering from the after-effects of the influenza she had had in the spring, and things might get better later on.

Sir James was still brooding wrathfully over the hot custard, but fortunately this reply, by reminding him of something else, distracted him from his grievance.

"Custance hasn't got over it either," he said. "Poor chap hasn't got much stamina really. D' y' know, George, he's getting quite bald?"

"Is he?"

"Noticed it this morning. Not in church, of course." He spoke as if this would have been irreverent. "Saw him outside, walking away from me, and he was distinctly bald. Poor old chap." Now that Mrs. Custance was not present he was able to make the most of it. "Not that he's really old," he added jubilantly. "Only sixty-one—and what's that, these days?"

"Not much really," George agreed, beginning to think of something else. His father, he knew, would now embark on a point-by-point comparison of his own health and Mr. Custance's; it was a comparison George had learned by heart so there was no need to listen very carefully.

He was not an unsympathetic son but he sometimes thought it would be better if he and his father lived apart. If he had had any sense he would have made the break when he was demobilized, for it would be difficult, now, to leave Mallin Hall without giving the impression that they had quarrelled; or indeed, without quarrelling in earnest.

But when he first got back to England he had not realized that his father would object so strongly to his going into business as a corn merchant, and he had been horrified by the neglected and derelict appearance of his home. By living at home, he had thought, he would be able to get things organized again, as well as keeping the old man company.

Sir James, at that time, had chosen to think of himself as quite worn-out, a man whose day was nearly done and who was only waiting for his son to take over. But things had changed since then. He still lamented his age, but he no longer wished to abdicate. George had his uses, of course. He could fill in forms and deal with the complicated accounts with the Milk Marketing Board, which neither Sir James nor his bailiff at the Home Farm really understood. He could garden in his spare time, for the garden had formerly employed three men and Thurstan couldn't possibly manage it all. But he must not think he could give orders about growing vegetables for sale or changing from Shorthorns to Friesians, because that was for his father to decide.

". . . so I told her he ought to go away."

Getting no response, Sir James repeated it in slightly different terms.

"Our parson needs a change of air, George."

"Does he?"

George was not really interested, for he was still thinking about himself, and whether a change of air—or at least, of residence— might not be beneficial both for himself and his father.

"Yes," said Sir James, puffing out his moustache so that its ends fluttered. When not being agitated it hung down in two walrus tufts, and he was very proud of it. "Yes. We must see that he gets it."

He waited, but still nothing happened. The boy seemed to be half asleep.

"They can't really afford it, y' know, but that's what he needs. A change of air. We must send him a cheque."

At the mention of a cheque George woke up.

He might have guessed it, he thought; his father was never as chatty as this without some reason for it. He did not have to ask where the cheque was to come from, since he already knew the answer. His mother's money—that fabulous fortune lying idle in the bank—would provide the cheque.

"I can't really afford it myself," he began. It was perfectly true, but it was quite impossible to get his father to believe it.

"Come, come, George, we mustn't grudge the poor chap a holiday."

"I don't, but—well, what about going fifty-fifty?"

Sir James made a regretful gesture. "My income—such as it is— goes back into the estate. Have to think of the future, y' know." Having reminded George of the sacrifices that were being made for him, he went on: "Just a small cheque, m' boy. Amy's a sensible woman—won't want to go rushing off to the Ritz. A fortnight by the sea for the pair of them."

George grinned, thinking of Mrs. Custance at the Ritz. "Doesn't Cassandra get a holiday?" he asked. But Sir James did not feel the same sense of responsibility for Cassandra. "You let me have it sometime this week," he said, "and then I'll see Amy—see them both—and tell them what we've decided. *Noblesse oblige*, y' know. What's Mrs. Dixon thinking of, sending in this stale bread?" He pushed the loaf away in disgust, and rose to his feet.

Following his father out of the room, George wondered whether he should make another protest. He wished he could convince his father that his mother's money was not a crock of gold to be dipped into at will. It had never been a large fortune, and in the post-war world it had dwindled considerably.

But in Sir James's eyes it had grown. Like a grievance of long standing—which, in a sense, it was—it had grown out of all proportion. He had persuaded himself that George was comfortably affluent, and since the money ought really to have come to him he felt justified in using it.

He generally used it for charity, and to make everything fair and square he spoke of himself, in these charitable actions, as 'we'. In this way, George was included; though Sir James sometimes thought the boy did not deserve it, for he seemed to have a mean streak in him.

He paused at the door of the library and looked back at George, who hesitated and then turned away towards the dusty lobby where they kept their oldest and most battered garments—the coats that even a Brigham could not be seen in, unless he was weeding the flower-beds.

"Going out to garden, eh? That's right, m' boy," he said approvingly. "Plenty to do out there. I must tell Thurstan about those gaps in the long border."

George was standing in the middle of the hall. Behind him hung a portrait of an eighteenth-century Brigham known as 'Spendthrift Charles', and the sight of this liberal ancestor smiling down over his son's head reminded Sir James that they had traditions to maintain.

"Don't make that cheque *too* small," he said. "Custance hasn't had a decent holiday for years. We must see that he gets a good one".

CHAPTER IX

THOUGH THE pessimists said it could not last, the fine weather continued, and old Birley's forecast of a hot summer now began to be quoted freely. Panama hats and cotton frocks made their appearance, the county council sent workmen to resurface the village street, and Mrs. Custance summoned a bevy of helpers to draw up plans for the Church Fête.

The Church Fête took place annually in aid of the church funds, but for the last two years it had not made much money. This was no one's fault; it was entirely due to the vagaries of the English climate. Rain had made it necessary to hold the Fête in the Parish Hall, a small and quite inadequate building, and the wet day had discouraged people from coming. The church funds were in their usual precarious state, and Mrs. Custance, relying on Birley's forecast, was determined that this year's Fête should be a very special one in order to make up for the two failures.

Her chosen helpers were the Misses Fenn, the headmistress of the church school, Miss Gregory from the post-office, Mrs.

Polegate and her daughter, and Isabel Templer. They were all females because Mrs. Custance believed that women were better organizers than men and wasted less time in talking.

It was true that the Misses Fenn talked a great deal, unless firmly handled, and that Isabel simply could not keep to the point; but the school-mistress was a very capable woman, Miss Gregory was ardently pro-Custance, and Mrs. Polegate was practically dumb. If ever she had any opinion to offer she told it to her daughter, who gave a brief summary of it to the meeting, under the heading, 'Mother says—' or, 'Mother thinks—' The daughter had no opinions of her own, because Mrs. Polegate did not permit it, but she was a useful, hard-working creature, and she positively enjoyed helping with the teas.

Mrs. Polegate, too, had her uses. Although she took no active part as a stallholder, she was a wonderful source of supplies. She had a nephew who manufactured hardware, and another relative connected with some wholesale haberdashers, and from them she obtained pots and pans, sub-standard handkerchiefs and lingerie ribbons and very gaudy ties, which always sold well. So both the Polegates deserved their places on the committee.

Mrs. Custance spoke of her helpers as a committee, but really they were only there to assist her. The Church Fête was her own affair, and before the committee assembled she had made her plans and had even begun to put them into operation.

Hitherto, unless rain prevented it, the Fête had been held in the vicarage garden; but this year she wanted it to be at Mallin Hall. Not in the house, of course—Sir James would never have consented—but in the grounds, or if the weather after all should be wet, in the empty stables and coach-house. The stables would not be very suitable, but it would be impossible to advertise the Fête as being at Mallin Hall and then transfer it, at the last moment, to the Parish Hall in the village. People would feel defrauded.

The gardens at Mallin Hall had not been open to the public since before the war, and Mrs. Custance felt sure people would come out from Mallinford to see them who would not trouble to come to a Church Fête in her own garden at the vicarage.

She had already written to Sir James. A written request, which gave him time to think it over, had a better chance of success; if one asked him verbally his immediate instinct was to refuse. But she thought he would consent to this, since it was for the church funds, and she gave her committee the impression that the matter was settled.

The committee was at first a little critical. Traditions die hard in country places, and Mrs. Custance, like many reformers, had to contend with an audience stubbornly opposed to new ideas.

"It's *always* been at the vicarage," said Miss Templer. "And there's such a pretty view of the church from your lawn at the back. I mean, it's pretty because you can't really see the church, only that it's *there*."

Miss Gregory, showing herself loyal but obtuse, said that the vicarage really seemed the right place, if they knew what she meant, and that it was a privilege they all enjoyed.

After a whispered colloquy Miss Polegate said that Mother thought Mallin Hall was too far away, and how were people going to get there?

This was a difficulty which had troubled Mrs. Custance herself. There were not many buses from Mallinford, and they only came as far as the village; so that patrons of the Fête would have nearly a mile of uphill walking before they arrived at the Hall. But she reminded the committee that before the war, when the gardens were opened in aid of the hospital, people had come from far and wide.

"I remember so well the last time it was opened," she said. "It was simply *crowded*. It was a lovely hot day, not a cloud in the sky, and they sat about all over the lawns."

"Mother thinks it might be all right on a fine day, but how will they get there if it rains?"

"We must all lend our cars," said Miss Templer, suddenly changing sides. "We could have a fleet of cars to take people from the bus stop to the gates, and charge them threepence each. I'm sure my brother-in-law would be delighted to help, and his car holds any amount of people."

Mrs. Custance felt doubtful about that, but she accepted the suggestion, and asked the school-mistress, when she had time, to make a list of car-owners who might be prepared to assist.

The Misses Fenn were invariably late and the meeting had begun without them, but now they suddenly appeared outside the french window and with girlish cries begged to be let in. Everything had to be explained all over again. It was really a good thing for the committee now had time to get used to the idea, and by the end of the second exposition they were becoming enthusiastic. 'Co-operative' was how Mrs. Custance thought of it; if they had not been co-operative she would still have had the Fête at Mallin Hall, but she liked to feel that they agreed with her.

Various other matters were discussed. It was agreed that the Fête should take place on the second Saturday in August. The school-mistress and Miss Polegate would do the teas, Mrs. Custance would be in charge of the Produce Stall, and Miss Templer in charge of the Needlework and Fancies (with Miss Gregory in charge of Miss Templer, who could not be trusted alone). The Misses Fenn would look after the Jumble and White Elephants. Other helpers would be invited to run sideshows and competitions, take the money at the gate, and act as assistants at the principal stalls.

All this had been decided by Mrs. Custance before the meeting began, and as the arrangements were much the same as they had been in previous years the committee did not question any of her decisions. The meeting progressed smoothly, until Dossie Fenn suggested that they ought to have a fortune-teller.

"In a tent with bangles and gold earrings, you know, to look like a gipsy. Of course, she needn't *be* a gipsy."

"I don't hold with gipsies," said Miss Gregory. "A nasty, thieving lot—and *dirty!*"

"I said she needn't be a gipsy. One of us could do it. I'll do it myself, if you like."

Dossie Fenn was the elder of the two. Like her sister, she had flashing teeth and a vivacious smile, but although they had once looked much the same the past few years had produced a striking difference between them. Daisy was a blonde, nowadays, while Dossie, by way of contrast, had very dark hair worn in turbulent curls all over her head. Her hair was naturally curly, she boasted, and it gave her no trouble at all—she only had to run a comb through it and there she was!

Even Miss Fenn's admirers sometimes wished that she would run the comb through more frequently. Her curious mop-like *coiffure* was perhaps better suited to the South Sea Islands than to an English village, but she evidently believed that it had gipsyish possibilities. "I'm probably the best person, really," she said. "I mean, I'd *look* right, don't you think?"

"Oh, I do," Daisy answered eagerly. "Just the job! You could wear that old black velvet of mine, and a little scarlet bolero!"

Not so little either, thought the school-mistress, but she kept this unkind comment to herself.

"And simply *strings* of coloured beads!"

"And my fingers crammed with rings!"

"English gipsies are much more subdued," said Miss Templer. "I suppose it's the climate. You ought to brown your face and smoke an old clay pipe."

This suggestion pleased no one, least of all the elder Miss Fenn.

"Mother thinks you're too well known," Miss Polegate announced dutifully. "It ought to be a stranger."

"I agree," said Mrs. Custance. "It's a good idea, Dossie, but everyone would recognize you." (And everyone would know that the gipsy's information came, not from cards or crystal-gazing, but from a lifelong study of local gossip. It would never do.) "Anyway, I'm not sure if the vicar would approve of a fortune-teller. I shall have to ask him."

Mrs. Custance knew that Edward could be brought to approve of almost anything, but she wanted time to think it over.

After the rest of the helpers had gone Mrs. Custance and Miss Templer walked round the garden together, ostensibly to settle a few details about the Needlework and Fancies, but in reality to give Mrs. Custance the pleasure of admiring her flowers and describing, at great length, the triumphs and disasters of her perpetual war against Pests.

Miss Templer was quite ready to listen. She never did any gardening herself, but she liked looking at other people's gardens and hearing her friends talk of pruning and weeding, of getting the roses sprayed, the raspberry canes tied up, and the lettuces pricked out. It seemed to her that a gardener's life was an unending struggle against superior forces, and she was often thankful that she had not been enslaved by the garden at Prospect House. It was nice to be able to sympathize with Amy about the greenfly and the ravages of the rabbit, without feeling that these or similar problems menaced her own happiness.

"Too dreadful!" said Mrs. Custance, pointing to what had been her carnation cuttings. "He lives in the shrubbery. I can't think how he got in."

The vicarage garden was enclosed by a stone wall, and Mrs. Custance had put wire-netting along the bottom of the gate to repel any rabbit who might be bold enough to come through the village and along the road. "But he *must* have come that way," she said. "The gate so often gets left open. I suppose he seized his chance."

Miss Templer pictured the rabbit hiding behind the war memorial until the coast was clear, and then making a dash for it.

"That reminds me of Mrs. Midge," she said, seeing a small but resolute animal with rather bulging eyes. "I meant to tell you after Dossie went, but I forgot. By the way, poor Henry had a very trying afternoon with Daisy, the day they went to Witling to look at the old rectory. At least, I conjecture he did, but he's one of those inarticulate people who can't really explain what happens to them."

"Perhaps he doesn't want to," Mrs. Custance said. "What about Mrs. Midge?"

She had a wild hope that Isabel was going to say Mrs. Midge was leaving Prospect Cottage.

"Oh yes. Mrs. Midge tells fortunes with cards, when she's in the mood for it. Mrs. Imber says she's quite good. Of course, she isn't in the least like a gipsy, is she? But if we had the tent quite dark, and dressed her in veils—?"

"More than veils," Mrs. Custance said sharply.

"Well, of course she'd have something underneath. I can't imagine Mrs. Midge without a good deal of stiffening. I don't suppose they'd be very agreeable fortunes—though if she really reads the cards they'd have to be, wouldn't they? I mean, if *they* said so, *she'd* have to say so," Miss Templer added explicitly.

"Anyway, I don't believe in that sort of thing." Unconscious of any inconsistency, Mrs. Custance added, "It wouldn't be much good if she can only do it when she's in the mood."

"She doesn't look moody. But of course no one does . . . only one mood at a time."

Mrs. Custance frowned. She wanted the Fête to be a success, but she did not want Mrs. Midge to play a prominent part. She was spared having to make a decision at once by the sight of an ancient red car coming slowly up the drive.

"That's Sir James," she said. "I suppose he's come to talk about the Fête. Don't go, Isabel."

But Miss Templer said she would slip away by the path behind the shrubbery.

Mrs. Custance took her guest into the drawing-room. She was glad to see him but she wished he had come at some other time, for it was getting late and she had meant to make macaroni cheese for supper. The macaroni had to be cooked, and supper must be punctual as Edward had a meeting afterwards.

Cassandra was home and she had begun to tidy out the drawers of Mrs. Custance's desk, and had reached the stage when everything was heaped on the floor. What with the contents of the drawers, and the chairs pulled into a circle for the meeting, the drawing-room appeared chaotically disordered. Mrs. Custance hoped their patron would not think it always looked like this; it was but seldom that he paid them a visit, and by some unfortunate chance he usually came when things were not quite as they should be.

"Do sit down," she begged. But Sir James planted himself on the hearthrug, saying he would not keep them long.

"Where's Custance?" he asked. "Ought to see him too, y' know. Feel he ought to be consulted."

Cassandra went off to find her father, who had observed the approach of his patron and was lying low in his study.

"He *was* consulted," Mrs. Custance said. "We both thought it would be an excellent idea. I do hope you agree."

"What's that, Amy?" Sir James looked grieved and perplexed, and she realized that he had not come about the Fête after all.

"Didn't you get my note?" she asked. But her guest pretended to be hard of hearing. He had come in the guise of a fairy godfather, and the other business could wait.

Mr. Custance appeared, shepherded into the room by Cassandra, who asked if she was wanted. Sir James told her to remain; he was pleasantly conscious of his benevolence, and a larger audience would not come amiss. When he had got them all grouped under his eye he felt in his pocket, and with a dramatic gesture he produced a sealed envelope. It obviously contained something important, but since the Custance family could not guess what it was the gesture fell a little flat.

"For you, Custance," said Sir James, offering the envelope to Mr. Custance but not letting go of it. "Just a small contribution, y' know, but it'll help, it'll help."

Mr. Custance, who did not know whether it was a contribution to the Bishop's fund, the Sunday-school outing, or Foreign Missions, made nervous, grateful noises.

"Don't say anything," Sir James continued. "You need it, Custance—noticed that myself on Sunday. It's all arranged, so don't say anything. All you've got to do is *go*. Get away the first week after Whit-Sunday. I fixed it for then, y' know, because it's easier to get a replacement."

For a moment Mr. Custance thought he was being pensioned off. But Mrs. Custance had a quicker mind and grasped at once what was intended.

"Is it for Edward's holiday?" she asked, giving her husband his cue. "My dear Sir James, it's very, *very* kind of you!"

"For the two of you, Amy. Do you both good. Now don't say anything—it's all settled and I won't hear another word."

But naturally he did not mean this, and he listened with increasing good humour while they poured out their thanks. To do good by stealth was not his way, for he considered that generous gestures and heartfelt gratitude were as closely connected as duckling and green peas, and neither was at its best without the other.

Cassandra noticed that her father, though suitably grateful, was also a little worried; and she sympathized with him. It was now the beginning of May and Whitsun was quite near; he would have to find someone to take the services in his absence, and he would also have to find somewhere to go.

"A fortnight by the sea—that's what you need, Custance."

"My sister went to a very nice place in Cornwall last year," Mrs. Custance said. "I've got the address. I'll write to them tonight."

She knew that Edward did not want to go away and that it would be very inconvenient, but she also knew that Sir James would be very much offended if they stayed at home. They would have to go; and since they had to, they had better make the best of it. She had not had a real holiday for years, and she suddenly began to look forward to it. The only sad thing was that Cassie would not be able to come with them.

Mr. Custance, however, was bitterly regretting his careworn appearance in church the previous Sunday. Brigham meant, of course, to be kind, and he was being uncommonly generous, but he seemed to forget that one could not just lock up a church and leave it.

The difficulty of finding another clergyman to take his place, the thought of having to alter and postpone all his engagements (how would he ever get things straight again?), and above all the horrid prospect of being torn from his home, his books, and his Greek commentary, made it impossible for Mr. Custance to exhibit unqualified delight. He did his best, but it was not a very good best. His wan smiles hardly masked the melancholy heart within.

It had happened before that the vicar had been so unfortunate as to annoy his patron in two ways at once; by disagreeing with him, and by not having the courage to state his opinion boldly. Cassandra and her mother both hoped that Sir James would not notice Mr. Custance's lack of enthusiasm, for it was precisely this mute, yet obvious, dissent which had so annoyed him on previous occasions. Cassandra joined in the conversation, trying to distract the guest's attention, while Mrs. Custance with quick glances sought to warn Edward of impending danger.

But happily their fears were groundless. Sir James did not fail to notice that Custance had something on his mind, but he was still playing the part of a fairy godfather, and he knew that his next words would allay his parson's anxiety. It was right and proper that a clergyman should be conscientious; it was quite natural for Custance to be worrying about what was going to happen in his absence.

"Hr-rmph!" he said loudly, puffing out his moustache. It was a signal to command their attention for his next announcement, and they recognized it as such. Cassandra broke off in mid-sentence, and Mrs. Custance stopped frowning at her husband and produced a politely alert smile.

"You'll be away two Sundays. Must stay a fortnight, y' know. A holiday's no good unless you stay a fortnight."

To his family's regret Mr. Custance began to explain that he could not possibly manage a fortnight. He did not, of course, mention his own dislike of leaving home. He said, very suitably and just as his benefactor had expected, that he could not leave his church unattended.

"Now don't worry about that, Custance," said Sir James. "You'll only be away for two Sundays, and I've borrowed a curate."

He spoke rather as if the curate were an umbrella, and Cassandra was hardly surprised when he added reassuringly, "Quite a sound one."

"Where from?" Mr. Custance asked sceptically.

"I borrowed him from Bingley."

Everyone was impressed. It was an historic fact that in a long succession of rectors Mallinford had had more than its fair share of difficult and quarrelsome clergymen, and Mr. Bingley, true to tradition, was very difficult indeed. Unlike Mr. Custance, he enjoyed travelling, and he was continually flitting away to conferences, where he spoke glibly about the need for peace and squabbled with his fellow-speakers. He also collected postage stamps, and made frequent visits to London to attend auction sales. With so many activities he had little time to look after his parish, but fortunately he was a man of means and could afford to employ a curate. This curate he regarded as his personal property, and he kept him fully occupied.

It was so unusual for Mr. Bingley to let his curate out on loan that the young man was virtually unknown to the neighbourhood.

"How clever of you," Cassandra said, voicing the general opinion. Sir James preened himself; he would have liked to tell them how he had played on Bingley's vanity and his snobbish weakness for titled landowners, but that might put Custance in a difficulty, since parsons, like doctors, were bound to stick together.

"Feller's name is Johnson," he said. "Quite young—only twenty-six. Glad to do it."

Cassandra was glad, too, that the curate had at least been consulted, but Mrs. Custance shook her head.

"Only twenty-six," she said. "He's much too young to be married."

She did not approve of married curates. In the old days at her father's rectory there had always been a curate, and she and her sisters had looked on him as a useful perquisite, an unattached man who could be asked to supper or tennis at short notice, and who often ended by becoming warmly attached to one or the other of them. This perhaps accounted for her view that all curates should be single; or perhaps she felt that by employing a married man instead of a bachelor Mr. Bingley was reducing the number of possible candidates for her daughter's hand.

Mr. Custance, who had now realized that the holiday was unavoidable, pulled himself together and said that, married or unmarried, he was sure Mr. Johnson would do very well and it was remarkably kind of Sir James to have taken the trouble to get him. On this happy note the visit ended. Sir James, stooping less than usual and almost forgetting to lean on his stick, walked out to his car and departed amid a final chorus of thanks. As soon as the car was out of sight Mrs. Custance and Cassandra turned to Mr. Custance and told him to open the envelope.

"Do you think I should have opened it before?" he asked, hunting for the envelope in all his pockets. "One doesn't want to look greedy, but I think perhaps he expected me to open it."

"He wanted you to say Oo-ah!"

"The other pocket, Edward. Yes—there. I don't know— perhaps it *would* have looked greedy—anyway, I'm sure he realized how grateful we are. Let me see."

Mrs. Custance took the envelope away from her husband, who was being maddeningly slow, and tore it open. "Well, that's really very generous of him," she said.

Cassandra looked over her mother's shoulder.

"Oo-ah!" she exclaimed. "I wish I'd been more gushing—on your behalf, of course. When he said it was a small contribution I thought it was something towards the railway fare."

Then she noticed something else. The cheque which Sir James had presented as his own, and for which he had been rewarded with so much gratitude, bore George's signature. The initials were the same as his father's, but the handwriting was different—sprawling, untidy, and looking as if it had been written in haste. George's signature had always looked like that. She knew it well for right up to the end of the war they had corresponded regularly.

"Why—" she began. And then she stopped. Neither her mother, who had looked only at the figures on the cheque, nor her father, who had not got his spectacles, had noticed this curious circumstance. The cheque was already being folded up and put away in Mrs. Custance's handbag, and Cassandra decided it would be better to say nothing. Her mother was now happily discussing the coming holiday. It would be a pity to spoil her pleasure by pointing out that it was George who was paying for it, and not his kind, generous father.

The thing to do, she thought, was to tackle George himself. There might be some perfectly simple reason for his signing the cheque instead of Sir James; and she hoped there would be.

"What were you saying, Cassie?" Mrs. Custance asked.

"Nothing, Mummy. Shall I start getting supper?"

CHAPTER X

MISS TEMPLER had a theory that it was better for children to be educated at home. Her brother thought exactly the opposite, or pretended to (one could never be certain with Eustace), and he was all for sending them to boarding-schools as soon as possible and keeping them there until they were grown up. He said it was much easier to grow fond of a child whom one saw only in the holidays, and that the child, for the same reason, learnt to appreciate its home.

These conflicting views had produced wordy arguments in the past, but finally a compromise had been reached; Isabel was allowed to keep the children at home until they were eleven and then each in turn went off to boarding-school.

Leonard was only just ten, but Miss Templer was already thinking of the parting; this meant that she viewed all his activities with a particularly indulgent eye, and in consequence he was getting dreadfully spoilt.

He was fond of Cassandra, but he welcomed any chance to escape from lessons, and when escape was impossible he had various schemes for distracting his governess's attention from the task of the moment. Cassandra seldom allowed herself to be distracted, but she sometimes wished that she had a less exhausting pupil. It was a pity that Leonard seemed to have made up his mind that education was a waste of time.

"I don't know how you can stand Leonard," Lily said. The morning's lessons were ended, and she had come into the dining-room to find Cassandra tidying the big cupboard where she kept the school books. Leonard had been rescued from this task by his doting aunt, who had sent him up to the garage to search in Henry Ashford's car for her handbag which had been missing since the previous day.

Cassandra protested that she was very fond of Leonard. "But he really ought to be at school," she added. "I think he'd do much better if he had some competition."

Lily said: "I hate competition, and team games, and all that dreary stuff about being a good influence. The thing is, one has to have a congenial environment before one can even begin to discover one's true qualities."

The last part of this statement sounded as if it was in quotation marks, and Cassandra had no difficulty in guessing its origin. "Did Lukin Midge say that?" she asked.

"Yes, he did, actually. But I think it's awfully true."

"The only thing is, if one doesn't know what one's true qualities are, how does one choose the environment that's going to suit them?"

"Well, I don't know. I didn't think of it like that. But really, Cassandra, Lukin is frightfully clever. He's a bit odd, too, but I think that's *because* he's so clever, and because he's got a terribly uncongenial environment so that he can't develop properly."

"But I thought Lukin and his Mama simply lived for one another. Mrs. Midge guards him as if he was the crown jewels."

"And Lukin can't escape. Don't you see? She has never let him grow up."

Cassandra put the last book in its place. "Poor wretched Peter Pan," she said lightly. But Lily pointed out that Peter Pan did not want to grow up, and Lukin did.

"What we must do," she said, "is to help him, but not too obviously because he's so sensitive. Don't laugh, Cassandra. Suppose Lukin turned out to be a budding genius, and afterwards he— he—"

"Budded. Or burgeoned, perhaps."

"Well, anyway, if he grew to be famous, it would be nice to know that you'd believed in him and helped him when he was poor and unknown."

Cassandra saw that it would be very nice, for Lily. She did not believe Lukin Midge was a budding genius, but she was interested to hear that he was entangled in a web of mother-love.

But for Lily's prompting, she would not have known it; for, as Mrs. Custance had complained, she was strangely indifferent to young men and she had never bothered to make Lukin's acquaintance beyond saying good morning or good evening when she encountered him. She had imagined that he was perfectly content to be his mother's darling, and therefore a person to be laughed at rather than pitied.

"Are you sure he wants to escape?" she asked.

"Oh yes. I told you, the other day. He's dreadfully repressed."

"Then let's help him," said Cassandra. "But how?"

Lily hesitated. She had no clear plans for Lukin's rescue, but after three visits to his workroom she longed to discuss him with some sympathetic friend. Perhaps it was because she herself was now grown up that Cassandra appeared younger and more approachable than she had done in the past, when a seemingly unbridgeable gulf had separated Leonard's governess and Leonard's schoolgirl sister.

"Actually, that's what I want to ask you," she said. "Come and walk round the garden before lunch."

She said it on the spur of the moment, but even as she spoke the dream-friend of her fantasies was acquiring Cassandra's face and smile. Cassandra, unaware of her promotion, debated whether she should correct Leonard's dictation or give up being a governess for the rest of the morning. But the sun was shining, and it did not take her long to decide.

"I'd love to," she answered; and the casual words established her, in Lily's eyes, as the right person to confide in.

Lily led her to a secluded spot behind the rhododendrons. The garden was wholly deserted, but she thought in terms of secluded spots and possible eavesdroppers. They lay down on the grass, and Cassandra pillowed her head on her arms and closed her eyes.

But she had not been brought there to sleep.

"You see, it's awfully difficult about Lukin," Lily said earnestly. "If I ask him here, Uncle Eustace is sure to find out he's a painter. And one doesn't know what his reactions would be."

"Bad, I should think," Cassandra hazarded.

Everyone who was well acquainted with Eustace Templer knew what he thought about painters.

He had once been a fashionable painter himself, he had quarrelled with most of his eminent contemporaries—carrying on a spiteful war in speech and print which had ended in his resignation from the Academy and his retirement from the London scene—and now he hated all painters, good, bad and indifferent. He no longer waged war on them; he simply avoided them as if they were lepers, and vicious lepers at that.

Fortunately there were no professional artists in the neighbourhood, and the only amateur was an elderly lady who was almost as eccentric as Eustace himself; she never left her own house so there was no danger of their meeting. If he found out that there was a painter at Prospect Cottage he would probably be furious—it would be worse than the time when he found a scorpion in his bed. Far worse, thought Cassandra; because Lukin, unlike the phantom scorpion, would not be able to evade retribution by simply ceasing to be.

"Bad," Lily agreed. "And it's no good asking him when Uncle Eustace is out, because Uncle Eustace has an uncanny instinct about that sort of thing. He always turns up just when he's not wanted."

The rhododendrons rustled as she spoke. There, at the end of the overgrown path that led to their retreat, stood the unwanted uncle. He was too far off to hear what had been said, but this striking proof of his instinct caused Lily and Cassandra to exchange glances of wonder and sympathy. His appearance at that moment did a good deal for their friendship. Cassandra was young enough to feel that youth and age were clear-cut divisions and that one must support one's own contemporaries, and now, faced with age in the person of Eustace Templer, she accepted Lily as an ally.

"Nymphs!" said Eustace Templer, advancing towards them. "Nymphs without shepherds. Where is your swain, Lily? Cassandra, where is Leonard?"

"I haven't got a swain," Lily answered pertly. She was accustomed to this sort of teasing, which always meant that he was in a good humour. "And Cassandra has been teaching Leonard all morning, so she deserves a rest."

Eustace took from his pocket a silk handkerchief, which he spread out on the ground. "My bones are sensitive to damp," he observed, sitting down carefully on the inadequate little square. "Why do you choose this shady bower, when the whole garden lies basking in the sun? Do you value your complexions so highly?"

"On the contrary, sunburn improves mine."

"And Lily's is so well farded that no sunlight could reach it. So, fearing not the heat o' the sun, you had some other reason for retreat. You came here to talk secrets!" Playful as a kitten, he made his little pounce, his voice shrill and sharp for an instant, as if the kitten were showing its claws. "Secrets," he repeated gently. "Schoolgirl secrets? Of course not, you're both past the age for such nonsense. Serious secrets, then. Enterprises of great pith and moment—plans to reform the world. Or some member of it in particular."

This time they dared not look at each other, and neither of them knew how to reply. They were both daunted by this latest manifestation of his almost supernatural talent for appearing when he was least wanted and joining in a conversation not intended for his ears. After a short but revealing pause Lily said they had been discussing Uncle Henry, and at the same instant Cassandra declared that they had been talking about lawn tennis.

"Come, come," Eustace Templer said amiably. "Did neither of you listen to the other? Two gushing streams running parallel, two flights of fancy falling on deaf ears! I should have been here earlier. I would have made an attentive audience."

Improvising rapidly, Cassandra said they had wondered if Colonel Ashford liked tennis, and had meant to ask him to play on the vicarage lawn, now that it was dry enough.

"To cheer him up," Lily added.

"Henry doesn't need cheering up," Eustace objected. "He's perfectly content with himself."

"But not with us, Uncle Eustace. We drive him to melancholia."

"Faults on both sides, my dear Lily. Faults on both sides. I leave you to discover your own, but I'll tell you what's the matter with poor Henry. He's too rigid. Isn't he?"

Uncle and niece now embarked on a critical analysis of Colonel Ashford's character, while Cassandra tried to look indifferent; for, as an outsider, she felt it wise to remain neutral. Her hatred of injustice sometimes made her feel rather sorry for Colonel Ashford. She did not care for him, but she saw that he had a lot to put up with.

It was after half-past one, and probably he was waiting impatiently for his lunch. Lunch, according to the too-rigid ideas of Colonel Ashford, ought to be at the same time every day; but at Prospect House it was a moveable feast which appeared on the table when Mrs. Truefitt was sure that the family was all assembled. The moveable feast interfered with Leonard's afternoon work, and this made it easier for Cassandra to enter into Colonel Ashford's feelings on the subject of punctuality.

"Bound to the wheels of time," Eustace was saying. "A prisoner in a minute-glass. The sort of man who ought to live by himself in a clockwork house and spend his well-regulated leisure hours filling in forms in triplicate. Yes, yes," he added thoughtfully, "Henry really needs a house of his own."

It was not the first time he had spoken of this. Henry Ashford's desire for a house of his own was no less evident than Eustace Templer's desire to be rid of him.

"Perhaps something will turn up," Lily said vaguely.

"Or be turned up. When you grow older, my dear, you will realize that things don't turn up of themselves. They need assistance."

Cassandra knew that Colonel Ashford had inspected every vacant house in the neighbourhood, and was only prevented from looking farther afield by his wife's wish to settle somewhere near her sister Isabel. She did not know how Eustace Templer was tackling the problem, but she strongly suspected that he had his eye on Prospect Cottage and was planning to dislodge Mrs. Midge.

Lily thought so too, and a little later, as they were walking back to the house, she whispered to Cassandra that Uncle Eustace had been twice to see his solicitor and had said after the second visit that lawyers were as hidebound as their books and as unenterprising as unborn babies.

The whisper was perhaps an unnecessary precaution, for Eustace had diverged across the lawn to speak to Todd the gardener. But Lily enjoyed the feeling that she and Cassandra were engaged on a dangerous mission—the rescue of Lukin—and surrounded by hostile forces.

"Tennis," she continued. "That's an awfully good idea."

Cassandra was puzzled. "Do you really think it would cheer him up? I only said it for something to say."

"Oh, I don't mean Uncle Henry—though perhaps it might. I mean Lukin. Cassandra, couldn't you ask Lukin to tennis next Saturday?"

"Well—I could." (Cassandra wondered what her mother would say.) "But does he play tennis? I've always been given to understand that he hated all games."

"But we've got to start somewhere. I don't think he has ever tried. But he might come if—if—Well, I might persuade him to come."

"If he's never tried he won't be very good," Cassandra said thoughtfully.

"That doesn't matter. It'll only be you and me and—Felix, I suppose. Yes, it will have to be Felix, but I'll have to warn him. Felix isn't much good anyway. Shall I ask him—Lukin, I mean—or will you?"

"You ask him." She saw that Lily was longing to do it, and that she evidently doubted whether Cassandra would prove sufficiently persuasive. "Only let me know soon, because I'll have to get the nets up and the court marked. It will be the first time we've played this year."

"I've got a lovely new pair of shorts," Lily said happily. "Pleated ones, and *really* short. I do hope it's fine on Saturday."

The vicarage tennis-court was rather overshadowed by trees, and badly in need of draining and levelling. Clover, plantains and moss competed with the grass on its surface, there were humps and hollows that caused the balls to bounce at unforeseeable angles, and except in a prolonged drought it never got really hard. Nevertheless, it was the only tennis-court in Little Mallin, apart from the two at Mallin Hall which, from the point of view of the community, hardly counted.

Mrs. Custance liked tennis, and when she had first come to the vicarage she had had tennis parties all through the summer, and had even got her husband to play; though Mr. Custance had never been anything but a severe handicap to the person he partnered. But since the war many of her contemporaries had given up the game; people who used to cycle over from Witling and other villages now made their increasing age an excuse for stopping at home, and their sons and daughters were never available. It was quite difficult to find enough people to make up a set.

It was a great pity, for it was still the thing she enjoyed best. But even if there had been plenty of other players, housework and parochial duties left her little time for it, and she knew that she was past her prime. She had never been a really good tennis player, but in the old days she had been quick on her feet, with a hard, accurate service and a forehand drive that won her local fame. Every autumn she declared she would give up playing, and every summer, as soon as there had been enough heat and sunshine to dry the grass, she found herself looking forward to an occasional game, 'just to get some exercise'.

Owing to the dampness of the lawn it was seldom possible, at the vicarage, to open the season before June. But this spring had been wonderfully dry and the ground was quite hard al-

ready. Mrs. Custance, returning from an inspection of the tennis-court, met her daughter coming on the same errand; Cassandra had only just got home, but for once her mother omitted
the usual inquiries as to how she had spent her day. "I've been
looking at the lawn," she exclaimed, "and I must tell Nutting to
mow it again tomorrow. It's beautifully dry, more like August
than May. I thought we might have some tennis on Saturday."

"I had the same thought, Mummy. I hope you don't mind—I
asked Lily and Felix."

"Felix isn't very good, but that doesn't matter. Perhaps we
might get your father to play. I'm sure he enjoys it really." Mrs.
Custance could not believe that anyone could fail to enjoy tennis. "Anyway, we shall have a women's four, because I've asked
Dossie and Daisy. How many is that?—six without Edward.
Well, perhaps he needn't play after all. Six is a good number,
isn't it?"

In the midst of her happy anticipations she noticed that her
daughter seemed ill at ease.

"What's the matter, Cassie?" she said. "Did you want someone else?" Making a rapid mental survey of Cassie's friends she
tried to think of a possible choice—how nice if Cassie was to say
that Dr. Atcherley's son was home on leave at Long Hampton, or
that she had met young Mr. Armitage, or the Lucas boy (or both
of them), and asked them to tennis on Saturday!

Mrs. Custance never ceased to hope that Cassandra might
suddenly turn into the kind of daughter who announced that
John Armitage, or Robert Lucas, was coming on Saturday, and
that Robert, or John, was taking her out the following week. For
a moment it seemed as if her hope was well-founded. Cassandra, looking confused and almost shy, replied that there might
be someone else, only she wasn't sure if he could come.

"Who is it?" her mother asked eagerly.

"It's—well, Mummy, I know you'll be surprised. It's Lukin
Midge."

"That wretched boy!" Mrs. Custance cried. "Cassie, you must
be mad. He doesn't play games, he's utterly useless—living at
home and letting his mother work! Of course she spoils him,

making out he's delicate and so on, but still no man with any self-respect would allow it!"

Cassandra had foreseen that her mother would not welcome Lukin's inclusion in the tennis party, but she had not expected such bitter opposition. She had meant to explain why he was being asked; she knew that her mother disliked Mrs. Midge and she had hoped that this would make it easier to convince her that Lukin needed a helping hand. But it was no good trying to explain things now, because it was quite evident that Mrs. Custance was not in a mood to listen to explanations. It was one of those times when explanations, however lucid and reasonable, were simply a waste of breath.

Neither Cassandra nor her father would have admitted that Mrs. Custance was hot-tempered, but they both knew that there were times when she would not listen to them and when any attempts to make her listen were better avoided. "Your mother is a little upset," Mr. Custance would say, and this charitable phrase served both as a warning, and as an excuse for his own shortcomings. If Mrs. Custance had not been upset it would not have mattered that he had forgotten to buy the fish, or spilt ink on his new flannel trousers.

The invitation to Lukin had upset Mrs. Custance more than either of these disasters, and it was clearly hopeless, at the moment, to try to win her sympathy.

Cassandra—a little upset herself—said she was sorry about it but perhaps he wouldn't be able to come after all, and her mother replied fiercely that she wasn't going to put off Dossie and Daisy for Lukin Midge. After this, by tacit consent, they let his name drop out of the conversation.

But it remained, like a small but irritating pimple, in Mrs. Custance's thoughts, long after she had recovered her outward good humour. The horrid shock of hearing what she did not want to hear, and the disappointing contrast between that and what she had hoped for, had caused her to speak with injudicious fervour. She admitted it. Her denunciation had been harsh and hasty, and she wished she had held her tongue.

Ever since the end of the war, ever since Cassandra and Lukin had grown up, she had had at the back of her mind the fear that they might fall in love. It had often occurred to her that her daughter was just the sort of girl to throw herself away on someone quite unsuitable; and this maternal anxiety was really what had made her set her face against Mrs. Midge and her good-for-nothing son. If there had been no Lukin she would have overlooked Mrs. Midge's faults as easily as she overlooked the faults of Dossie and Daisy Fenn.

It was true that the young people had never shown much interest in each other, but that did not prevent Mrs. Custance from worrying. She had a sort of presentiment that sooner or later Cassie's foolish indifference to the male sex would yield place to an equally foolish infatuation for a man who could not possibly make her happy.

And now Cassie had asked Lukin Midge to play tennis; and she herself, by showing open hostility, had probably encouraged Cassie's incipient interest. She knew that fierce parental opposition was always a mistake.

She could not unsay what had been said, but she resolved that from now on she would make the best of Lukin, and would give him no chance to appear unwelcome or ill-used. But it went dreadfully against the grain. Why, oh why did Cassie have to be so perverse—and why was there no other young man who might serve as a counter-attraction?

She thought at once of George Brigham. But it was a long time since George had played tennis on the vicarage lawn.

The last time had been in 1945, when he had come home on leave shortly after V-E Day. Cassie had just left school, and no one had begun to worry about Russia. She had been so happy and confident then, so full of plans for the golden future. She had been almost sure that George and Cassandra would get married and live happily ever after.

Instead of which, George had returned to Italy and had almost instantly become engaged to an Italian countess. It seemed to Mrs. Custance, looking back, that he had behaved with the utmost duplicity—one moment he was playing tennis with Cassie, and the next he was writing buoyant, boastful letters (which Sir James had shown her) proclaiming his own good fortune. It was then that she had changed her mind about George, and although the Italian engagement had not lasted long his subsequent behaviour had proved her right. The war had quite spoilt him.

He had turned out fickle, ungrateful and conceited. He had neglected his old friends and disappointed his father. It would be quite impossible, nowadays, to ask him to her tennis parties; and even if her principles allowed her to do so, he would be certain to refuse.

George was a very good tennis player. She thought, regretfully, of the splendid games they had had in the past, and she thought, more practically, that Lukin would look ridiculous if he were matched against a player like George. She remembered—delving into an even remoter past—that nothing was more disillusioning than to see the loved one making a fool of himself in public.

At this she stopped short, telling herself not to be silly. She could not yet be sure that Lukin was loved by anyone. Except, of course, by Mrs. Midge.

CHAPTER XI

ON SATURDAYS Mrs. Midge did not go to the shop, except in the holiday season when business was extra brisk. But she sometimes went to Mallinford for her own pleasure, to meet one of her new friends for coffee and to buy food for the week-end.

She liked to idle away an hour at 'Peter's Pantry', wearing her best clothes and a little more make-up than she used on other days, as if she were one of those leisured women who did not have to work for their living, and while she played this rôle she still felt smugly superior, because few people had had such a hard life as herself and made such a success of it. So she had the best of it both ways, and usually returned from a Saturday morning expedition in an excellent humour.

This morning she was later than she had intended. The friend whom she met for coffee was lunching with some people at Witling, and offered her a lift home; she accepted the offer before she realized that Mrs. Howell had a lot of shopping to do first, and then had to take the parcels back to her flat and collect her dog (who was so looking forward to a nice afternoon in the country), and pay her 'daily', and change her shoes for thicker ones so that she could take the dog for a walk in Witling woods. The luncheon party at Witling was not till half-past one and she had plenty of time, but Mrs. Midge thought regretfully of her own lunch; Mrs. Nutting would have prepared the vegetables, but they would still have to be cooked, and the fish as well, and there would hardly be time to make pancakes.

Still, she enjoyed the drive, especially as Mrs. Howell went out of her way to take her up the hill to Prospect Cottage instead of setting her down at the criss-cross in the village. Prospect Cottage was looking its best, with the tulips and forget-me-nots a blaze of colour, the early Banksia rose almost hiding the windows with its creamy clusters, and the little lawn a trim patch of green. "How charming!" her friend exclaimed. "You lucky, lucky woman—I had no idea it was like this!"

She had, in fact, expected it to be larger—for Mrs. Midge had somehow given the impression that it was a small Queen Anne house standing in its own grounds—but since this dear little cottage was a much more desirable residence than the house she had pictured her praise was quite genuine.

"Can't you come in for a minute?"

"My dear, I must fly. I'm late already. But I'd love to come another time."

"You must come to tea," Mrs. Midge said, beaming hospitably. It was at this moment that she noticed Lukin's white trousers hanging out of his bedroom window. Being rather short-sighted she had mistaken them at first for densely covered sprays of the Banksia rose, and it was only when one leg flapped suddenly in the breeze that she realized her error.

Her smile became a little strained. She could not bear untidiness, and this was worse than untidiness, it was almost vulgar.

She moved closer to the car, to block out, if it were not too late, the lamentable sight, and gave her friend some rather confused instructions about a gate higher up the lane where she could reverse. As soon as the car had started she shot into Prospect Cottage and hurried upstairs to remove the trousers so that they should not be visible if Mrs. Howell stopped for another look on her way back. She did not pause this time to tap lightly on Lukin's door, and her abrupt entry surprised him in a state of *déshabillé*.

"Mama!" he cried, leaping for cover like a startled faun. But Mrs. Midge sped to the window and pulled the offending object inside. She just had time to lean out and wave her hand as the car went by, a happy, carefree wave to show what a nice person she was, in her nice cottage with the nodding tulips and the clustering roses. Then she turned to Lukin and became, in the twinkling of an eye, the personification of a Superior Being.

"Lukin," she said, "Mother has often asked you to be more considerate. She works very hard to give you a good home, and you ought to remember it and try to show a little gratitude. You know how it hurts Mother to see untidiness, and yet you can go and do a thing like this. Hanging your—your clothes out of the front window as if we lived in a slum. Mother is really upset!"

By this time Lukin had modestly donned his dressing-gown.

"I was changing," he said. He attempted a wistful smile. In his dressing-gown, and with his hair rumpled, it was quite easy to be little Lukin, yet for once the boyish charm went unnoticed.

"So I see. But that's no reason for hanging your trousers out of the window."

"I thought they might be damp."

Mrs. Midge hesitated. Lukin, like herself, was liable to chills, and she had trained him to be very careful about changing his socks in wet weather and never putting on clothes which had not been well aired.

"I thought, if I hung them in the sun they'd get aired," he continued, quick to follow up his advantage. "You see, I haven't worn them since last year."

She realized that these were Lukin's best white flannels, the trousers she had bought him a year ago for his visit to Pentalloch. He had hurt her feelings by refusing to take them to Pentalloch, so really they had hardly been worn at all.

"But, Lukin, they're much too good for the garden," she said.

She turned to leave the room, thinking as she went that she would have to open a tin of fruit and have the pancakes tomorrow instead. "Put on your grey ones, darling," she said. "And that thin blue shirt, if you're too hot."

"I'm playing tennis at the vicarage," Lukin said abruptly.

Mrs. Midge was halfway through the door, and for a moment she thought she had not heard him aright.

"You're doing what?"

"Playing tennis."

Just at first there was silence—the ominous silence that precedes a thunderstorm. Mrs. Midge was so surprised that she quite forgot to be Mother. Lukin, who had been wondering for three days what her reactions would be, drew a deep breath and shut his eyes. He knew that his sensitive nature was about to undergo a dreadful buffeting.

How easy it would have been, three days ago, to say that Lily had asked him to play tennis at the vicarage. Even yesterday—even this morning—it would have sounded simple and natural. So he thought now, while the storm-clouds gathered round his head.

He had meant to tell her when they were both in a cosy, affectionate mood, sitting together over their knitting and embroidery in the evening. But for some reason these moods were becoming infrequent; and he had been hampered by the convention that he always told his mother everything. (It was a convention he had privately rejected some time ago, but he still lacked the courage to reject it openly.) He could not have spoken of the tennis party without mentioning Lily's visits to his workroom, and she would certainly have wanted to know why he had not mentioned them sooner.

If Lukin had not been suffering acutely from the feeling that he was misunderstood at home, Lily would not have found it so easy to persuade him to play tennis. He wished, now, that he had never consented; yet the consenting had had a symbolic importance. It was a gesture of independence. It was necessary. He saw himself, not as a trim little figure waving a tennis racket, but as a heroic rebel waving a flag of freedom.

Still keeping his eyes shut, he tried to calm his nervous apprehension by controlled deep breathing. But he wished he could shut his ears as well.

Mrs. Midge began with a patter of repetition, in which the words 'tennis' and 'vicarage' rattled like hailstones. Lukin couldn't play tennis, he didn't know how, it wasn't good for him to run about and get overheated, and he had always pretended that he didn't like games. The vicarage was not a house *she* had ever wished to visit, the Custances were frightfully stuck-up, the girl was as dull as ditch-water, and they hardly knew anyone.

Having said this several times over, with increasing emphasis, she became sad and reproachful. She only lived for her son, and she had believed that he loved her; anything he wanted, anything which would help him, she would obtain, even if she had to work her fingers to the bone. All she asked—and it wasn't much, was it?—was that Lukin should trust her and not shut her out of his life. For that would be more than she could bear—and more than she deserved, after what she had done for him.

"After all, darling, I am your mother," she said in a noble generous voice which was the prelude to a grand scene of forgiveness and reconciliation.

"And Mothers always know best," said Lukin, opening his eyes and suddenly feeling very brave.

"What do you mean?"

"You want to dominate me, to tell me what's good for me and what isn't. And to keep me in a gold cage—"

"Lukin!"

His little spurt of courage died away. Perhaps it had been a mistake to look at her; for Mrs. Midge, like the basilisk, had a death-dealing glare when she was really roused.

"I know you don't mean it," he temporized. "But really, Mama, why shouldn't I play tennis if I want to?"

There was really no reason why he shouldn't; even Mrs. Midge saw that. But that wasn't the point. It was his treachery, his underhand behaviour, that mattered. Making new friends, getting himself asked out—and never telling her a word about it.

Of course, he would be sorry for it later. In fact, he was sorry already, she could see that. He looked half pleading, half petulant, and in a very short time he would be ready to apologize.

She raised her hand to her forehead and spoke in the voice of one who is near breaking-point.

"I can't talk about it any longer. I've got a frightful headache and I'm going to lie down. You can get your own lunch, Lukin. Nothing for me, please. I suppose," she added bravely, "it's the heat."

She went to her own bedroom, where she drew the curtains, took off her frock, and lay down on her bed. Presently, she thought, Lukin would creep up with a cup of tea, and then they would have a loving talk and all would be well. Soothed by this prospect, she actually dropped off to sleep, and in spite of the absence of lunch and the agitations of the preceding hour she slept soundly.

She did not wake till four o'clock, when hunger and alarm brought her out of her room without waiting for the cup of tea. A quick inspection of the cottage, the garden, and the *atelier* showed her that Lukin was not on the premises; and his white flannel trousers were missing too. And as if this were not enough, her shopping basket stood just where she had left it on the hall table, and the chocolate éclairs smelt strongly of fish.

"That's better," Cassandra said kindly, as Lukin smote the ball over the net. The shot, like most of his shots, went out, and they lost another game. But Cassandra did not mind this, since Lukin seemed to be enjoying himself and the afternoon had gone better than she had expected.

Felix, from the other end of the court, served two double faults in succession, and Mrs. Custance, who was looking on, gave a sharp mutter of impatience. If Felix had not been nearly as bad as Lukin the set would have come to an end long ago, as it deserved to. She did so want a women's four before the light failed, but if Lily and Felix could not win this game it would be five-all, and then they might go on for ever.

Dossie Fenn, sitting beside her, said that those two boys ought to take lessons. Daisy said she wouldn't mind coaching them herself, if Mrs. Custance would let them have the court. But Mrs. Custance would not agree to this. Fond though she was of Dossie and Daisy, she felt it would not be right to encourage their pursuit of young men—and Felix was only a schoolboy—by lending them the vicarage lawn, so she made some implausible excuse and changed the subject. Neither Dossie nor Daisy bore her any malice for it; they looked on her as a sort of mother and therefore as belonging to a different generation from their own, so naturally she was bound to be a bit stuffy about fraternization between the sexes. The Misses Fenn still saw themselves as dashing young things, and everyone older than themselves as relics of the Victorian era.

The set had come to an end at last. Lily and Felix had managed to win their game, and now they were all looking for a lost ball among the rhododendrons. Mrs. Custance stood up and called to them not to bother.

"We'll find it afterwards. I want one of you girls for this set".

She pulled off her cardigan and walked happily on to the court. Lily said it was Cassandra's turn, and Cassandra was too tactful to protest.

Mrs. Custance was pleased, because Cassie was the better of the two, and with a Fenn on either side they would have a good game. She took Dossie for her partner, saying good-humouredly, "Age against Youth—and I'm sure we'll give them a beating."

Dossie giggled loudly at this remark but felt, inwardly, a little hurt—for after all there was only a year or so between herself and Daisy and they could have passed for twins if their hair had been the same colour.

Lily said to Lukin, "Would you like to see the garden?" She had left it late in the day to ask this question, thinking that Cassandra or her mother might want to show him the garden themselves, but since neither of them had done so she felt justified in suggesting it now.

Lukin accepted her offer, but she had to wait a few moments while he wrapped himself up carefully in a sweater, a tweed jacket, and a long green scarf. Felix asked him if he caught cold easily, and he explained that he was nervous of taking a chill; and would have gone on to explain in detail how the chill affected him, if Lily had not interrupted by asking Felix to look for the missing ball. She had noticed that Lukin was not nearly as shy as she had expected, and was quite ready to talk when the conversation was about himself.

There was not a great deal to see in the vicarage garden but what there was looked flourishing and healthy, and Lily was surprised that her companion found so much to criticize. Not having been brought up by gardening enthusiasts she was unaware of the fierce rivalry that exists between gardeners, and she could not guess that Lukin had been smitten with jealousy by his first sight of Mrs. Custance's broad beans and early potatoes.

They were far ahead of his own, but he comforted himself by finding fault with the lettuces, which needed thinning. He shook his head over the roses and said they hadn't been pruned properly; and the big clumps in the herbaceous border wanted splitting and dividing. The summer annuals, on the other hand, ought to be massed together, not dotted about haphazard. And all the shrubs were a very bad shape.

At the end of their tour Lily decided that Lukin was really very like his mother. Mrs. Midge had the same disparaging sniff, the same way of implying that things could be done much better than that, if people would only take the trouble *she* took. Thinking of Mrs. Midge, she said to Lukin:

"I suppose you and your mother look after your own garden together?"

It had an alarming effect. Lukin shuddered and closed his eyes, and for a moment she thought he really had caught a chill—or could it possibly be sunstroke? But the next instant he recovered himself enough to give a wan smile. "Don't speak of it," he said. "It makes me feel a traitor."

"Oh, but why?"

"If I tell you, you'll think I'm heartless. I'm not—the trouble is, I'm fighting for my very existence. It's only lately that I've come to see what's happening to me."

Lily felt gratified, for she was sure that this awakening must be due to her efforts. She had been quite right, what he needed was to meet more people, to talk to someone of his own age, and to overcome his painful self-consciousness and his morbid concern with his own health. She meant to give him a hint not to talk so much about his health, but it was rather difficult to do this without antagonizing him. For the present she prepared to be a sympathetic listener.

Reassured by her obvious interest Lukin embarked on a long, involved, and not altogether accurate account of his difficulties, and in particular of the fearful crisis which had preceded his coming to the tennis party. He dwelt on his sufferings, on the terrible nervous prostration such scenes produced, and he told her that he had not had any lunch, because he could not face it, and that he had only forced himself to come to the vicarage because he realized the symbolic importance of his action as a step towards freedom.

Lily kept her sympathetic expression to the end, but once or twice in the course of his narrative she wondered if things were really as bad as he supposed.

She was truly sorry to hear that he had gone without his lunch—but she remembered that he had made up for it by eating a very hearty tea. And although he spoke of the tennis party as an ordeal, a necessary means to an end, he had appeared to be enjoying himself in a perfectly normal way. She liked Lukin, and she still wanted to help him, but she began to see that it would not be enough to rescue him from his mother. He would have to be rescued from himself.

But it was rather late to begin now, and she felt too that it would be better to consult Cassandra first. It was not that she believed herself incapable of rescuing Lukin single-handed, but she looked forward to the discussion of his character, the making of plans—in short, the sharing of this interesting problem with her friend.

She said to Lukin that they had better go back to the tennis lawn, and as they walked through the shrubbery she realized that they had been away a long time. She hoped Mrs. Custance would not think it odd.

Mrs. Custance, however, had benefited from their absence. The first set had been a short one, and since Lily, Lukin and Felix were all out of sight when it ended she had suggested 'a return', and this had developed into a splendid struggle in which she and Dossie had eventually triumphed, after a succession of exciting deuce-games.

Flushed, panting and happy, she was now receiving the congratulations of her opponents; while Dossie, who even in the hour of triumph was mindful of her appearance, endeavoured with the aid of an inadequate little powder-compact to restore to her face the peach-bloom of an earlier hour.

"Now that's what I call tennis!" Daisy said rapturously. Daisy was the weakest player of the four, but she made up for it by exhibiting a great deal of *joie de vivre*, leaping about, running up to the net as often as possible, and keeping up a constant patter of encouragement or commiseration. "You ought to have been watching," she told Lukin. "I always say you can learn a lot by watching better-class players."

Apart from this, no comments were made on their absence, and Mrs. Custance assumed that they had all three been together. Felix, who had wandered off to the house to talk to Mr. Custance, reappeared while they were collecting the balls and folding up the deck-chairs. It was too dark to play another set (no vicarage tennis party ever ended until darkness or rain made further play impossible), but everyone except Lukin agreed that it had been a wonderfully enjoyable afternoon, and that the lawn was extraordinarily hard for the time of year.

Dossie and Daisy made their farewells and departed on foot. Lily and Felix had bicycles, and Lily supposed that Lukin had a bicycle too, though he had come late and she had not seen him arrive. But he explained that he had walked, and added that cycling gave him vertigo.

Mrs. Custance overheard this remark, for she had gone down to the gate with her daughter to speed the parting guests. As soon as they were alone she said that it was a wonder Lukin could play tennis at all, since every kind of activity appeared to have some harmful effect on this or that part of him.

"But of course it's very sporting of him to try," she added quickly, remembering her decision to be kind and tactful. "You must ask him again."

"He wasn't bad, was he?"

He was as bad as he could be, Mrs. Custance thought indignantly. But she kept the angry protest to herself.

CHAPTER XII

ON THE WEDNESDAY after Whit-Sunday Mr. and Mrs. Custance started off for Cornwall.

Mrs. Custance had meant to take the car, but the tyres were in such a bad state that she thought better of it and decided to go by train. Cassandra was to drive them into Mallinford, and it would mean two changes and a long wait at the junction, but fortunately Edward liked watching trains so he had readily agreed to this change of plan. It was really a good thing, Mrs. Custance thought, that they were going by train, because now Edward would have something to cheer him up at the very start of the journey.

She herself did not need cheering up, she was looking forward to the holiday with real pleasure, and she had bought a new hat and a pair of white shoes. She would have liked a white handbag as well but she could not afford it, and in fact there was nothing the matter with her navy-blue one except that it reminded her, every time she looked at it, that she was a vicar's wife; it was so exactly the sort of bag that vicars' wives carried.

Wednesday morning was warm and cloudless, with a heat haze shimmering in the valley and the needle of the barometer pointing to Set Fair. Mrs. Custance, wearing the new hat, came into the kitchen where Cassandra was cutting sandwiches for their lunch, to give her daughter some last directions about watering the sweet peas and the lettuces and remembering to lock the back door when she returned to Prospect House.

Cassandra was not to be allowed to remain alone in the vicarage in her parents' absence, though neither her mother nor anyone else could produce any good reasons against it. "I shouldn't be easy in my mind," Mrs. Custance had said, and Miss Templer had agreed with her that it would be better if Cassie stayed at Prospect House; she could easily slip down on her bicycle in the evenings to see that everything was all right at home.

So it had been arranged, rather against Cassandra's will, and now all she had to do, after she had driven her parents to Mallinford and seen them off, was to come back and collect her own suitcase, take it to Prospect House, bring the car back again (and remember to lock the garage), and then return to Prospect House on her bicycle.

Going through these arrangements, in case Cassandra might somehow have forgotten them, Mrs. Custance remarked happily that at least Cassie would get a rest from that daily ride up the hill, and her daughter had not the heart to point out that she would have the ride just the same, only in the evenings, if she had to water the lettuces every night.

"And Nutting is coming two mornings a week. I've told him to keep the lawn mown, so that you can play tennis. If this weather goes on Lukin ought to get a lot of practice."

Again the strangely benign reference to Lukin; it was really wonderful, Cassandra thought, that her mother had taken Lukin so well. It had not been necessary, after all, to explain why he had been asked—and this was a good thing because if she had told her mother about Lily's scheme of rescue Mrs. Custance would probably have told Isabel Templer, who might easily have repeated it to Eustace.

Mr. Custance appeared at the door, holding a book in his hand and asking if Amy could find room for it in her suitcase. Mrs. Custance answered blithely that he would not need books in Cornwall; they would go for long walks and there would be other people to talk to in the evenings. Since he already had several books secreted in his own suitcase and in his coat pockets Mr. Custance took this rebuff bravely, and shortly afterwards, when they were putting the luggage into the car, he told Cassandra that he was looking forward to Cornwall because he had remembered that a friend of his, a man he had not seen since he was at Cambridge, was the rector of a parish close to where they were going—or it might be the actual place, he could not be sure—and he intended to visit him and see what sort of a library he had collected in the forty odd years since their last meeting.

Cassandra was pleased to see both her parents so happy, her father buoyed up by the thought of a library, and a classical scholar to talk to, her mother thinking about food not prepared by herself, new acquaintances with whom she could conduct a discreet search for mutual friends, and perhaps an excursion to Newquay, or a day-trip in a steamer, as highlights of the holiday. She waited on the platform till the train left, and waved vigorously until it got to the curve; but not until it was out of sight, because Mrs. Custance firmly believed that it was unlucky to do so.

Turning away before she should imperil her mother's safety, she walked out into the station yard, which lay blank and empty in the morning sunlight.

Mallinford was at the end of a branch line from the junction at Bramchester, and its station was a charming relic of the past, combining cast-iron *chinoiserie* with Victorian-Gothic doors and windows. Even the presence of two cars hardly diminished the feeling that one had strayed back into the eighteen-forties. There ought to have been a trap waiting for her, with an old family groom standing at the horse's head; or perhaps a low-slung victoria with two cream-coloured ponies, like the one her great-grandmother was driving in the faded water-colour drawing that hung in her mother's bedroom.

Thinking about the cream-coloured ponies and the peculiar difficulties their anatomy had presented to the amateur artist, Cassandra walked slowly to the car. She had left it in the shadiest place she could find, in an angle between the main building and the parcels office, and now she saw that another car had been drawn up behind it, in a position which made it impossible for her to get it out. She looked at the second car and recognized it as George Brigham's.

She had not yet had a chance to ask George about the cheque; or perhaps it would be more exact to say that she had done nothing about it. She had meant to ask him when she next saw him, knowing well that they were unlikely to meet by chance, and yet persuading herself that it would be better to wait for a casual meeting than to seek him out. Now that the opportunity had come she felt embarrassed, and if it had been possible she would have driven away leaving the problem unsolved. She told herself that it was silly to bother about it now; her father had paid the cheque into his account without noticing the signature, and no one but herself had any doubts about Sir James's benevolence. But while she was thinking these things George came out of the parcels office and approached the car.

"Hullo, Cassandra," he said. "Sorry to keep you waiting. I thought I'd be through before you came back."

"Hullo, George. I've been seeing my parents off on their holiday."

"So I guessed. I knew they were starting today."

"Everyone knows everything in Little Mallin."

The conversation flagged. Cassandra sat in the open car, George stood beside it, and the sun beat down on the scene with relentless brilliance. Probably, she thought, the sun was like that in Italy— and perhaps George, who appeared to have gone into a trance, was thinking about Italy. It seemed a pity to wrench his thoughts away from that romantic subject by asking him about the cheque.

"I'd better be getting back," she said.

"Hope they enjoy themselves. They ought to, if the weather keeps like this."

"Oh, I'm sure they'll enjoy themselves immensely. They were both looking forward to it."

"Good," said George. Then he looked down at her and spoke in a different voice, the friendly, teasing voice of the past. "I hope you're not just being polite."

"What do you mean?" She knew perfectly well what he meant, but she chose to appear unresponsive. The past was like a distant country; she often thought about it, but she did not want to return there.

"Well . . . your father is the last man, from what I know of him, to enjoy being taken away from his books and dumped down in a seaside resort with a pier and a band."

Cassandra replied with dignity that he was quite wrong. Her father had told her only that morning how pleased he was to be going to Cornwall.

For a fleeting moment it seemed as if George was going to question this and set himself up as a rival authority on Mr. Custance's likes and dislikes. His look reminded her, against her will, of the friendly but obstinate George with whom she had had so many cheerful arguments in the past. But her own determination to remain in the present had its effect; the lurking twinkle vanished and he answered rather lamely that he was glad, to hear it.

Cassandra knew that she had cheated, and this made her feel annoyed, both with herself and—most unfairly—with George. It was with the deliberate intention of setting a trap that she said:

"We're all very grateful to Sir James. Father and Mother could never have afforded a holiday if he hadn't helped them."

George replied gruffly that he was sure it made his father happy to be able to help.

"He's very generous, isn't he?"

"Yes, I suppose he is pretty generous."

"*Very* generous. Do you know how much he gave them?"

"Not exactly."

"But it was your signature on the cheque."

"Damn!" said George, looking both injured and angry.

Cassandra had the satisfaction of feeling that at least there were faults on both sides in the matter of truthfulness. "It was your cheque, wasn't it?" she said.

"The stupid old man. I didn't mean him to show it to all of you. I suppose he got you all together and made a public presentation!"

"Not exactly. Well—I looked at it afterwards."

"Our initials are the same, so I thought they wouldn't notice."

"They didn't—and I didn't tell them. Sir James pretended it came from him. It was really very kind of you, George." To spare our feelings, she meant, though naturally she could not say this aloud.

Nor could George explain the circumstances in which the cheque came to be written. He saw that Cassandra believed he had tried to do this kind action surreptitiously, because Mrs. Custance would not have cared about taking money from a person she disliked (and he knew quite well that she disliked him), and he saw too that Cassandra herself, though bound to express her gratitude, hated having to do so.

He felt the embarrassment of being thanked when he did not deserve it, but it would be even more embarrassing for Cassandra if he told her the true facts. So he could only say, quite honestly, that it was his father's idea, and less honestly, that it didn't matter who provided the money, the thing was that Mr. Custance had really earned a break.

"But I don't agree," Cassandra said. "He did need a holiday, but there's absolutely no reason why you should have to provide it. I mean, it's frightfully kind of you but—Well, look, will you let me pay you back? I could manage it perfectly easily if I did it a bit at a time."

It would have to be a bit at a time because most of her own salary went to augment her father's inadequate stipend, and to withhold it would involve awkward explanations.

"Don't be silly," George said forcibly. "I wouldn't dream of it. I wanted him to have a holiday and he's having one," he continued, flinging honesty to the winds. "So don't spoil it now by making a fuss about nothing."

Cassandra's cheeks grew pink. It was not a fuss about nothing, and unless George was completely obtuse he should know that his philanthropy was most unwelcome. But of course he was obtuse. Moreover, he was proud and conceited and fickle—as well as being a great disappointment to his father. She wished desperately that she had never mentioned the cheque.

"Oh, very well," she said. "I didn't mean to sound ungrateful, and it's really most awfully kind of you—"

"Please don't say that again."

Aware that she had at least succeeded in making him angry, and feeling, for some reason, faintly cheered by this achievement, she desisted; and said instead that she hoped he would have equally fine weather for his own holiday, when the time came.

"Are you going sailing again this year?" she asked.

Among George's friends—the new friends he had made since the war—was a fortunate rich family called Malloch, who lived in a seaside fishing village about twenty miles down the coast. Or rather, they lived there for the summer months, and spent the rest of the year in a comfortable flat in London, thus making the best of both worlds but remaining objects of suspicion to impoverished country-dwellers.

But they did not mind, for the seaside village was full of people like themselves who came and went with the season. It was a gay place in the summer, full of striped umbrellas and sleek, polished cars; in winter it was almost deserted. The few permanent residents viewed the annual invasion with disfavour, but they were left with a rich harvest of anecdotes and rumours to brighten their dull lives until the following year.

All the summer migrants were manifestly rich, since they possessed other homes and quantities of exotic beach clothes, but none was richer than the Mallochs. They had two cars and a sea-going yacht; and it was in this yacht, last year, that George had spent his summer holiday.

"I don't think so," he said. "I haven't made any plans yet. I'll probably spend it catching up with the garden. And that reminds me that I ought to be catching up with my work."

It was clear to Cassandra that he had no wish to pursue the subject of yachting, though she did not for one moment believe that he meant to spend his holiday at home. Perhaps he had plans that could not be discussed; perhaps, she thought scornfully, he was hoping to get engaged to yet another enchantress.

George's sailing holiday last year had resulted in his becoming engaged to one of the Malloch daughters. The engagement had not been announced publicly, but the news had reached Little Mallin from a reliable source; the date of the wedding, and even the names of the bridesmaids, had been common knowledge. The wedding was to have been in London, in the early spring, and they were going to the south of France for the honeymoon. One version of the story said they were going to Italy, but this was felt to be unlikely and unsuitable.

Then came a report that the wedding had been postponed; it was thought that Miss Malloch was ill, or alternatively that Malloch *père* had quarrelled with Sir James Brigham over the marriage settlements. Finally, when these and other speculations had failed to account for the delay, a strong rumour sprang up that the engagement had been broken off because George Brigham had transferred his affections elsewhere.

Thinking of all this Cassandra replied coolly that she too had better be going, if he would kindly move his car. George hesitated for a moment, as if he had not expected this sudden dismissal. He said:

"I see you've started tennis again."

"Yes, we've played quite a lot." She leant forward and fiddled with the ignition key.

"There's just one place on the road, at the top of the hill, where you can see the tennis lawn," he explained. "It's rather odd, because you'd think the lawn would be quite hidden, with all those trees round it."

"You would, wouldn't you?"

"I haven't played this year. Never seem to have time for it."

Cassandra said, "I expect you have lots of other things to do."

She did not intend it as a parting shot, but it had the effect of one. George dropped the subject of tennis as abruptly as he had dropped the subject of sailing, and bade her the coldest of good mornings.

He got into his own car and reversed it fiercely into the middle of the station yard, where he waited while Cassandra in her turn backed out of the shady corner. Then occurred a ridiculous contest in politeness, in which each gestured to the other to proceed, and neither would take advantage of the other's courtesy. It ended in their both starting at the same instant and converging on the station entrance like rivals for the winning-post, but they were saved further embarrassment by the arrival of a large van, whose driver, finding his approach blocked, hooted at them impatiently. The contest in politeness was abandoned, and George drove out of the yard at a speed that Cassandra considered highly dangerous.

As she followed him at an increasing distance, up the narrow street, she told herself that it had been a thoroughly unsatisfactory morning.

"Just in time!" called Dossie, shooting out of her garden gate with a total disregard for other traffic. She advanced towards Cassandra at a gallop and leant heavily on the door of the car, which gave a sad protesting squeak.

"I kept my little eye open, but I thought I'd missed you. You've been ages. Did you go shopping after you'd seen them off?"

"No, I mean yes. But I couldn't get what I wanted," Cassandra replied, conscious that Dossie's little eye was raking the car for parcels.

"Mallinford's hopeless. Did they get off all right?"

"Oh yes. Both quite happy. Father had a long talk with the engine-driver."

"Splendid. And now you'll be able to have a gay old time on your own." Identifying herself, as usual, with riotous youth, Dossie seemed to assume that the vicarage could now be given over to Bacchanalian orgies. When she heard that Cassandra was to stay with the Templers she wrinkled her nose in sympathy and said it was a shame.

Cassandra laughed. "Mother thought burglars might come in the night and knock me on the head."

"Well, you're only young once," Dossie remarked ambiguously. "I mean, even burglars would be something."

"Being knocked on the head would be something, but I don't suppose I should enjoy it."

"Nothing like that ever happens in Little Mallin—worse luck!" said Dossie, whose yearning for male society included even burglars. "One gets so absolutely browned off. I sometimes think it's just like being in a nunnery."

Cassandra could not believe that life at The Moorings bore any resemblance to life in a nunnery, but she did not say so. It was a waste of time to argue with Dossie Fenn, and she had already wasted quite enough of the morning. She still had to collect her suitcase, and even at Prospect House a guest should endeavour to be reasonably punctual for lunch.

But Dossie was propped against the car, and it was hardly possible to drive away without hurting her.

"The thing is this," she said. "Daisy and I thought we might go for a picnic on Saturday, and we wondered if you could come with us and perhaps take the car. We'd thought of Witling or Long Hampton, but anywhere would do. How about it?"

Cassandra had no particular wish to go for a picnic with Dossie and Daisy, but she did not know how to get out of it, especially as they had no car of their own and were probably asking her because they could then enjoy the use of hers. "I think I could manage that," she said. "I'm sure Miss Templer won't mind. The car is pretty decrepit, but you wouldn't want to go far. It ought to be able to get to Witling."

Dossie said Witling or anywhere, the thing was they both felt absolutely morbid being stuck in the village the whole time, and even to get a couple of miles away would be marvellous. Cassandra thought privately that the Misses Fenn might have managed this distance on their own feet, but she agreed to pick them up at three o'clock on Saturday, unless it rained, and to take them to any spot they fancied within a twenty-mile radius of Little Mallin.

"And we'll bring the eats," Dossie said. "And you won't mind, will you, if we ask someone else? There's room for four."

"No, but don't ask more than one, because the springs and the tyres are both in a bad way."

"Righty-oh. And look here, Cassandra, the thing is this—" She paused.

"Yes. What?" Cassandra spoke with a trace of her mother's brisk impatience. One had to be firm with Dossie or she would stay there for ever.

"If by any chance one of us should have a date—*you* know—for Saturday, you wouldn't mind if just the other came? You wouldn't feel we were letting you down?"

"Of course not." She knew too that if by some minor miracle both Dossie and Daisy should acquire 'dates' for Saturday, they would without hesitation abandon the picnic and herself. "Only let me know," she said, "if you want to put it off."

Dossie said there was no question of that, they were both looking forward to it enormously and there was nothing she personally liked better than being all girls together.

CHAPTER XIII

ON FRIDAY EVENING Miss Templer spent an enjoyable hour hunting for a Hungarian blouse which she had bought in 1927 at a market-stall in Budapest, and which had been recalled to her mind that morning by an illustration of a totally dissimilar market-stall in a travel book about Spain. She thought the blouse might be put away in the tallboy on the landing, or perhaps in one of the trunks in the attic, and she summoned Lily and Cassandra to assist her in the search. Looking for long-lost treasures was always a beguiling pastime. One never knew what might turn up.

They did not find the Hungarian blouse, but they found, among other things, a large shady hat that tied under the chin with pink ribbons. Lily tried it on and thought it rather becoming, in its antiquated way.

"It looks like fancy dress," she said.

"So will your new one, in forty years or so," Cassandra prophesied. But Lily did not believe her.

"I wore that hat at a picnic once," Miss Templer said thoughtfully.

It was characteristic of her mental processes that the sight of the hat should make her think of sitting on a fallen oak in a wood full of bluebells, and that the bluebells should remind her of Dossie and Daisy Fenn who had sent her a Christmas card of a blue bell wreathed in holly and surmounted by a robin. Not the same kind of bell, of course, but that did not matter; Dossie and Daisy, bluebells, and the pleasures of picnicking, were now linked together, and she said gaily:

"Why shouldn't we *all* go?"

"Go where?" Lily asked.

"It is tomorrow, isn't it, Cassandra? And it's really more fun with more people. If I can persuade Henry to take us."

"Oh, I see. Yes, it would be more fun. Family outings are always more fun."

"Go where?" repeated Lily, who hadn't seen, and could not be expected to guess because she knew it was hopeless to try to follow Aunt Bella's thoughts. Lukin's thoughts were on a different level, and she made great efforts to keep up with him; but naturally one did not make these efforts for aunts.

When Miss Templer and Cassandra had explained things she agreed that it would be fun to go for a picnic.

"Only I'd better warn you," Cassandra said. "They may be bringing someone else—but I don't know who it will be."

"Mister X. Certainly *mister*. Well, that will make it more exciting."

After some discussion it was settled that Miss Templer should call on Dossie and Daisy the next morning on her way to Mallinford and break it to them that the picnic was to be a family outing. She would provide tea for her own party, and they would all meet at Witling wood. After tea they might drive on to Shingle Street and see if the motor-boat was running.

"That will please Henry," Miss Templer said. "He was asking about the motor-boat. And I shan't tell him Dossie and Daisy are coming, if you don't mind, because of the day he took Daisy to Witling rectory."

Cassandra and Lily wanted to know what had happened on that day, but Miss Templer answered evasively that it wasn't what had happened, it was only that Henry was not accustomed to it.

Like Cassandra, Colonel Ashford could find no good reason for refusing to go for a picnic, and he became mildly enthusiastic at the idea of going out in the motor-boat. But he asked rather apprehensively how many were coming. He knew that Bella was quite capable of inviting ten or a dozen people and expecting them to sit piled up in his car, endangering each other and the springs.

Miss Templer assured him that it would only be themselves.

"Cassandra isn't coming with us," she said. "And I don't suppose Eustace will come either, because of the scorpions. He says they're more abundant in woods."

Colonel Ashford gave an uneasy cough. He didn't like the way she spoke, as if the scorpions were real.

"Pity to encourage these morbid thoughts," he said stiffly. "Far better persuade him to come. Then he'd see there weren't any."

"But we shouldn't enjoy the picnic. Suppose you were picnicking where there might be a tiger, Henry. Even if the tiger didn't appear you'd be wondering about it and telling us not to loiter. It's just the same with Eustace."

He could not see that it was at all the same, but neither could he imagine himself picnicking where there was a tiger. The trouble with Bella was that she was completely out of touch with reality.

On Saturday morning Miss Templer told Felix and Leonard about the picnic, and Felix immediately reminded her that he was going to Bramchester that day to meet his friend Powys.

It was true that he had spoken of it before, but she could not remember that he had said Saturday. She sometimes thought that Felix's friend Powys, whom none of them had ever met, was a phantasm of his imagination, like Eustace and the scorpions. But not quite like that, for Powys was a useful phantasm; he lived in Bramchester and enjoyed watching cricket matches and going to concerts, and he only came to life when Felix wanted to escape from his family.

"Couldn't you telephone, and go next Saturday?" she suggested. But Felix said Powys was not on the telephone and he couldn't let him down. Miss Templer then gave him his railway fare and told him not to miss the seven-thirty that evening, and he went off to catch the bus to Mallinford.

That left only Leonard and Lily and herself; and Henry's car could easily hold six. It was a beautiful day and there must surely be other people who would enjoy a picnic in Witling wood and a trip in a motor-boat.

She had meant to go to Mallinford on the early bus, but when Felix started she was not ready. She had never yet succeeded in going to Mallinford on the early bus, though she always tried to; either she mislaid her purse or her spectacles, or else she simply forgot to watch the clock. Today, of course, she would have to call on Dossie and Daisy first, so it was just as well that she had not hurried off immediately after breakfast—for they would probably have been in bed, or at the stage of facial undress when they did not care to appear at the door.

When she finally set off down the hill she was still wondering whom she could ask to the picnic; and it only needed the sight of Prospect Cottage to answer the question. Though she had never made friends with Mrs. Midge she felt vaguely sorry for her, whenever she remembered her existence. A picnic in a bluebell wood, on a fine summer's day, would surely come as a welcome escape from the fixed routine of business, housework and gardening that seemed to encase Mrs. Midge as tightly as her stiff tweeds and whatever she wore underneath them.

The invitation took Mrs. Midge by surprise. She told herself that it was just like them, plotting and planning to turn her out of her home and then coming in as friendly as you please and asking her to go off for a picnic. And probably when she got there Miss Templer would have forgotten the tea, or there would be something funny about the sandwiches.

Hiding all this behind a frosty smile she replied that she would have loved it, but unfortunately she had a friend coming to tea that afternoon. It was quite true. Mrs. Howell was coming, and the whole cottage was being intensively cleaned and polished by Mrs. Midge and Mrs. Nutting, while Lukin was busy rolling and mowing the lawn.

"Then what about Lukin?" said Miss Templer, turning towards him as she spoke. He had stopped to empty the grass cuttings into the barrow and was standing within earshot, but he did not reply directly. He looked at his mother.

"Lukin must please himself."

He always does, said Mrs. Midge's face; even Isabel Templer could not help noticing that it was not the face of a loving mother, and that the frosty smile had become several degrees colder. Feeling sorry, now, for Lukin, she did not press the invitation—for she did not want to get him into trouble—but just as she was saying good-bye he announced that he would very much like to come to the picnic.

He spoke defiantly, almost heroically, as if he were volunteering for some perilous mission; but since Isabel did not know that her picnic had a symbolic importance she was only reminded of a Pekinese puppy called 'Foofoo', which she used to meet on Hampstead Heath.

Later in the morning—a good deal later, after she had called on the Misses Fenn, taken the bus to Mallinford, and done most of her shopping—she met George Brigham. Whatever Amy Custance might say, she had always liked George, principally because he was tall and good-looking and resembled a young man she might have married if he had not quarrelled with Eustace, long ago in the past. But she liked George, too, for his own sake, and she was pleased when he offered her a lift to Little Mallin and insisted on driving her all the way up the hill to Prospect House.

Cassandra and Lily, who were sunning themselves on the lawn, heard the car come up the drive, and at lunch Cassandra asked Miss Templer who had brought her home.

"George Brigham. He told me Sir James had had a very nice letter from your mother. Quite delighted with the place, and such wonderful weather."

"Yes, I had a postcard this morning." Cassandra thought of her mother sitting down to write a polite thank-you letter to Sir James; of Sir James taking all the credit for their holiday; of George in the background, unthanked and perhaps regretting his kind impulse. Quite suddenly she felt she had behaved very badly, the day they met at the station, and she wished she could have an opportunity of seeing him again and saying she was sorry for it.

She did not know that her wish was about to be gratified, because Miss Templer quite forgot to mention that she had asked George to the picnic.

Shortly after three o'clock Cassandra drove up to The Moorings. She was a little late but it did not matter, as Dossie and Daisy were always late for everything. Three chintz cushions and a rug were heaped outside the front door, showing that preparations were toward, and from inside the house came shrill cries, bursts of girlish laughter, and an exuberant masculine voice that she could not identify.

"Mister X," she said to herself. She got out of the car and walked up to the door. Her first knock went unanswered, but at the second Dossie opened her bedroom window and leaned out, clutching a dressing-gown round her with one hand and waving a powder-puff in the other.

"We're just a weeny bit late," she cried. "Come in and talk to Rupert—that'll give poor us a chance to get ready! Of course we meant to be ready *ages* ago, only he came early, and now he will keep on interrupting. He's such a scream!"

Cassandra supposed that Rupert must be Mr. X. She opened the door and walked in, to find herself face to face with a toothy stranger who exclaimed, "Aha, the fair unknown!"

"Good afternoon," she said.

"Good day to you. A blessing on this meeting." Rupert made her a low bow, and then turned to call up the stairs, "A-pace, a-pace, the hour has struck!"

Peals of laughter greeted this remark, and Daisy replied, more prosaically, that they wouldn't be two ticks.

"My tongue runs on," Rupert prattled happily. "You mustn't mind me, my friends say it's incurable." His beaming smile belied the apology; it was all too clear that he was one of those men who delight in being the life and soul of the party. Cassandra felt that her own conversational efforts would fall far short of Rupert's standards, and she wondered how she was to entertain him. But she need not have worried, for he was perfectly capable of supplying all the *joie de vivre* that was needed.

"Why do we linger in this dungeon?" he cried. "Come into the garden, Maud. Come and improve the smiling hour!"

"Shining," she said automatically. But Rupert did not hear, or if he did he paid no attention. He pranced off down the narrow hall, and opened a door which he seemed to assume would lead into the garden. He was confronted by a very small room filled with an extraordinary collection of discarded clothing, broken furniture, and cardboard boxes; and as he flung back the door several of these objects were displaced by his impetuous action and fell clattering about his feet.

"Aha, the skeleton in the cupboard!"

Stooping, he endeavoured to shove the skeletons aside and close the door, and at this moment the Misses Fenn came bounding down the stairs and wanted to know whatever he was doing.

"Up to no good, of course!" cried Daisy, while Dossie exclaimed that it wasn't safe to leave him alone for five minutes. They evidently considered Rupert a very dashing character, and he returned the compliment by treating them both as dangerous enchantresses.

Cassandra felt herself *de trop*, and she was very glad it was to be a family outing so that she would not have to spend the whole afternoon laughing at Rupert's sallies and agreeing with Dossie and Daisy that he was a scream.

When they got outside there was a slight delay while the enchantresses bickered amiably over the seating arrangements in the car; during this pause she was able to look at Rupert, who, in full sunlight, appeared rather less dashing and debonair than he had seemed in the house. He was wearing white flannels and a remarkably vivid sports jacket, his fair hair gleamed with oil and his smile was unflagging; but his figure was, to put it kindly, mature, and the lustrous hair grew rather sparsely on the top of his head. She wondered who he was and where Dossie or Daisy had met him, and why he was being brought on a family picnic instead of keeping a 'date' with one or the other of them.

On the way to Witling wood she decided that it must be because they were determined to share him. Daisy had won the coveted place in the back of the car, but Dossie spent most of the time screwed round at an uncomfortable angle so that she should miss nothing of his sparkling wit. Occasionally she unscrewed herself and talked to Cassandra, but it was generally to repeat what Rupert had just said, or to exclaim, in a voice only slightly subdued, that she couldn't understand why his wife had left him.

Cassandra hoped that Rupert could not overhear Dossie, but her own sympathies were all with his wife.

It was not until they reached the lodge gates of Mallin Hall that Miss Templer remembered about George, and then only because he was standing at the end of the drive. "Stop, stop!" she cried, and Colonel Ashford pulled up hastily, thinking that Leonard was being sick; a disaster which had happened on another occasion when he had taken them all for a nice outing.

"I'm afraid we're late," Miss Templer called to George, who was walking towards them.

It took Colonel Ashford a minute or so to realize that this was an addition to the picnic party. He wondered bitterly how many more houses there were between here and their destination, and how many more people would be standing waiting for them.

Already they had had to stop at Prospect Cottage, where an oddly silent young man had popped out from behind the hedge, looking, in Colonel Ashford's opinion, like an overdressed for-eigner. Lukin's blue and white check shirt, the scarlet pullover he carried and the floppy linen hat that shielded him from the sun, had produced an unfavourable impression; but at least he sat speechless and did not distract the driver's attention.

But now the seating arrangements were all to be altered. Miss Templer, from the back of the car, told George to get in beside Lukin, and then changed her mind and said it would be better if he sat behind, and Leonard in front. At the same instant Lily declared that she would sit in front; and Leonard protested fiercely that it was his turn. No one consulted the owner of the car, and while they were arguing about it the minutes were tick-ing by. It seemed unlikely to Colonel Ashford that they would ever get to Witling wood, let alone to Shingle Street and the mo-tor-boat. He kept glancing at his watch, until Miss Templer no-ticed it and settled the argument by taking the front seat herself, sitting bodkin between her brother-in-law and Lukin.

"There's plenty of room," she remarked happily, squeezing Henry a little farther into his corner. "Now you three get in be-hind—give me that basket, George, it's got the milk in it. I won-der if Cassandra has started yet."

"She went past just as I got to the gate."

"Oh, dear—and I said we'd be there first. I thought we had plenty of time, Dossie and Daisy generally take so long to get going."

A small poignant sound came from Colonel Ashford's lips, neither a groan nor a curse but something between the two. "How many people," he asked coldly, "are coming to this picnic?"

"Only ourselves, Henry, and Dossie and Daisy Fenn and Cas-sandra. Oh, and Mister X, of course. He's sure to be there."

"Who is Mister X?"

"I don't know, but that makes it more exciting. There might even be two Mister X's, but I don't suppose that's likely. Did you notice, George?"

"There was one Mister X, on the back seat."

Colonel Ashford let in the clutch with a jerk and the car bounded forward. He didn't know what they were talking about, and he didn't want to. Nothing that Bella said ever made sense, and it was entirely typical that she should have asked one or more total strangers to the picnic, as well as that young woman with the teeth. That dreadful young woman. Deplorable as Lily was, in many ways, it was not right that a girl of seventeen should be exposed to bad influences, and Bella ought to have thought of it.

Outwardly stern and composed, inwardly glowing with virtuous indignation, Colonel Ashford drove on in silence, and Isabel Templer talked to Lukin about picnics, different sorts of cake, and the effect things had on his digestion. One subject led quite naturally to the next and soon Lukin was doing most of the talking, while his hostess listened with the specially attentive look that signified, for those who knew her, a completely inattentive mind.

Lily noticed this. She was glad her aunt wasn't paying much attention to Lukin, whose account of his digestive processes might have repelled a more heedful listener. She still maintained that he was a very interesting personality, but she understood what Cassandra meant when she said it was Lukin, and not his thermometer, that needed shaking.

"Are we at Witling wood yet?" Leonard asked for the sixth or seventh time. George replied that they had still to pass through Witling village, and Leonard asked rather anxiously how long it would take.

"If you're feeling sick," Lily said kindly, "we can stop while you are."

"I'm not feeling sick, only a little queasy."

"I knew a man once who used to feel queasy in tanks," George said.

Lily did not think this a very tactful remark but it had a great success with Leonard, whose questions about tanks continued unabated for the rest of the journey. Not until they had turned into the lane that led to Witling wood did he remember his own queasiness, and then he merely said that the back of a car must be worse than any tank, and it was a jolly good thing they were nearly there.

CHAPTER XIV

ONE PICNIC is very like another, and it is usually the weather that makes or mars the day. When they set out the weather had been perfect, with a gentle breeze to temper the brilliant sunshine, but in Witling wood it was airless and oppressively hot. Everybody remarked on the heat, and from marvelling at it they soon passed on to saying it was unnatural. Only Miss Templer and Leonard, like salamanders, continued to feel that this was the best kind of weather for picnics. Miss Templer sat happily sunning herself, and wishing she was young enough to wear a frock without sleeves or shoulders, while Leonard made his companions feel even hotter by running about and shouting.

"Isn't it *hot!*" Dossie or Daisy would exclaim at short intervals. But it was not the heat alone that oppressed and fatigued the picnickers. It had been, from the beginning, an ill-assorted party.

Tea was no more uncomfortable than picnic teas always are. They sat on cushions and rugs and spiky bits of bracken, flies fell into the cups, and Leonard upset the milk. Colonel Ashford helped himself to sugar, and then found it was salt; Mr. X knelt on one knee, offering buns with a knightly gesture, and overbalanced on to a plate of tomato sandwiches. The onlookers laughed at these incidents, and at times the talk grew animated, but in spite of talk and laughter everyone seemed glad when tea was over.

In her vague way Miss Templer got on well with most people, and it never occurred to her that her various acquaintances would not mix. Never, that is, until she had assembled them in a spot from which they could not escape; and even then, being an unobservant person, she took a little time to discover that they were not enjoying themselves.

She had known, of course, that Henry disapproved of Daisy Fenn. One could not expect to please Henry anyway, so she had simply hoped for the best. But as the afternoon wore on it gradually became clear, even to Miss Templer, that things were not going well. It was not only the heat, the flies, the minor disasters of spilt milk and squashed sandwiches; it was not only Henry, glowering and looking at his watch. It was something indefinable, but unmistakeable, in the way people looked and spoke. Even the glittering smiles of Dossie and Daisy had lost some of their sparkle.

After tea the party had split up, and instead of splitting up into congenial groups it seemed driven to divide itself awkwardly. Dossie and Daisy had temporarily abandoned Mr. X and were talking to Colonel Ashford, who obviously did not want to talk to anyone. Cassandra was being monopolised by Lukin. Lily had wandered off to pick bluebells, and Mr. X and Leonard were conducting a laborious conversation about railway trains. Miss Templer alone had a companion who suited her; for George was helping her to pack up the remains of the tea. But although she approved of his good manners she wished he would not bother. It would have been much better, she thought, if he had talked to Lily or Cassandra.

Poor Lily, picking bluebells by herself and hoping vainly for masculine assistance! Poor Cassandra, listening so politely to that dull, egotistical young man! It was for them that Miss Templer felt sorry; the others were less deserving of sympathy. Still, it was a great pity that the party was not being a success.

"I think it must be the heat," she said.

One of her reasons for liking George was that he did not look blank or ask her to explain herself. Though she knew her own mind to be volatile and illogical, she often thought that other people were curiously slow-witted. But George nearly always understood her.

"It's partly Mr. X," he said now.

"Wretched Mr. X. How exhausting—having to be so high-spirited all the time."

"It seems to come natural to him."

"But it's more than that," said Miss Templer, meaning that the disintegration of the picnic party was not entirely the fault of Mr. X. "Perhaps large ones aren't always the best."

George proved his worth as a listener by following this lead without apparent difficulty. "Small ones are even riskier," he said. "A picnic party of three people is almost bound to end in a cry."

"Perhaps you're right. But even if this one doesn't end in a cry, no one could say it was being a huge success."

"Well, I'm enjoying myself. So are Fizz and Pop, and Cassandra and Lukin Midge. I wouldn't say as much for your brother-in-law."

"Henry never looks as if he were, so one can't tell, except of course that I know he isn't. And Cassandra isn't, either."

"She looks quite happy."

George spoke with perfect good humour, and there was no reason to suppose that he meant more than he said. Nevertheless, Isabel Templer was immediately reminded of another picnic, and of a girl wearing a hat with pink ribbons who had made a young man extremely jealous by talking all afternoon to his rival.

The present situation was different . . . or was it?

She looked at George, who was fastening the straps of the basket with meticulous care, and the first thought that came into her head, characteristically jostling aside more rational ones, was— 'This isn't going to suit Amy'.

The thought remained unspoken, and the long brooding silence that followed his last remark made George wonder if his hostess had gone to sleep. She was sitting propped against a tree-trunk, and her face was turned away from him. She seemed still to be gazing across the little clearing at Lukin and Cassandra; but it could not have taken her all this time to decide whether Cassandra was looking happy.

"Are you awake?" he asked softly.

"Of course I'm awake. I was just thinking of something. When I'm asleep I snore."

"Then I shall know in the future."

"I was thinking about Amy Custance."

Happily unaware that the thought of Mrs. Custance had anything to do with himself, he remarked that the Custances were being lucky in the weather.

"The weather is like everything else, for Amy. Either very good or very bad."

George laughed. "The weather in Little Mallin must surely be the same for everyone."

"I don't mean that. I mean, that's how she sees it. She can't be neutral."

"A clergyman's wife is bound to take a strong line, isn't she?"

"But not such a wobbly one, George. Amy's line may be strong, but it isn't straight. Look at Dossie and Daisy."

This time George unaccountably failed her, and instead of continuing the discussion he looked across the clearing at the Misses Fenn. Miss Templer sighed over the misunderstanding; but perhaps it was just as well. In another minute she might have been saying—'Look at her attitude to you'.

The check brought her mind back to the picnic party, which was now being organized, by Mr. X, into two teams for a guessing-game. No one wanted to play, but Rupert's cheery determination made short work of excuses. He had invited Colonel Ashford and Leonard to choose sides, and even the fact that he and Lukin were the last to be chosen had not dimmed his dazzling smile.

As Rupert came bounding towards them, crying out to them to join in the revels and explaining that Miss Templer belonged to Leonard's team, and George to Colonel Ashford's, she wondered if George had really misunderstood her. Perhaps it was simply that he did not want to discuss Amy's prejudices. Oddly enough, this idea seemed to confirm her intuition; and although, as a strong believer in intuitions, she did not feel that they needed confirming, it was nice when other things fitted in.

As well as believing in intuitions, Miss Templer believed in romance. She was all for it, and the faintest breath of romance in the air made her feel that life was well worth living. In her eyes the unsuccessful picnic had suddenly become delightful, and it took her some minutes to realize that most of the party were, at best, indifferent to the pleasures of a guessing-game.

No one but Rupert wanted to impersonate historical characters, and none of his companions had listened to his explanations or knew what the game was about. Dossie and Daisy were indulging in jealous asides, because one was in the team that contained Rupert, and the other was not. It was hotter than ever in the wood, a clinging, clammy heat that suggested thunderstorms, and even Leonard had flopped down on the grass as if he had had enough of picnics. But it was the way Henry looked at his watch that brought Isabel Templer back to the present.

"The motor-boat!" she exclaimed happily.

The motor-boat came as an unpleasant surprise to Rupert, whose talents flourished best on dry land, but to everyone else it appeared as a long-wished-for deliverance from bluebells, guessing-games and heat. At Shingle Street there would be a breeze, they said hopefully; and even the thought of it put them all in a better temper. The rugs and baskets were collected, the last limp lettuce leaves were stuffed out of sight down a rabbit hole, where Leonard hoped they would gladden the heart of some poor rabbit that had never eaten lettuce before, and soon the whole party was walking back to the lane where they had left the cars.

Miss Templer was pleased to notice that George walked beside Cassandra.

The lane was a narrow one, and since it took Colonel Ashford a little time to reverse—for, as Miss Templer had explained to Mrs. Custance, he was not very good at it—she was able to regroup the party as she wished. She suggested that Lily and Lukin and George should go with Cassandra, whose car was already facing the right way, while she and the others waited for Henry.

"Then Dossie and Daisy can sit with Mr. X in the back," she said cunningly to Cassandra. "There isn't room for three in the back of your car."

"Very well," Cassandra said. "But hadn't I better take Leonard? We shall get there first and he does so like to be first."

For once Miss Templer ignored Leonard's wishes. She explained that he would take up less room, sitting three abreast, and that Henry needed plenty of room and always thought he was being squashed—though that was just nonsense, but still it was his car and one didn't want to upset him.

Aware that she had little talent for plotting and was far too apt to say the first thing that came into her head, Isabel thought she had been very clever. It only remained to see that George sat in front with Cassandra, and Lukin with Lily; she did not know how she was going to manage it, but fortunately Lily managed it for her, by getting in and calling to Lukin to join her. This left George no choice but the front seat.

No sooner were they all seated than Miss Templer was waving them off, fearful lest something might interfere with her scheming. It was not until the car was out of sight that she remembered she had meant to ask Cassandra exactly how one got from Witling wood to Shingle Street. But probably she would recognize the turnings when she came to them.

It was not necessary to go back to Little Mallin; there was a more direct way, through a network of small lanes, and she had told Henry quite confidently that she had often been that way before. This was true; but on previous expeditions there had always been someone else who knew the way, and she had never had to decide whether one went left or right.

At first all was well. The village, the common, the pink-walled farm with the duck-pond, the steep lane that led to Gallows Hill— she remembered them perfectly. But then came a crossroads where her memory faltered. The signpost did not mention Shingle Street and each road looked familiar and yet different.

"I think it's down *that* way," she said. "Yes, yes, it is! I remember the little gorse bush on the right."

But at the next cross-roads there was another little gorse bush. Henry Ashford began to doubt their value as landmarks, for this time Bella insisted that it should be on the left and forced him to take a road that seemed to lead back towards Witling.

Soon after this the lane plunged down a steep hill and they came to a ford. He stopped the car.

"Where is Shingle Street?" he asked. His passengers, pointing vaguely, said that it was over there.

"Then this stream must be flowing away from the sea," he said gloomily.

It was a pity that his passengers were all too stupid to appreciate the force of the argument, and that no one could agree whether they were on the right road or not.

Bella said there hadn't been a ford there before, but perhaps it had been dried up. The Misses Fenn added helpfully that the wells in Long Hampton often ran dry in a hot summer. Rupert proclaimed himself a stranger to the district, and Leonard declared that they must cross the river twice.

Leonard's only reason for saying this was that he wanted to drive through the ford, but he said it so loudly and so often that it began to sound convincing. Colonel Ashford wanted to be convinced, he did not want to reverse his car up the steep hill, and perhaps the whole way back to the cross-roads, and he knew he could not turn it in this narrow lane. He walked down to the stream and inspected the ford; it looked quite shallow, especially if he kept well to the right.

"We'd better go on," he said. "This lane is bound to lead somewhere."

Anyone with more knowledge of English lanes would have known better than that, thought Miss Templer; but she did not disillusion Henry, who was really behaving quite well considering how precious his car was to him.

"Can I stand on the running-board, Uncle Henry? Can I see if the water comes up to my feet?"

"No," said Colonel Ashford.

"Well, can I paddle across and watch if it comes over the tyres?"

"No. Get in the car."

They all got in the car. He started slowly, keeping well to the right. "There's a great big stone," Leonard shouted, bouncing up and down on the seat. "Look, look, we shall be wrecked!"

Distracted by his nephew's cries, and anxious to avoid the big stone, Colonel Ashford turned the car still farther to the right. The ford was roughly paved, but suddenly the offside wheels slipped off this paving and embedded themselves in soft mud. The car gave a gentle lurch, and sank to rest.

"We're wrecked! We're wrecked!"

Colonel Ashford was too well-disciplined to indulge in wanton ferocity, but at that instant he would have thrown Leonard to the sharks, if sharks had existed. He made two or three efforts to drive on and only succeeded in churning up a lot of mud, while shrill cries from the back seat assured him that the wheels were sinking in. The car was now tilted sideways and Bella and Leonard were leaning heavily against him. He switched off the engine and sat for a moment in silence, not because he had nothing to say, but because they were things that could not possibly be said aloud.

Shingle Street consisted of three or four old cottages, a decayed jetty, and a wooden café and boathouse. It could be reached from Little Mallin by a road along the river bank, or by the winding lanes from Witling and Long Hampton. In the holiday season the motor-boat, which belonged to the proprietor of the café, brought people across the river from Mallinford, and the little terrace blossomed with striped umbrellas, but today the place was empty; the motor-boat lay at its moorings and the café was being painted by its owner and his children.

It was a peaceful scene, and there was a faint breeze coming off the river, just as they had hoped. They waited, at first, near the car; Cassandra had driven quite slowly and they all expected that Colonel Ashford would be close behind them. But presently Lily and Lukin strolled away towards the jetty. Lukin did not feel at ease with George Brigham, whom he suspected of not liking him.

George walked over to the café, to ask if they could hire the boat. He explained that they were waiting for another car, and that there were ten of them altogether. The owner said the boat only held eight, along with himself, and that they couldn't have it without him. He then went off in a dinghy to bring the boat in from its moorings.

"It won't matter," said Cassandra, when George had reported this conversation. "I'm sure Miss Templer won't mind staying on shore, and I'll stay with her."

George said he would stay on shore as well; he added that Leonard would probably be sick and that Lukin Midge did not look a good sailor either.

Cassandra laughed. "Poor Lukin—he does have a lot of things wrong with him!" She was not really thinking about Lukin; she was thinking that this was her chance to tell George she was sorry about the meeting at the railway station.

It had not been possible during the drive (in spite of Miss Templer's clever scheming), because of Lily and Lukin in the back seat. The ancient car was so noisy that one had to shout to be heard, and she did not want them to hear her shouting to George that she had behaved badly.

Now that it had come to the point, she did not want to speak of it at all. She felt that it had been a very trying day and that it would be a pity to spoil this peaceful interlude. Somehow it seemed all too probable, if once they began talking about the cheque, the holiday, and her parents, that things would go wrong again.

But she had been unfair, and she ought to admit it.

"They're taking a long time," George said.

He gave Cassandra a cigarette, and lit one himself. He asked who Rupert was, and she said she didn't know.

"Mr. X. That's all he'll ever be. We shall never see him again."

"Do you want to?"

"Well, no," Cassandra said. "Not particularly. But it's very odd the way Dossie and Daisy produce these Mr. X's, and then they simply disappear into limbo."

"They run for their lives," George said darkly. "Remember Herbert the Hatter?"

Again Cassandra tried to look as though the past was a blank wall, but it was no good. She could not help remembering Herbert the Hatter, and she could not help laughing.

He had been a mild little man with a brown moustache and rimless glasses, who, in the summer before the war, had been briefly engaged to Dossie Fenn. He used to come out from Mallinford on Wednesday and Saturday afternoons, and it was George who first noticed the splendid variety of his headgear.

After that they used to watch for him from the field that sloped down to the river opposite The Moorings, and being robust, unsentimental children they had invented a drama in which he married first Dossie and then Daisy, and murdered them as he had murdered his six previous wives. This drama had lasted them the whole of the summer holidays; but by Christmas Herbert the Hatter had disappeared from the scene and Dossie's engagement was broken off.

"I wonder what really happened to him," Cassandra said, after they had recalled some of the more bloodthirsty ways in which he had committed his eight murders.

"He rushed off and joined the army, or the fire service. Or anything. The war came just at the right time for him."

"I wonder if Dossie minded very much."

Somehow one never thought of Dossie as 'minding'; and probably she didn't. Probably she and Daisy were like ardent anglers who did not care whether they caught anything or not, provided they enjoyed good sport.

But George was not interested in Dossie's reactions when the fish got away. "What I'm wondering," he said, "is what has happened to the rest of the picnic."

It seemed odd to Cassandra that she had forgotten the rest of the picnic, and she was startled to see how the shadows had lengthened. She looked at her watch. It was nearly two hours since they had left Witling wood.

Lukin and Lily were sitting on the end of the jetty, apparently as forgetful as herself. The owner of the motor-boat had taken it back to its buoy, and was now walking up the shingle bank towards them.

"Can't hang about any longer for your party, sir," he said grievedly. "If they want a trip in the boat they must come earlier, that's all."

"They *meant* to—" Cassandra began. But George took the aggrieved owner aside and solaced his anger with money. It seemed rather hard, she thought, that George, who had been invited as a guest, should have to pay for hiring—or rather, not hiring—the boat.

"Lily!" she called, and after two or three shouts Lily turned round and scrambled to her feet. Cassandra and George walked down the bank to meet her.

Neither Lily nor Lukin had noticed the time. Lukin, when he realized how late it was, looked fretful and said his mother would be getting worried. But no one paid much attention. George suggested that they should drive back to Witling and see if the other car had broken down. But both Lily and Cassandra were convinced that they had simply got lost.

"Aunt Bella could get lost anywhere," Lily pointed out. "And Leonard would *make* them get lost if he could."

"And Dossie and Daisy would be too busy talking to notice."

Finally they decided to return to Little Mallin, which was much nearer, and if there was no sign of the wanderers to drive out to Witling by the main road.

When they reached the village Bryce was getting his car out of his garage. It was a large, powerful car, which did duty both as a taxi and as a breakdown van. "Stop and ask him," said George. "He's probably just off to the rescue."

"Telephoned from Long Hampton, someone did," Bryce informed them. "Telephoned to Miss Gregory at the post-office, and asked her to come down and tell me." It was one of the village grievances that Bryce was not on the telephone and could only be summoned, at times of crisis, by sending messengers running with notes or verbal entreaties.

"Half-way over to Long Hampton, they are," he went on. "Stuck in that ford they calls Mucky Crossing. Though how they come to be stuck there I can't rightly make out. Can't be much water in that little stream this weather."

"Uncle Henry won't be pleased," Lily said thoughtfully.

Bryce did not approve of picnics, holding that meals should be eaten at table, and that fresh air, if it was wanted, could be had in one's own garden. Nevertheless, he liked any job that was out of the ordinary and he was obviously quite pleased to be called to the rescue of a car that had got itself stuck in Mucky Crossing.

"I reckon I can tow it out," he said. "If not, I'll bring them back in this one and the car must wait there till Monday. Not likely to be much traffic that way—it don't go nowhere."

"Perhaps one of us had better come with you—or shall I come in the car? Then I could drive some of them straight home."

"No, Miss Cassandra," Bryce said firmly. "There's no reason for any of you to come. And if I can't do the job with this big car of mine, it's not likely that little one of yours 'ud be much help." Bryce always treated Cassandra as if she was about nine years old.

"I'll drive you home first, George," Cassandra said, when Bryce had departed. "And then I'll drop Lukin on our way back to Prospect House. Do you think I could keep this car there for the night, Lily, to save coming back to the vicarage? It could sleep out in the yard for once, couldn't it?"

Lily said it could. "If you're as hungry as I am you must be longing for supper. Why do picnics always make one hungry?"

"It can't be because there wasn't enough to eat," said George. "We all ate plenty."

"But that doesn't seem to count. Aren't you hungry?"

George said he was. Cassandra said it must be much worse for the others, stuck in the ford. Lily said they had the picnic-baskets in the car, and there was still a lot of cake left when they finished tea.

Lukin, who had been fidgeting nervously at this time-wasting chatter, began to say something about his mother. He was not hungry himself ("I have a very poor appetite"), but his mother would be worrying about him. His remarks seemed to fall on deaf ears; they all went on talking, and Lily, feeling that the duties of hostess had now devolved on her, invited George to come back to Prospect House and have supper there.

"There's sure to be enough to eat," she explained ingenuously, "because Mrs. Truefitt knows we're always hungry when we come home from picnics." Thinking that this did not sound quite right she went on to say that Uncle Eustace would be delighted to see George; he always liked seeing people when they did not come too often.

But George replied gravely that he ought to return home. With an unkind glance at Lukin, he added that his father would be worrying about him.

CHAPTER XV

THE CUSTANCES, obedient to Sir James's wishes, had gone away for a fortnight, and so they missed what came to be known as 'the week it rained'. They were fortunate, and in Cornwall they enjoyed good weather. But in Little Mallin the long succession of warm days was broken, the Sunday after the picnic, by a heavy thunderstorm, and it rained intermittently for most of the following week.

The thunderstorm occurred in the morning. Cassandra had gone to church with Miss Templer, Lily and Colonel Ashford, and although Mr. Johnson proved an eloquent preacher their minds were distracted from his sermon by thoughts of Colonel Ashford's car, still embedded in the mud at Mucky Crossing and now exposed to torrential rains and a rising river.

When Bryce came round with the offertory bag Colonel Ashford threw him an imploring look, a look which beseeched him to forget the Sabbath and hasten to the rescue. But Bryce was a strict believer in the fourth commandment, and even if the car had been sinking into a bottomless bog he would not have broken his rule.

It was not until Monday afternoon that the car was extricated. Wet and tired, Colonel Ashford returned to Prospect House on foot. He had refused to take Felix with him and no one dared at first to ask him what had happened. But Cassandra met Bryce that evening in the village and learnt that the car was in his workshop, 'and a proper mess too'. They had had to tow it back after spending most of the day digging it out of the now swollen stream, and it would have to stay where it was until Bryce had time to get round and clean up the engine.

Deprived of his car, and unable to forget that it was Bella and Leonard—but chiefly Bella—who had caused the disaster, Henry Ashford became a very difficult guest. Everyone was relieved when he announced one morning that he was going up to town to visit Barbara and find out for himself how she was getting on.

He proposed to stay in London for the present. He would let them know when he was coming back.

"But I'm sorry for Bonny," Miss Templer said to Cassandra. "It's such a nice nursing-home and she's having such a wonderful rest. No, it's not where she had the operation—she left that one because of the cats. This is one of those patent places where they feed you on fruit, like a hotel but cosier."

"It sounds wonderful," said Cassandra, wondering what Miss Templer meant.

"She's going to stay there as long as she can afford it, and then she's coming here. I do wish I could find them a house."

They were driving back in the vicarage car after taking Colonel Ashford to the station, and had reached the hill out of the village. Both their heads turned towards Prospect Cottage as they passed it.

"I do wish there were some *nice* way of getting rid of her," Miss Templer said.

In Prospect Cottage the barometer was no longer Set Fair; the needle wavered between Change and Stormy. There had been two reconciliations but neither had been as satisfactory as Mrs. Midge had hoped; that is to say, Lukin had been sorry but not sorry enough. He had been sorry when he came back late from the picnic and found her tearful and anxious; but he had accepted Lily's invitation to practise his tennis. It was the rain, and not his mother's wishes, that kept him at home.

Mrs. Midge disliked all the Templers, but it was now Lily, rather than Eustace or Isabel, whom she disliked the most. That fat little thing with the painted face, she called her; but she had sense enough not to say this to Lukin. Like Mrs. Custance she knew that one could say too much.

Lukin noticed that his Mama was no longer prostrated with a headache when he wanted to leave her, and he confided to Lily that the walls of his prison were opening out.

"That's marvellous."

Lily waited for him to say that it was all due to her, but Lukin went on to speak about his own will-power.

"I have to fight the whole time. It's terribly exhausting. I feel like a soldier who spends his days and nights defending a citadel. The citadel of my integrity."

Defrauded of her due, Lily became captious. She pointed out that he could not feel like a soldier and be certain he was getting his feelings right, because he did not know anything about soldiering. His many ailments (and a sympathetic doctor) had secured his exemption from National Service. Far from defending a citadel, he had not even learnt to march in step.

Lukin bore this criticism without flinching, because, as he explained, she had a literal outlook and no sense of real values. It was more important to apprehend the emotional aspects of a situation than to know how to fire a gun. People doing things were simply raw material for the mind to work on.

Lily reported this conversation—or as much of it as she could remember—to Cassandra.

She was very much enjoying Cassandra's visit to Prospect House, because it meant that she could go to her bedroom at night and indulge in long, delightful talks. Cassandra's bedroom, although furnished with the usual Templer haphazardness, had a window-seat and a wicker chair, and Lily liked to curl up on the window-seat and imagine herself in some foreign land, the garden transformed by dusk to exotic beauty, and her sympathetic friend sitting at her side listening.

Of course, Cassandra was not the ideal friend of the fantasy, but Lily realized that this dream-paragon represented a perfection she could hardly hope to encounter in actual life. Cassandra, in some ways, was more fun.

Cassandra said: "'People doing things' provide Lukin with his bread and butter. At least, Mrs. Midge does."

"There's the alimony too."

"Oh, is there? I often wondered how she managed so well. That awful Gifte Shoppe doesn't look as if it could support Mrs. Midge and Mrs. Imber in comfort."

"I used to wonder too," said Lily. "She was always talking about hard times and hard work, and how she worked her fingers to the bone for Lukin. I used to think they were quite penniless except for what she earned. How much does alimony come to, Cassandra?"

But Cassandra, whose experience of matrimonial disputes was limited, did not know.

"It must be quite a lot," she said. "I expect divorce is more paying than just being widowed. But don't tell my mother she's divorced."

Lily promised to keep it a secret. A vicar's wife was bound to be fussy about that sort of thing, she thought, not understanding that Mrs. Custance could easily have overlooked a divorce if she had been fond of the people concerned.

"I wonder what Mr. Midge is like," Cassandra said.

"Lukin can't remember. He thinks he had a black beard, but he says that may be his subconscious something-or-other influencing his vision."

"How peculiar. Surely you'd remember a black beard, and not go adding it on to a face that hadn't got one."

"*I* shouldn't," said Lily. "But Lukin paints what his Unconscious sees, so I suppose he gets muddled between real beards and symbolic ones."

Cassandra wanted to know what Lukin's painting was like, and Lily had to explain that the things his Unconscious saw were hard for other people to identify.

"Especially at present, because he has to put in the prison bars and you can only see bits of the other things, outside. Of course the prison is just a symbol."

Cassandra yawned. Lily would go on talking about Lukin till the dawn, if allowed to, but she was impractical and vague when it came to making plans for his future. She seemed to think that one day, by some miracle of intuition, critics and art dealers would flock to Little Mallin to proclaim his genius. The more practical Cassandra saw that it was Lukin who would have to make the first move.

"He ought to get away," she said. "Back to that Pentalloch place you talked about."

"He didn't like it."

"Well, London or somewhere. If he's to become famous, people have got to *see* his paintings. Has he ever sold a picture?"

"Not exactly. I mean, he's thought about it, but even if he asked his mother to get Mrs. Imber to put one in her shop window"— this had been Lily's idea—"I don't suppose anyone would buy it."

"I don't suppose they would, but they might in London."

Cassandra did not believe that even in London people would want a picture of something seen dimly through prison bars, but she had suddenly realized that if Lukin could be persuaded to go to London his mother would certainly accompany him.

And then Prospect Cottage would be empty.

After Colonel Ashford's departure she enjoyed her stay with the Templers. It had been difficult, up till then, for a neutral visitor to remain on good terms with everyone, and it had been difficult for the Templers themselves to ignore the excessive gloom, the chilly accusing glances, of their relative.

After he had gone they were able to laugh about the picnic, which had hitherto been unmentionable, and Felix made several visits to Bryce's workshop to look at the car. He reported that Bryce had found a great deal wrong with it, apart from the damage done by mud and water.

"Henry doesn't understand machinery," said Eustace, who didn't understand it himself but didn't pretend to. "Everything he touches goes wrong. Look at the mower. No—no need to look at it. Listen to it."

"We can't until Uncle Henry comes back."

"So nice and peaceful without it," said Isabel. "If I'd had nerves it would have got on them."

"It certainly made a lot of noise."

Eustace said that was what he meant. "An abominable amount of noise, and getting worse every day. A peculiar grinding noise. Other people's mowers don't make noises like that."

His sister said mildly that she had never listened to other people's mowers and she didn't think there was another motor-mower in the village. Eustace retorted that there was one at Mallin Hall.

Lily took advantage of the uncle-and-little-niece convention to ask him boldly if he had been visiting Sir James Brigham, and Eustace, with one of his sly and tantalizing looks, replied that he had gone there for advice.

"From Sir James or George?"

"Sound, practical advice from one landowner to another. But I was disappointed. The old man was courteous but singularly unhelpful. He could only talk of his own troubles. His servants have established a dictatorship and refuse to give him enough to eat, or to clean the rooms, or even to mend his clothes."

"Mrs. Dixon and Sarah?" Cassandra asked incredulously. It was a long time since she had encountered them, but the legend of their loyalty was firmly believed in Little Mallin.

"I remember meeting George in Mallinford," Miss Templer put in. "He was buying wool to darn his socks. Quite the wrong colour for anything."

"Oh, but this isn't a question of *George's* socks," Eustace said gaily. "They haven't darned George's socks for years, but this is much more serious. Sir James's own socks, and his vests. And— d' y' know—his pants."

"Mrs. Truefitt sometimes goes over to have tea with Mrs. Dixon," said Miss Templer. "I do hope they won't go putting ideas into her head."

On the afternoon of the day when Mr. and Mrs. Custance were due to return Cassandra and Lily went to the vicarage to prepare for their homecoming. They made up the beds, which had previously been well aired by Mrs. Nutting who believed that one could not be too careful, even in summer, and Cassandra lit the kitchen range and prepared the supper. While she was doing this Lily picked flowers and arranged them in vases, which she proceeded to place in spots where no vicarage flower-vase had ever stood before—a bowl of lupins on the drawing-room mantelpiece (hiding a Maitland miniature), a larger bowl of mixed flowers on the Sheraton table, a vase of roses on Mr. Custance's desk in the study. She thought it would make a nice welcome for them.

Cassandra meant to move the vases as soon as Lily had gone, but Lily dawdled and in the end she had to hurry off to the station to meet her parents. So the first sight that greeted Mrs. Custance's eyes when she entered her drawing-room was a profusion of flowers crammed tightly together, standing on her precious table where only the Dresden shepherdesses were ever allowed to stand.

Darting across the room she observed that there wasn't even a mat to protect the polished surface. "Cassie, how could you!" she cried, lifting up the bowl and discovering that it had already left a wet ring on the table. "Fetch a cloth, quickly! And take this bowl out to the kitchen—it's simply brimming over."

Then she turned round, and saw the other bowl on the mantelpiece. It too was brimming over, and had left a wet mark. It too was banished to the kitchen.

It was an unfortunate homecoming. Cassandra explained that it was Lily who had arranged the flowers, but Mrs. Custance was hot and tired after her train journey, and she replied crossly that Lily had no sense and Cassie ought to have stopped her. Then Mr. Custance appeared and confessed unhappily that he had knocked over the little vase on his desk, and in trying to save it he had also knocked over the ink.

Cassandra sped to and fro with dish-cloths and blotting-paper and furniture polish. She remembered how calmly the Templers took such everyday accidents—no fuss, no lamentations—and she forgot that the mattress had been lumpy and the bedroom door would not shut properly. Prospect House, now that she had left it, seemed a haven of peace and quiet.

By the time they sat down to supper Mrs. Custance had got over her annoyance. She began to talk about the holiday, and said over and over again that it was a great pity Cassie had not been with them.

"There were some very pleasant people staying there—the sort of people one likes to meet," she said. "There was a Mrs. Hughes— such a nice woman—and her son. And it turned out that she lives quite near Aunt Mary and knows her well. Wasn't that odd? The son is a doctor and at present he is an assistant to his uncle, but I gather they're going into partnership quite soon."

Mrs. Custance had decided not to say too much about young Dr. Hughes, but his name kept straying back into the conversation. He had a car and had taken them for a picnic and several nice drives. His manners were excellent, not a bit like some of these modern young men. He was a bachelor. She did not mention her talk with Mrs. Hughes (who had told her that she disapproved of possessive mothers and only longed to see Tony happily married), but she said that Mrs. Hughes had asked her to come and see them the next time she stayed with her sister.

"And she said she'd love to see you too," she told her daughter. "If you go to Aunt Mary in August you must certainly look her up."

From the start Cassandra had known that Dr. Hughes must be an eligible bachelor. The more she heard of his niceness, his good manners, his rosy prospects, the more she disliked this paragon. Nothing, she thought, would induce her to visit Aunt Mary; and she decided to write to Joan as soon as possible and fix it up about the caravan. In a spirit of mischief—and to provide a contrast to Dr. Hughes's perfections—she said that she had seen quite a lot of Lukin Midge in the past fortnight, and his tennis was really improving.

"We couldn't play much last week because of the rain, but we played on Monday evening and yesterday. I thought we might have a tennis party next Saturday, but I haven't asked anyone yet."

"Next Saturday is impossible because it's the Sunday-school outing."

Mrs. Custance positively blessed the Sunday-school outing, which would give her a reprieve from having to be nice to Lukin. Cassandra was talking about the picnic, and she knew from her letter that Lukin had been one of the guests. Her fears returned, and now there seemed some reason for them; Cassie had spent a lot of time in his company, and had introduced his name into the conversation. In Mrs. Custance's abbreviated idiom this was 'a sure sign'.

At the first pause she pushed back her chair, saying she must go upstairs and unpack. She had hardly been listening to her daughter, who was describing the catastrophe at the ford.

"You ought to have gone first and shown him the way through," she said.

"But, Mummy, we weren't *there*. I've just been telling you—we were at Shingle Street, waiting and waiting. George wanted to go back and see what had happened, but of course we would never have found them because they were miles off the right road."

Mrs. Custance stood still. "George Brigham?" she said. "Was he with you? You didn't tell me."

"Didn't I? I thought I did. Yes, George and Lily and Lukin. The others were with Colonel Ashford."

"The slough of Despond," Mr. Custance said suddenly, wondering if he could bring it into a sermon, or if it would seem too personal. His wife and daughter paid no attention. Mrs. Custance was revising her ideas about the picnic and trying to decide whether she was glad or sorry that George had been present.

It was funny that Isabel should have asked him—but of course not really; Isabel would have asked anybody, even Miss Gregory from the post-office, even Bryce, if she had happened to meet them and had been in the asking mood. In her own mood of alarm and dejection Mrs. Custance felt that George's presence had been, on the whole, a Good Thing. At least it meant that there had been someone else for Cassie to talk to, besides Lukin.

She did not count Colonel Ashford, because he was a married man; nor did 'someone to talk to' include females and children. And no man who had been brought to a party by Dossie or Daisy could be counted either. The Misses Fenn would have seen to that.

Cassandra was thinking of her own deceitfulness. She knew she had not mentioned George's presence in the letter she wrote about the picnic. Again, she had let her parents think that their holiday was provided by Sir James Brigham. And yet again, she had told George that her father was glad to be going to Cornwall, concealing the fact that he had only been moved to a last-minute gladness by the thought of meeting his dear old friend and escaping from the pier and the band.

These were but minor matters, but they weighed on her conscience.

The minor matter of showing a particular interest in Lukin Midge did not weigh on her conscience at all. She had done it to tease her mother and she could not guess what an effect it had had. She was not thinking about Lukin when she said, a little later on, that she had thoroughly enjoyed her stay at Prospect House.

But Mrs. Custance thought of him at once. What other reason could there be for Cassie's enjoying herself so much? The Templers were old friends and she saw them every day anyway, and no one could say that Prospect House was comfortable.

Kneeling by her suitcase, surrounded by little piles of clothes that would all need washing and ironing, part of her mind already occupied by thoughts of meals, the Sunday-school outing, and the damp patch on the bathroom wall, she gave a deep sigh, a sigh worthy of Sir James Brigham himself.

"Let me unpack," Cassandra said. "Or shall I unpack for Father?"

"Yes, would you? If the water is hot I shall have a bath, and then I shall go to bed early. I'm quite tired."

She did not often admit to being tired, and her daughter said sympathetically that it must have been the railway journey.

"But it was a lovely holiday," Mrs. Custance murmured. "Something to look back on."

"There's the rest of the summer to look forward to."

"It's going to be a very busy summer—very busy indeed. I shall want you to help me a good deal, Cassie."

"Of course I will."

Cassandra was surprised to hear that it was going to be a busy summer. She could not know that Mrs. Custance had that very instant decided that an active life, with a multitude of urgent tasks and no time for brooding—better still, no time for seeing a lot of that wretched boy—was what her daughter needed.

CHAPTER XVI

MALLIN HALL was a long, low house, well suited to its position. It stood at the top of a gentle slope, backed by trees that sheltered it from the north, and its gardens were laid out in broad terraces to the west and south. About 1840 a new wing had been added to the house, but fortunately this was at the back and did not mar the symmetry of the garden aspect; from the terraced lawns one saw only the sun-bleached gold of the original stone.

In 1720, when the house was built, they had quarried the stone forty miles away, and teams of oxen had dragged it through miry lanes, through Long Hampton and Witling, to the new site on the slope of the hill. The reigning Brigham in 1840 did not go to all this trouble; he used brick, which was cheaper and, in his opinion, just as good. Later generations of Brighams had done their best to hide his addition under ivy and Virginia creeper, but it remained an eyesore. Sir James and his son thought differently about many things but they both agreed on one thing—that the 'new wing' was a mistake. Even Sir James, who valued his possessions, preferred not to look at it, while the more ruthless George wanted to pull it down.

The new wing contained a billiard-room, a gun-room, and two small dank rooms looking north which no one had ever used. Overhead were several bedrooms, for the wing had been built to accommodate the large family of the reigning Brigham, and a bathroom which had been installed about 1890, but in which, for some unfathomable reason, the water never ran hot. All these rooms were now unfurnished and abandoned to damp.

Since Sir James disliked the new wing he did not mind its being neglected, but it was a different matter when Sarah gave up dusting the library. The books left dirty marks on his hands, and he complained of it to George.

George said: "Well, look at the brasses! Look at the hall! Actually the library is the cleanest room in the house. I think it still gets dusted sometimes."

"What's that, m' boy? What d' y' mean?"

Sir James sought and found his long-distance spectacles. He did not often make use of them, believing that they would ruin his eyesight, but now he put them on and went off for a tour of his house. What he saw upset him so much that without consulting George he opened the green baize door and penetrated into the servants' sitting-room, where Mrs. Dixon and Sarah were tatting away at their crochetwork over the inevitable pot of tea.

It was a mistake, he admitted afterwards; he ought to have rung the bell and interviewed them in the library. But George pointed out that ringing the bell was a waste of time. Sarah no longer answered bells, except the front-door bell, and she only answered that when she knew that he and his father were both out.

The interview in the servants' sitting-room put Sir James at a disadvantage. He knew the rules; he knew that the sitting-room was, so to speak, a sanctuary, and that he had no right to be there. The mute reproachful faces of his staff; the obvious trouble it was to them to put aside their sewing and their tea-cups and rise to their feet; the way Mrs. Dixon clasped a chair to support her trembling knees—all this made him pause and feel guilty. When he spoke he did not say that the house was like a spiders' mausoleum and must be given a damn' good cleaning straightaway; instead, he remarked apologetically that he was just having a look round.

To add verisimilitude he looked round the room as he spoke, and Mrs. Dixon at once pointed out that some of the plaster was off the ceiling and one of the bars in the grate was broken. Sarah asked him to be sure and notice the lino in the passage—it wasn't hardly safe in that state—and they both assured him that it took them half the morning sometimes to clear the waste-pipe from the pantry sink. There was something wrong with it, it got choked up no matter how careful you were, and the sink itself was cracked so that the water dripped through and was making a rotten place in the boards underneath.

At the first pause in their lamentations Sir James made soothing promises and withdrew to his own territory, where he poured out the whole sad story to George.

"So now we've got to repair a ceiling and buy a new grate and a new sink," George said, "and put new boards in the pantry and do something about the lino. Oh yes, and get the plumber to look at the waste-pipe."

"There was something else as well," Sir James growled. "Something about the cistern keeping them awake at night going bubble-bubble. I didn't listen. D' y' know, George, they were using that tea-caddy that used to be in the drawing-room? Remember it well, though you won't. Your grandmother always made the tea herself."

"We shall be doing that soon. Except that we shan't have any tea to make it with."

By taking the offensive, Mrs. Dixon and Sarah won the day. Nothing was said about their own deficiencies; their employer had been glad to escape before they could tell him about the kitchen range and half a dozen other things. But either they had sensed his dissatisfaction and were punishing him for it, or else they were extending their plan for a serene old age; whichever it was, after the interview they ceased to mend Sir James's clothes. Instead, they occupied their leisure hours in making an elaborate tablecloth of crochet lace and hairpin work.

This masterpiece was kept out of sight. Sarah told her employer, when he asked her to sew on some buttons, that her eyes had been troubling her and she really couldn't afford to touch a needle at present.

It was shortly after the Sunday-school outing that Sir James called his son into the library and announced that something would have to be done. He had said it before; but except for his one unsuccessful attempt he had left it to George to take action. Now, puffing out his moustache and looking both indignant and mournful, he told George that a firm talk—civil, y' know, *but firm*—must be given to the servants, and if things didn't improve, they must go.

"And what will happen then?" George asked.

He did not ask who was to deliver the firm talk, but he wanted his father to understand what its result might be.

"Hr-rmph! Get some more. Not foreigners, though, I won't have 'em in the house. And no young women either—they're never trustworthy. Couple of middle-aged women, that's what we want. Not too old, y' know. *Healthy* women," said Sir James, thinking of his present staff's infirmities. "Sensible, middle-aged bodies. Pair of sisters, perhaps, but not a widow-with-children."

"But—"

"Harrap tells me they had a widow-with-children and she was a damn' nuisance, always saying they were coming out in spots and rushing them off to the doctor. The children, I mean, not the Harraps. Then one of them swallowed a teaspoon and there was a fearful fuss. Middle of the night, too."

"Queer time to swallow a teaspoon," said George.

"One of Harrap's own spoons. An Apostle, I think he said."

George hoped they had got it back. But he pointed out that the Harraps were now without any servants, widowed or otherwise.

There was a long pause. His father said mournfully that he didn't know what things were coming to. Did George mean they wouldn't be able to replace Mrs. Dixon and Sarah?

"I think it might be difficult. We're a mile from the bus. Still, we shouldn't be much worse off without them. Perhaps we could get someone daily from the village."

He felt sorry for his father. Sir James had spoken confidently of the two middle-aged bodies, but now, thinking of the servant-less Harraps, he looked dejected and unsure of himself. There was a button missing from his coat and a large hole in the heel of his sock. George forgot his father's tiresome ways, his obstinacy and his foolish pride in his family; he remembered that his father was sixty-nine and had not been brought up in a world where one darned one's own clothes.

"Why not ask Mrs. Custance about it?" he suggested.

"Ask Amy, eh? Well, I might."

"Ask her what the chances are of getting someone from the village. Then we shall know how strong a line to take with Mrs. Dixon."

Sir James made no direct reply, but nodded his head to show that he had heard. He would not admit that it was a good idea, because that might have made George conceited.

"I was talking to Templer about it the other week," he said. "Feller came up to see me. There I was with my old coat off—not this one, y' know, the other one—trying to stick the pocket on again. Had to say something, so I told him about Sarah's eyes. Not that I believe that clap-trap. Thing is, she doesn't *want* to mend my clothes."

"And what did he say?"

"He said Batts."

"He said what?"

"Batts. Plenty about, he said, and they soon learn English. Jabbering away like parrots in no time."

"Oh," said George. "I see what you mean. At least, I think I do. Well, what about trying for some Batts?"

"I've told you before, George, I won't have any foreigners about the place. Bad enough having those Ites in the war."

Whoever the Batts might be, the Ites were Ey-ties, and George said he couldn't agree with him more.

The servant crisis had drawn them together, and later in the afternoon, when he had had his nap and looked through *The Times*, Sir James thought he would go out and give George a hand in the garden. He exchanged his fairly good coat for the old one, put on a Panama hat to shield him from the sun, and then went out by the front door to collect his dandelion spud, which he remembered having left under the cedar tree that overhung the drive.

While he was crossing the drive a car appeared; he saw it approaching and at first he thought of taking cover behind the cedar and waiting for whoever-it-was to depart, but it was too close and they might have already spotted him. He stood his ground, telling himself that he never had a moment's peace, but his hostility lessened when he recognized Mrs. Custance.

She was alone, and as a matter of form he asked after her husband and Cassandra. Mrs. Custance explained that Edward was watching the Little Mallin cricket XI, which contained no less than four of the choir, and Cassandra was practising the organ.

The regular organist was the school-mistress, and Sir James wanted to know what had happened to her.

"Nothing," said Mrs. Custance, "but she's dreadfully busy just at present and she was telling me the other day that she never got time to go and see her married sister in Bramchester. So I suggested that Cassie should take over for a bit. I know she isn't as good as Miss Nelson but she can manage all right if we have easy hymns."

"Very good of her to do it."

"It's very good *for* her," said Mrs. Custance, meaning exactly what she said. "I hope I'm not disturbing you. I was on my way to Witling and I thought I'd look in and find out where you want us to have the Fête. I mean the stalls and the tea-tables."

"Better come and have a look round. Just wait while I get my spud. D' y' know, Amy, it's a good thing you came today. George is at home and he'd better know what we're planning. Got to get the place looking tidy."

Mrs. Custance had purposely come on a Saturday afternoon, when she knew George would be at home. Whatever she thought of him, his co-operation would be necessary; and it would be a pity if he was told nothing until the last moment, and then refused to help.

She had decided that the stables could only be used as a last resource; if it was possible they would have the stalls under the colonnade in the garden and serve the teas in the empty billiard-room, which could be entered from the garden without going through the rest of the house. She would have liked a marquee, but of course they could not afford it, and the billiard-room would do very well once it had been cleaned and aired. It was really a good thing that Sir James had got rid of the billiard-table when he shut up the 'new wing' in the second year of the war.

Tact would be necessary. Sir James would not consent to the use of the billiard-room unless he could be persuaded to think of it for himself. As they walked round the end of the house Mrs.

Custance began to talk about the weather. It was almost too perfect. It could not possibly last, but she did hope it would be fine for the day of the Fête.

"It will be quite a tragedy if it rains," she said.

"Have to have it in the stables. I'll tell George he must get those farm-carts out of the coach-house. Give it a coat of white-wash, perhaps."

"Oh, that's too much trouble for you. We shall manage quite well. We'll brush the spiders away!"

"Spiders!" cried her host, speaking in so loud a voice that Mrs. Custance jumped. "Thing is, Amy, I've got to talk to you. Look at my coat!"

She looked, and saw that the patch pocket had been half torn away, and was now held in place by a criss-cross of cellophane tape.

"That's only temporary," he said, tweaking at it. "Templer's idea—and I don't think much of it. Stuff was on my desk and he said it would do—said we'd never thread the needle if we tried till Doomsday. And as for spiders, the whole house is full of 'em. What I want to know is, can we get a replacement from the village?"

For once Mrs. Custance was at a loss. The spiders, the cellophane tape, the unexpected intrusion of Eustace Templer, made it difficult for her to guess what sort of replacement her old friend needed.

Assuming a face of shocked sympathy she said, "Tell me all about it."

Half an hour later they resumed their tour of the garden. In the course of his narrative Sir James had had occasion to dwell on his old age and what was due to it, and now, remembering that he was frail and elderly, he walked very slowly, using the long handle of the dandelion spud as a substitute for his stick. The grating of the pronged end on the paved path attracted George's attention; he looked across the lawn and was surprised to see his father talking to Mrs. Custance and making expansive gestures with his hands, as if he were pointing to invisible objects.

George was hot and tired. He had been working in the kitch-
en garden, and had only come down to the lower lawn to see
how the sweet peas were getting on in the long border and to
finish some weeding. He did not want to talk to Mrs. Custance,
or to anyone else, but his father had seen him and was calling
to him to join them. He walked across the lawn, noticing as he
went that his father had spotted a dandelion and was busily
prodding it out of the turf.

George wished he wouldn't. The long-handled spud made it
easy for Sir James to get the dandelions out, but since he did
not like stooping he left them lying on the ground for George or
Thurstan to pick up later. He seldom managed to get the dandelion out in one piece and from its broken root another would
soon appear, so that the operation was rather a waste of time.
And if the mangled corpses were not collected he complained
that the lawn looked untidy.

After greeting Mrs. Custance George stooped to retrieve the
dandelion Sir James had just uprooted. As he stood up his father said, in a sort of gloomy triumph: "Your shirt's slit. Just at
the back of the neck. Saw it as you bent down."

Though he realized that his father had taken his advice and
consulted Mrs. Custance, George did not care to be used as a
living example of Neglect. "This is my gardening shirt," he said.
"Only fit for a jumble stall—if that."

"*Anything* will do for a jumble stall," Mrs. Custance said. "I
thought we might have it over there."

She pointed.

Sir James said, "More in the corner," and pointed in a slightly different direction. George gazed at them in astonishment.

"Of course, if it's wet . . ." Mrs. Custance murmured anxiously.

It took George a minute or two to grasp that they were talking
about the Church Fête, but when he had done so he understood
at once why he had been called over to talk to Mrs. Custance.
The old farm-carts would have to be moved, the stables cleaned
and whitewashed; the whole garden must be looking its best;

and Mrs. Custance hoped he would be able to help them on the day itself.

"It's for a good cause," she said firmly, to forestall argument.

George said, "It had better be fine, or no one will turn up." He looked as if he would not much mind if no one did turn up.

Mrs. Custance said to herself that this was just what she might have expected. He was being difficult. He had no sense of duty (so different from his father) and he wouldn't care if the church fell into ruins.

But before the end of her visit she came to feel that things might have been worse, and that George was really more practical than his father. It was he who suggested that the stalls might be set out under the covered walk they called the colonnade, and with very little prompting he added that it would be easier to use the new wing than the tumbledown stables.

"Can't have people tramping through the house," Sir James said decisively. Mrs. Custance made haste to soothe him. "Of course not," she said, "I wouldn't dream of it. Though the billiard-room would be nearer the colonnade and the gardens . . . but still, I quite agree with you about letting them through the house. It wouldn't do at all."

She held her breath lest George should intervene at this critical moment, and willed him to be silent. Either the power of her will or his own common sense kept him quiet. Sir James, having been given time to think about it, produced his own solution with the happy air of one who has triumphed over great difficulties.

"D' y' know, Amy, there's no reason for them to come through the house. Why shouldn't they come in by the garden door into the gun-room? Have the tea-tables in the billiard-room, y' know, and a woman selling tickets in the gun-room. Make the tea in that little room at the end. All those rooms are empty—might have been made for it!"

Mrs. Custance said that was a wonderful idea. She pretended that she had not known about the garden door, or had forgotten its existence. She said that she and Mrs. Nutting would come and clean the rooms before the day, and she would arrange for a van to bring the chairs and tables and crockery from the Parish

Hall. Having got this settled to her satisfaction she looked at her watch and exclaimed that she must be off.

"Where are you going?"

"Over to Witling—and I'm very late. They're having *their* Church Fête this afternoon and I promised to go, because of course one must go to the others or else they won't come to ours."

"Taking in each other's washing," said George. But his voice was friendly; he could not help admiring Mrs. Custance for the way she had got round his father. He opened the door of the car for her, and as she turned to bid him good-bye he said quietly, "When did you decide to have the tea in the billiard-room?"

Mrs. Custance laughed. "Never you mind. Will you be able to help us, on the day?"

"I'll do my best."

At that moment she nearly forgot that she had changed her mind about George. She nearly added, "And will you come to tennis next Saturday?" But before she could utter these words Sir James appeared at the other side of the car and said loudly, "Don't forget, Amy—must be someone who can sew."

Mrs. Custance nodded. She said good-bye to both of them and drove off to Witling.

After Mrs. Custance had gone Sir James explained to George that she had not been very hopeful about getting help from the village but she had promised to make discreet inquiries and let him know if there was anyone who would be prepared to come daily.

That meant they would have to get their own breakfasts, he added gloomily; since Amy had assured him that none of these daily helpers ever arrived before nine o'clock.

George replied that he would guarantee to provide a better breakfast than they were getting at present. But his father did not believe this, and moreover he did not like the idea of daily help, though of course it would be better than nothing. He still thought that a firm talk might bring Mrs. Dixon and Sarah to their senses, and then everything would go on as before.

"After all," he said, "we know that Mrs. Dixon *can* cook. Trouble is, she won't."

"And we know that Sarah could dust, once," said George. "Trouble is, she's probably forgotten how."

Later that evening, still brooding over the situation, Sir James decided that what Mrs. Dixon and Sarah needed was someone to keep an eye on them. He was an old, worn-out man, George took no interest in his home, and naturally their servants, for lack of supervision, had grown idle and neglectful. He remembered his own father complaining, long ago in the past, of the laziness of the lower orders; and he remembered too that his wife used to spend some time each morning interviewing the cook, or closeted with the head-housemaid in the linen-room.

He played with this theory for some time, and the more he considered it the more sensible it appeared. What was needed was not daily help from the village, but someone to keep Mrs. Dixon and Sarah up to the mark; someone who would insist on fruit pies being cold, and potatoes being mashed or fried instead of always plain boiled; someone who would tell them to turn out rooms and polish brasses when the right day came round. Mrs. Dixon and Sarah were not so very old—years younger than himself—and with a little tactful supervision they would soon have things straight again.

He coughed gently, then a little louder, until George looked up from his book. He found his father staring at him with a critical eye, as if he were assessing the good points and the bad.

"Anything wrong?" he asked.

"D' y' know, George, it's quite time you got married."

Since George could not guess how his father had reached this conclusion he was considerably startled. Rather to Sir James's annoyance he asked sharply:

"Was that Mrs. Custance's suggestion?"

"No, no. An idea of my own."

"Oh," said George. He remembered their earlier conversation; he looked at his father's torn coat, and thought of the bread pudding they had had for supper. Following his father's train of thought, he slowly, almost reluctantly, began to laugh.

"Nothing to laugh about," his father said. "And nothing to do with Amy Custance either. Though between you and me, George, I've often thought you and Cassandra might make a match of it. No money, of course, but she's a Maitland on her mother's side. I've often thought, y' know, that you might go further and fare worse."

George had stopped laughing, but when he spoke his voice sounded half-mocking, half-angry. "She wouldn't have me," he said.

Sir James gave an indignant snort. He had temporarily forgotten that George was a disappointment to him and that he had confided his disappointment to everyone in the neighbourhood. He remembered instead that George was a Brigham, the heir to a modest estate and a fine (though sadly neglected) house.

"Don't be a fool," he said. "She'd have you tomorrow."

CHAPTER XVII

TO THE STRANGER Little Mallin appeared a small, rather dull village. Kind-hearted visitors, searching for an appropriate adjective, often ended by describing it as 'peaceful'. Peaceful it looked, in the golden warmth of a fine summer, but there were plenty of disputes and grievances which now and then, throwing off red sparks like a smouldering bonfire, provided the residents with conversation or, better still, with a dramatic spectacle.

Dramatic spectacles were compared, to their detriment, with the unsurpassed spectacle of twenty years ago when Crowe's Bakery had burst into flames through the fault of Mrs. Crowe, who, brandishing a rolling-pin in anger, had knocked over an oil-lamp; when the fire brigade, dashing to the rescue, had become involved in an argument about tolls with the bridge-keeper, and a small boy, standing on the parapet to get a better view, had fallen into the river. The Affair of the Fence, as Miss Templer called it, was trivial compared to this, but it brought quite a lot of residents out of their own houses and gave several people an opportunity to say what they thought about Bryce, or alternatively, about the Misses Fenn.

Dossie and Daisy had frequently told Bryce that the party fence needed mending, and Bryce had as frequently assured them that he would see to it when he had time. The fence was five feet high and massively constructed, and the noise of its fall, when it collapsed along its whole length into the Misses Fenns' garden, brought the nearest neighbours to the spot in time to see Dossie and Daisy scrambling over its ruins to begin their assault on the bell and knocker of The Anchorage.

It was a Saturday morning, and Bryce had stayed at home to see to his cistern, which had something wrong with the ballcock. He was dealing with it when the fence collapsed and it took him a little while to climb down from the attic and open his front door. While they waited, Dossie and Daisy told everybody within earshot that they had had the fright of their little lives, and that Daisy might easily have been killed cos she'd been out in the garden only just before and if she hadn't come back to get a blouse she would have been exactly where it fell.

Though baffled by the reference to the blouse, which seemed to imply that Daisy Fenn had gone out without one, everybody was sympathetic. When Bryce appeared he had to face a hostile audience as well as the shrill owners of twelve rose bushes all squashed flat. But he counter-attacked by saying, as soon as he saw what had happened, that they had no business to fasten their clothesline to his fence and then go blaming him when the weight dragged it over.

"Stands to reason you're pulling it that way, putting wet sheets and blankets on it—and other things too, if you'll excuse me, *ladies*," Bryce said sternly. "Been weakening it for years—"

"We've *told* you, over and over again!"

"Not sheets and blankets, we always send them to the laundry—"

"—and now it's gone, and quite a big job setting it up again, which will have to wait its turn."

"Don't be ridiculous, Bryce. You can't leave it like that!" Dossie went on to point out that the fence lay across their path and stopped them from opening the front gate. Daisy said tearfully that two nighties and their summer undies couldn't hurt any fence, and she had been going to hang out her best blouse and if she had it would have been ruined too, and look at the ends of the posts all rotten like the state of Denmark.

The argument was still going on when Mrs. Custance drove down the hill. Accompanied by Miss Templer she was on her way to Mallinford, where they were to buy plimsolls for Leonard and new socks for Eustace, collect Edward's best summer suit from the cleaner's, and search for cheap articles for the sixpenny dip at the Fête. But seeing the knot of spectators outside The Moorings and The Anchorage she naturally stopped to find out what was happening.

She crossed the road, and the spectators moved aside, allowing her a view of the ruined fence and the three disputants. The Misses Fenn were in full cry, and Bryce, as she saw at a glance, was in his most difficult mood. With a Fenn on either side of him, both shouting, he could not be heard, but his sallow face was creased into lines of obstinacy and disapproval.

Mrs. Custance thought at once of the Fête. It would never do for Bryce and his neighbours to quarrel now, so close to the Day. She had had enough experience of village feuds to know how disrupting such a quarrel could be; everyone would take sides and it would be impossible to get the co-operation she needed. She stepped forward, smiling briskly and impartially at Bryce and the Misses Fenn.

Dossie and Daisy stopped shouting at Bryce and began to tell her what had occurred. Bryce stood his ground, waiting, and as soon as they paused for breath he said shortly that it was the washing, and those that pulled the fence over had better be the ones to set it up again.

Having said this he stepped round Daisy Fenn and walked into his own house, shutting the door behind him. Mrs. Custance sighed, but she did not hesitate. She turned to Isabel Templer, who had followed her across the road, and whispered to her to take Dossie and Daisy into The Moorings and calm them down.

Then she entered the front gate of The Anchorage and knocked boldly on the door which Bryce had just slammed.

The spectators had retreated but were still hovering in the background, and she had a moment's fear that Bryce was not going to open his door. She saw the story in headlines—'Church-warden defies Vicar's Wife'—and she thought how dreadful it would be if she had to turn round and walk back down the path. But just as she was wondering if she should knock again the door opened.

"Can I come in for a minute?" she asked. "There are or two things I wanted to see you about."

Bryce looked suspicious. "If it's about the fence, it's like I said—"

"Not about the fence," Mrs. Custance said hurriedly. (Something would have to be settled about the fence, but she could get to that later.) "About the Fête. The tub for the sixpenny dip, and the bran. Did you say you could get us some bran?"

"Have to be sawdust. That I *can* get, and nice clean stuff too."

Mrs. Custance expressed her gratitude, and Bryce, relenting slightly, added that he had an old barrel that was just the job for the dip and he'd been painting it up; it was out in the garden at the back, if she would care to see it.

Mrs. Custance followed him into the house, telling herself that she wouldn't get to Mallinford that morning but that didn't matter; all that mattered was to coax Bryce into a better humour, so that they could come to some agreement about the fence. She hoped that Isabel, next door, had realized what was at stake, and was devoting herself to the same good cause.

Without feeling, as Mrs. Custance did, that it all depended on her, Miss Templer was vaguely aware that she ought to be tactful and kind and not let Dossie and Daisy make fools of themselves. She clambered over the fence, saying something about wanting to see how it looked from their side, and the Misses Fenn followed her; as soon as they had regained their own garden Miss Templer, like a fussy sheepdog, herded them into the house, and urged them to sit down.

"What about a cup of tea?" she suggested. Daisy, whose emotion had now taken the form of tears, was looking for her handkerchief, and Dossie said loudly that she needed something stronger than tea. She then opened a cupboard and produced a bottle of sherry and three rather dusty glasses.

Miss Templer did not mind the dusty glasses, but after she had taken a sip of the sherry she wished she had insisted on tea. However, it seemed to have a good effect on the Misses Fenn. Daisy stopped crying, and Dossie stopped shouting, and although they continued to speak harshly of Bryce they were no longer, as Miss Templer expressed it to herself, 'screaming for blood'.

"But he'll have to pay for the roses," Dossie declared firmly.

"Perhaps they'll survive. After all, roses get pruned right down to the ground—don't they?" Miss Templer was not sure about this, for she had never pruned a rose in her life, but she was pretty certain that the Fenn roses, like their owners, could weather any storm.

"How can we tell? They're all under the fence!"

"I might have been under the fence too!"

"But you're not," Miss Templer pointed out. "And you never have been, and you never will be. You're not accident-prone. Some people aren't—I was reading about it the other day. Liable to accidents, I mean," she added; for the word 'prone' seemed too closely associated with the fallen fence.

"Aren't I? Well, p'raps I'm not," Daisy said, taking it as a compliment.

"I'm not either. In fact, I'm frightfully lucky, in some ways," Dossie said proudly. "Do you remember, Daisy, when the bus went into the shop window in Mallinford? I'd been standing right outside that window only just before, and if I hadn't remembered about getting the fish I might have been there when it happened. You see—"

"And do you remember that other time—"

Neck and neck, each striving to outdistance the other, Dossie and Daisy raced away with reminiscences of various occasions when they had been miraculously preserved from threatening danger. Isabel Templer drank her sherry as slowly as possible, saying at intervals, "How wonderful!"—or—"That's what I meant". She looked impressed and attentive, but she was thinking about Amy next door, and the total ruin of their shopping expedition. The things for the Bran Dip . . . the Fête itself. . . .

"Has anyone spoke to Mrs. Midge?" she asked suddenly.

"Good gracious, what about?"

"I'm so sorry, Dossie—it was the Bran Dip, and that made me think of the little tent."

Fortunately the Misses Fenn regarded Miss Templer as slightly mental, so they did not take offence. Daisy gave a suppressed giggle, and Dossie repeated her question.

"About fortune-telling," Miss Templer explained. "She does it with cards, you know, and I saw George Brigham the other day, and he said there was a little tent put away in the stables which would do beautifully. But she'll have to be asked."

"But I thought fortune-telling was *off*," said Dossie, correctly linking the Bran Dip and the little tent with the Church Fête.

"I thought Mrs. Custance said—"

"No, she didn't. She said it couldn't be you."

"I don't see why it should be Mrs. Midge."

"It couldn't be you," Miss Templer said, "because everyone would recognize you. Mrs. Midge is such a furtive little person that no one would expect it to be her. Of course, we'd have to dress her up, and pretend she was a total stranger."

Dossie tossed her turbulent curls in triumph. The description of Mrs. Midge as a furtive little person, in comparison with herself, had had its effect. "That's quite an idea," she agreed. "I said from the very begininng—didn't I?—that we ought to have a fortune-teller. Only will she do it?"

"How did you find out she told fortunes?"

"What will she wear?"

While they were still debating it, Mrs. Custance appeared. She had expected to find them bemoaning the fence; she had expected that a great deal of tact, sympathy and cunning would be needed, as it had been needed next door. Everyone knew that Bryce was a difficult man, but she had finally succeeded in calming him down; and they had agreed, over a cup of tea, that he would set the fence on its feet again if his neighbours would promise not to fasten their clothes-line to it. But Dossie and Daisy must now be persuaded to treat Bryce nicely, and not to undo the good Mrs. Custance had done by urging him to make haste, or by alluding to squashed roses or muddy underwear.

With this difficult task in front of her she was agreeably surprised to find Dossie and Daisy in such a good humour. Their grievances seemed forgotten; they were merrily discussing what Mrs. Midge should wear, in her rôle of fortune-teller at the Fête. At any other time Mrs. Custance might have taken strong exception to their interfering with what was, committee or no committee, her own concern; but the relief of seeing them comparatively calm and good-tempered was so great that she forgave them. Besides, a fortune-teller would be a great asset to the church funds.

Isabel told her about the little tent. Dossie volunteered to approach Mrs. Midge. Daisy said she had a friend in Mallinford who would lend black velvet curtains and a crystal, to give the right atmosphere.

Mrs. Custance listened and approved. But there was still a fierce hostility in her heart towards Mrs. Midge, the mother of that wretched Lukin, the unevictable and unwanted resident who ought, long ago, to have gone back to her London suburb. It was only the thought of the church funds that kept her from saying that fortune-telling, like gambling, was impermissible at Church Fêtes.

But gambling did not include raffles, or guessing the number of sweets in a jar or the number of cherries in a cake; and by a similar piece of reasoning fortune-telling was not illegal if it was done on a private lawn, and for the good of a deserving cause.

When everything had been settled—except for the minor detail of getting Mrs. Midge's consent—Mrs. Custance brought the conversation back to the fence.

By this time the Misses Fenn had had three glasses of sherry apiece. They seldom touched anything stronger than ginger-ale and only kept a bottle of sherry in the house in case some mas-

culine acquaintance should appear unexpectedly; and consequently they were now in a mellow, forgiving mood, and quite
ready to let bygones be bygones, if Bryce would repair the fence.

"Poor old Bryce," said Daisy. "I feel quite sorry for him really, though we did tell him about it, over and over again!"

"Over and over again . . ." Dossie echoed.

"But that's got to stop," Mrs. Custance said firmly. "Don't say
a word, and don't try to hurry him. You know how touchy he is.
Just keep out of the way and let him get on with it."

"Wouldn't hurt Bryce's feelings for the world," Dossie protested.

"We'll be absolute mutes!"

Rather doubting it, the mediators stood up to go. While Dossie and Daisy were talking to Mrs. Custance in the narrow hall
Miss Templer got rid of her second glass of sherry by feeding it to
a pink geranium which lived in an imitation majolica flower-pot
on the window-ledge. It smote her conscience, the next time she
visited The Moorings, to see that the geranium had died.

It was now too late to go to Mallinford. Mrs. Custance reversed the car and drove Miss Templer back to Prospect House.
On the way they discussed the Affair of the Fence. Mrs. Custance
said it was a good thing they had been passing at the time, or
there would have been murder done.

"As it is, I don't feel at all happy. They won't *mean* to upset
him, but they're both much too—too—what can I say?"

"Squiffy," Miss Templer suggested, fishing out of her vocab-
ulary a word that had lain dormant for years.

"Oh no, Isabel, I don't mean that. I'm afraid they *are*, just a
little bit, at the moment," Mrs. Custance admitted calmly, "but
I was thinking of their everyday selves. They can't leave well
alone. I'm so afraid they'll annoy Bryce, and then he'll be sulky
for the Fête."

Not until then did it occur to Isabel that Amy's intervention,
her desire to patch up the quarrel and avoid possible bloodshed,
was not sheer altruism but, as one might put it, enlightened
self-interest. The Church Fête was, for Amy Custance, the most
important event in the year; moreover, following on two lean

years, it was absolutely essential that this summer's Fête should be a success.

"Like the lean kine and the fat kine," she said aloud. "No, I've got it the wrong way round."

"What's that, Isabel?"

"Anyway, I drank the sherry in a good cause. Only not the second glass—even the most deserving cause couldn't sanctify two glasses of sticky brown poison. Wasn't it dreadful?"

"I didn't have any," Mrs. Custance answered, abandoning the riddle of the fat kine and the lean kine. "Bryce gave me a cup of tea; he insisted on making it, and it was dreadful too. As black as ink."

"We deserve medals. But perhaps it had better be soda-mints," said Miss Templer, her mind leaping to sodamints, because like medals they were round. "Don't bother to drive up the drive, Amy, it's got a sort of hole half-way up. Quite a deep hole. Cassandra says it's subsisting."

Since this statement purported to come from her daughter Mrs. Custance did not query it. "I expect I can manage," she said, swinging in at the gateway. "There's more room to turn round at the top."

The hole was undoubtedly deep, but she edged the car past it and drove up to the stable-yard. Here they found Eustace Templer talking to Todd the gardener, and before Mrs. Custance could prevent it Isabel jumped out of the car and embarked on a lively, dramatic account of the Affair of the Fence.

Such a pity, Mrs. Custance thought; for the less said about the fence, the better. But she comforted herself by reflecting that, even if Isabel had not spread the story abroad, there were plenty of other people who would be doing the same.

She ought to have been more grateful to Isabel, who had provided Dossie and Daisy with a fresh interest that kept them from brooding too much over the morning's catastrophe. Good and bad luck, clairvoyance, the casting of horoscopes, and fortune-telling in general, were subjects dear to their superstitious hearts, and they regarded a person who could read the cards, or

diagnose one's character from the lines in one's palm, as someone worthy of respect.

Neither of them possessed what they spoke of as 'the gift'.
When Dossie had volunteered to tell fortunes at the Fête she
had meant—as Mrs. Custance anticipated—to rely on her own
knowledge of local affairs, with a little guesswork thrown in,
to carry her through. As she said to Daisy at lunch-time, she
wouldn't have proposed it if she had known that there was
a *real* fortune-teller in the neighbourhood.

The only ground they had for believing that Mrs. Midge was a
real fortune-teller was Miss Templer's vague report of what Mrs.
Imber had said; but this was enough. They liked fortune-tellers.
They believed because they wanted to believe, and already their
opinion of Mrs. Midge had undergone a quick change.

"I always said there was something about her," Daisy maintained. "She's been sort of aloof, hasn't she, all this time? No
one's ever really got to know her."

This was a thing that could be remedied.

That very afternoon Dossie walked up the hill to visit Mrs.
Midge. The Affair of the Fence, which had threatened the success of the Fête by imperilling good relations between Bryce and
his neighbours, was, after all, proving useful. But for this disaster Mrs. Midge might never have been asked to play the rôle
of soothsayer; for if Dossie and Daisy and Isabel Templer had
not practically settled the matter over the sherry, Mrs. Custance
might have let her dislike of Lukin's mother outweigh her zeal
for the success of the Fête.

Even if she had decided to ask her, Mrs. Custance would have
issued the invitation herself, and it would have been couched in
the form of a royal command. It is doubtful whether Mrs. Midge,
who had never recognized Mrs. Custance's authority in village
life, would have accepted her allotted rôle; and the church funds
would have suffered by her absence.

But Dossie's enthusiasm, her ready respect for someone who
had 'the gift', was so flattering that Mrs. Midge hardly liked to
refuse her.

"Of course, it will be a great strain," she said.

Dossie said she quite realized that; it must be absolutely exhausting. She had read of mediums who had to rest for hours after a séance, because they had used up all their vitality. Other people didn't understand, but she did, for she had always been interested in psychic manifestations.

Mrs. Midge's gift had never been extended to psychic manifestations or séances; a little reading of the cards, and a scrutiny of the palms of her friends' hands, was all she had attempted. But she preened herself and said that she was very sensitive to atmosphere.

"I can't live in a place where I'm not in harmony," she said. "I feel *chilled*. My whole life has been a search for the right place—the place where Lukin and I can both be happy."

"And now you've found it," Dossie cried encouragingly.

Her hostess pursed up her mouth and made a small gesture with her hand, as if to indicate that Little Mallin, charming though it was, had not an unimpeachable claim to be considered the right place.

"I hope so," she replied.

CHAPTER XVIII

"WE don't seem to have done half the things we meant to do," Lily said.

Cassandra answered sadly, "I've been much too busy."

It was now less than a week to what all Mrs. Custance's acquaintances had learnt to call 'the Day', and naturally there was a great deal to be done. But Cassandra was thinking of the past month or more, during which a succession of tasks had kept her fully occupied. Choir practices and her own private struggles with the organ; making costumes for the children who were to dance at the Fête; tending the vegetables for the Produce Stall and re-papering the vicarage dining-room, had left her little time for tennis or picnics.

Then there had been the visiting. Mrs. Custance, as a rector's daughter and a vicar's wife, was an accomplished visitor. She believed in it and what was more she enjoyed it. She visited all her husband's parishioners regularly, the old and infirm once a fortnight and the others whenever she could fit them in. But this summer, since her return from Cornwall, she had found herself exceptionally busy, and she had delegated a lot of the visiting to her daughter, in spite of Cassandra's protests that she felt awkward and could never think of things to say.

Cassandra was a dutiful daughter, but she had resented the visiting, and she was now on such friendly terms with Lily that she was able to relieve her feelings by telling her what a nuisance it had been.

"Good works often have that effect," Lily said. "They don't make one *feel* good."

"It isn't all good works I mind, it's just this one. What makes it worse is that I know Mummy simply loves visiting, so it seems very perverse that she should get me to do it instead of going herself."

They considered it, and it was to Lily that the inspiration came.

"There must be a reason," she declared. "She must *want* you to go. Cassandra, do you think she wants to separate us?"

As she spoke Lily was visualizing herself as a dangerous influence in someone else's life; but Cassandra spoilt the illusion by laughing. She assured Lily that Mrs. Custance was very fond of all the Templers and not least of Lily herself.

"Mummy either likes people very much, or else she totally disapproves of them," she said. "And I always know how they stand with her. She likes Fizz and Pop, for instance, but she can't bear Mrs. Midge."

"And she likes Sir James, but she can't bear George."

"Yes," said Cassandra.

She believed it was true. Nevertheless, Lily's bald statement sounded unconvincing; its very baldness, perhaps, made it unjust to both parties. Cassandra could remember a time when George, far from being disapproved of, had been Mrs. Custance's favourite.

"I wonder why she feels like that about George," Lily said.

Cassandra did not answer at once. Sitting beside Lily on the dry grass she looked down the sloping hillside, seeing the valley with the river glinting in the sunlight, the toll-bridge in the distance, the outskirts of Mallinford beyond it, hazy in the heat, and on the nearer bank the small cluster of houses that was Little Mallin. On the flank of the hill stood the church, almost hidden by trees, and just below it the vicarage, where George had once been a welcome guest.

"It's because she's fond of Sir James, I suppose," she said at last. "George has been a great disappointment to him."

"Why?" Lily pursued.

"Oh . . . lots of ways, I suppose."

It was Lily's turn to look unconvinced, and Cassandra felt guilty. It occurred to her—and not for the first time—that George had been badly treated. Mrs. Custance's reasons for changing her mind about George were largely based on a misunderstanding; but it was a misunderstanding, her daughter felt, that could not possibly be put right now without involving them all in an embarrassing scene. Or perhaps a whole series of embarrassing scenes; for she could not be sure what action her mother might take should she change her mind about George again. Better, far better, to leave things as they were.

"How is Lukin?" she asked, less from a desire to know than to divert Lily's interest.

"Very busy, too. He's painting a most peculiar picture. At least, one can't judge it at present because it isn't finished, and I've no right to criticize it when I don't understand anything about the Unconscious," Lily replied, obviously quoting Lukin himself. Reverting to her own character, she added, "Honestly, Cassandra, it's fearfully difficult to know whether he's a genius or—or what."

"What, I should think. Is the picture just another maze of circles?"

Cassandra had been permitted to see one of Lukin's earlier efforts, and it had led her to believe that his genius, if it existed at all, was a geometric genius gone astray.

"Oh no, it's quite different from the others. I mean, one can recognize everything in it, only they don't make sense. There are some sea-monsters, and a bridge upside down, and pink sunflowers growing out of a tomb. That's as far as it's got, at present."

"It seems quite comprehensive already."

"I don't like to ask Lukin too many questions, because he gets cross. You see, he's just made a great step forward, and naturally it's annoying when other people don't—don't—"

"Don't notice that he's moved."

"Well, yes," Lily agreed, laughing reluctantly. She was proud of her two new friendships, and already felt herself a different person from the schoolgirl she had been six months ago. But Cassandra's mockery of Lukin, and Lukin's constant disparagement of Little Mallin and all its inhabitants, were confusing. Far from influencing other people, she found herself the prey of two influences totally opposed; and sometimes she wished she could find a third friend—someone with more experience of the great world beyond Little Mallin—to tell her which of them was right.

"We've not done anything, really, about rescuing Lukin," she mused.

Cassandra did not believe in his genius, but she was quite ready to discuss Lukin's rescue.

"But we can't do anything," she said now, "unless Lukin really wants it. Did you ask him about selling his pictures?"

"I keep on about it, and he does see, in a way, that it's important. If he could sell even one picture Mrs. Midge would sit up and take notice."

"But has he *done* anything?" Cassandra repeated, a little impatiently. Lily was always quoting what Lukin had said; but his flow of talk never led to any action. "Has he tried to sell a single one of those pictures?"

"He doesn't like any of them now, except the one he's painting. He says they're the result of undigested experience and only useful as a chart of his development. He says that their only meaning is for *him*."

Cassandra thought this was the most sensible thing Lukin had ever said. But she reminded Lily that no painter could become famous if his paintings were never seen.

"It's a pity we can't ask your uncle how one starts selling pictures," she added.

"I thought of that, but it's a bit risky. Uncle Eustace is so terribly perspicacious, when one doesn't want him to be."

The discussion of Lukin's future drifted away into silence. Lily lay back on the grass, thinking of the new dress she would wear at the Fête and wondering if she could persuade Aunt Bella to buy her the white shoes, with very high heels, she had seen in Mallinford that morning. After a time Cassandra looked at her watch and said she must be going.

"It's much too early," Lily protested. "Can't you stay for supper as well?"

Since Leonard had started his holidays Cassandra no longer came daily to Prospect House. She had been too busy at home, for the past week, to visit the Templers, and consequently she had not told Lily that Joan Baker-Wright was coming to stay at the vicarage.

She told her about it now, and explained that Joan was arriving that evening, and had to be met. Lily's face clouded; she remembered Joan Baker-Wright only vaguely, as a person to be avoided because in manner and appearance she bore a resemblance to one of the mistresses at her own school. Besides, she knew that Joan and Cassandra had been friends for a long time, and this rather dimmed the lustre of the friendship between Cassandra and herself.

"How long is she staying?" she asked.

"A week, I think. Till after the Fête, anyway. She'll like that, and she'll be a tower of strength. Then I may be going away with her, to a caravan—only she's not sure yet if she can have the caravan in August."

"Oh," said Lily. She half wished Cassandra would say, "Couldn't you come too?"—but she had to admit that she would not like being in a caravan with Joan Baker-Wright.

A little later, having watched Cassandra cycle off down the hill, she wandered back to the house to find Aunt Bella and sound her about the shoes. Everyone had been in for tea, but now the house seemed deserted. She went upstairs to the disorderly room where Miss Templer worked at her lampshades, she looked in the bedrooms and in all the rooms downstairs, and finally she went to the kitchen, where she found only Mrs. Truefitt, who hardly ever left the premises, and the lazy dog Barker.

Mrs. Truefitt did not care for children, but she still treated Lily as a child. She did not go so far as to say, "Run along now and don't bother me," but she managed to imply it, while informing her that she hadn't seen Miss Templer or either of the boys, and probably they'd all gone for a nice walk.

Lily left the kitchen and searched the garden for Felix, who was seldom to be lured away for nice walks. After a fruitless search she discovered her Uncle Eustace, placidly asleep in a deck-chair. She did not particularly want to talk to Uncle Eustace, but before she could retreat he woke up, as bright-eyed and self-possessed as a cat that has been roused from its nap by the faint, distant scratching of a mouse.

"You're looking quite mumpish," he announced. "But it's not unbecoming, that mournful droop of the lip—you should try it before a glass. I've no doubt you will. Don't overdo it; don't forget that pouting petulance is only effective when you're very young." Lily did not care for her uncle in this captious mood, but she could not help being interested when he continued:

"How old is Lukin Midge? I don't know, but he's too old to pout all the time. Have a look at him—it's an object-lesson—next time you see him."

"I will," she promised. She would not have admitted it, but she almost agreed with her uncle about Lukin's pouting.

"I don't suppose he pouts for nothing, mind you. It probably works all right with his mother, who is even more of a fool than most mothers. But just imagine what he'll look like, pouting like that, when he's middle-aged and bald."

"Perhaps, instead of being bald, he'll have lovely white hair."

Eustace ran his hand through his own hair. "Mine was always much thicker than his," he said complacently, "and of course I didn't ruin it by all this clipping and cutting. Nothing worse for your hair than clip-clip-clip every week, year in, year out. Takes all the strength out of it. No, no, Lukin will be as bald as Aeschylus, and just as vulnerable."

"But men must cut their hair," Lily said, wisely ignoring Aeschylus. "They can't wear it long."

"I could," said Uncle Eustace. "In my day—a day which seems to you as remote as the antediluvian age of Noah's young manhood—it was, in my profession, a recognized custom. Painters, poets and musicians could wear their hair as long as they pleased. Of course the fashion was changing, even then, and beards were already extinct, except in a few individualists whose individuality, I always suspected, masked a dearth of chin. But long hair was perfectly permissible. And my hair, as you can see, does credit to Bohemia."

"Your hair is wonderful, Uncle Eustace."

She said it fondly, reverting to the uncle-and-little-niece relationship. She felt that fate had given her a splendid opportunity, and she meant to make use of it.

Seldom did Eustace allude to his former profession; seldom was it possible to mention art, or artists, when one talked to him. But now he seemed to be looking back at the past with tolerant gaiety. Now, if ever, was the time to lure him into reminiscences of an artist's life; and in particular of his early struggles, and how he managed to sell his pictures when he was young and unknown.

Lily set about it with great tact, allowing him his digressions but bringing the conversation back, whenever she could, to his youth. The status of little niece gave her an advantage; it was possible to ask bold, direct questions, as she had done when she was a child and he told her stories, without seeming too inquisitive. It was natural, too, for a little niece to show more interest in the earlier part of Uncle Eustace's career, when he was seeking his fortune like the hero of a fairy-tale, than in his later, prosperous middle age.

She thought she managed very well. The colour of his hair, when he was a boy, did not detain them long, and after he had warned her against dyeing her own hair she was able to ask him if he could always tell, when he painted people's portraits, whether their hair was dyed or not.

Uncle Eustace was in such a benign mood that he did not deny he had once painted portraits; and so, by slow degrees, they came back to his early career, before he had made his name as a painter of fashionable women and successful men.

Once or twice in the conversation she thought she had failed. Uncle Eustace's voice grew shrill, and his answers became erratic. But quite suddenly, and for no reason that Lily could see, he recovered his good humour. After that it was easy. Never had she found it so easy to control and direct a conversation, and never had her eccentric uncle been so ready to answer questions.

The important question had still to be asked, and Lily tried to sound casual and natural as she led up to it.

"What did you do with the pictures you painted, before people started asking you to paint them?"

"How should I know, after all these years? Stacked them round the walls, showed them to friends, sold them when I was lucky. I remember throwing one out of a window at a cat, but it was a wretched daub. A botched monstrosity—and so, for that matter, was the cat."

"But the ones you sold . . ." Lily said dreamily. "How do—how did you start selling them?"

There was a short pause, during which she had to sustain her pose of not being particularly interested. Eustace was still reclining in his deck-chair and she was lying on the grass beside him; she was conscious of his bright gaze as he answered.

"Sell them to art dealers, of course—if they'll take 'em. Or send them to exhibitions and hope some rich idiot will decide to patronize you. Or curry favour with the critics and get yourself talked about, and then give a one-man show. Ask your Aunt Bella how to sell pictures."

"Aunt Bella!" Lily exclaimed.

"When I was a young man," Eustace said, "sisters were there to assist. Bella took a great deal of trouble, in the early days, to sell my pictures. Tramping round to the dealers, blowing my trumpet, persuading her friends to buy. I can't see you doing as much for Felix or Leonard—or am I underrating your sisterly qualities?"

Lily wriggled uneasily. Uncle Eustace's voice was silken smooth, but she sensed that he was laughing at her. She wished very much that she had thought of consulting Aunt Bella.

"Times have changed," Eustace said. *"Tempora mutantor nos et mutamur in illis.* Perhaps it is no longer necessary to be a sister."

He smiled his cherubic smile.

At the vicarage they had a late supper, which was still further delayed because the train bringing Joan Baker-Wright to Mallinford was half an hour behind time. Mrs. Custance, rightly distrustful of the railway, had planned a cold meal, and consequently she had nothing to do but listen for the returning car and see that Edward brushed his hair.

"I do dislike being kept waiting," she said.

She had come in from the garden at half-past seven, and now that she had changed her old skirt and blouse for her second-best summer frock she could not go back to the weeding and watering.

Moreover, the person who was keeping her waiting was Joan Baker-Wright. Of course, it wasn't Joan's fault that the train was late, thought Mrs. Custance, but she might easily have travelled earlier in the day. It was inconsiderate of her to arrive in the evening.

She said so to Edward, who, brushed and clean and tidy, was sitting with her in the drawing-room. He seldom sat there unless there was a Mothers' Meeting or a tea-party that required his presence, and he had unconsciously assumed the kindly, but rather anxious, smile he always used for drawing-room functions. But at his wife's remark the smile changed into an expression of genuine interest.

"She has no choice," he said.

"Of course she has," said Mrs. Custance.

"No, no, Amy, it's like this. Coming from Yorkshire, she couldn't possibly get to King's Cross in time to cross London and get the 12.20 from Paddington. She might get the 2.30, but that's a bad train. The 3.30 doesn't stop at Bramchester, so probably she'd wait for the 4.10. Unless, of course, she came on the 3.30 and changed at—"

"She isn't coming from Yorkshire," Mrs. Custance said.

Some years ago, when Joan had been at school with Cassandra, her parents had lived in Yorkshire, and Mr. Custance could never remember that they did not live there still. Crestfallen—for he had looked forward to discussing with his guest a long and intricate railway journey—he remarked sadly that his memory was not what it had been.

"It's simply lack of concentration," Mrs. Custance said. "You remember what interests you, Greek dates and all that sort of thing—"

"Yes, yes, I always had a good memory for dates. I remember, just after I left Cambridge—let me see, that must have been in 1912—or was it 1913?"

"*Greek* dates, Edward. It's odd, but you seem to find it easier when they go backwards," said Mrs. Custance, to whom the centuries marked B.C. appeared topsy-turvy. "But that's not much use when you can't even remember the date of your own birthday, let alone mine or Cassie's."

Mr. Custance looked flustered. Various classical anniversaries sprang to his mind; but his daughter's birthday hovered vaguely between the Harvest Festival and Advent. He remembered that Amy had been twenty-eight when he married her; but when, exactly, had that been?

"October," he hazarded. "Cassandra's birthday—let me see—"

"November the second," said Mrs. Custance. She sighed. "And she'll be twenty-six."

Knowing what was coming, Mr. Custance sighed too.

"I sometimes think we're wrong to keep her at home," his wife said plaintively. "And yet, if she were to go off and teach in a school, it would be far worse. I don't care for this friendship with Joan, it's so—so unsettling."

She paused. Though she was, of course, fond of Edward, she was not in the habit of consulting him, being firmly convinced that he was the most unpractical of men. But now, perhaps only because they were alone together with no parish problems to distract them, she felt an impulse to ask his advice.

"I sometimes wonder if I made a mistake," she said.

This unnatural remark drew Mr. Custance's attention away from the Peloponnesian War, and he looked at her almost in alarm.

"I was so disappointed," she went on, "and of course he *did* behave badly. But if I'd simply taken no notice—if I'd just gone on as before . . . After all, it's come to nothing. And there's something very likeable about him."

"Who?" Mr. Custance asked anxiously.

But he was left without an answer. At that moment a loud, grinding noise, punctuated by toots from the horn, proclaimed the arrival of the vicarage car. Mrs. Custance sprang up and hurried to the front door. Whatever she thought of her guest it was her duty to welcome her with a smile.

"Hullo, Aunt Amy!" Joan cried. Springing from the car almost before it had stopped, she embraced her hostess heartily, giving her a resounding kiss and a thump on the back. "The train was absolutely the end!" she exclaimed. "I thought I should never get here!"

It was the custom in Joan's family to have honorary aunts, and the mothers of her dearest friends were all in this category. But Mrs. Custance could never bring herself to regard this big, fat, bouncing young woman as an honorary niece.

"You must be hungry," she said, freeing herself from the bear's hug. "Did you get any tea? Never mind, we'll have supper as soon as Cassie has put the car away. Come inside."

She had known Joan since she was twelve. Wherever she travelled from, whatever time of day she arrived, it was always safe to assume that she would be hungry.

CHAPTER XIX

ON THE MORNING after Joan's arrival the weather showed signs of changing. The signs were not definite, just a few clouds in the sky, a cooler breeze rustling the poplar trees at the end of the vicarage garden, but Mrs. Custance shook her head mournfully, and said, with unusual agitation, that she didn't know *what* she would do if it was wet again for 'the Day'.

She made this remark at the breakfast table. Joan, who had forged her way through porridge and bacon-and-egg, and was now enjoying a liberal allowance of toast and marmalade, besought her to cheer up, adding brightly that the weather in August was always a bit tricky, and hadn't she ever considered having the Fête in June?

This did not please Mrs. Custance, especially when her guest went on to say that where *they* lived the Church Fête was always in June, and this year they had made nearly a hundred pounds.

"I wasn't there, of course, as it was in term. I was sorry to miss it, because I simply adore village revels. You must let me help in any way I can, Aunt Amy, and never mind if it's rough stuff. I'm a mass of energy," Joan declared, brandishing her toast so energetically that a blob of marmalade flew off on to the cloth.

Taking advantage of this generous offer Mrs. Custance decreed that Joan and Cassandra should spend the morning sorting and pricing the stuff for the Jumble Stall, which had been accumulating all summer in the vicarage stables.

"I asked Dossie and Daisy Fenn to do it," she said, "and they promised to come yesterday, but they never turned up."

Cassandra hoped they were not having Fence trouble again. "All right, Mummy, we'll do the jumble," she added. "If Joan doesn't mind."

"Just lead me to it! I hope you've got masses, because it always sells so well. We had a Do at the school last term, in aid of our mission, and I was absolutely staggered at the old junk people bought. Of course, it wasn't *all* rubbish, there was some quite good stuff there, and the kids had set it out very well—"

"There's some quite good stuff *here*," Mrs. Custance said firmly, rising to her feet. "You'd better go and look at it."

At Prospect House they breakfasted later than the Custances, and since Leonard's summer holidays had begun it was no longer necessary to leave the dining-room free for his lessons. At ten o'clock Eustace and Isabel were placidly enjoying their coffee, and Isabel had only just realized that the children had all had their breakfasts and gone.

"Did you see them?" she asked. "Are they doing anything special? I meant to take Leonard into Mallinford this morning, to buy him some new sandals and vests. Those sandals I got were much too small, but they said they'd change them."

Eustace shook his head. "Too late," he said decisively. "Leonard has joined the Boy Scouts, and Felix too—though rather, I gather, against his will. Today they are performing a good deed."

"Bonny says they'll be here for tea," said Miss Templer, who had begun to open her letters. "But Henry's postcard, yesterday, said they'd arrive at six-thirty. I suppose Henry knows best."

"Henry always knows best."

"What did you say the boys had joined, Eustace? I hope it isn't one of those shirt things—though they're all banned now, aren't they?"

"Shorts, not shirts; and I spoke metaphorically. Felix and Leonard have gone to Mallin Hall to wash the windows."

"Oh dear, I do hope they won't fall off the ladders. Can't Sir James afford a proper window-cleaner?"

"The windows of the empty wing, where they are serving tea on the Day of Days. I understand that Amy Custance called for volunteers to clean it up, and Bryce press-ganged the local boys into a window-washing squad."

"But Leonard is much too small," Miss Templer said indignantly. "Even if he doesn't fall off the ladder, he'll get so tired. They shouldn't have asked him."

"They didn't," said Eustace. "Leonard asked himself. No one who really wished for clean windows would ask Leonard to undertake the task."

"Oh well, as long as he's enjoying it . . ."

Reassured about Leonard's happiness, Miss Templer turned back to her sister's letter. "Bonny says Wednesday, and I'm almost sure Henry said Thursday. And she says, too—Listen, Eustace!"

But Eustace was not listening, and a glance at him showed her that he was not going to listen. He had left the table and was walking up and down the room, humming a tune. He walked briskly, giving a little skip now and gain, and each time he reached the window he drummed with his fingers on the glass. He was smiling his cherubic smile.

An expression of anxiety appeared on Miss Templer's face. This was what she called 'his war-dance'; and it usually meant trouble. It meant that Eustace had decided on some course of action, and that the action was about to start.

She waited, pretending to be immersed in her letters, and trying to think what could have happened, in the past few days, to provoke him. No one had written to him, he had not been into Mallinford, none of his *bêtes noires* had visited the house. The long dry spell, of course, was conducive to scorpions, but Eustace hadn't bothered about scorpions lately, and moreover the war-dance suggested a larger quarry. In her previous experience, the war-dance had always been directed against human beings.

Without warning, as suddenly as it had begun, the war-dance came to an end. Eustace stood facing her across the table.

"Where's the nearest painter?" he asked.

She drew a breath of relief; for painters were phantom opponents, like scorpions—not like the rector of Mallinford, or, as she had feared, the tenants of Prospect Cottage. Painters (she did not make the mistake of thinking he meant house-painters) were, in this district, remarkable for their scarcity.

"There's no one this side of the river," she answered in a matter-of-fact voice. "Unless you count old Lady Gracey at Long

Hampton, and no one has ever met her because she never goes out, so we don't really know if she is one."

"I don't mean her. There's someone else. Some struggling young genius, misunderstood by his family and a failure in all eyes but his own."

"But, Eustace—" she began. He swept her aside.

"I say 'he' because it's undoubtedly a male. And of course, though all-but-friendless, he has managed to attract a fond foolish female sympathizer who admires his pictures—which are probably chaotically unrepresentational—and longs to assist him. Now then—who is it?"

Miss Templer shook her head. "There's no one like that in Little Mallin," she said soothingly.

"Pay attention, Bella. I've drawn his portrait for you. Are you sure you can't put a name to it?"

"Perfectly sure. But I'll ask Amy Custance, if you like. She knows everyone for miles round, so if there was anyone she'd have heard of him. I shall go to the vicarage this morning, as I can't take Leonard to Mallinford."

She had learnt long ago that it was no good arguing with Eustace about the reality—or otherwise—of his phantom enemies. Argument only excited him.

"Not miles away," Eustace said. "You have forgotten the female sympathizer. I confess, Bella, it had occurred to me that you yourself, though past the age of folly, might have connived at this secret. But I exonerate you."

He gave another little skip, reminding her of a dreadful day when he had nearly got himself involved in a libel action.

"I exonerate you," he repeated. "Blissful ignorance—that's your characteristic. Blissful ignorance! How charming, but how useless. Now, cognizance—that's a very different thing. That's going to be very useful."

The shrill, staccato voice, the bright eyes and the cherubic smile, all these, like the war-dance, were danger signals. But Miss Templer could not see where the danger lay. There wasn't a painter within reach, unless he chose to walk fifteen miles to Long Hampton; and she was quite sure he wouldn't do that. He must have read something in a book, she thought, or gone back, in dreams, to his belligerent youth. Or perhaps it was simply the long, hot summer making him restless.

Outwardly calm, and inwardly only slightly perturbed, she collected the breakfast china and carried it through to Mrs. Truefitt. After that she made her bed and packed up several things destined for her Fancy Stall at the Fête; she would take these with her to the vicarage, and then there would be no fear of their being mislaid before the Day.

Fifteen minutes after she had gone down the lane Eustace set off after her. He was wearing a cream-coloured gaberdine suit and a tidy shirt, and he carried a panama hat. He looked cool, genial, and not a little pleased with himself. Every now and again, like a child contemplating a treat, he gave a little skip of excitement.

It was not far to Prospect Cottage. When he reached it Eustace halted at the gate for a long stare.

So neat, so trim . . . so eminently suitable, in every respect, as a home for Henry Ashford. That lawn, so smooth and weedless, that closely-clipped hedge, those horrible little flower-beds, each star and lozenge clearly defined against the grass . . . why, it was made for him! But there was still the question of getting these midgets to quit.

He entered the garden and advanced towards the front door. From the porch he could look down the length of the garden, and his attention was caught by the wooden building at its farther end —a building approached by a well-trodden path and obviously in use. "That's the place!" he said aloud, and nodded his head in triumph.

The door was opened by Lukin himself, who, at the sight of Mr. Templer, showed embarrassment and alarm.

"Good morning," Eustace said blithely. "Why do I never see you?"

Lukin goggled at him.

"I asked myself that question last night. Why, when we're such near neighbours—and, as you might say, legally bound to one another—do you never visit us? Is it my sister—or myself? Is

Leonard too young for you, or Felix too intellectual? Don't you like the shape of Lily's nose?"

"I—" said Lukin. "I—"

"Or can it be that you have something to conceal? Don't imagine that I'm accusing you; solitude, in the country, is always suspect. If you want to be solitary you should live in London."

Still talking, Eustace advanced into the narrow passage without waiting to be asked, while Lukin retreated before him. The door of the sitting-room stood ajar, and Lukin—perhaps with some idea of taking cover—dodged into the room. But his visitor entered too, and stood in the doorway, looking about him with interest.

"As a landlord," he said, "I can congratulate myself. Such careful tenants—no wear and tear—not even a mark on the walls. It's quite extraordinary."

"We distempered this room last April," Lukin said sulkily.

"You did it yourself? I can see you did. It's better done than Bryce's rooms. But these bare walls—didn't they tempt you? When I was young I never looked at a wall without seeing it as a possible background for a picture. One of my own, of course."

Eustace laughed amiably as he made this confession. He was now standing in the middle of the room, and looking quite at home.

"I was conceited, you know," he went on. "I wanted everyone to see my pictures. And, to be honest, I wanted to sell them. No sense in denying it, money's damned useful. It's delightful to be famous, but it's even better to be rich; then, if your reputation dwindles, you can still be comfortable."

As he spoke he looked about him at the small, neatly-covered chairs, each in a stiff cretonne overall with a hard little cushion to match it. No one who was looking for comfort would have chosen to sit in any of them; but until this moment Lukin had not realized how uninviting they appeared.

"Comfort," said Eustace, sitting down gingerly. "It's not a thing that matters much at your age—I can see that. But there are other things, you know. Oh yes, it's better to sell bad pictures than to paint good ones; and, of course, you may be lucky enough to sell the good ones too."

This cynical pronouncement drew from Lukin a small, half-stifled snort. It showed, at least, that he was listening, and that was all the encouragement that Eustace needed.

"You don't agree?" he said. "My dear boy, I don't expect you to. At your age, one's out for fame. But they're not mutually exclusive, fame and fortune, and you mustn't forget that money is *useful*. Enormously useful. It takes you to places. It buys canvases, paint—and friends. Don't shake your head. I haven't come here to tell you how to paint, or what to paint, for I'm perfectly aware that you, like Lily, regard me as a superannuated delineator of superficial likenesses. I am only telling you—what you must know for yourself—that paintings have got to be hung, and looked at, before they get you anywhere."

"Yes," said Lukin. "I see."

He felt slightly dazed. It was difficult to recognize in this talkative but friendly stranger the unscrupulous and deranged landlord whose existence he had so often deplored.

"Of course you do. But seeing isn't enough. Do noble deeds, not dream them all day long. Or, to apply it to yourself, painting isn't enough. Paint like a genius—who's the current genius, by the way?—but don't think that's the end of it. It's only the beginning."

Every word the visitor uttered made it clearer that he knew all about Lukin's painting—and yet he showed none of the fierce hostility that Lily had predicted. Lily had said her uncle hated all artists. His mother had said Mr. Templer was mad, dangerous, and gave her the shudders. But if Lily were mistaken—and it seemed like it—then his mother might also be mistaken. So Lukin reasoned; and having convinced himself that his mother was mistaken about a great many things he found it easier to believe that she might also be mistaken about Eustace Templer.

He still had misgivings, but presently, as Eustace went on talking without showing any sign of breaking out into frenzy, he so far overcame them as to ask him how he knew about the painting.

"I guessed," Eustace answered, beaming at him. "Only last night, as a matter of fact. You may think it was a particularly brilliant guess—and so it was! But of course, it was simply the last of a whole chain of guesses. There had to be a painter somewhere."

"I don't understand—"

"Of course you don't. But does it matter? Where do you work? I've guessed that as well—in that hut at the end of the garden. Not difficult, you'll say, to guess *that*. No, of course it isn't, it's all part of the chain. One guess leads to another."

Lukin gave it up. As his visitor had remarked, it didn't matter. What mattered (and he could not help feeling pleased about it) was that Mr. Templer, after making the brilliant guess, had come hastening down the hill to talk to him.

He had come, by a happy chance, at exactly the right moment. Lukin was increasingly dissatisfied with his life in Little Mallin; the trouble was that he did not know how to change it. He sometimes felt bold enough to defy his mother, but he was still dependent on her, and he knew that she regarded his painting as a child's pastime, something to keep him quiet and contented at home. He liked Lily, but he could not feel much confidence in her judgement; she was too obviously ignorant when it came to practical details. He had lately begun to wish for a different audience, for someone who would not only admire his paintings, but tell him what to do with them.

And here, in the unlikely person of Eustace Templer, was the answer to his wish. Eustace seemed to be exactly the man he needed, even though he was a little eccentric (one could not call it mad), and undoubtedly, as a painter, worthless. In spite of these drawbacks, he had a great deal of practical experience; and, judging by his cynical conversation, he believed that pictures ought to be sold.

All this, and much else, passed slowly through Lukin's mind, while outwardly he remained sulky, silent, and—as his visitor gleefully noted—pouting.

Other visitors might have been discouraged; but not Eustace. Lily had often remarked his uncanny instinct for knowing what was going on and joining, unprompted, in a conversation not intended for his ears. Now, without needing to be told, he knew that Lukin was anxious to display his paintings.

When, at last, he asked to see them, the pouting modulated into a tremulous smile.

"Well . . . you can if you like," Lukin said, unconsciously assuming the rôle of Little Lukin and speaking in the diffident voice that seldom failed to charm his mother.

With no further demur he led the way to his *atelier*, and there, forgetting to be diffident, he treated Mr. Templer to a long discourse on the true aspirations of an artist, and the profound gulf between painting mere outward appearances and painting the subjective reality.

Beginning with the early murals, Eustace was shown nearly everything Lukin had done. He said very little; as he told Isabel afterwards, it wasn't necessary, because the midget, like all other patent self-inflating geniuses, never listened to any voice but his own. But the little he said was satisfactory. He did not presume to criticize, contenting himself with approving grunts and gestures—varied by a faintly malicious twinkle which Lukin quite failed to observe.

Seldom had Lukin had such an agreeable morning; but it is doubtful whether he enjoyed himself more than Eustace.

"My dear boy, you can't stay here," Eustace declared.

This was precisely the thing he had come to say; and he timed it so well that Lukin never noticed it was his landlord speaking.

"I know . . . I've known it for a long time. But, you see, I'm not free. I can't just walk out."

Implying that he would not be so heartless as to abandon Mrs. Midge, Lukin gazed despondently at the floor.

"Take her with you," Eustace said heartily, as if the idea had just occurred to him. "Why not? Women are useful—like money. Mothers, sisters, you've only got to get them interested in your career, and they'll do anything for you. Cooking, sewing, all the tiresome time-wasting mechanics of life—"

"But she isn't."

"Isn't what?"

"Interested in my career. I mean, she doesn't believe in me. You see . . ."

Shyly, reluctantly (but with increasing zest), Lukin embarked on an account of his difficulties, his unfortunate childhood, his too-possessive Mama, and his total dependence on her income.

"She treats me as a child," he said. "When I went to that place in Wales, she just thought of it as a nice holiday. I came back. But if I said I was going to London, and not coming back, she'd—she wouldn't take it seriously."

'She wouldn't stump up the railway fare,' was the thought in both their minds, though Lukin did not put it in those words.

"She has no confidence in you. Of course she hasn't; women are all alike, they judge by material success, and you've done nothing, as yet, to impress her. Sell a picture, sell several pictures, and she'll start to believe in you. That's the way!" Eustace cried happily.

"But who—I mean, how does one begin?"

"With me!"

Lukin stared goggle-eyed. It was too good to be true, in one way; in another, it was merely what he had always expected would happen.

"Now this isn't charity, my boy." No need to say that, Eustace thought; the midget won't wither away at the sight of a cheque. "I admire what you've shown me this morning. Unlike your mother, I am already persuaded that you've got a future before you, and I'm ready to back my judgement. I'll give you twenty guineas for that picture. No, not that one—the one by your foot."

Forgetting what the picture symbolized, he simply pointed to it, and Lukin picked it up in a dazed way and stood it on a chair.

"And I'll also see what I can do about interesting other people. Mind you, I make no promises. I'm a fossil, and fossils get pushed into a corner, dusty, forgotten. But I'll do my best."

Lukin thought of art dealers, those half-legendary figures for whom Eustace Templer had once, presumably, been a person of consequence. In theory he had no use for them. But all the same, a few introductions might be very helpful.

But Eustace was thinking of his brother-in-law. If Henry became the tenant of Prospect Cottage, an ideal home and far better than anything he could have found for himself, it would be on condition that he bought one, or possibly two, of the midget's productions. It would do Henry good, he thought, to fork out twenty or thirty guineas for a conic section of a lighthouse surrounded by magenta tombstones.

CHAPTER XX

OWING TO THE imminence of the Day, everything seemed to be happening very fast. Everyone connected with the Fête was busy with preparations, and so there was less time than usual for exchanging news and putting two and two together.

Eustace Templer's visit to Prospect Cottage, which could not have failed to excite interest and speculation, went unobserved, because Mrs. Nutting had abandoned her daily work for Mrs. Midge in order to 'lend a hand' at Mallin Hall, where the new wing was being got ready. Several of her friends had also volunteered to help, and they all enjoyed themselves much more, and worked far harder, than they would have done if they had stuck to their routine employments. It was only the employers, bereft of their 'dailies' without, in most cases, a word of warning, who grumbled a little at Mrs. Custance's enthusiasm and her unscrupulous use of other people's domestics.

By Thursday the new wing, or at least its ground floor, had been thoroughly scrubbed and aired. The parquet shone with beeswax, the windows glittered in the sunlight, and the spiders were all exterminated. It only needed the chairs and tables, the tea urns and the crockery; which Bryce was transporting, the following day, from the Parish Hall.

"So now we shall be all right if it rains," Mrs. Custance said, in a falsely cheerful voice.

"Teas will be served in Mallin Hall," said Cassandra. "We ought to have put that on the posters—it would have been such a draw."

Joan Baker-Wright, who prided herself on a democratic outlook, said it was pretty quaint, really, to think there were still people who would trail miles across the countryside to have tea in an ugly old barn like this, just because it belonged to the Brighams.

Both Mrs. Custance and her daughter resented this remark, though their reasons for resenting it differed, and Mrs. Custance replied sharply that no one was being invited to have tea in a barn. She would have said more, but Joan, realizing that her Aunt Amy was upset, hastily volunteered to go and ask George Brigham about the flowers.

She and Cassandra had just brought the last load of jumble to Mallin Hall, straining the springs of the vicarage car to their utmost limits, and they had meant to detach Mrs. Custance from whatever she was doing and take her back to the vicarage for tea. But it appeared that Mrs. Custance still had several things to see to, and among them was the question of flowers.

She had found, hidden away in one of the dark rooms at the back, a number of large and hideous vases. If they were washed, and if George, on Saturday morning, could provide some flowers and evergreens, it would make a pleasing floral background for the teas. He must be asked about it now, because she knew he was at home, and if she left it till later she might forget.

"He's in the kitchen garden," Joan said. "I saw him going through the door in the wall when we were putting that stuff in the coach-house."

Mrs. Custance had meant to ask George herself, but Joan was off, bounding like an overweight gazelle across the empty room, and only pausing, at the garden door, to call back, "Don't forget, Cass, about the exhibition!"

"What did she mean?" Mrs. Custance asked, when Joan was out of sight.

"It's Sir James—we met him in the drive. He's having an exhibition. He's only just thought of it, and he's awfully pleased, so of course we said we were pleased too. A shilling entry fee, and the money goes to the church funds. Joan and I thought we ought to warn you."

"I don't know what you mean, Cassie. Surely Sir James can have an exhibition if he wants to. It's very good of him to bother."

"But it's to be in here."

"Here!" Mrs. Custance cried, looking at her daughter in horror. "Oh no, I can't possibly have it here. I—"

"Not in this room, Mummy, but in this wing. The gun-room, I think."

"That's where we're putting all the cakes and sandwiches, and the urns. Oh dear, I don't want to upset him, but it would be dreadfully inconvenient. What is it, and why didn't he tell me before?"

"Because he's only just thought of it. Objects of interest, I gathered, connected with himself or his ancestors."

"Oh, dear!" Mrs. Custance repeated. "That will be dreadful too —if it's dull, I mean, and no one wants to pay a shilling to look at it. He'll be so hurt and offended."

She had been working quite as hard as Mrs. Nutting and her friends, and she was hot and tired. If anyone else had suggested the exhibition she could have ignored it (for it was much too late to alter all their arrangements for the teas), but she could not ignore Sir James. She would have to appear enthusiastic and agreeable, and somehow she would have to coax him into abandoning or modifying his plans. The thought of it was so exhausting that she looked round for somewhere to sit down, and if she had been alone she might even have burst into tears.

But the room was empty of furniture, and Cassandra was watching her.

"Couldn't you persuade him to use one of those little rooms at the back?" Cassandra suggested. She could see that her mother was on the verge of being seriously 'upset'. Joan had upset her to begin with, and now it would take very little to reduce her to tears—or temper. But of course it was because she was tired out; if she had thought of it sooner she would have kept the news of the exhibition till the morning.

"I don't know," Mrs. Custance said crossly. "It's too bad. Something like this always happens, right at the last moment."

Before Cassandra could reply George Brigham appeared on the path outside the windows. He was carrying in both hands a large flower-pot containing a well-grown palm, and it was obvious that he was bringing this to the garden door.

"That stupid Joan!" Mrs. Custance lamented. "She must have told him we want the flowers *now*. I hope he hasn't cut them—they'll all be dead by Saturday."

Hot and exhausted and ruffled, she did not pause to think that there had not been time for George to cut the flowers—or that it was his home and he had a right to cut them if he chose. Nor did it occur to her that it was not his fault if Joan had made a muddle of the message. As he opened the door and bore his trophy into the room she exclaimed:

"Not on the clean floor, George, *please*! What's the good of bringing them now, when I said Saturday? And what's all this about an exhibition, you know we want the gun-room for the urns. You should have stopped him."

George, clutching the flowerpot, was invisible behind palm leaves. "Urns?" he said in a puzzled voice. "It seems a bit morbid to exhibit urns, though the gun-room is undoubtedly the place. Who ought I to have stopped doing what?"

Cassandra began to laugh. Mrs. Custance, whose sense of humour had totally deserted her, said:

"The exhibition, not the urns. I *want* the urns, *in* the gun-room. If the exhibition's there it will be too far to carry the trays—and anyway a shilling is too much. If you can't stop it, at least we must have it in the little room at the back—"

"Tea urns," Cassandra interrupted, trying to explain things and only adding to the confusion. "Do put that plant down, George, it looks so heavy."

"I will not have that flowerpot on the floor," Mrs. Custance cried fiercely. "Here we've been cleaning the place all week, and you and George just standing about and laughing. Take it away—and if you've cut the flowers you must put them in buckets in the cellar till I've washed the vases, though you ought to have had more sense even if Joan hasn't!"

Even as she spoke she was aware of her own voice, much louder than usual, echoing through the empty room. She knew she had said too much, but she could not, at that moment, bring herself to unsay it. She walked swiftly to the door, and just managed to restrain herself from banging it behind her.

"There's some newspaper in that corner," George said. "Spread a bit out on the floor, will you, Cassandra? . . . Thank you."

He set the plant down carefully on its protective mat, and he and Cassandra exchanged cautious glances across its spiky leaves.

In his younger days George had been well accustomed to these sudden explosions of wrath. Though he had never addressed her as Aunt Amy, he had known Mrs. Custance much better than Joan did. He knew that she could generally manage to control herself in front of strangers, and that it was her nearest and dearest who suffered most when she lost her temper. It seemed to him now that by provoking an explosion he had somehow become on better terms with Mrs. Custance.

This thought, illogically comforting, drew him back to the past, as her words had done. How often, in past moments of domestic crisis, had he and Cassandra been accused of standing about and laughing!

"Too frivolous," he said aloud. "Just standing there laughing, when the water's pouring through the ceiling and my bedroom carpet ruined!"

"Oh, George!" said Cassandra, remembering too.

The next instant they were both laughing. Mrs. Custance, if she had been present, might well have thought that her favourite accusation was justified.

"I meant so well," George said. "I didn't know you were still here, and I thought I'd get the fireplace banked up with greenery, to save time on the Day."

"But it will be all right. I'll explain to her. You see, Mummy thought you'd cut the flowers, because she asked Joan to tell you—I mean, Joan said she would ask you—only it was for Saturday—"

"Steady," said George. "Could you go back to the beginning? I haven't been asked anything, by anybody. I haven't seen this

Joan you keep alluding to, and I still don't know what exhibition I've got to stop."

"Joan Baker-Wright. She's staying with us."

"Oh, is she?"

Cassandra remembered that George had never cared for her friend Joan. Not that it had mattered, in the past; for Joan was so overflowing with general good-will that she seldom noticed other people's reactions, and George had kept his dislike to himself, except on one occasion. Even then, Joan had not perceived that she wasn't popular. . . .

Shying away from the thought of it, and hoping that George had forgotten the incident, Cassandra said hastily, "The exhibition is a scheme of your father's—"

"It would be. Exhibition of what?"

She hesitated. "Oh, I don't know. Old things, perhaps—"

"Old things," George said, in the teasing voice which Cassandra had once, at the railway station, pretended to ignore, and to which she listened now with ridiculous pleasure. "*Valuable* things, you mean. Collector's items from the Brigham repository. The surviving boot that *didn't* get lost at Sebastopol, the tunic that went to King Edward's funeral, the Hun helmet that failed to preserve the Hun. Splendid relics of the glorious past."

"Quite right," said Cassandra. "And there was something about a nightcap, too."

"The one my intrepid great-grandfather shot a burglar in. Well, you know what I mean. But I haven't seen that nightcap for years. I think it got the moth."

"Shame. After so much notoriety."

They catalogued all the other relics they could remember, and invented several that did not exist. But presently George said thoughtfully:

"You know, it's not going to be easy to stop it."

"But you needn't stop it. What upset—I mean, all that matters is that it shouldn't be in the gun-room."

"It will probably matter a lot to Father that it *should* be in the gun-room."

"Then they must settle it between them," said Cassandra, who had begun to think that it didn't matter much anyway.

George grinned, and reminded her that the whole success of the Fête would be imperilled if their parents came to blows. Then, too, they would be forced to take sides; for each disputant would expect his or her offspring to join in, and both parties would abuse them if they didn't. Parents expected complete loyalty from their children, he said tolerantly, but it didn't always work the other way round.

"Father goes about telling everyone I'm a great disappointment to him. He doesn't say how, but the impression has got round that I'm Spendthrift Charles and Black Bartholomew rolled into one."

Cassandra laughed, thinking of the family portraits. The next moment it occurred to her that there was a great deal of truth in that statement; and that George, though he spoke lightly, was speaking seriously. But she did not know how to reply.

"Has he ever said that to you?" George asked abruptly. Casandra shook her head. "No, but I'm afraid he often does say it, to other people." (And they've repeated it, she thought, and it's helped me—everyone—to believe all the other rumours.) She looked at George, who was leaning against the mantelpiece in an attitude of studied indifference. Carefully avoiding her gaze, he remarked: "Of course, I know I *have* been a disappointment. One gets—pigheaded about things. Idiotically determined not to give in."

"Yes," Cassandra said. "I know."

"Do you?" said George, wheeling round to face her. "Do you, Cassandra?"

It was not Joan's fault that she chose this moment to burst in through the garden door, as suddenly, and almost as noisily, as an express train emerging from a tunnel. If George and Cassandra had been looking they would have seen her on the path outside; as it was, they were taken by surprise, and neither of them could instantly summon up the welcoming smile and casual words that her advent demanded. It was Joan herself who broke the silence.

"Well, well!" she cried, panting slightly. "I've been looking everywhere for you, George, and here you were all the time! You might have given me a shout, Cass. How are you, George? It seems years since we met."

Beaming, breathless but unresentful, she advanced to shake him by the hand and assure him of her own excellent good health. Without a pause she went on to ask about the flowers, a subject which George and Cassandra had entirely forgotten; and then she reminded Cassandra that it was after half-past five, and that Aunt Amy had said she must be home by six, because the schoolchildren were coming to try on their costumes.

"Where is she? Washing the vases, I suppose. I'll go and tell her," said Joan, whose boundless energy was such that she positively enjoyed running with messages.

"No, I'll go," Cassandra said firmly. She would have preferred to stay, but she felt that it had better be herself, rather than Joan, who fetched Mrs. Custance from her retreat.

The taxi from Mallinford station, chugging up the hill to Prospect House, had already been observed by Dossie and Daisy at the toll-bridge, and by Bryce as it passed his workshop at the end of the village street. "That must be Colonel Ashford and his wife," said Daisy, advancing to the front gate for a better view. Bryce said nothing, but thought triumphantly of Colonel Ashford's car, which had now been restored to life and which he had returned to Prospect House two days ago. It wasn't often he had a job finished and delivered before the customer was ready for it.

Approaching Prospect House the driver had to swerve to avoid the deep hole in the drive, and Colonel Ashford and his wife, a dressing-case, two cardboard boxes and a lively puppy, were jolted into disorder. As the taxi drew up Miss Templer rushed out and flung open its door, and the puppy, escaping from the mêlée, hurled itself upon her. Barbara followed; the boxes were tumbled on the ground; Felix and Leonard appeared from nowhere and greeted their aunt with warmth, and the puppy with shouts of enthusiasm. All was noise, tumult and chaos.

Isabel alone remembered her manners and assured her brother-in-law that it was nice to have him back again. But it was not the right moment for compliments; he had to settle with the taxi-driver, and collect the cardboard-boxes, and see the heavier luggage unroped and stacked in the hall. By the time he had finished these tasks the rest of the family had disappeared. He stood at the front door, looking out at the neglected garden, and wondering when—if ever—he would obtain a home of his own.

It would not be a home with dogs in it, he thought decidedly. Barbara had bought the puppy without consulting him; but perhaps, when the time came, she could be persuaded to give it to Leonard or Felix. But would it ever come? Was there, anywhere, a house that was neither much too big nor much too expensive? His gaze wandered over the familiar landscape; but the trees hid Prospect Cottage from his sight.

From these gloomy thoughts he was rescued by Mrs. Truefitt, who came out to tell him that Todd would be along presently to help carry the trunks upstairs, and that there was a kettle boiling if he would fancy a cup of tea.

It was late for tea, but Colonel Ashford accepted her offer with gratitude. Sitting at the kitchen table, drinking his tea and absentmindedly eating plum cake, he grew, if not more cheerful, more resigned to his lot. Next Saturday was the Fête, said Mrs. Truefitt, and once that was over things would be back to rights. And Bryce had returned the car, and it looked as good as new.

He was delighted to hear it; it almost made up for the puppy. Mrs. Truefitt, tactful as ever, suggested that he should go and have a look at the car, and perhaps take it out for a trial on the road. To give him an excuse for doing this she added that Miss Lily was down at the vicarage, and if he went and fetched her home it would save her the walk up the hill.

Armed with this excuse, Colonel Ashford got the car out, negotiated the deep hole, and drove to the vicarage. Unencumbered by luggage, the puppy, or his wife, he felt, for the first time for days, a free agent, and as he approached the house his contentment so nearly became *joie-de-vivre* that he executed a short fanfare on the car's horn.

The fanfare brought the vicar to the door. Mrs. Custance, with her daughter and Joan and Lily, was busy in the big room at the back of the house, where sixteen schoolchildren were trying on their costumes for the country dancing; and Mr. Custance had been instructed to listen for the bell, and given messages for Dossie Fenn, and Miss Polegate, and Miss Gregory, all of whom were expected, and told to discourage other visitors from entering, because Mrs. Custance was much too busy to see them.

He had written the messages down on a scrap of paper, but it had unfortunately got mislaid in a book. He was so relieved that this was not one of the expected visitors that he greeted Colonel Ashford with warmth, and had got him into his study before he remembered the embargo on visitors who were not expected.

"No, I haven't seen Lily," he answered, a little shaken by this blunder. "But if she's here—and probably she is—she'll be helping with the children. One hardly likes to disturb them, especially as they will all be undressed, or at least partially unclad. I should explain that they are preparing for our festivities on Saturday."

Colonel Ashford did not see why these preparations required his niece Lily to be undressed, or even partially unclad. But he agreed to Mr. Custance's suggestion that he should wait a little while.

"My wife will probably send the children away, quite soon," the vicar said hopefully. "She will know when it is their bedtime."

Colonel Ashford nodded his approval; for that was the sort of thing women might be expected to know. He looked about him. The sun had now reached the stained-glass window, and the study mantelpiece was spot-lit by red, blue and yellow rays, which showed it to be thick with dust.

"Yes, indeed," said Mr. Custance, following his glance. "I had already observed it—you and the sun arrived together, visitors both welcome and admonitory, or rather, let me say, respectively . . ." Despairing of this sentence, he seized his duster and made an ineffectual onslaught on the bronze bell in its bamboo frame.

Colonel Ashford reminded himself that he was a visitor. But after a moment he was forced to intervene.

"Not like that," he said.

"I beg your pardon? As you see, the sun reveals one's sins of neglect. *Lux in tenebra—*"

"None of my business, really, but you've missed out the tobacco-jar."

"So I have. I am well aware that my thoughts are, too often, elsewhere."

"It's far quicker, you know, to take everything off the mantelpiece, instead of trying to dust round them."

The vicar paused to consider this idea. "Is it?" he said doubtfully. "I should have thought—"

"Of course it is. Dust each one as you put it back. Then you miss nothing, and you don't waste time doing them twice over."

"Quite so," Mr. Custance replied, dusting the Parthenon for the second time.

A few minutes later he was sitting at his desk, while Colonel Ashford, duster in hand, made a methodical tour of the room. As he worked he gave lucid directions; pictures first, then tables and chairs; and don't forget the chair rails, and the mouldings round the door panels.

A delightful visitor, Mr. Custance thought. So kind, so helpful and instructive . . . if only one could remember what he says.

But after this, he thought happily, the room won't need dusting for a very long time.

CHAPTER XXI

Isabel Templer, as she would have been the first to admit, was not a person who could fix her mind, for long at a time, on a particular object or situation. The arrival of her sister Bonny had diverted her attention from the Fête, just as the preparations for the Fête had kept her from worrying too much about finding a home for Bonny and Henry. People might say she was forgetful, yet nothing was completely forgotten; thoughts were simply covered up by layers of new thoughts, like silting sand in a rock-pool, and there they stayed until some chance disturbance brought them swirling to the surface.

It was while she was telling Bonny about the picnic, and its dreadful disastrous ending in the ford, that she revived her romantic speculations about George and Cassandra. She had done what she could, at the picnic, to bring them together; and she had done nothing about it since. Thinking of this, she grew a little pensive, and forgot to answer Bonny's questions, until her sister remarked kindly that, if nothing was the matter with Isabel herself, she supposed it was the children.

"No, it's not," Miss Templer replied, when this remark had drifted through to her. "I was just thinking about happy endings."

She thought about them, off and on, during the rest of the morning. Bonny retired to her bedroom after lunch, to lie down, excusing herself for this idleness by saying that she must take things easy today, in order to be fit and strong for the exhausting programme of the morrow. This reminded Miss Templer that she had promised to be at Mallin Hall at three o'clock that afternoon. She could not remember what she was to do when she got there, but as it was already ten minutes to three she set off in some haste.

At the foot of the hill she encountered the Misses Fenn, also bound for Mallin Hall. They hailed her with delight. It was a jolly good thing, said Daisy, that she was late too; now Mrs. Custance couldn't say it was always them.

"Of course I wouldn't breathe a word against her, to anyone else. But just lately she has been a bit—well, sort of edgy, hasn't she?"

"We're as keen as mustard, really, about the Fête, only we do rather resent her thinking we've got absolutely nothing else to do!"

Miss Templer reminded them that they would be free after tomorrow. To soothe them, she agreed that Amy Custance had been rather difficult lately, and as a loyal friend she made excuses for this behaviour. Mrs. Custance had been working very hard; the success of the Day meant a great deal to her; she was worried because it still looked like rain, and in this fine summer she had counted on a fine day for the Fête.

Dossie and Daisy soon forgot their wrongs. But Miss Templer, walking between them and absent-mindedly agreeing with all they said, continued to think of Amy Custance—and, in particular, of Amy's strong views on men who got engaged to Italians, and neglected their old friends, and disappointed their aged parents. It seemed probable that Amy would make things very difficult for George, if, after committing all these crimes, he aspired to marry her daughter.

No, she thought, it certainly won't suit Amy.

But would it suit Cassandra? She could not tell; and yet, in her fond romantic heart, she was already convinced that it would. There was so much about the present-day Cassandra, when one came to consider it, that was slightly out of character.

"Of course, they might have quarrelled," she said aloud, arriving at this conclusion after an erratic retreat into her own past.

The Misses Fenn, not unnaturally, wanted to know what she meant. But fortunately she was not compelled to invent an imaginary quarrel, for at this moment, as they entered the stable-yard, they were hailed by Mrs. Custance herself, and were at once dispersed to the tasks awaiting them.

Miss Templer's task was the easiest; she was to go and assist Sir James, who was setting out his exhibition in one of the little rooms at the back, and who needed someone to write labels, and hold things, and listen to him.

"And don't forget to admire the *room*," Mrs. Custance whispered urgently. "It isn't the one he wanted, so we must all be very tactful about it."

The little room, though Miss Templer did her best to admire it, was dark and overcrowded. Three tables, spread with white damask dinner cloths, left only a narrow passage for visitors, and at the moment this space was taken up by the various things which were to be set out on the tables.

Sir James, surrounded by family trophies, was trying to decide how they should be grouped.

"Thing is, to keep people moving," he said. "No use having all the showy stuff on one table. Swords, y' know, and helmets—that's what one always looks at first."

With dim memories of the Roman Museum at Bramchester, into which he had once wandered on a wet afternoon, he selected three swords, together with the Hun helmet, a battered topee and the plumed shako which a former Brigham had worn as colonel of the local militia. After hearing the history of these objects, Miss Templer was allowed to put a sword and a headpiece on each of the tables. But almost at once Sir James thought of another, and better, system.

"Come to think of it, that won't do," he said, lifting them back on to the floor. "We ought to put the early things together. Begin at the beginning, and work up, with the dates on labels. And Arrows."

"Arrows?" She had been thinking of the Crimea, but now her mind jumped to Agincourt and she began to search hopefully among the dusty relics. "Is there a bow with them?" she asked.

"Not bows-and-arrows. *Arrows*. On bits of paper, y' know, to show people which way the time goes, and make them go that way too. There's a special name for time in an exhibition like that, Carlovingian or something."

"Chronological," she suggested. Sir James nodded his approval. "D' y' know," he said, "it's a good thing you mentioned bows-and-arrows. Reminded me, there's a pike somewhere about, and that would do nicely for the first table. Or we might hang it on the wall to hide that bad place."

Bit by bit, the exhibition took shape. In spite of frequent misunderstandings—as when Miss Templer visualized the pike as an early angler's record catch—they got on well together. She listened patiently to a great deal of family history, and by half-past five the tables were set out, the arrows drawing-pinned to the walls, and a few dates-on-labels, mostly inaccurate, scattered among the exhibits.

They stood admiring their achievement.

"Pity it has to end with me," said Sir James, glancing with melancholy pride at the biggest table, where the Hun helmet had the place of honour. "But there it is. Young men are all too busy making money, nowadays, to bother about this sort of thing. D' y' know, I asked George last night if he'd got any stuff that would do. War stuff, I meant of course—bomb fragments or even a bit of ruins—"

"A bit of ruins?"

"See that blue tile, with the chipped corner? That's a bit of ruins —brought it home myself, from France, in the other war. Well, as I was saying, I asked George, and he told me he hadn't got anything —unless I'd care for a sack of corn with the firm's name on it. Brigham and Tunk!"

"But he meant that as a joke," Miss Templer said hastily, seeing that her host had taken it to heart. "It's just the sort of thing a boy would say, in fun. He didn't mean to hurt you."

"George isn't a boy any longer," Sir James declared. Nevertheless, he grew calmer, and it was in quite a genial voice that he added, "It's time he got married."

This remark, coming so unexpectedly amid reminiscences of war and the glorious past, took Miss Templer by surprise, and before she could stop herself she exclaimed:

"What a good thing it would be if Amy could break her leg and be out of the way for six weeks so that George and Cassandra—"

At that point she bit the words off her tongue; but it was already too late.

"Amy—break—her—leg!" Sir James echoed slowly. "What d' y' mean? What's Amy got to do with it?" Since his companion had made her meaning ail too plain he did not wait for an answer. "Interfering, is she? *Hr-mph!* I should like to know what she thinks—"

Miss Templer cried, "She's not! She's not!" but the interruption went unheeded. Sir James, in a state of melancholy agitation, was deaf to all voices but his own.

"Old friends—known them for years. Helped them whenever I could. And now . . . !" He stood with bowed shoulders; then, suddenly abandoning his grief, he said fiercely: "What has Amy got against George, anyway? Answer me that. Look at what he's done for them—holidays in Cornwall and Heaven knows what else! If she thinks he isn't good enough for Cassandra she must be out of her mind. And I shan't hesitate to tell her so!"

At this frightful moment Miss Templer heard footsteps—almost certainly Amy's footsteps—approaching along the passage. If there had been another door she would have run away; as it was, she stood rooted to the spot, regretting her own indiscretion and appalled at the thought of the major crisis which now seemed inevitable.

"Not till after the Fête!" she entreated as the door opened. *"Please!"*

Whether the extreme urgency of this cry made its effect, or whether he needed more time to prepare his reproaches, she did not know; but the explosion, though it still threatened, was delayed. Sir James was angry, and showed it, but Mrs. Custance supposed that he was vexed at having to relinquish the gun-room. She did her best to placate him, admiring the exhibits and exclaiming at the symmetry of their arrangement, while Miss Templer, in the background, supplied a twittering accompaniment of half-finished sentences and inapposite phrases, partly out of nervousness, partly because she felt that any pause in the conversation might well be fatal.

"If you've finished, I think we might call it a day," Mrs. Custance said at last. "I've got the car, Isabel, so I'll drive you home. Just come and look at the tea-room first. It really looks very nice."

Miss Templer did not want to look at the tea-room. She felt it her duty to stay with Sir James and persuade him that she had not said what he thought she had said; or at least, persuade him to let things alone. But Sir James was in no mood to be persuaded of anything; he had had quite enough of Amy Custance and her managing ways. With marked coldness he bade them good evening, and walked away down the long passage to his own territory.

It was tacitly agreed that Mallin Hall, apart from the new wing, was out of bounds; and Miss Templer realized that she could hardly pursue him without exciting curiosity. Meekly she followed Mrs. Custance to the tea-room, and praised the tables and tablecloths, the polished floor and the spotless china, with indiscriminate zeal.

Once they were in the car she relapsed into a preoccupied silence. But Mrs. Custance barely noticed it; she knew that Isabel was incurably vague, and she herself had a great many things to think about. The weather, still doubtful, with clouds heavy on the horizon . . . the tiresome last-minute dispute between Miss Gregory and Miss Polegate . . . the non-arrival of a large iced cake, which she had been expecting from an old friend in Bramchester, and for which she had already sold a good many raffle tickets.

Should she telephone about the cake, or wait to see if it came tomorrow morning? But, if it didn't come, there would be no time to get a substitute. Could Cassandra and Joan manage the Produce Stall, if she herself helped Isabel with the Needlework and Fancies—which would release Miss Gregory to help with the teas? They really needed someone else for the teas, because two people had failed her; and if, after all, the day turned out fine, teas would be in great demand.

"Amy, I've done the most terrible thing," Miss Templer said suddenly.

Mrs. Custance, still obsessed with her own problems, asked if it was something to do with the Fête, and when Isabel said, no, not exactly, she advised her to forget about it, at least until after the Day. She was too busy multiplying loaves into sandwiches, and wondering if there would be enough, to inquire what terrible thing her friend had done. Isabel being what she was, it was probably something quite unimportant and trivial.

"Three sandwiches each, and four pieces of bread-and-butter," she said. "Just a minute—I'm counting."

Miss Templer abandoned the idea of warning Amy. With any luck, she hoped, Sir James would have no opportunity, on the Day, to speak his mind.

Sir James Brigham had played at being a disappointed father for so long that one would have thought he could not easily relinquish the rôle. One would have expected him to sympathize

with people who disapproved of George—or at least to understand why they did so.

But although a Brigham might criticize a Brigham, no one
else had that right; and although a father might be disappointed
in his son, it did not follow that every Tom, Dick and Harry (or
their female representatives) could turn up their noses at the
heir to Mallin Hall.

From being a disappointed father Sir James had become a
proud and angry partisan; and from being a disgrace to the family, George had become a good, hard-working boy, a Brigham
every inch of him, and an excellent husband for any girl who was
lucky enough to attract him.

This startling change in his status had not yet been revealed
to George, who was working late in the garden in a final attempt
to get everything tidy for the Fête.

In the library, where he had taken refuge from Amy Custance
and her friends, Sir James sat brooding over his wrongs. Strictly
speaking, they were George's wrongs; but that made no difference. He wished now that he had 'had it out' with Amy in the
first flush of his anger, because anger was a useful emotion that
sharpened the tongue, and one needed a ready tongue when arguing with women. Especially with a talkative, managing woman like Amy. But at the time, even in the midst of his wrath,
Miss Templer's plea had reminded him that it would be rash to
quarrel with Amy on the very eve of the Day. The Fête, since it
was for the benefit of his own church, and was being held in his
own grounds, was nearly as important to Sir James Brigham as
it was to Mrs. Custance.

So he had kept silent. But anger, when it had to be suppressed, did no good at all; in fact it did positive harm, giving
him indigestion and a twinge of gout. No one cared. He was an
old man, sitting alone in a dusty room, neglected, practically in
rags, and suffering from hunger, thirst, indigestion and pent-up
rage. After a life of conscientious endeavour he deserved something better than this.

His eye fell on the bell-rope, a thick, faded cord with a frayed
tassel, hanging from the picture-rail. Someone had looped up

the tasselled end, knotting it round the top part of the cord to keep it out of the way, and he felt sure it had not been like that the last time he looked at it.

It must have been done quite recently—as if Sarah, after months of slow rebellion, had finally decreed that bells should be obsolete.

"Good Gad!" said Sir James. He looked again. He saw, not only the bell-rope, but all the other things—the drawing-room teacaddy in the servants' sitting-room, the gong in the kitchen passage, the tarnish on the brasses, and the holes in all his socks. He thought of the miserable little cutlet he had had for lunch. His anger needed an outlet, and Heaven knew that Mrs. Dixon and Sarah needed reproof.

He pulled himself out of his chair, picked up his stick—though not to assist his faltering steps—and strode across the room. Reaching up with the stick he hooked down the furled bell-rope and tugged at it, vigorously.

At first nothing happened. But after the second or third assault he heard Sarah coming across the hall. She was walking quickly, and as she entered the room she showed curiosity and alarm, peering about as if she expected something strange, or horrible, that would account for this summons.

Sir James spoke with assurance. "I want some tea," he said. "Tea and hot toast. You can bring it in here."

Sarah paid no attention to this demand. She was looking at the bell-rope, which now hung full-length, still swinging from side to side after its brutal treatment.

"We thought you must have been taken ill," she said. "Mrs. Dixon she said to me, 'Oh, Sarah, whatever is it?', and I came as fast as ever I could, though with my feet what they are I can't run like I used to. A dreadful shock it was to both of us—Mrs. Dixon she turned as white as a sheet, I reely thought she was going to faint, and I left her sitting holding her heart on a chair. 'Just you stay there,' I said to her, 'while I run and see what's happened to the master.' There was the bell going like mad all the time, till we couldn't hardly hear ourselves speak!"

This speech, with its veiled reproaches, was designed to bring the listener to heel. Often enough, in the past, Mrs. Dixon and Sarah had won the day by producing bigger and better grievances, and producing them quickly, before their employer could name his own.

But suppressed rage, hunger and fatigue had had a fearful effect on Sir James. He was indifferent to Mrs. Dixon's palpitations; he did not care whether Sarah's feet hurt her or not. He was not going to be intimidated by his own servants.

"That's enough of that," he said. "All this fuss because I want something to eat. . . . Might think no one had ever rung a bell before. All I want is some tea and hot buttered toast. Now go and get it."

Sarah's sallow cheeks turned faintly pink. Using the privileged voice of an old family retainer she said:

"It's half-past six, and you'll be having your dinner at half-past seven. And with Mrs. Dixon so upset, I don't rightly know—"

"I don't care if it's half-past six or midnight. I'm hungry, and I'm not going to wait for what you're pleased to call dinner. Half a sausage and a potato, with bread and cheese afterwards, and everything lukewarm!" Sir James snorted very loudly as he said this, for it was a particularly sore point. "D' y' know, Sarah, you and Mrs. Dixon have been getting very slack lately. Just look at this room—look at all the rooms—dirt and spiders everywhere, sheets all in holes, and not a decent pair of socks to my name! All this damn' nonsense has got to stop!"

"I'm very sorry I'm sure, sir," said Sarah, obviously not meaning it. "Of course, if you're not satisfied, there'll have to be a change."

"That's what I'm telling you. A very big change. Or else you'll have to go."

For a moment Sarah stood gaping, wondering if the master had taken leave of his senses. The threat of departure was *her* threat, and very useful it was too; though neither she nor Mrs. Dixon had any intention of leaving, not after all these years.

"Me—to go?" she faltered.

"*And* Mrs. Dixon," Sir James said ruthlessly. "Plenty of other people who can do the work, if you can't. Heard of two women, only the other day, who'd come any time. You tell Mrs. Dixon what I've said, and tell her I want my meals when it suits me, not when it suits her. I want my tea *now*. And don't stand there goggling!"

Almost before the last words were spoken Sarah was gone, departing with a scurried apology of which the words, "Yes, sir, no, sir," were borne back to him on the breeze of her haste. In less time than one would have thought possible she returned, with a tray on which the silver teapot, the crested muffin dish, and the Rockingham china jostled one another for pride of place.

She set the tray down tenderly on a small table beside her master, as if it were a votive offering intended to propitiate an angry deity. Sir James received it with a noncommittal grunt.

"Omelette!" George remarked, surprised by the change from bread and cheese. His father gave him a warning glance, and waited till Sarah had left the room. Then he said:

"I spoke to Sarah this afternoon."

"You—what?"

"Spoke to her," Sir James said simply, as if it was the easiest thing in the world.

Inwardly, however, he was tingling with pride, and when they had drunk their coffee (strong and clear and boiling hot) he took George into the library and spent a happy evening telling him all about it, with considerable embellishments, and making elaborate plans for his future well-being.

This took so long that there was no time left to tell George about the plans for his own future, and how his father proposed to deal with Amy Custance and her unwarranted objections to a Brigham alliance.

Just as well, Sir James thought sleepily, as he bade George good night at the foot of the stairs; just as well to keep it to myself, until after the Day.

CHAPTER XXII

DRAWING BACK the curtains, Mrs. Custance took one look at the day and exclaimed, "It's going to be all right!"

The cloudless yet hazy sky, the white mist shrouding the garden, the colour creeping into the landscape as the sun's warmth dispersed the mist—all this foretold a perfect day. "It's going to be wonderful!" she cried, too happy and excited to think of going back to bed, or to care that she had woken Edward from a dream of ancient Greece.

The promise of the early morning was fulfilled. At midday the sun blazed down in August splendour; and Mrs. Custance's assistants, hot and sticky from their labours, were glad to forgather in the gun-room where Miss Polegate gave them cups of tea. Mrs. Custance did not altogether approve of this relaxation (though Miss Polegate had provided the tea, milk and sugar out of her own resources), but she said nothing. After all, they had worked very well; the stalls were nearly ready, the side-shows were set out—clock golf, buried treasure, hoop-la, and the rest—and really there was little more to do, except for cutting sandwiches and arranging the cakes, which could not be done till later.

Refusing a cup of tea for herself, Mrs. Custance went out into the deserted garden. She walked through the colonnade, casting a sharp eye over the Gift Stall and the Needlework and Fancies, where she made a trifling rearrangement so that the hideous embroidered tea-cosy and tray-cloth, sent by the Honourable Mrs. Piggott (and believed to be the work of her own hands), should appear to greater advantage. Mrs. Piggott was coming to the Fête, and she would certainly expect to see her contribution in the place of honour.

As the day was flawless they had decided to have the other stalls out in the open. The Produce Stall was at the edge of the shrubbery, shaded from the sun by a large chestnut and conveniently near to a garden tap. The flowers were standing in buckets of water, to keep them fresh, and the lettuces were lying *perdu* under the bushes behind the stall, for the same reason.

"I must remember to tell Cassie they're there," Mrs. Custance thought; and then her thoughts were diverted by the sight of a peculiar box-like structure, rather like a bathing-tent, on the opposite side of the lawn. As she gazed at it George, accompanied by Cassie and Joan, came into view, and behind them, all talking at once, the Misses Fenn and Mrs. Midge.

The six of them approached the little tent, and Mrs. Custance, perceiving that something was being done without her knowledge, went across the lawn to join them.

It is said that we forget the things we do not wish to remember. Certainly she had forgotten, until that moment, that Mrs. Midge would need a shelter, and a table and chair, to practise her fortune-telling. But someone else, without consulting her, had got everything organized.

"Isn't it a *dotey* little tent?" Daisy was saying.

"Just the job, really."

"And we've only got to drape the black curtains round inside—"

"—and hang that long embroidered thing across the entrance—"

"Won't it be rather hot?" Mrs. Custance interrupted.

She did not really mean to find fault; but this was *her* Fête, and no one had told her about the tent.

"Oh, I don't think so, Mummy. We could lift up the canvas at the back, to get a through draught."

"Dark, warm and mysterious," said Joan. "That's what it *ought* to be."

Dossie and Daisy, speaking in chorus, assured Mrs. Custance that the tent was absolutely perfect, and that it was wonderful of George to have thought of it.

These replies, which were intended to be soothing, only irritated Mrs. Custance. It was a perfectly ordinary tent and quite suitable for its purpose, but she ought to have been consulted before it was put up.

She said that the tent was right in the sun and that she was thinking of Mrs. Midge, who would have to sit there the whole afternoon. Mrs. Midge, not to be outdone, replied that they mustn't worry, she would bear it somehow, and it was all for the good of the cause. She indicated that she was used to bearing things.

Mrs. Custance, now committed to championing Mrs. Midge against the rest, asserted that the tent ought to have been put in a shady place.

"But it's here!" Dossie cried unnecessarily. "And it looks so twee, on the edge of the lawn—"

"If only you'd thought of asking me first," Mrs. Custance said, speaking more in sorrow than in anger. She was determined to keep her temper; yet, in spite of good resolutions, she knew that it would be very easy for her to lose it.

It was a moment fraught with peril. Dossie and Daisy were plainly offended by her criticisms, and even the unobservant Joan had grasped that something was amiss. Mrs. Midge, in a voice full of odious sympathy, said that they hadn't even asked *her* where she wanted the tent; and this piece of presumption might have wrecked everything if George had not intervened before Mrs. Custance could speak.

"I'll move the tent," he said, addressing Mrs. Custance and ignoring Mrs. Midge. "There's a place under the copper beech that might do—have you time to have a look at it?"

The situation was saved, and no one felt more thankful than Mrs. Custance herself. It was a way out, an escape from the circle of hostile faces and from her own folly. Now she could walk away, and give herself time to calm down. She could not express her gratitude openly, but it coloured her thoughts, and her lingering disapproval of George dwindled into insignificance.

Almost without realizing it, she had changed her mind again.

Local custom decreed that a church fête should be opened by a member of the clergy, or his wife. It had been easy enough, in the old days, to get the rector of Mallinford, who had sped round the countryside all summer opening church fêtes in the surrounding parishes. But the present rector was not only 'difficult', but notoriously stingy, and since the year when he had opened a fête at Long Hampton and bought nothing but a bag of cooking apples he had not been in great demand.

From the beginning Mrs. Custance had determined not to invite him to open *her* Fête. But this year, since it was to be a grander affair than usual, none of the other local clergy seemed suitable. At one time she had thought of asking the Bishop, but the mere mention of it had reduced Edward to such a melancholy state that she had given up the idea. She had to admit, too, that a church fête in Little Mallin was not likely to appeal to the Bishop, who preferred a more fashionable setting for his rare personal appearances.

In the end she had written to the wife of a canon at Bramchester, who was an old friend of hers, to ask if the canon would officiate. Mrs. Powlett had replied that her husband was already engaged on that day, but had offered to come herself; and so it had been arranged. A canon's wife, as Mrs. Custance pointed out, would at least be a nice change.

Mrs. Powlett was too tactful to accept the invitation to luncheon which Mrs. Custance had felt compelled to issue. She drove herself from Bramchester, in a car nearly as old as the Custances' car, bringing with her a twelve-year-old niece and a fat, lethargic poodle. She explained to Mrs. Custance that the niece and the poodle could look after themselves, and that it was much too beautiful a day to leave them at home.

At three o'clock the platform party—Mrs. Powlett, Sir James Brigham, Mr. and Mrs. Custance, and the two churchwardens— emerged on to the upper terrace. The gardens were filling up, and someone had just told Mrs. Custance that crowds more people were coming up the hill from the village. The sun shone brilliantly, the stalls had an inviting appearance, the side-shows were already attracting customers. Everything was perfect—so perfect that Mrs. Custance, in the midst of her happiness, had a sudden, superstitious fear that it couldn't possibly last.

It was Isabel Templer, of all people, who remembered that Mrs. Midge had not had any tea.

"Poor thing, she's probably quite worn out," she said, thinking to herself what a strain it must be to go on inventing dramatic futures for people, all afternoon, when one glance must have shown that for most of them life was static and humdrum.

Mrs. Custance, who was busy re-grouping what was left of the Needlework and Fancies (what a pity they had not managed to sell the tea-cosy!), replied that Mrs. Midge could go to the tearoom if she needed refreshment.

"But she may not like to come out of her tent, all dressed up like that," Miss Templer pointed out. "If you could just stay here, Amy, I'll fetch her some tea on a tray."

"Better find out, first, if she's had any. Someone else may have thought of it."

Miss Templer hurried away. At least, she meant to hurry, but she was delayed by meeting Henry and Bonny. Bonny had her new puppy with her, and the puppy had attracted a number of admiring children who were trying to teach it tricks. Isabel stopped to laugh and applaud, and to ask Bonny if she was sure she was enjoying herself, and not getting tired. She did not ask Henry if he was enjoying himself, because it was obvious that nothing but a sense of duty had brought Henry to the Fête.

When she reached the fortune-teller's tent she had to wait for a client to leave. Then she made her way inside, and was confronted by a veiled, impressive figure, hardly recognizable, in the gloom, as the brisk tenant of Prospect Cottage.

Whether her undoubted popularity, in the rôle of soothsayer, had mellowed Mrs. Midge, or whether she was simply tired and glad to relax, Miss Templer could not tell; but Mrs. Midge was clearly in a good humour. She did not want a cup of tea ("I never take anything," she explained, "while I'm doing this"), but she would love a cigarette. Fortunately Miss Templer had cigarettes in her bag. After they had peeped out and made sure there were no clients waiting they settled down, one on each side of the table, for a smoke and a chat.

Cassandra thought the Fête was being a great success, but she wished her mother had not decided to leave the Produce Stall entirely to her and Joan. Flowers and vegetables, homemade jam and bottled fruit, were all in great demand; they were kept busy, and they had no time to look at the other stalls or to walk about the garden and talk to friends.

Resigned to being a vicar's daughter, she did not mind this so much for herself, but she minded it for Joan, who had worked so hard, and been so resolutely jolly—and whose energy and jollity were now, alas, proving a little wearisome.

"Sixpence more for the Cause," said Joan, dropping the money into the wooden bowl.

At the start Cassandra had laughed at this jest, then she had smiled, and now she ignored it.

"I'll get some more lettuces," she said. The reserves of lettuces were still hidden in the shrubbery, to be fetched out as the stall emptied. "I think they're nearly all gone," Joan said over her shoulder, busily weighing out plums. "But I tell you what, Cass—there are some lettuces in the kitchen garden, here, that George said I could have if we ran short. I asked him about them this morning."

For some reason this speech vexed Cassandra, though it only showed how practical Joan was, compared to herself. It had not occurred to her, that morning, to look ahead and arrange for an extra supply of lettuces; and even if she had thought of it, she would have hesitated to ask George, who had already done so much for the Cause. . . . But that's silly, she thought, because it wouldn't be asking for oneself. . . .

"Hist!" Joan said loudly. "Wake up, Cass—you were miles away. If you'll hold the fort I'll just pop off and get my lettuces."

"You stay here. I'll get them."

She knew that this, too, was silly, yet she resented the proprietary way in which Joan spoke, as if the wretched lettuces belonged to her.

"You don't know where they are."

"Of course I do."

Without giving Joan time to argue she picked up an empty basket and walked off.

The kitchen garden was surrounded by a high wall. It lay at the back of the house, behind the stable-yard, and consequently the visitors to the Fête had not discovered it. Cassandra came through the green door, and, seeing no one, shut it behind her with a slam, as if she were shutting out the chatter, the crowds and the fatigue of the Day. She walked slowly down a path between cordoned apple trees. At the end of this path there was a small herb garden enclosed by a yew hedge, where she and George, as children, had sometimes taken refuge from their elders and betters.

It had been an excellent hiding-place, for you could not be seen unless the person seeking you took the trouble to walk down the long path and enter the enclosure. She was thinking about this as she stepped through the archway in the hedge. Absorbed in memories of the past, she did not at once perceive that the herb garden already had an occupant.

"Hullo," George said quietly.

Cassandra, taken by surprise and, for obscure reasons, at a disadvantage, cried his name aloud, and then added quickly, "How you startled me!"

"I'm sorry. But you startled me, too."

"I—I didn't mean to disturb you," she said, as if George was a fractious invalid. "I mean, I really came to get some lettuces."

"A good excuse for getting away from the Fête."

It was quite true, but she perversely chose to deny it. "We *need* the lettuces," she declared. "They're selling very well, and we've hardly any left."

"You must be making a lot of money."

"Oh, we are! Pounds and pounds."

"Splendid for the church."

Cassandra wondered why she and George were talking in this unnatural and ridiculous manner, like mere acquaintances grasping at conversational straws. But although she regretted it, a stiff self-consciousness forced her to continue.

"Mother will be awfully pleased," she said.

"She deserves a success," George answered dutifully, "after all she's done."

"And Joan too; Joan has worked so hard. She's a wonderful saleswoman."

"I can quite believe it."

Surprisingly, this innocuous reply put an end to the exchange of polite platitudes.

"What do you mean?" Cassandra demanded.

"Just what I said."

Because Joan had got on her nerves, Cassandra was obstinately determined to defend her. It wasn't fair that George should make fun of her when she was working so hard—and when he had crept away from the Fête to laze in this secluded spot.

"You were laughing at her," she insisted. "Pretending that she bullies people into buying, and—and—"

"I didn't say so. But anyway—"

"That's what you meant. I know from your voice."

"You know me too well," he answered. "Or you think you do."

Cassandra was uncertain what to make of this; she did not know, now, whether George was laughing or not. Perhaps he was angry. It would not be the first time she had driven him to anger; but on this occasion the thought brought her no consolation.

"I'm sorry," she said.

"And about time too," said George.

It was not what she had expected him to say. But why had she said, in the first place, that she was sorry? She felt confused, almost panic-stricken, by the thronging memories that her own words, and his reply, had somehow conjured up; it was as if the garden, in broad daylight, had revealed its ghosts.

There was a prolonged silence; a silence in which each looked back at the past.

"All right, I was laughing at her," George said at last. "But it isn't so funny really. If you hadn't had that Amazon for your best friend, you might not have turned me down."

He spoke without bitterness, as if he were simply stating a fact. But Cassandra stared in astonishment, feeling that George s recollection of the past must be totally different from her own.

"But that's absurd," she cried. "I know she interrupted us, but that was afterwards—and anyway she didn't mean to."

"Meaning to or not meaning to, she has an absolute genius for coming in at the wrong moment."

"But Joan had nothing to do with it. I know I was proud and silly, but it wasn't because of her—it was because you took everything for granted, and Mummy kept hinting and hinting. I don't suppose—"

She broke off, forgetting what she had been going to say in the sudden realization of what she had already said.

"Were you?" George asked, in a voice that no longer mocked her. "So was I. Very proud and very silly."

Cassandra heard herself declaring that it was all her fault. But whether it was she who had been proud and silly, or George, or both of them, mattered not at all, since pride and silliness were now relegated to the past; and George, for the second time in her life, was asking her to marry him.

She supposed, afterwards, that she had said Yes. She must surely have said something, she could not have just stood there, silent with happiness, nor could George have proposed to her in dumb-show. But what he said, and what she answered, escaped her memory; happiness blotted out everything else.

"But I didn't think you still loved me," she said later.

"I tried to pretend I didn't. I was so certain you didn't love me."

Each had long regretted their estrangement, and each had been ready to believe that the other was fickle or indifferent. From these misunderstandings they were set free; and although they allowed themselves the luxury of repentance, they were too conscious of the present to trouble overmuch about the past.

The past was not ignored, but it no longer had the power to hurt them. Nor did they wonder (since the rest of the world had grown invisible and the Fête had ceased to exist) whether other people, and one person in particular, would be equally ready to forget and forgive. The nearest they got to discussing it was when Cassandra reproached herself for the harsh and scornful way in which she had rejected George's earlier proposal.

"I was so horrid to you," she said.

"I deserved it, didn't I? The conquering hero, returning home, thinking it a foregone conclusion that you would marry me as soon as I asked you."

"Darling George, don't exaggerate! That's only partly true, and anyway I would have been quite ready to marry you, if only—"

"If only you hadn't felt you were being pushed into it."

"Well, yes. Such obvious scheming and matchmaking. I felt like an eastern slave, up for sale."

Safe in his arms, she could laugh at it now. It was a pity, she said, that her mother had never known about that earlier proposal, because in her ignorance she had blamed the wrong person for the failure of her hopes. But George thought it better that he should be blamed than Cassandra.

If Mrs. Custance had known that George, home on leave at the end of war, had proposed to her daughter and had been refused, she might indeed have sympathized with him. But it is doubtful whether she would have understood that pique, and wounded pride, were responsible for the engagement that followed, so soon after his return to Italy.

But Cassandra understood too well how resentment and pride could act; for if he had behaved foolishly, so had she. She had chosen to feel slighted, she had met him with a cool indifference that forbade allusions to the past, she had persuaded herself that he was heartless, and that he had never loved her. It had not been possible, even at the height of her anger, to persuade herself that she did not love him.

"I was so unhappy," she confessed. "And it's been getting worse and worse, ever since I began to admit that it was mostly my own fault. I feel now that I couldn't have borne it much longer. If you hadn't proposed to me I should have proposed to you."

George said he was almost sorry he hadn't waited to be proposed to, especially as his own effort had been breathless, clumsy and abrupt.

"I meant to stage it much better than this," he said. "I was only waiting till after the Day."

"Oh, George, that's what everyone has been saying for weeks, about everything. 'After the Day.' Feuds, tea-parties, shopping . . . and even asking me to marry you!"

"Only because I wanted your undivided attention."

"But nothing could possibly distract me—" she began.

Smiling at his dear Cassandra's anxiety, George assured her that nothing had. "Even the lettuces," he said, "have had a reprieve."

"Good gracious, the lettuces!"

The confessions of past stupidity and the avowals of present happiness had taken a considerable time; but Cassandra, like the spellbound heroine of a fairy-tale, was unaware of passing time. "I'd better get some lettuces," she continued. "Joan will be waiting for them."

"Unless she's gone home."

For a moment Cassandra looked blank. Then, seeing the long shadow of the yew hedge and the changing light in the evening sky, she understood, and tried with no great success to feel penitent and ashamed. After all, the Fête was an important event, and she had been brought up to take it seriously.

"Never mind, my love," George said teasingly. "It isn't everyone who gets engaged at a church fête."

"And it will give the committee something to talk about, when the accounts won't come right," she replied, ignoring the fact that no committee which included Dossie and Daisy had ever been known to run short of conversation.

CHAPTER XXIII

THE COUNTRY-DANCING by the schoolchildren was a popular spectacle and always attracted a large audience. No charge was made for the entertainment but it took place late in the day, after tea, so that people who might otherwise have left early were induced to remain, and to while away the time by eating ices, or spending a little more money on side-shows and competitions. The only drawback to the arrangement was that the performers themselves sometimes suffered from a surfeit of ices before their hour of glory arrived; but this year the schoolmistress had insured against the danger by promising them a feast of ices and left-over cakes when the dancing was ended.

When the Fête was held at the vicarage the children had to dance on the tennis-court, and Mrs. Custance could not really enjoy it for thinking of the damage their stamping and leaping would inflict on her mossy grass. At Mallin Hall, however, the performance was to take place on the lower lawn, so that everyone could watch from the upper lawn and the steps, and she was looking forward to it with pleasure. It would be the final triumph of a long, successful afternoon.

This made it all the more disappointing that she had to forgo the spectacle. The dancing began, and Miss Templer was still absent; the dancing progressed, and she did not return. Miss Gregory had been sent to help with the teas and had stayed to do the washing-up, and Mrs. Custance was far too conscientious to leave the Needlework and Fancies to look after themselves. Her constancy was rewarded when a total stranger, whom she never managed to identify, came up and bought Mrs. Piggott's tea-cosy, remarking that it was just what she wanted; but although this was, in its way, a tribute to good salesmanship, it did not compensate for Isabel's defection.

Before the dancing ended she glanced across the now empty garden and noticed that the Produce Stall, like her own, had only one attendant. It was Joan; so Cassandra must have gone to watch the schoolchildren. She thought no more of it, for just then an outburst of clapping proclaimed the finish of the performance, and people began drifting back across the upper lawn.

A few minutes later Miss Templer came hurrying through the colonnade. Mrs. Custance thought that Isabel was hurrying to atone for past neglect, but she was wrong.

"I've had a most absorbing conversation," Isabel whispered breathlessly. "Extremely confidential, of course—why is it that people like Mrs. M., who normally keep one at arm's length, will suddenly unbosom themselves . . . oh dear, that's all arms and bosoms, it's because we've been talking about painting. Anyway, why did she pour it all out to me, when I'm practically a total stranger?"

"Talking of total strangers—" Mrs. Custance began.

"Yes—why does one? I mean, what makes a stranger a total one? Surely—"

Losing patience, Mrs. Custance said loudly that it didn't matter. "You've been away for hours," she declared untruthfully, "and I missed the dancing."

Then, feeling a little ashamed of her petulance, she added, "But I sold the tea-cosy."

"How clever of you, Amy! I couldn't have done that. Who bought it?"

"A total stranger," Mrs. Custance repeated firmly. The phrase went unnoticed this time, for Isabel wasn't listening. "I can't get over it," she said, as if Mrs. Custance had not spoken. "If I'd known at the time—! But of course I did know—at least I knew that something was up, because of the war-dance. Only of course I didn't know it was a *real* painter."

Mrs. Custance was busy selling the last three lavender-bags. "There wasn't a war-dance," she answered, speaking partly to Isabel and partly to the woman in front of her. "Unless they did one as an encore."

"I don't mean that. I mean Eustace."

"That'll be ninepence change. Thank you so much."

"Ever so pretty, the dancing was," said the buyer of the lavender-bags, and embarked on a long account of it. When she had gone several other acquaintances came up to bid Mrs. Custance farewell and congratulate her on a wonderful afternoon. The Day was drawing to its close, there was a general movement towards the gates, and the crowd on the lawns was perceptibly thinner. Mrs. Custance straightened her back and surveyed the scene. She was tired but triumphant, and almost sorry that her splendid, successful Fête was nearly over.

"To think of Eustace buying a picture!" Miss Templer remarked. "It just shows, doesn't it, that one's nearest and dearest are much cleverer than one expects. I'd never have credited him with so much cunning."

"What picture?" Mrs. Custance demanded. "What are you talking about?"

"About Mrs. Midge and Lukin. Did you know, Amy, that Lukin is a painter?"

"That wretched boy!" Mrs. Custance exclaimed automatically.

Then, piecing together Isabel's disjointed remarks, she realized that something out of the ordinary must have happened. "Tell me from the beginning," she said.

"That's just what I am doing, but you aren't listening. It was cunning of him to buy the picture, because now Mrs. M. thinks Lukin could sell more pictures, if he was—what did she say?—'in the swim'. And of course he isn't in the swim, down here. So she is seriously thinking of moving."

Mrs. Custance drew a deep breath of satisfaction. She could not make head or tail of Isabel's story; the war-dance, the 'real' painter (could he be Lukin?), and Eustace's behaviour, were baffling mysteries; but here was something concrete, and greatly to her liking.

"That will be a very good thing," she said. She would have gone on to say more, but her attention was diverted to the Produce Stall. Now that the crowd had dwindled she could see it plainly once more. But she could not see Cassandra.

The Produce Stall was still doing business, for it was the custom, at the end of the Day, to sell off cheaply what flowers and vegetables remained, and several buyers had gathered round in the hope of last-minute reductions. Joan, in a bright yellow frock, was easily identified, and none of the other figures could possibly be Cassie. She was not there; and she had not been there at the time of the country-dancing.

A sudden misgiving assailed Mrs. Custance, though she told herself that there couldn't possibly be anything wrong. "I must just see what's happening," she said aloud. "Yes, Isabel, I think we can begin packing up now. But I must just have a word with Joan first."

When she reached the Produce Stall her misgivings were justified by Joan making questioning faces at her over a customer's shoulder. As soon as the customer had departed Mrs. Custance edged round behind the stall and asked, "Where is Cassie?"

"Honestly, Aunt Amy, I haven't an idea," Joan replied, as if she had been accused of kidnapping Cassandra. "I just can't *think*. I mean, I'm not complaining, because I absolutely adore this sort of thing and I'm always ready to hold the fort just as long as I'm wanted. Only it seems—well, a bit much, doesn't it, just to walk out on me?"

She gave a laugh, which, to her credit, was tolerant and even jolly, and added that a friend was a friend but all the same Cass was straining the bonds of friendship pretty thin.

Mrs. Custance interrupted impatiently to ask when Cassie had gone, and where.

"Absolutely ages ago, just after tea. Actually, I didn't have any tea, but I'm not complaining, because—"

"*Where* did she go?" Mrs. Custance said ruthlessly. Joan explained about the lettuces, and pointed out that it couldn't have taken a quarter of an hour to pick them and bring them back. "I thought at first she might be having a look round the other stalls," she said. "But I've kept my eyes skinned, and I haven't caught a glimpse of her."

It was this suggestion that made Mrs. Custance think of Sir James and his exhibition. Cassie might well have looked in to see how he was getting on; and perhaps, if he was alone and disconsolate, she had found it difficult to escape. Of course, it was very wrong of her to leave Joan for so long—but it was equally wrong of Joan to be giving herself such airs and talking about not complaining, when she was complaining with every second breath.

"You stay here," she commanded, "and I'll go and look for Cassie." Joan started to say that she would be quicker, but at the sight of her Aunt Amy's face she broke off, and said instead that she would just go on holding the fort.

Mrs. Custance made her way to the house. The front door stood open, and she went in that way to avoid Miss Polegate and her assistants. But as she crossed the hall Sir James came out from the long passage that led to the new wing, and since she had assured him that no one would set foot in Mallin Hall (apart from the new wing), she felt at a slight disadvantage, and began by apologizing for her presence.

"No, no, Amy," he protested. "Glad to see you any time." But he spoke in a perfunctory way, and she noticed that he was stooping more than usual—a sure sign that something was amiss. Before she could ask him if he had seen Cassie, he announced that the exhibition was closed, and that he had only taken thirty-seven shillings, in spite of making it half-price after tea.

"That's not at all bad," she answered, thinking to herself that it was more than she had expected. "I'm sure you must be tired, but it's well worth it. Have you been there all the time?"

"Practically the whole afternoon."

This was not quite true, for he had installed Mrs. Dixon as his deputy while he had tea, and a short nap, in the library, but it seemed to him that many weary hours had elapsed since the opening of the Fête.

"Didn't see many of my old friends," he continued. "Custance came, of course—brought Mrs. Who's-it, the one who did the opening. And then old Piggott came, and we had quite a talk. I haven't seen old Piggott for a long time, not since he had the measles."

"I hadn't heard about that," said Mrs. Custance.

"Must be six months ago. Serious business at his age. Real ones, y' know, not German." Caressing his moustache, Sir James added in a voice of subdued triumph that the measles had aged old Piggott considerably.

"Did Cassie come?" Mrs. Custance asked.

"Cassandra? No, she didn't. D' y' know, Amy—"

"I can't think where she's got to."

If she had not been worrying about Cassandra Mrs. Custance would have known better than to interrupt him. Although she ranked as an old friend she was, after all, the wife of his parson; and although she was a woman, Sir James's conventional respect for the fair sex did not interfere with his belief that women should be seen and not heard.

"Hr-mph!" he said loudly; so loudly that Mrs. Custance, who had been about to continue her search, decided that she had better wait and hear more about the exhibition. Perhaps she had not asked enough questions, or perhaps she owed him an apology for not having been to the exhibition herself. Of course she hadn't had a moment, but he had probably expected her to come.

"If I hadn't been so busy I would have paid you a visit," she said. "I know I saw it yesterday, but I meant to come today as well. I'm sure Edward found it very interesting. All those swords and—and other Brigham relics."

"Wouldn't have interested *you*, Amy," Sir James said, with a melancholy emphasis that puzzled her. "Brigham relics! Well, well—I suppose the Brighams were all right in the past. Not good enough for the present—eh?"

Mrs. Custance could only suppose that fatigue and disappointment had engendered in him the morbid humour that led, if one was not careful, to talk of tombstones, the hymn he wanted for his funeral ("It's marked in my big hymn book"), and the unlikelihood of George's doing anything about that window in the church. To avert this conversation she gave a brisk laugh and said cheerfully that she was always interested in family history, but it did no good to compare past and present.

"Things have changed so completely," she declared. "It's not the same world, and naturally we all think we're much worse off. Now, Mrs. Powlett was telling me . . ."

Sir James was fond of discussing his acquaintances, and an anecdote about someone else's misfortune often distracted him from his own sorrows. But this time it had no success, and he listened with obvious impatience to the tale of the Bishop's difficulties in maintaining his unwieldy palace.

"What's that got to do with it?" he burst out at the end. "Feller didn't *have* to be a bishop, did he? No, no, Amy, that's not what we were talking about."

He looked at Mrs. Custance accusingly; and she, in her turn, looked despairingly at the grandfather clock that stood at the foot of the stairs. She ought to be thanking her assistants; she ought to be saying good-bye to Mrs. Powlett; and she still hadn't found Cassandra. But even as she started to frame a sentence that should be at once soothing and valedictory, Sir James turned away and walked across the hall to the library door.

"Talk better in here," he said over his shoulder. He held the door open for her. and after a moment's hesitation she followed him across the hall and entered the room.

"I mustn't stay long," she said.

"The Fête's over, isn't it?" Sir James retorted. "I said I'd wait till after the Day, and so I did. Now, I just want to have a word with you."

'Which of us is it?' thought Mrs. Custance. But she had no real doubt of the answer. It must be Edward.

On previous occasions it had always been Edward who, through tactless zeal or sheer forgetfulness, had succeeded in enraging his patron to the point of 'having a word'—which meant a great many words—with one or the other, and bringing them both into disgrace.

Looking as meek as she could, she sat down on a straight-backed oak chair. Sir James was standing at the window, and beyond him she had tantalizing glimpses of the garden, where her assistants were joyfully discussing the Day's events and reckoning up their takings. She longed to be with them; but if Edward had committed some fearful blunder it was essential that she should find out what it was and, if possible, put things right.

Sir James embarked on a preamble, in which the words 'old friends', and 'known each other for years', occurred more than once. This was his usual way of approaching a grievance. Mrs. Custance did not listen very attentively (for she was busy formulating possible blunders), until he said:

". . . and then I hear *this*. In my own house, too. He's not good enough for you—eh? Good Gad, Amy, you've no business to say a thing like that. It's—it's worse than unkind. It's downright untrue."

Because her mind was occupied with Edward, Mrs. Custance leapt to the conclusion that it was Edward who wasn't good enough for her. "But who said so?" she expostulated. "Who told you such a thing?"

"Miss Templer. Didn't mean to let it out, I dare say. But when I thought it over, y' know, I could see she was right. You've always had a down on him, ever since after-the-war."

"Isabel!" Mrs. Custance cried.

"Said you ought to break your leg. Just a figure of speech, her saying that," Sir James added chivalrously. "Women always exaggerate. All she meant, y' know—"

"*Isabel* said I ought to break my leg!"

"—to keep you from interfering. But that's all wrong; they make you walk about these days. Thurstan's wife broke her leg last year, and they puddled it up with plaster and she was as spry as a grasshopper. It was just a figure of speech."

To Mrs. Custance it was not a figure of speech, but the blackest treachery. She stood up, and said in a voice of wrath:

"I'd like to know what Isabel means—"

"Thing is, Amy, you had no business to criticize him. Think of all he's done for you. It's so damned ungrateful."

"—break my leg. How dare she! And gossiping about me behind my back—"

They were both speaking at once, and Mrs. Custance had quite forgotten that she had come there to intercede for Edward. The shock of finding that it was herself who had incurred Sir James's displeasure had been intensified by his monstrous accusation, which had not a word of truth behind it—or only the absurd distortion of truth that Isabel might have drawn from wifely grumbles.

Each antagonist felt grievously wronged; and neither listened to the other. Mrs. Custance's voice grew shriller and shriller. Sir James, who was determined not to be shouted down by Amy, boomed out sonorous phrases that echoed round the room like the reverberations of muffled drums.

George and Cassandra, entering the house to look for their respective parents, stopped half-way across the hall and exchanged questioning glances. The sounds that filtered through the library door were undoubtedly sounds of dispute.

"Something seems to have upset them," George said tolerantly.

"Could it be us?"

"I don't see how they could know. Anyway, we'd better find out."

"Darling, how brave," Cassandra mocked him.

"I am brave," said George. "Come on."

"What's the matter with the boy?" Sir James roared suddenly, as the library door opened. This question, delivered *fortissimo*, reached Mrs. Custance's ears even above the sound of her own voice—as George said afterwards, it was probably heard at the toll-bridge—and reduced her to a bewildered silence. For few people, and certainly not Sir James, would think of referring to Edward Custance as 'the boy'.

For a moment Sir James was silent too, not because he had no more to say, but because he had seen George and Cassandra at the door. He had been about to catalogue his son's virtues, but he could hardly do this now that his son was in the room. He coughed, and frowned meaningly at George, indicating that he should withdraw and take Cassandra with him. But George stood his ground.

"But you said—" Mrs. Custance began.

"Tss, tss!" said Sir James, turning the meaning frown in her direction and augmenting it with hand signals. She looked over her shoulder and perceived her dear daughter advancing towards her. Even in the midst of her bewilderment and anger it struck her that Cassandra was looking very pretty.

"Cassie! Where on earth have you been?" she exclaimed.

"Well, Mummy . . ."

Having got so far, Cassandra stopped, feeling that it was not the best moment to break the great news. But George, living up to his reputation for courage, said triumphantly, "We've been getting engaged."

The silence that followed this announcement was not perhaps as long as it seemed. But it allowed Cassandra and George time to contemplate a runaway marriage; while Sir James wondered what Amy would say now.

None of them expected that she would exclaim, "Oh, George! Oh, Cassie!" in tones of heartfelt joy. Yet this is what occurred.

She then turned to her late opponent and said, wasn't it splendid? Sir James confirmed once for all in his belief that women were quite unpredictable, agreed that it was.

"And how wonderful," Mrs. Custance exulted, "that it should happen on the Day!"

CHAPTER XXIV

"I'LL DRIVE you home," said Joan Baker-Wright, seeing that Miss Templer and her niece Lily were preparing to walk. Felix and Leonard had gone home with the Ashfords, and most of the helpers who had stayed behind to clear up were now ready to leave.

"But the Custances aren't ready yet—goodness knows what they're doing," Joan continued. "I haven't seen Cass since teatime, and I only saw Aunt Amy for a sec. and now she's gone back into the house—anyway, I know they won't mind if I take the car. It's a bit dusty, I'm afraid, from the plants—"

Miss Templer said mildly that they could perfectly well walk, but Lily, like Joan, thought it foolish to walk when there was transport available.

Overborne, Miss Templer got into the vicarage car, choosing the spiky discomfort of the back seat so that Joan and Lily might sit together in front. She thought that the young people would prefer to talk to each other; she also thought that she had had quite enough female conversation for one day.

Joan reversed the car in the stable-yard. Just as they were starting Mrs. Custance appeared under the entrance arch and hurried towards them waving her hand.

"Stop, stop!" she called. "I've been looking everywhere—Oh, it's you!"

"I'm just taking Miss Templer home. I was sure you wouldn't mind, Aunt Amy—you see, there's the walk up the hill, and—"

"I'm looking for Edward. Have you seen him?"

Although she could not be bothered to listen to Joan's explanations it was fairly clear that Mrs. Custance was not 'upset'.

"Have you seen him?" she repeated. "Oh, dear, how tiresome of him to vanish like this, just when he's particularly needed."

Tiresome Edward—and yet not tiresome. Only Isabel Templer noticed the happy excitement in Amy's voice; the others were too busy recalling when, and where, they had last seen Mr. Custance. Only Isabel suggested that he might have gone home; but her suggestion was not heeded. It was his duty, Mrs. Custance pointed out, to stay till the very end. Probably he was wandering round the garden.

"Well—we'd better buzz off," said Joan, who could not bear to sit in a car unless that car was in motion. They buzzed off. The verb was so peculiarly applicable to Joan's driving that Miss Templer, holding on to the side of the car and bracing herself against the bumps and springless shudders of their progress, was hardly able to think clearly.

But she did not need to think clearly, or to think at all; her intuition had already informed her that George and Cassandra were engaged. Nothing else could account for Amy's behaviour—her prolonged absence, her almost perfunctory thanks and smiles for her assistants, when at last she reappeared, and her obvious desire to get everything tidied up as quickly as possible.

Not for a moment did Isabel doubt her intuition. She had been quite right, the day of the picnic, when her intuition told her that George was in love with Cassandra. But she had been wrong, she admitted honestly, in thinking that Amy would object to the marriage. And yet it was strange; for Amy had certainly disapproved of George, and what in the world could have induced her to change her mind?

Absorbed in these interesting speculations, she became aware that the car had stopped. They had reached Prospect House, and Henry was standing at the front door, looking, as usual, at his watch.

Of course they *were* rather late, but what did it matter? Supper was a cold meal, they could have it when they pleased; and Henry was being much too fussy. Standing there to draw attention to their lateness, as if he had the right to do it. As if it were his own house.

'His own house!' she thought suddenly; and in one swift leap she had abandoned George Cassandra and Amy, and was thinking instead of Henry and Bonny at Prospect Cottage, so near and yet not too near, and Lukin making his fortune in London—at least one hoped so—and Eustace doing the war-dance in the dining-room.

"We must all have a drink to celebrate it!" she cried aloud.

Joan supposed that 'it' was the Church Fête, but she nobly refused the drink, to which she had not really been invited. Aunt Amy, she said, would be wanting the car. As the car rattled away down the drive Colonel Ashford looked at his watch again. Looking at his watch had become so much a habit since he came to Prospect House that he was quite surprised when his sister-in-law implored him not to.

"Not till we've had our drink," she said. "After all, you'll be able to have clocks in every room and all the Greenwich time signals."

Without explaining this remark, whose meaning totally eluded him, she led the way into the house.

Eustace was in the library. Isabel flung open the door, calling over her shoulder to Lily to fetch the sherry and tell Aunt Bonny they were home. "Bring it in here, Lily, and if the glasses aren't on the shelf they'll be in the cupboard with the egg-cups."

"Let us celebrate by all means," said Eustace. "But what are we celebrating?" His bright glance took in Bella's animation, Henry's bewilderment; he stood up, a courteous host making them welcome, and in the fading sunset light his white hair gleamed like silver. He looked almost benign.

"You," Isabel said. "Your cleverness."

It was almost too much for Henry. Even a silly woman like Bella could hardly suppose that Eustace was clever. He gave a little cough of disapproval; but it went unnoticed.

"Very gratifying," Eustace was saying. "But why this evening, of all evenings? A church fête is not my *métier*, and I claim no part in your triumphs. I'm simply the man who stayed at home."

"Mrs. Midge didn't stay at home. She was in a tent telling fortunes, and I had a long talk with her."

Eustace gave a shrill laugh, and, to Henry's disgust, clapped his hands at his own reflection in the mirror.

"I begin to understand," he said. "Did she tell you the fortune I predicted for the midget?"

"It's odd, but what really impressed her was the twenty pounds."

"I thought it would. And I'm sure you agree, Bella, that it was cheap at the price?"

Now it was Isabel who laughed. Henry Ashford, looking from one to the other, wondered what the joke was about; but the arrival of his wife with her puppy, and Lily and Felix with the sherry, diverted his attention from this puzzle.

"What are we celebrating?" Lily asked, when the glasses had been filled.

"My cleverness," Eustace answered quickly, with a gleeful look at his brother-in-law. "Or, if that offends you, call it by another name. Insight. Tact. Good timing. And, of course, a certain element of luck."

"Yes—but what have you *done*?"

"I have bought a picture."

Lily cried out in surprise, and even Felix looked impressed. A picture was the last thing Uncle Eustace could have been expected to buy.

"How nice," said Bonny, whose long residence abroad had made her forgetful of Eustace's peculiarities. "Is it by some local painter? Or an old one?"

An old picture, she meant, her thoughts hovering vaguely round the eighteenth-century flower paintings she so much admired. But Eustace, smiling his cherubic smile, answered gaily:

"Local and young. A youthful genius, desperately misunderstood, who wastes his sweetness on the desert air. Yes—if I hadn't intervened, he'd have stayed here for ever. But now, let us hope, I've got him going."

"London," said Isabel. "Rather sad for Mrs. M., now that she's getting so tweedy. But I can't pretend to be sorry, when it's so exactly what you want and just the right distance."

Having thus, as she believed, made everything clear, she waited for Henry and Bonny to show their gratitude and delight. But since she had not told them that the youthful genius was Lukin Midge neither realized that Prospect Cottage might soon be vacant.

Lily had guessed it at once. She was torn between a guilty fear that she had somehow betrayed Lukin to his enemies and a wild hope that she had been—though inadvertently—of great service to him. True, Uncle Eustace couldn't abide painters, and was apparently planning to rid the neighbourhood of this one; yet he had bought a picture and used the word genius.

"Is he going to be famous?" she cried, curiosity overcoming discretion. Uncle Eustace might be maddening but he was still, for Lily, an authority on art, an oracle whose answers were trustworthy. The difficulty, as with all oracles, was that the answers were often obscure, flippant or irrelevant.

This evening, mellowed, perhaps, by his own excellent sherry, Uncle Eustace spoke quite plainly.

"Lukin will be to his generation what I was to mine—if he's lucky. A popular exponent, glib and dextrous, of what it calls culture. I painted their faces and he will paint their subconscious impulses. He's really in a stronger position than I was. No one liked to tell the Emperor that he had no clothes on, and no one will like to tell Lukin Midge that *his* subconscious doesn't harbour anything so entertaining as a crimson nude and a view of the Admiralty Arch upside down. Yes, my dear, I expect he'll make a good thing of it."

"But is he a genius?"

"At my age," Eustace said, "the word has little meaning. We were all geniuses once; it's a thing you grow out of very quickly. I'm quite content, myself, with a happy ending."

• • • • •

The happy ending of the Day was only marred, for Mrs. Custance, by having to keep the great news to herself. She longed to announce it straightaway, or at least whisper it to her closest friends—which would have come to much the same thing. But naturally Edward must be told first, that was only right and proper; and Edward, living up to his unlucky talent for being in the wrong place at the wrong time, was simply not to be found.

The last of the helpers had departed while Mrs. Custance was searching the more distant parts of the garden. When she returned to the house she had to admit that Isabel Templer's suggestion was probably correct; Edward must have gone home. Even this desertion did not ruffle her temper. She was far too happy for that. But still, as she pointed out, he ought to have stayed till the End.

"But it *was* the end," said George. "He'd done his duty by the Fête, and he couldn't have guessed about us."

"The End comes right at the end, not just the minute it's over," Mrs. Custance replied. Having delighted her hearers by this definition she added with sudden candour, "I'm as bad as Edward—I hardly noticed what was happening, this evening, and I'm sure I didn't thank them properly."

"Oh, Mummy, you mustn't worry. It was all a huge success, and anyway I know they'll forgive you when they hear why."

Mrs. Custance knew it too. Her face beamed with maternal pride. George and Cassandra said hastily that they would go to the vicarage and break the news to Mr. Custance. They both realized that it would be difficult for Mrs. Custance to restrain herself from crying it aloud, if she should chance to meet any of her friends on her way home.

"I'll drive Cassandra," George said, "and you can follow us, with Joan. Give us a little time."

Joan might as well have stayed to drink the Templer sherry, since Mrs. Custance had forgotten her existence. "Where is she?" she asked. George explained that his father had taken her to see his exhibition, and Mrs. Custance said in that case she had better go and see the exhibition herself, because Joan was so tactless and would certainly be arguing about the dates and annoying poor Sir James.

She wondered why George and Cassie laughed, but since they were newly engaged, and since Cassie had turned out to be the right kind of daughter after all (and was looking quite as pretty as her Maitland forbears), she left them to enjoy their joke in peace.

Mr. Custance knew that his wife and his parishioners thoroughly enjoyed their annual Fête, and he often wondered why. For him it was less a festivity than a penance, or a yearly testing of all the qualities in which he least excelled.

A vicar, presiding at a church fête, is expected to look cheerful, confident and enthusiastic, and to have a word for everybody. Mr. Custance found it difficult to look cheerful when he was feeling exactly the reverse, and his lack of small talk was an even greater handicap.

He envied the vicar of Long Hampton, who had a talent for *badinage* and a widow's cruse of respectable little anecdotes. The jocular approach, however, was a style he himself had never been able to master, and anecdotes, when he essayed them, had a way of losing their point. For small talk he was forced to rely on the weather, and people's health.

Only there were so many people, and he found it so hard to remember who they were. If he knew their faces, he could not think of their names, and if he knew them by name ("Don't forget that Mrs. Piggott will be there, and old Lambton who used to live in Bigg's Row before he moved to Witling"), then he failed to recognize them in their best clothes.

This particular Day had been worse than usual. To begin with, it was at Mallin Hall and not in the familiar setting of his own garden. Then there had been a record number of people, some of whom turned out to be total strangers who showed surprise and alarm when he asked after the health of their non-existent wives or offspring; and others, probably, had been hurt or offended by his neglect. Moreover, he had had Mrs. Powlett on his hands the whole afternoon, in spite of Amy's promise that she would join them for the country-dancing.

Mrs. Powlett did her duty by the Fête, staying until the last dance had ended and then delaying her departure to spend another two shillings on the Hoop-la. When, at last, he escorted her to her car, where her niece and the poodle were placidly awaiting her, it seemed to Mr. Custance that he too had done his duty.

"Good-bye," he said. "So kind of you—the long distance . . . my wife and I . . . a real pleasure . . ."

Mrs. Powlett, correctly interpreting this as a speech of thanks, replied that she had really enjoyed herself, and added that she was quite sorry to leave, only it was getting late and she had the long drive back to Bramchester.

It was getting late. . . . The words fell suggestively on the ear, and as he waved his farewells to the departing car Mr. Custance found little difficulty in convincing himself that this marked the end of the Day. The Day had lasted an interminable time, but now everybody seemed to be leaving. The long shadow of the great cedar stretched over drive and lawn, and it was getting late. . . .

He went by the field path, meeting no one, and before he reached the first stile his thoughts had detached themselves from the Fête and he was back among the minor Greek poets of the Hellenistic Age. He was faintly surprised to find the front door of the vicarage shut and locked, but fortunately he remembered that the key would be under one of the flower-pots that flanked the steps. There it was; an excellent proof, he thought, that his memory did not always play him false.

Safe in the empty vicarage, safe in the shabby, comfortable chair in his study, he leant back for five minutes' relaxation before resuming work on his commentary . . . and there, peacefully asleep, George and Cassandra found him an hour or so later.

George had an idea that he ought to ask Mr. Custance for his consent to the marriage. But it proved difficult to put this request to a man who was only half awake, and who had somehow got the notion that George and Cassandra were each announcing their engagements to other people and not to one another.

"What a coincidence," Mr. Custance said, struggling politely with his yawns. "So strange—and yet so delightful. Your father will be pleased, George. Though of course we had heard rumours—"

"But, Father, it's *me*."

"Yes, yes, as I was saying, a delightful coincidence. And you haven't yet told me, Cassandra, the lucky man's name. I should know it, indeed I should," Mr. Custance babbled guiltily, racking his brains for the name he could not recall. "Someone I know quite well—"

"But it's George!"

"George too. Remarkable. And yet, in life, coincidences are not uncommon. As I was saying—"

"Cassandra is going to marry *me*. We have just got engaged, to each other," George declared, forgetting all about asking Mr. Custance's consent.

This assertion only added to Mr. Custance's bewilderment, and before he could stop himself he said: "But, my dear George, you *are* engaged, aren't you? My wife was telling me about it, last year, I think. You were going to be married in London."

Cassandra laughed. George replied calmly that he had been engaged once, but it was a long time ago and he hoped Mr. Custance would overlook it.

He had already confessed to his beloved that the rumour of his second engagement was false. It was Anne Malloch's sister who had got engaged, against her parents' wishes, and some hint of this secret romance had become known to the leading rumourmonger of the neighbourhood, who had added names to make it more interesting. He and Anne had thought it amusing, and neither of them had realized how vivid and detailed the story had grown, nor how far it had spread.

He did not trouble to explain all this to Mr. Custance, since it would only have added to his confusion. Cassandra assured her father that they meant to be married in Little Mallin church, and this definite statement finally convinced Mr. Custance that George and Cassandra were betrothed, not to shadowy strangers whose names he ought to have known, but to one another.

"This is wonderful news!" he exclaimed. He kissed his daughter and shook George by the hand; they were both dear to him, and he was genuinely delighted that they should have found happiness. But at the back of his mind anxious questions presented themselves, and after a few more ejaculations of delight he asked:

"Does Amy—have you told your mother?"

"Yes," said Cassandra, understanding perfectly and wishing she had reassured him sooner. "And she's very pleased."

"So is my father."

Mr. Custance drew a deep breath. He did not altogether believe it; it seemed almost more than one could hope for. But Cassandra and George looked quite at ease, and surely they would not laugh like that if they had suffered thunderbolts of parental wrath and disapproval.

"Wonderful news," he repeated.

It was not only the engagement that was wonderful.

Mrs. Custance slipped her shoes off her aching feet, putting them neatly together beside her chair so that she could step into them if the door-bell rang. But it was late; no one would come tonight.

The first gay celebrations were over. George had gone home, and Joan and Cassandra were already upstairs. She had made her usual tour of the house, fastening doors and windows, and now she had come to tell Edward that it was past his bedtime. But Edward was rounding up the notes for his morning sermon, which had got scattered all over his desk, and while she waited for him to finish this essential task she was glad to sit down.

'I'm not as young as I was,' she told herself; though it was only her feet that seemed to be feeling their age.

Edward, too, was not as young as he had been; the bald patch showed clearly in the glow from the reading-lamp as he bent to retrieve a fugitive paper from the floor. She had known for years that Edward would never be a bishop, and by now she had ceased even to hope that he might become a canon or the rector of an important parish. Probably they would stay here for the rest of their lives.

Mrs. Custance smiled, for the prospect no longer displeased her. A prolonged vista of Harvest Festivals, Sunday-school outings, Church Fêtes, stretched away into the future; yet for her the future was sunlit and golden.

"I wonder if they'll live at the Hall," she said.

It would be a pity not to, with all those fine rooms, even though they would have to share it with Sir James.

"But perhaps they could divide it," she went on. "Make a flat—or just have half each."

Mr. Custance nodded, not listening. Among the bits of his sermon he had discovered an old envelope that must have got there by mistake. He held it to the light and read the faint pencil scrawl in his own handwriting.

"Compare with Poseidippus."

He shook his head sadly, for he could not remember who or what was to be compared with Poseidippus.

"Are you ready?" Mrs. Custance asked, warned by wifely experience that Edward was no longer intent on his sermon. That faraway look always meant Greek.

"Yes, yes, my dear. Quite ready."

After a moment's thought he put the envelope into the tobacco-jar, which was full of other cryptic scrawls awaiting clarification. Then he walked to the door, where his wife, practical as ever, stood waiting to switch off the lights.

Fatiguing as the Day had been, it was over at last.

THE END

FURROWED MIDDLEBROW

FM1. *A Footman for the Peacock* (1940) . . . . RACHEL FERGUSON

FM2. *Evenfield* (1942) . . . . RACHEL FERGUSON

FM3. *A Harp in Lowndes Square* (1936) . . . . RACHEL FERGUSON

FM4. *A Chelsea Concerto* (1959) . . . . FRANCES FAVIELL

FM5. *The Dancing Bear* (1954) . . . . FRANCES FAVIELL

FM6. *A House on the Rhine* (1955) . . . . FRANCES FAVIELL

FM7. *Thalia* (1957) . . . . FRANCES FAVIELL

FM8. *The Fledgeling* (1958) . . . . FRANCES FAVIELL

FM9. *Bewildering Cares* (1940) . . . . WINIFRED PECK

FM10. *Tom Tiddler's Ground* (1941) . . . . URSULA ORANGE

FM11. *Begin Again* (1936) . . . . URSULA ORANGE

FM12. *Company in the Evening* (1944) . . . . URSULA ORANGE

FM13. *The Late Mrs. Prioleau* (1946) . . . . MONICA TINDALL

FM14. *Bramton Wick* (1952) . . . . ELIZABETH FAIR

FM15. *Landscape in Sunlight* (1953) . . . . ELIZABETH FAIR

FM16. *The Native Heath* (1954) . . . . ELIZABETH FAIR

FM17. *Seaview House* (1955) . . . . ELIZABETH FAIR

FM18. *A Winter Away* (1957) . . . . ELIZABETH FAIR

FM19. *The Mingham Air* (1960) . . . . ELIZABETH FAIR

FM20. *The Lark* (1922) . . . . E. NESBIT

Made in United States
Troutdale, OR
12/20/2023

16218720R00146